Praise 1

MW00624823

"An authoritative, emotionally satisfying, deliciously complex mystery in courtroom drama. I devoured it from the first pages to the surprising finale."

JAMES PATTERSON, #1 *New York Times* bestselling author of *The 24th Hour*

"In the tradition of great courtroom novels *Anatomy of a Murder* and *Presumed Innocent*, McLachlin's *Denial* captures the life of a defence lawyer embroiled in a high-stakes murder trial, with twists and turns to the very last page. Jilly Truitt is a character readers are going to cheer for over and over again."

ROBERT ROTENBERG, bestselling author of *What We Buried*

Praise for *Full Disclosure*

"Gripping, intricate, and full of heart, *Full Disclosure* is a bold debut by the former Chief Justice of the Supreme Court of Canada. Novelist Beverley McLachlin is a force to be reckoned with."

KATHY REICHS, *New York Times* bestselling author of *Fire and Bones*

"Totally compelling: McLachlin brings her wit and intelligence—and unrivalled experience—to this courtroom drama, which brilliantly illuminates the games lawyers play and the risks of wrong choices. The main character, Jilly Truitt, is a woman I want to meet again."

CHARLOTTE GRAY, bestselling author of *Passionate Mothers, Powerful Sons*

"McLachlin puts her experience on the Court to good use, writing a taut legal thriller with great twists and turns that will keep readers guessing to the very end."

CATHERINE McKENZIE, bestselling
author of *Have You Seen Her*

"A well-crafted page-turner in the vein of international bestsellers like Sarah Vaughan's *Anatomy of a Scandal*, and is packed with courtroom drama, intrigue, plot twists, and fascinating details about our criminal justice system. Written in an accessible voice, with a fast-moving narrative, this is beach, cabin, and airplane reading at its best."

Vancouver Sun

"For page-turning legal thrillers, it's hard to do better than this one, and not just because it's by the ultimate insider: the recently retired Chief Justice of the Supreme Court of Canada."

Maclean's

"A great read . . . Has sequel written all over it."

CBC's *Sunday Edition*

PROOF

A NOVEL

BEVERLEY McLACHLIN

PUBLISHED BY SIMON & SCHUSTER

New York   London   Toronto   Sydney   New Delhi

SIMON &
SCHUSTER
CANADA

Simon & Schuster Canada
A Division of Simon & Schuster, LLC
166 King Street East, Suite 300
Toronto, Ontario M5A 1J3

On page 310, "There speaks a devil who is sick of sin" is taken from Wilfred Owen's poem "Dulce et Decorum Est," published in *Poems*, by Chatto and Windus, London, 1920.

This Simon & Schuster Canada edition September 2024

SIMON & SCHUSTER CANADA and colophon are trademarks of Simon & Schuster, LLC

Simon & Schuster: Celebrating 100 Years of Publishing in 2024

For information about special discounts for bulk purchases, please contact Simon & Schuster Special Sales at 1-800-268-3216 or CustomerService@simonandschuster.ca.

Manufactured in the United States of America

1   3   5   7   9   10   8   6   4   2

Library and Archives Canada Cataloguing in Publication

Title: Proof / Beverley McLachlin.
Names: McLachlin, Beverley, 1943- author.
Identifiers: Canadiana (print) 2023046601X | Canadiana (ebook) 20230466079 |
ISBN 9781668003619 (softcover) | ISBN 9781668003626 (EPUB)
Classification: LCC PS8625.L33 P76 2024 | DDC C813/.6—dc23

ISBN 978-1-6680-0361-9
ISBN 978-1-6680-0362-6 (ebook)

For all the children

PROOF

PART I

CHAPTER 1

THE PHONE ON MY NIGHTSTAND pings. I feel for it—welcome relief from my sleepless state—and bring it to my face, squinting at the bright screen. It's not an Emergency Alert. British Columbia reserves those for the tsunami that will roll in any year now and destroy us all. But the message makes my heart thud.

CHILD GONE MISSING, the AMBER Alert reads.

Instinctively, I reach for the bassinette by my bed where my baby daughter sleeps. I find Claire's face to trace the warm, smooth skin of her forehead. Somewhere, a desperate mother is weeping for her lost child, but my little girl is here, with me, safe. Gently, so not to wake her, I lift Claire out of the bassinette and draw her to my chest, stroking her tuft of hair—dark like mine in the pre-dawn light—and will my heart to stop pounding. She stirs for a moment, then settles, her chest rising and falling with each breath. She's fifteen weeks old.

Jilly Truitt, criminal defence attorney. If only they could see me now. In the old days, I would be rising, tugging on sweats for my pre-work run, and rehearsing questions to skewer a prosecutor's witness in the courtroom. But that was then, and this is now. After a few moments, I place Claire back in her bed and lay down on my side, gazing at my baby girl. I blink away the exhausted remains of a sleepless night.

Postpartum depression. That's what Edith says I have. Wise Edith, the social worker who rescued me as an orphaned baby and shepherded me through foster homes. I didn't argue with her, but I know it's more than that. It's grief. Motherhood wasn't something I craved, nor was it something I swore off. I always thought, though, that when I took that leap, I'd have someone by my side. I'd have Mike. But a bullet changed that.

If only I hadn't taken Vera Quentin's case.

Last month marked the one-year anniversary of his death. I woke up that morning feeling out of sorts, out of alignment. I had a weight on my chest, a pain that I couldn't shift. Later, I realized. My body remembered what my brain forgot. Gone a year, and yet when I close my eyes I still see Mike's long face and beaky nose, the shift of his cool grey eyes from dark to light when he smiled at me. We met in first-year law and passed the next decade plus as best friends and occasional lovers. Mike wanted more, kids and the whole bit, but I wasn't ready. Then when a disgruntled client put out a hit on me last year, I ran to Mike for help—and the killer got him instead of me. Mike saved my life but lost his own.

Postpartum depression. And grief.

A month after Mike died, I found out I was pregnant. *I will keep this child*, I told the doctor, *it's all I have left of him*. I held myself together throughout the pregnancy, but when they slipped

Claire into my arms, I broke down. Mike would never see his daughter, and I had to raise her alone. Tough as nails in the courtroom, I feared I would fail as a parent.

I long for Mike, for his presence, for his strength and understanding, for him to tell me that the bullet that killed him wasn't my fault. Above all, I long for him to tell me that it will not happen again, that Claire will be safe, that she'll live a long life. Depression, grief—labels can't make the fear of losing what I love go away.

Go back to work, Edith tells me. That will cure me. Each week, I think I might be ready. Each Monday, I force myself to my closet. I finger the dark court suits, preserved in protective plastic for the day when I will need them again, and turn away. I have no time for keeping the people who do bad things out of jail. That's why I lost Mike. Some day, I will be a lawyer again. But not today.

I cup Claire's head. Somewhere, a mother has lost her child.

CHAPTER 2

I MUST HAVE DRIFTED OFF BECAUSE I am awakened by a slash of sunlight cutting through my window.

As the room comes into focus, I reach for the bassinette, but Claire's not there. Panic rises inside me, then I hear her gurgling laughter downstairs, and my heartbeat slows. Mab, my new live-in nanny, has her. She must have come in and changed Claire's diaper then brought her downstairs.

I check my beside clock: 10:41 a.m. I can't remember the last time I slept so late. Throwing back the covers, I get up and cross to the window. Green leaves, warm sun. It's September, but it feels like summer. Still, it's hard to trust. Here on the west coast, the clouds and dark days of rain are just around the corner. Despite the weather, the gloom inside me persists. Resisting the urge to crawl back under the covers, I pull on my robe and pad down the stairs.

In the kitchen, Mab is humming a lullaby as she wipes the marble counter. Claire babbles in her baby chair on the table. The kitchen has never been this clean, nor, it pains me admit, Claire so contented. And it's all thanks to Mab, who is as precise with her nannying as she is with her appearance. Twin wings of black hair swing from her centre part as she cleans.

"Good morning, ma'am." She's Irish, and her voice has a lilt.

"You should have woken me up," I say.

"Not my job," says Mab, taking in my robe and unwashed hair. "I changed Claire's diaper and gave her some formula."

I feel the sting of her disapproval. *Breast is best.* I'd tried, hadn't I? But my milk was too thin. Guilt clouds the edges of my mind: for failing the breast test, for sleeping through Claire's best waking hours.

I cross the room and plant a kiss on Claire's forehead. I stand a moment, taking in the marvel of my daughter before I pour myself a coffee. The alert that woke me in the wee hours hovers at the edges of my mind. Somewhere out there, a child is missing.

I look at Mab, furiously scrubbing the marble now. Straight off the boat, Mab is my third nanny in three months. Seems I'm a failure at keeping nannies happy, too. Anxiety rises like bile in my empty stomach. I can't do this alone; I need Mab to work out.

"Did you hear about the little girl who went missing?" I ask, trying to make amends with some conversation.

"Yes, terrible thing. The police are still searching, that's all the radio says." Mab's words are clipped, but I sense her softening. "Her name is Tess. Just five years old. I can't imagine how her parents feel. Her father is that pop singer Trist."

I know that name. Tristan Jones, or Trist as he's better known, is a local musician who made it big. His songs play in cafés and elevators, soft rock underpinned by rap rhythms. Mike would play that song of his, "Goin' Down on Love," when we were heading to Whistler in his Porsche—which was high praise coming from Mike, who occupied his evenings playing Ravel and Mozart on the piano. The piano that sits in the sitting room now, untouched by Mab's dust cloth.

When Mike died, he left me this house. With Claire on the way, it made sense to move out of my condo, but the memories that come from every corner hit me hard and often. The sitting room where he played the piano. The dining room where no one dined. The foyer where he died.

It took months before I could walk through the door without hearing the sharp whip of bullets. I shake the thoughts from my mind and focus on what Mab is saying.

"Trist's fairly famous, isn't he?" she asks. "Do you think she was kidnapped? Maybe for a ransom?"

I think about the people I defended. Child molesters, child beaters, purveyors of pernicious porn. Some were innocent and some were guilty. It turned my stomach, but my job was to defend, not judge. My duty was to give them the best defence the law allowed. Strangely, no child abduction case had ever crossed my path.

"Could be ransom kidnapping," I say. "Sometimes those turn bad, though . . ." I trail off, unable to voice the possibility that little Tess might turn up dead. I look at Claire, who has started to doze peacefully, and feel a shiver down my spine.

"Just terrible," Mab says, wiping the coffee ring I've left on the counter. She doesn't want me here.

With Claire in her baby chair in one hand and my coffee in the other, I head into the den. Another stab of guilt: boxes of Mike's things still sitting in the corner, more boxes of my stuff

9

half-unpacked. I push aside a mess of papers, set Claire's baby chair on the desk. I slump into the big office chair and fish my cellphone from the pocket of my robe. I start scrolling news.

The headline proclaiming the disappearance of Tess Sinclair-Jones dominates the list of news notifications. I click and suck in my breath—Tess's opalescent eyes of sea blue stare up at me. Her light-brown complexion is splashed with freckles, and her blond Afro circles her head like a halo. She's serene, almost ethereal, I think, then I look more closely. She's not smiling. That's odd. Usually when a child goes missing, the news digs up joyful family shots, the better to tug at the public's heartstrings. I look again at Tess's eyes, glazed and expressionless. This is a paparazzi shot, I realize with a jolt.

I don't follow celebrity gossip, but a memory of Tess on the cover of a tabloid at the grocery counter floods back, and the horror of the abduction hits me in the stomach. The missing little girl is not some faceless child, she is *this* child, a child I know, beloved of the media, caressed by the cameras. Bits and pieces are coming back to me. There was a big media circus when Trist and his wife, Kate, had their baby. Trist's fame as a popstar was beginning to rise and the entertainment news was fixated—unnaturally so—on their beautiful biracial baby, Tess. And now, she's missing. Could someone have kidnapped her, like Mab said? Could someone have wanted her so much they plotted to snatch her away? I think of the perverts I have known, repress a shudder.

I scroll down, scanning the article.

There's another photo—a wider shot. Tess is in between her parents, one hand in each of theirs. Trist is smiling for the camera through the blond mane that half-obscures his handsome features. Kate's focus is on Tess, her free hand in motion as if to cover

Tess's face as she bends to protect her from the camera's gaze. Kate is beautiful with a high forehead and sculpted cheekbones; here though, her green eyes glare at the camera and her lips are parted in a hiss: *Leave my child alone.* I recall photos of her hair flowing dark and loose, but on this occasion, she has slicked it back into a sleek chignon. Identifies as Black, I recall hearing, but you wouldn't know by looking. The media fawned over the little girl and her famous father, but not so much Kate. *Came from no-where, gold-digger, unstable*—the ugly phrases echo in my mind. *Not like us*, they signalled, *not to be trusted.*

I stare at the photo. I see only a frightened mother trying to protect her child. Where is Kate now? What anguish is she suffering?

I keep reading. The details are scant. Tess was playing with her father on a beach on Bowen Island when she disappeared. I flip to other reports. Most are pictures—Tess's face everywhere—and offer the same details. One mentions that Trist and Kate had separated last year. I must have missed that in the fugue of my own grief over Mike. Apparently, he was with his new girlfriend, Lena Rodriguez, on Bowen Island, where they'd rented a house for a few days.

There aren't many mentions of Kate in the coverage, and so far, the press doesn't seem to be pointing the finger at the parents. The child is missing. There's a whiff of kidnapping, but nothing more.

Claire snuffles in her baby chair, and I sit back, awash with gratitude that she is safe with me. But my mind keeps going back to little Tess. I sip my coffee, flip through my recent call list.

Once, my life was full of people and talk—courtroom gossip, legal chatter, and quiet moments with Mike. Now the space I inhabit is silent, reduced to cursory exchanges with this month's current nanny. Debbie, Jeff, and Alicia—my law colleagues—are too busy keeping our little firm on its feet to bother me, or I them. My foster mother, Martha, has taken up permanent residence on Naramata Bench, five hours distant. My only solace is Edith. Edith, ten minutes away through tree-shaded streets and always available by text and phone. I click on Edith's name, and the phone rings.

Now firmly retired from four decades of grueling social work, Edith fills her life with her garden and volunteer work. But she always has time for me. No one claimed me when I was born—no mother, no father. The state, in the guise of Edith, took over. Edith found me my first foster home with a retired United Church minister and his wife. Then when they passed away within months of each other. Edith found me another foster home, and another and another, because I kept running away. At thirteen, I was on the streets, begging for change and dabbling in drugs. Once more, Edith tracked me down, rescued me, and placed me in the home of Brock and Martha Mayne. This time we clicked.

The Maynes and their four boys loved me as their own. I went to law school, became a lawyer. Edith could have—*should* have, according to the book—cut ties, but she hovered in the wings, lunch here, a coffee there, to stay in touch. When I lost Mike, she fully re-entered my life, helping me through grief and pregnancy, counseling and comforting, and on my dark days, reminding me how far I had come.

Edith's face fills my small screen now. Faded blond hair clipped short to her chin, round wire-rimmed glasses, soft eyes that go hard when tough love is required, Edith is what she has always been—my compass, my rock, my refuge.

"Jilly," she says, her voice brisk and businesslike, belying the vulnerability she spent four decades hiding. "I was just thinking about you. How is our little Claire?"

"Peaceful as can be," I reply, flipping the camera on my phone so Edith can see her. "Oblivious to the world's woes, lucky child."

"As she should be," Edith says. "It's good to see you smile," she adds when I flip the camera back.

"I'm lucky," I say, and I mean it.

"You're thinking about that missing girl, Tess, aren't you?" Edith guesses. "It's all over the news."

Edith knows me well. "I'm finding myself a bit obsessed with the story," I say. "The pictures are everywhere, but there aren't many facts. Just that she was playing on the beach near the house her father had rented."

Edith nods. "I saw Trist outside the police precinct on this morning's news. He was broken up. Said something about how he stretched out on a beach recliner and must have fallen asleep, then the lawyer he had with him whisked him away."

"One little mistake and your child is gone." I suck in a breath.

"Nobody seems to be blaming him, though. Not yet, anyway. He's the golden-haired rockstar dad who can do no wrong. I imagine they'll have less sympathy for the mother, Kate. The press don't like her."

Claire stirs, and I rock her chair, lulling her back to sleep. "I hadn't realized they separated," I say.

"Oh, yes. Quite the custody battle, too. My social worker friends know all about it. Both parents wanted full custody, but Trist won. Later, he got an order so that Kate can only see Tess on supervised visits."

I feel a tug of an old instinct. That thing they call a gut. Tess hasn't wandered off. Someone took her. Trist is too high profile for this to be unrelated to his fame. But this bit about the custody battle niggles, too.

Edith interrupts my thoughts. "I wouldn't be surprised if they suspect Kate stole her back."

"The press knows better than to report that without evidence," I say.

"Yes, but social media is full of it. Check your Twitter."

"I don't do Twitter, or X, or whatever it's called now. A habit from the old days when they skewered me for defending murderers and sexual predators. For some reason, people refuse to understand that it takes a prosecution *and* a defence to do justice."

Edith nods. "As someone who checked her sites this morning, let me fill you in. Social media is not being kind to Kate. Even if the police don't charge her, she'll be destroyed. They'll dig up the dirt from the custody fights. Say she was an unfit mother. However this plays out, it will be her fault."

"The world is hard on mothers," I say before my forensic mind kicks in. "None of the articles I saw said where Kate was when Tess disappeared."

"That remains unclear," Edith replies. "The police will start feeding out details. They'll be talking to your old friend Cy about what charges to lay."

"Too early to bring the Crown prosecutor in—they need to find Tess first." *Or a body*, I think, then block the thought. "Besides, Cy's not my friend. More like foe."

"He was there when you lost Mike," Edith gently reminds me.

"A fleeting gesture of humanity," I say. Cy found me in the hospital waiting room after Mike was shot, later stood at my side by Mike's open grave and gave me a single red rose to place on the coffin. But apart from a note congratulating me on Claire's birth, he's been absent.

"Don't be harsh, Jilly." Edith's tone has shifted. "I've got to go. I've got a guidance session at the hospital for families with children undergoing cancer treatment."

"You shame me with your good works."

"It's not much. We do what we can. Keep in touch. I'll drop by to see you and Claire some evening. By the way, how is the new nanny working out?"

"Not bad," I lie. "Early days."

"Okay." A pause. "Hang in there, Jilly."

I put the phone down. I never could fool Edith. Claire squirms in her chair, as if she, too, senses my dishonesty.

"There, there," I coo, lifting her out and bouncing her in my arms. Outside, the sun is still shining. Why am I still here in this gloomy house? I feel a flash of determination. Today, I will bundle Claire up, put her in her baby carrier, and take her for a long Saturday walk. We will stop in the park to soak up the sun. Just my girl and me.

"Claire and I are going out," I announce to Mab as I come through the kitchen and round the corner to the staircase.

Halfway up, my phone rings. Edith calling me back? Distracted, I fish it from my robe pocket and answer. "Jilly Truitt speaking."

There's a rustle on the other side, then a voice I know well. I lower the phone.

"You there, Jilly?"

There's no avoiding this. I lift the phone back to my ear. "Yes, Cy. I'm still here."

CHAPTER 3

"**G**LAD I GOT YOU," CY says.

The voice I know so well, baritone tending to tenor, a voice made to calm and persuade, belongs to Cy Kenge, Prosecutor Numero Uno. My one-time mentor, longtime foe. He taught me everything I know about the practice of criminal law, including the shady parts, like the tricks lawyers play on each other. Slippery Cy, they call him in the corridors of justice, and not for nothing.

I skip the niceties. "What do you want, Cy?"

He barks a short laugh. "Gracious as always, Jilly. You never disappoint."

"Glad to oblige," I say as I trudge up the stairs to my bedroom, my phone mashed between my shoulder and face as I carry Claire. I imagine him leaning back in his plastic chair in the spartan office the state provides its prosecutors, the overhead light beaming on his great bald head as he executes whatever strategy occupies his mind today.

"In fact, I do want something. More precisely, I have a message to convey."

I take a deep breath. "Just so you know. I'm not working. Parental leave. You may have heard of it."

"Even I know the term. How's little Claire?"

I look down at burbling Claire, brush her sweep of dark hair along her forehead, and I soften. "Little Claire is lovely."

"And you are still wallowing in the delights of motherhood?"

Wallowing? Yes. Delights? Not so sure.

Cy pushes on, not waiting for my answer. "Word has it you've not been doing all that well. You know how people like to talk."

I bristle and strive for calm. "I'm a woman in a man's world. They've been talking since the first day I donned my robes." Jilly Truitt, the girl who scrabbled up from nowhere to the highest courts of the land, is finally going down. What the streets couldn't do, motherhood has. I sigh, weary of the world's tongue-wagging. "Half the world says stay home longer; half says get back to work. People will judge no matter what I do."

"I'm concerned. You've been through a lot. Mike . . ." Cy trails off, and I can tell he's thinking about his own wife, Lois, who died three years ago. Perhaps I'm too harsh, as Edith said. Cy's been there for me in rough times. "Are you sure you're okay?" he asks, and I can tell he means it.

"I'm fine, Cy. Thank you for asking."

"Glad to hear it. Depression is not your style." Without missing a beat, Cy pivots to business. "I wouldn't bother you, Jilly, but I have no choice."

"Explain," I say, bringing Claire to the diaper table for a change.

"It's the Tess Sinclair-Jones case. The girl who went missing yesterday. You must have heard—"

I cut him off, wet wipe in hand. "Whatever you want, I can't help. I told the firm and my clients that I would be taking six months' leave."

"Let me finish. The police have taken Tess's mother in for questioning. Kate Sinclair-Jones. She's being held under suspicion. The most obvious explanation for Tess's disappearance is a ransom demand. But so far, there's no demand. So the police are looking into all possibilities. Obviously, they need to talk to the parents. They've talked to Trist, and they need to talk to Kate. She's hysterical and won't talk to them. They can't push until she has a lawyer to hold her hand and protect her rights. We need someone she'll trust. I thought of you."

So, they are going after Kate, I think, then remind myself that questioning the parents is routine. I button up Claire's onesie. I'm not ready to go back. Not yet. I'm still bruised from my last case, a doctor accused of murdering his wife. Seven months pregnant, I stood before the jury and pleaded my defence—his wife was wielding a butcher knife against him and he acted in self-defence. Sure, in 99% of the cases, the woman is the victim, but this case was different. I thought we had a chance—the wife was bigger and stronger than her husband, and his evidence of how it happened wasn't shaken in cross-examination—but the jury didn't buy it, and now the doctor is in jail for life. Cy shot me a look when they read the verdict: *You've lost it, Jilly.*

"My mat leave is not over," I say. "Get someone else. I can think of ten defence lawyers who would kill to be part of a high-profile case like this."

"We haven't got time to hunt for another lawyer. This is an emergency."

"No," I say for the third time.

Cy's voice drops to an angry whisper. "I can't believe you're saying this, Jilly. What's happened to you? You used to care, a little."

"I got boundaries, Cy." But my curiosity wins out, and I hear myself saying, "Tell me what you know."

"I don't have time to explain, but Coles Notes: The police have a witness who says he saw Kate with Tess late yesterday afternoon after she went missing. Police went to Kate's place, but Kate wasn't there. Didn't turn up until this morning. That's when they brought her in for questioning. She's at headquarters now. The police want to run a lineup to confirm the identification and question her. But they also want anything that could help find the child." Cy pauses. "Or find out what's happened to her."

My mind races ahead. They have a witness. *Is he reliable? I wonder. What isn't Cy telling me? And why does he want me so badly?*

"If Ms. Sinclair-Jones wants me to act for her, she can pick up the phone and ask me," I say.

"I can have her do that if you want, Jilly," he says tightly. "But we'll be wasting time. Kate is upset, not thinking straight. That's why the police got me involved. They thought it would be quicker if I contacted you. You can reason with her."

Of course she's upset, I think. *Her child is missing, for God's sake.* "My job is not to help the police. My job is to protect my client's rights."

"Let's cut to the chase." I don't know why Cy needs me, but it's forcing him to keep his cool. "The police have evidence that Tess was last seen with her mother. The police need to talk to the mother—now—but for that, she needs a lawyer. You're here and available. You come down to the station and make sure everything is done right. Save us precious hours, Jilly." Cy pauses, and when he speaks again, the anger is gone from his voice. "I'm not asking you to take her case for the long haul, just to make sure her rights are respected during the interview. I need you to do this. For Tess. For her parents. For everybody who's sweating bullets as you dither. A little girl's life is in the balance. If she's alive, we need to find her. If she's not alive, we need to know what happened."

His words hit home. I'm not used to being asked to save a life—I'm usually pushing the mop post-crime. I swallow. I feel myself relenting—is it my growing obsession with Tess's fate, or something else?

The thrill of a case.

"Jilly, you there?"

"Yeah, I'm here." I chew my lip. It's a routine interview to see what Kate knows. Nothing more. I can do that. "Okay, I'll come down to the station. But no promises going forward."

"Thanks, Jilly. We'll take what we can get. I'll have an RCMP car sent round to pick you up. Twenty minutes."

"RCMP?"

"The child disappeared on Bowen Island. In the gulf, off Vancouver. RCMP territory. They're putting a joint task force into operation, but for now it's the RCMP."

I look at Claire. This time, I will do things right. This time, I will keep the danger far from my family. I clear my throat.

"Send the car," I say.

CHAPTER 4

TWENTY MINUTES, CY SAID. I run the numbers. Fifteen to dress, run a comb through my hair, and dab on lipstick; five to negotiate child-care with Mab. There is no telling how long the police interview might go. So much for my stroll with Claire, I realize, as I struggle to do up the button on my pre-maternity business slacks.

Mab's face goes blank when I tell her I might be late, but I take her silence as assent.

"I appreciate this, Mab. It's about the missing little girl."

Her eyes soften, but her lips remain a thin line.

I breathe in Claire's sweet smell, then hand her to Mab. "I've just changed her, and there's more formula in the fridge," I say. "You have Edith's number if anything happens. I'll be back as soon as I can."

With one last look at my little girl, I turn to the door.

In the back seat of the police cruiser, I shift as we leave the tree-lined suburban streets of Shaughnessy. I'm distressed, and it's not just the unaccustomed tightness of my waistband. I've never left Claire before. And Mab is new. Will they be okay? I repress my worries. Mab likes Claire, Claire likes Mab, and all will be well. I take a calming breath, but new doubts emerge. It's been months since I stepped into a courtroom, let alone a police station. To steady my thoughts, I pull together what I know.

One: Yesterday, Tess disappeared from a secluded beach on Bowen Island under Trist's supervision.

Two: Later in the day, Tess was sighted in the custody of Kate.

Three: The police couldn't find Kate until early this morning.

Four: The police have not found Tess.

And five: The court of public opinion does not favour Kate.

In the cruiser, I google her name again. The images that come up are tabloid shots. There's Kate in happier days, looking up adoringly at Trist as they enter a theatre; Kate emerging from the courthouse after the judge gave Trist custody, tears streaming down her cheeks; Kate shouting at paparazzi, her face twisted with anger. Their private struggles have played out on a public stage that demands villains and heroes, and the result is clear: Trist is the good guy; Kate, the inadequate mother.

Like all police stations, this one is garishly lit on the assumption that bright lights banish secrets, but it also thrums with a state of urgency. Someone has tacked a huge portrait of Tess on a corkboard, and uniforms race around in a frenzy to do something—anything—to find her.

The female officer who met me at the car directs me toward the sorting station down the hall, elbows out to fend off the traffic. I reel back. I haven't been in a police station for a while. I've forgotten about the cacophony and chaos.

I find myself standing before a counter shielded with plexiglass. On the other side, a woman looks at me as though she's been expecting me. Her name tag says Officer Nurjehan Nathan. The turquoise embroidery on her elegant headscarf sends my fingers scratching through my own rumpled hair.

"Ah, Ms. Truitt," she says. "A moment while I inform Detective Kan." She mumbles into the tiny microphone attached to her headset, then looks back at me. "He'll be out as soon as he can. Chaos in here today."

Minutes tick by, and I tap the heel of my pump, annoyance growing. I don't like police. After years in defence, I've learned not to trust them. Today, they rush me here and make me wait. So much for losing time. I need to get this done and get back to Claire.

Finally, I hear a door slam and look up. A man is moving toward me across the shiny tiles. Detective Kan, I presume. He has a broad face and grey eyes, and he's tall, 6'6" at least. His black suit tapers from his massive shoulders, and his white collar gleams in the fluorescent lights. He looms over me, lips grimly pursed.

"I'm Jilly Truitt," I say. "Here to see Kate Sinclair-Jones. Cy sent me."

"Kan. Igor Kan." His voice is deep and gravelly, like sandpaper.

He ignores my extended hand and gestures for me to follow him. I suppose this isn't the time or place for pleasantries. Or maybe he doesn't like lawyers. Even if they've been sent to help him do his job.

I follow him down a corridor to what turns out to be his office. It's a small room, with a big Russian icon on the wall behind the desk. Black almond eyes glow ominously at me from the tarnished gold background. Is Kan religious? Or is the art calculated to cut through the defences of whomever occupies the chair in which I now sit?

Kan speaks first. "We haven't got time to waste, Ms. Truitt. We want to do a physical lineup and we want to question Ms. Sinclair-Jones. She is—how shall I put it?—distraught, refusing to cooperate. She has asked for a lawyer." He looks at me and seems to remember his manners. "Thank you for coming. Cy said you know how to look after your clients."

I ignore the compliment if that's what it is. "I'll talk to Ms. Sinclair-Jones, do what I can to help. But first, I would appreciate some background. Cy was rather circumspect on the phone."

"Someone took Tess from the beach in a boat; we have the marks where it beached in the sand. A little later, a vacationer on the island saw a woman and child matching Kate's and Tess's descriptions in a boat in the next cove. He has identified Ms. Sinclair-Jones in a photo lineup." His words come out one by one, like he's rolling them around in his mind before uttering them. His jaw is strong and square.

"That's not surprising. Ms. Sinclair-Jones is a celebrity. Her photo has been all over the press for years. Show a witness a set of photos, he's programmed to pick out the face he's familiar with."

"He also *took* a photo of the woman and the child in the boat," Kan says.

Cy hadn't told me about that. This is more serious. "May I see the photos?"

"Later. Right now, we need to run the physical lineup."

So they have photo evidence. The next step is to talk to Kate and see what she has to say. He's hiding something.

"What's the rush?" I ask. "You haven't even interviewed my client and you're going for a physical lineup?"

"I have my reasons," Kan growls. "As you will soon appreciate."

I feel a chill. Kan is going to use the lineup to intimidate Kate. This will not be an interview; it will be an interrogation. Kan is rising, giving me no choice.

"Very well, Detective. But first, I need to confer with my client."

CHAPTER 5

KAN WALKS ME DOWN ANOTHER long corridor, this one lined with doors to interview rooms. He stops at the last one, punches in a code.

"Ten minutes," Kan says, pushing the door open.

It's clear he intends to run this show. Fine, let him think he is. For now.

I step into the room and close the door softly behind me.

The room, like all interrogation rooms, is windowless and bleak and beige—from the walls to the linoleum floor. Plastic table, plastic chairs. And a figure. Kate. Her head is bent, her black hair spilling out over the tabletop.

"Ms. Sinclair-Jones," I say quietly, slipping into the chair opposite. "You asked for a lawyer. I'm here."

No response.

"My name is Jilly Truitt," I try again. "I'm a defence lawyer. It's my job to help you, ensure your rights are protected."

Slowly, she lifts her head. "My rights?" she says hoarsely. "I thought this was about finding Tess."

She pushes back her hair, and I see her face. The face I recognize—high forehead, wide eyes, and full lips I remember from the photos—but now heavy with sorrow. She's only in her early thirties, I guess, but small lines are showing at the corners of her green eyes. She looks at me and wipes a tear from her cheek.

"Tell them to find Tess," she rasps, a low, animal sound.

How do I tell this woman, consumed with fear and worry for her missing daughter, that the police are already presuming the worst and have set her up as their number one suspect? Looking at her red-rimmed eyes and defeated expression, I wonder if they're right.

"They are searching," I say. "But they want to talk to you, find out if you know anything that might help them find her. That's why I'm here. You asked for a lawyer."

"I know nothing! Tess was with my ex-husband when she disappeared," she says bitterly. "I knew when they took her away from me that something terrible would happen. I tried to tell the judge, but she only gave me that look—*poor deluded thing.* 'Custody to Mr. Jones,' she said. Four little words." Kate wipes away fresh tears. "And now Tess's gone."

I reach across the table and cover her hand with mine. I read her grief; I've had my own. Losing Mike, and my fear that I will lose Claire, too. I lower my voice.

"We don't have much time. You have a choice. You can ask me to sit beside you to make sure the police treat you as the law requires. Or you can send me away and face them on your own. It's up to you, Ms. Sinclair-Jones."

"I don't trust the police. Outside the courthouse, after the custody hearing, they took my baby from my arms and left me there, screaming for her." Her low voice rises and eyes pierce mine. "I don't trust anyone."

I lean toward her. "You can trust me. I've been practising criminal law for well over a decade. I know the rules and the system, and I've handled difficult situations. I'm tough—I won't let them push you around." And before I realize what I'm saying, I blurt: "And I'm a mother, too."

I may not entirely believe my self-promo, but if I'm going to help her, I have to win her confidence. I study her face, wait for a response. If I'm going to act for this woman, I need her consent.

"Yes," she says at last. "Call me Kate."

I look at my watch. Kan will be banging on the door any moment now.

I need to forewarn her about where the police might go with their questions. I decide to ask the big one first. "Kate, tell me the truth. Do you have any idea where Tess is?"

"No, I haven't seen Tess since two weeks ago when we had our last supervised visit."

"Good," I say. "When the time comes, tell them that. Now, the police say they have a photo of a woman and child matching your and Tess's description in a boat yesterday afternoon shortly after Tess disappeared. They have a witness who they say has identified you both. They may ask you about that. Do you have an alibi?"

She tilts her head. "I don't know anything about a boat. I was at the university. It wasn't me. I told you: I haven't seen Tess for two weeks."

"Well, the police want to be sure. They're going to take you into another room in a few minutes for a lineup. You will be put in a line with seven or eight other women behind a one-way glass mirror, and the person who thinks he saw you will be on the other side. He'll be asked if he recognizes anyone in the lineup." I think back on the photos I've seen. In most, Kate's hair was tied back. Today it's loose. That could work in our favour, making her less recognizable.

I would ask her how she was wearing it yesterday in the boat, but she's denied being there. If the girl in the boat had her hair loose, our odds have worsened.

"And then?" Kate asks.

"And then they'll bring you back here and ask you questions. Don't worry. I'll be here with you. I will protect your rights. But they're entitled to ask you questions. They need to find out what happened to Tess."

"I told you," Kate says, her voice rising. "I don't know what happened to Tess. She was with her father. They should be talking to him."

I try to calm her. "I'm sure they are. They want to cover all the bases."

But Kate isn't listening. "If I knew where Tess was, I would run to her and never let her go. Tell the police to stop this charade and find Tess—that's their job." Her voice trembles. "They should never have taken her away from me. I would have kept her safe. I knew something would happen. I want my baby. I want my baby."

Kate wraps her arms around her small body and rocks in her chair. I could comfort her, but that's not my job. I reach for a Kleenex box on a shelf and hand her a tissue.

"Here," I say gently. "I know you're hurting, Kate. I can't imagine the pain you're going through. But when you're in the lineup, you need to look like you don't have a care in the world. Can you do that?"

A knock on the door. Detective Kan.

"We need another minute," I call through the door. I expect him to barge in anyway, but he doesn't. Maybe I'm running the show now, or maybe he's being polite. I turn back to Kate. "Can you do that?" I repeat. "For Tess?"

She blinks up at me, her eyes watery but determined. "Yes, Ms. Truitt. I can do that."

"I think you can, too. Okay. Take a moment."

She wipes her nose with a tissue, takes a breath. "I'm ready."

CHAPTER 6

THE BOOTH WHERE DETECTIVE KAN and I sit is dark. He folds his large hands in his lap and takes pains to respect my personal space.

Misidentification is the criminal justice system's dirty not-so-secret secret. People think they are good at remembering faces, but science tells us they aren't. Prisons are filled with people someone mistakenly said they recognized in a lineup. I don't have much confidence in the process that's about to unfold, but I don't get to choose. The only thing I can do is make it as fair as I can. It's been a while since I worked a lineup; I feel my muscle memory coming back.

The parade enters. Eight women. Two with tied-back brown hair, the rest loose: three with medium to light brown, two blondes, and Kate. Kate, with her loose jet-black hair, stands out starkly. Not good. There should be two other women with hair colour like hers, one at a minimum. I could let it go and complain to the judge at trial, but I decide not to.

I motion to Kan to exit. We huddle in the hall.

"The lineup's not fair," I say.

"Excuse me?"

"I'm doing you a favour, Detective. You need at least one person with loose black hair, maybe two. My client is the only person in that lineup with jet-black hair. The judge will take two seconds to throw this out if it ever gets to trial. And there goes your identification." I snap my fingers. "Not to mention, this lineup may already be compromised by my client's celebrity status. She's the one who will look familiar, the one who your witness is likely to pick."

Kan folds his arms. "I'm entitled to this lineup. I *need* this lineup. Save your arguments for the judge. We haven't got all day. A child is missing." He turns to go back in.

I resent his implication I've got my priorities wrong. "A false identification won't help you find her."

Kan stops. The set of his shoulders tells me he knows I'm right. "Fine. Let's go shopping."

He instructs the officer with him, a winsome thing with a brush cut, to recall the lineup women, then we make our way to the reception area.

I scan the room for women with jet-black hair, come up empty—lots of Asian faces, but that won't fix the problem. Kan does the same, shakes his head. He's about to move on when his eyes land on Officer Nathan—the woman with the headscarf who greeted me at the outset. Kan moves toward her and says something I can't hear.

"You know I can't do that, Detective," she says, her hand going to her scarf at her throat.

Kan presses on, undeterred. "I know you have jet-black hair, Officer Nathan."

"How would you know?" she hisses.

"I read the civilian staffing report. You agreed to be photographed for the job without your head covering. Remember?"

The plexiglass is between them, yet Kan leans in. "I know you can't bare your head before men. But I don't count. Consider me your brother. And the witness who will see you doesn't count either. This is a life-and-death situation. A little girl's life is at stake, Nurjehan."

Officer Nathan casts a glance at the poster of Tess on the wall. "Very well, Detective," she says finally. "For the child."

"Thank you," says Kan, then he straightens and swivels back to me. "Satisfied, Ms. Truitt?"

No, I'm not. Kan has outmanoeuvred me. This woman, with her tan skin and black hair, is too close to Kate. Even the set of her jaw and her lips resemble my client's—and it's the relationship of the mouth and jaw that is the clincher in facial recognition, I remember reading somewhere. If we ever get to trial, Officer Nathan's presence will doom any attempt to argue the lineup was unfair. If the witness is unsure, he may gloss over Kate and pick Officer Nathan. But something tells me this witness, whoever he is, will not be unsure.

Bottom line: I've made a mistake. I should have let Kan run his illegal lineup and saved my complaints for the judge.

"Let's go," I say.

Kan motions to Officer Brush Cut, who has reappeared, and tells her to take Officer Nathan to the prep room. "Do you need to see the lineup again before we bring the witness in, Ms. Truitt?" he asks politely.

I shake my head, but they're already there as Kan and I enter the booth—eight figures in nondescript outfits clutching numbers to their chests behind the one-way glass. Officer Brush Cut has swapped out one of the brunettes for Officer Nathan. I note her hair is indeed jet black, and loose like Kate's. I find Kate's face. The resemblance is imperfect—Kate's features are more delicate—but no judge would throw out this lineup.

"Bring the witness in," Kan orders, and a figure enters the booth. "Dante Bocci, Ms. Truitt."

We stare at each other in the dim light. Dante is thin, with wisps of faded red hair pasted over his pate. I put him at forty, perhaps older. His shoulders twitch, and when I meet his eyes, he looks away. Dante Bocci is nervous. Why, I don't know. He's already picked Kate's face out of a photo lineup.

Dante runs his expert eye over the assembled cast. He passes over the first four, pauses at Officer Nathan. For a moment, I dare to hope, and then Dante's eye scans on. I hold my breath as he comes to Kate, standing wan and strained before us. Her number wobbles in her hands; only I know the super-human effort she is making not to shake.

Dante peers forward. I see him nod, and I know it's over.

"Number six," he says.

"Are you sure?" asks Kan, all graciousness now. "Take your time. Be sure."

Dante whirls on Kan. "Of course I'm sure," he insists. "I'm a professional photographer. I take pictures of women's faces for a living. I never forget a fucking face."

Whoa. Is this guy nervous or is he unhinged?

If Kan is taken aback by Dante's sudden aggression, he doesn't show it. He simply nods and turns to me, a terse smile on his face. "Well, Ms. Truitt," he says. "There you have it. Any complaints?"

I should say no, but I won't give him the satisfaction. He and I both know this lineup was as perfect as they come. I can still play the celebrity angle if it comes to that, but given the resemblance between Officer Nathan and Kate, it won't get me far.

"I'll save my comments for the judge if it comes to that. Which it won't."

"Time will tell," says Kan. "Now, I have some questions for your client."

CHAPTER 7

BACK IN THE STERILE INTERVIEW room, my heart feels low and heavy as I wait with Kate. My client has been identified as the person with Tess after she disappeared, and the witness is a photographer who never forgets faces. It can't get worse.

Unless it does, I think, as the door swings open and Kan and Brush Cut enter. *Don't call her Brush Cut,* I remind myself. Her name is Ellen Burr.

Cops do interviews in pairs: one nice guy to lure the suspect in, one heavy to come down hard when defences are weak. Kan could play either role. The only question is how Sergeant Burr will come on. I don't have to wait long.

Burr, having started the recording and read Kate her Charter rights—the right to remain silent, the right to counsel, and then the kicker, she doesn't have to say anything but anything she says can be used against her—is all sweetness and light.

"We understand how you must feel, Ms. Sinclair-Jones," she begins. "We understand you are upset. I think we can all agree we need to find your daughter, make sure she is safe. And we need you to help us."

Kate looks at me. I nod, and she whispers, "Okay. Anything to find Tess."

As if on cue, Kan comes in. "Let us be frank, Ms. Sinclair-Jones. We have reason to believe you know what happened to your daughter. We have photos of a woman in a boat with a child we believe to be Tess, taken at 3:36 yesterday afternoon a few hundred yards from where Tess was last seen. And that woman has been identified—twice—as you."

Kan reaches for a plastic envelope, extracts three photos, and fans them out over the table. His eyes move from the photos to Kate, who is staring at the pictures in shock. I lean forward.

As Kan said, the photos show a woman and a child in a boat, some distance from the forested shoreline looming behind. The details are indistinct, but I make out a boat, a small steel barque, perhaps eighteen feet long, three slatted seats at the most and what looks like an engine hanging over the back. Sunlight glimmers on the surface of the water, and in the foreground, the shore forest looms. The photos are lovely in a romantic way, but for trial purposes they are all but useless: grainy and indistinct. Dante wasn't using a telephoto lens, which for a photographer is odd, unless he was going for artistic effect. I tuck that factoid away and focus on the pictures.

Despite the low quality, the first shot catches the woman's profile as she bends to touch the little girl's hair, the second as she lifts her face to the sun. The third captures her as she turns to manoeuvre the tiller on the small motor. The woman is tanned with dark hair, loose around her shoulders, but the face isn't clear. It could be Kate, or it could be someone else, someone who looks similar—there must have been hundreds of dark women with long hair in the area that day. This is good news for my client.

However, there can be no mistaking the child. Light-brown skin and a blond Afro—it's undoubtably Tess. There's little chance of a look-alike at that time in that place. And something else. I peer closer. Even with the graininess, it's apparent the little girl in the photo is relaxed with the woman. *The child knows the woman*, I think. *The child loves the woman.*

I want to reach for Kate's hand, but the protocols of professionalism don't allow that. Instead, I straighten and address Kan. "These photos aren't identification. They could be of any dark-haired woman."

"You are here to assist your client, not to comment on the quality of the evidence, Ms. Truitt," Kan says tightly, his grey eyes cold.

"Of course." I smile sweetly. I have done what I set out to do—tell my client this isn't as bad as Kan is making out.

But if Kate has taken note she shows no sign. She traces the face of the child in the nearest photo. Tears start down her face.

"Ms. Sinclair-Jones," I say softly, and she pulls her eyes from the image. *Stay calm*, I will her. "My client is in shock," I tell Kan.

"Your client needs to help us."

"My client denies she was the woman in the boat," I reply.

Kan gives me a hard look. "Again, you are here to advise your client, Ms. Truitt, not to tell her what to say. I was told you know your business. So let's stop wasting time. A little girl last seen with your client is missing—"

"Unproven," I interject.

"—this is a matter of life and death," he continues. "Your client needs to start talking. Now."

Kate's words come out in a tearful torrent. "That's not me. That woman"—her hand sweeps over the photos—"has the same build and hair, but that isn't me. I wasn't there!"

"Then can you tell us where you were yesterday afternoon, Ms. Sinclair-Jones?"

I nod at Kate to answer.

"I was at the university," she says. "UBC. I had an early morning class."

"You're attending UBC?" Kan prompts.

"Yes, when things fell apart with Trist and he got custody, I was so alone. I had lost my husband and my baby, and I hadn't spoken to my parents since Trist and I married." She bows her head. "I went through some dark times, I admit it. Eventually I pulled myself together and went to see my parents, told them I wanted to get my life on track. They welcomed me and Tess—I had her on weekends then—back into the family. And then the court took away my weekends and I slumped again. This time Mom and Dad didn't let me go. Mom got me help and suggested I should go back to school, get a teaching degree so I could make a living. I was a basket case for a while, I don't deny it. But I was trying to pick myself up."

I shoot Kate a glance of respect. She may be stronger and more resilient than I thought.

Sergeant Burr is all sympathy. "We know you've had emotional ups and downs. But let's get back to the case. Is there anyone who can corroborate you were at the university?"

I hold my hand up. "I'm instructing my client not to answer that question. My client is not on trial here. She's speaking to you out of concern for her daughter."

Kan takes back the reins. "What Ms. Sinclair-Jones can tell us about where she was yesterday when Tess went missing may assist us in finding her. Ms. Sinclair-Jones, what did you do after your class? Where were you yesterday afternoon?"

I gesture for Kate to answer.

She tucks her hair behind her ear. "I was at the university, like I said. After my morning class, I went to the library and sat in a carrel all afternoon working on a paper. How to structure lesson plans for kids learning band instruments."

"Did any friends see you, talk to you?" Kan asks. "Maybe you took a book out of the library with a time stamp proving you were at the university at the time Tess disappeared?"

"I instruct Ms. Sinclair-Jones not to answer," I say, but Kate is already speaking.

"Nothing I can remember. I mean, there were people around. Just no one I can remember."

"And where were you last night, Ms. Sinclair-Jones? We know you weren't at your home in Jericho Beach. The police sat in your driveway all night waiting for you. You didn't return until 7:35 this morning."

We're in uncharted waters now. I don't know what Kate will say, and Kan is determined to make her answer.

"My house," Kate says quietly, looking down at her hands. "It's the only thing I salvaged from my marriage to Trist, but it's filled with so many memories. Some good. Some bad." She raises her head. "I prefer not to spend time there. It's painful."

I allow myself a sympathetic glance at her in front of Kan. I know where she's coming from.

"So where were you last night?" Kan presses, but his tone is softer now.

"My parents' house. My mother called me about seven, as I was about to buy a sandwich at the machine. I had planned to stay till ten and finish the paper, but my mom said I was working too hard and I should come over. She'd gone to Riddim on Commercial Drive when she got off work—she's an ESL teacher—and got callaloo and patties. I love Jamaican food—that's where we're from, originally—so I said yes. Besides, I could tell she was worried about me. And to be honest, I didn't want to be alone. So I went over to their place and spent the night. It's not a big house, but they keep a room for me. They know how lonely I am without Tess."

"Where is it?" mutters Kan. I send him a warning glare.

Kate gives him an address on Everett Crescent in Burnaby. "It's a little seventies bungalow."

"Our search didn't turn up that address," Kan says, glancing at Sergeant Burr, who is already texting the police team.

"It used to be my grandfather's home, my dad's dad," Kate explains. "When my grandfather passed away last year, my parents downsized, and they moved in. That's where I was last night. This morning, I got up before my parents woke and went back to my house." She gives Kan a baleful look. "Where your officers were waiting. I had turned my phone off. I didn't even know Tess was missing. I had to hear it from the police."

Good, I think. She's recovering from her shock, fighting back.

Kan shifts gears. "You said your mother was anxious, Ms. Sinclair-Jones. Did she mention Tess yesterday?"

"Her only grandchild? Yes! She's always at the top of our minds. My parents thought it was terrible the court had taken my weekend access away, wouldn't even let me see her without a social worker in the room. They love her as much as I do. My mom loves to tell Tess island stories." A sob escapes Kate's throat. She pauses, swallows her tears. "Sorry."

"Did your mother seem worried about Tess?" Kan asks. "More than usual?"

"She is always worried about Tess. She doesn't think Trist is a good parent."

"Do you agree with her?"

Kate sighs. "It's complicated. Trist loves Tess. Do I agree with his parenting all the time? No. Tess is always in the spotlight. Too much. The paparazzi are relentless, following Trist and Tess everywhere, shouting at her to smile for pictures. Trist and I have very different opinions about privacy. I've always been afraid something would happen. My parents, too." She straightens, looks Kan in the eye. "And something did."

Kan replies, "We'll get to the bottom of this, you may be sure. I have officers on the way to your parents as we speak."

Kate nods. She's tired, but she's holding up better than I hoped.

Her story has the ring of truth. But she's not out of the woods, even if they confirm she stayed overnight with her parents. No one can vouch for Kate being at the university that afternoon. The woman and child in the boat were photographed around four. Lots of time for Kate to have done whatever she did, ditch the boat in some cove on the mainland, and get back to her parents' house that evening.

"Then are we done here?" I ask. "My client is exhausted, and she's cooperated with your interview."

"A few more questions," Kan says. "Ms. Sinclair-Jones, we know you were deeply angry the courts had taken away your custody and weekend rights. We know you told people you would get

Tess back, whatever it took. And we know Tess had been rejecting you, screaming at you, throwing tantrums."

I look at Kate, whose face has drained of colour.

"Put your question, Detective," I say, but Kan's voice cuts through mine.

"Do you deny your daughter was rejecting you?"

Kate shakes her head.

"Speak up, Ms. Sinclair-Jones."

"No, I don't deny it. The separation was hard. Tess didn't understand why she couldn't be with me anymore. She blamed me."

"Hard for her, hard for you?"

Tears form in Kate's eyes. "Yes, it's tearing me apart."

"And when Tess started rejecting you, it became still harder for you?" Kan presses.

Kate covers her face with her hands. Her shoulders begin to shake with sobs.

"You are badgering my client, Detective," I say. "Any mother would grieve at being separated from her child. And any child would resent the separation. None of this will help us find the child."

But Kan's focus is on Kate. "Trist is planning on moving to Vegas, isn't he? Which would mean fewer visits for you and Tess. Isn't that true?"

This is news to me. I suck in my breath and wait.

"No, no," Kate cries.

"I can understand how you must have felt," Kan goes on. "Tess moving to a different country. I understand how you might wish Tess had never been born."

"Stop badgering," I hiss to Kan, but Kate has jumped to her feet.

"No! No, you're wrong. I could never have wished that, never,

never, never. I told you I didn't take her. It wasn't me, why don't you listen?" Kate cries.

"Humour me," says Kan, "and sit down. You say you weren't the woman in the boat. But an eyewitness says you were. What if he's right? That would leave two possibilities. You took Tess somewhere to hide her . . ."

Kate has sunk back in her chair. "No, no."

"Or maybe something bad happened that wasn't your fault. And Tess is dead." Kan leans in, beseeching. "Help me, Kate, which is it?"

I slam my hand down on the table. "This interview is over, Detective. You've gone too far."

"No," Kate screams over my words. "No, don't say that! Tess is alive. I feel it, I know it."

The room falls silent, Kate's voice echoing in our ears.

"Unless you plan to lay charges against my client, we are done here," I say, rising.

Kan's face is expressionless, but I know he's calculating what to do next.

Option one: Keep grilling Kate until she disintegrates completely and tells him what she's done with Tess. But the odds aren't good. I won't let him, and anyway, Kate is fixed in her story and unlikely to budge.

Option two: Arrest Kate and put her in jail. But he doesn't have enough. The photo is blurry, and if Dante can produce a better one, we haven't heard about it. And going on Dante's identification alone is risky—eyewitness identifications are notoriously unreliable. Assuming Kan could prove it was Kate in the boat, the most he could accuse her of—without evidence Tess is dead—is taking her child contrary to court order.

Which leaves option three: Let Kate go. Watch and wait. If

Tess is alive, Kate will lead them to her sooner rather than later. If Tess is not alive, well, in that case, time doesn't matter much.

Kan meets my gaze. "Ms. Truitt, the police regard your client as a person of suspicion. But I'm releasing her. On condition that she not leave the Lower Mainland or Gulf Islands."

Option three it is. Kan is leaving Kate lots of room to move around. She can return to the island. She can drive a hundred miles to the north, south, or east. Everywhere she goes, she will be watched. Run, Kate, run. Let's see where you go.

"Very well. Kate?" I place my hand on her shoulder. She looks up at me, her face bleak. She gets it. The police say they want to find Tess, but what they really want is to pin her daughter's disappearance on her. "Let's go."

"Stop the recording," says Kan, and Sergeant Burr pushes the button.

CHAPTER 8

IREQUEST A SIDE ROOM SO Kate and I can do a post-mortem, then go to grab some food for Kate. She's been here since eight a.m. and it's almost five p.m. At the vending machine, I buy two granola bars and two bottles of water. I glance at my phone. No messages. Claire and Mab are okay, fingers crossed.

"What happens now, Ms. Truitt?" Kate asks when I return. Her voice is flat.

I open a water bottle, pass it to her along with one of the bars. "I know you're probably not hungry, but you need to eat."

Reluctantly, she takes a bite, chews. And I do the same. I feel the sugar hit my bloodstream. *How did I used to do this job?* I wonder.

After finishing the bar, I take a sip of water, then clear my throat. "What happens next depends on what new evidence turns up. As it is, they don't have enough to charge you with anything."

"What about the photos? What about that woman in the boat with Tess?"

"Even if it was you—"

"It's not."

"—the police have no proof any harm has come to Tess. The most they could do is haul you into family court for breach of the custody order, assuming they could link you to the boat." I pause. "Do you have any idea who that woman in the photo could be?"

"It's too blurry—it could be any number of people. Lena, Trist's new girlfriend, or Selma—she's the nanny—but neither of them makes sense. Why would they want Tess? They have her already." Kate shakes her head, and her eyes well up again. "If Tess doesn't turn up, they'll blame me. And I will pay. I always do. The press, the public—they've been against me since Trist and I got together, and it was even worse when we split up. *Crazy Kate,* they said. *Kate the bad mother.* Like it was wrong to protect my child's privacy. The police already think I did it. They've zeroed in on me when they should be looking for Tess. My beautiful, beautiful baby." Kate wipes a tear from the corner of her eye. "I used to worry she was too perfect for this world. And now—" She stifles a sob.

I'm listening, but my fingers are busy on my phone. A tabloid picture of Lena and Trist fills the small screen; Lena is dark and slender. I scroll on, hit a photo of Tess with her hand in the hand of a different woman, presumably her nanny; I can't see the woman's face, but she, too, is slender and dark. Any of these women could have been the woman in the boat. Still, Kate has a point—she is the one with the motive. She was heard saying she would get her baby back, and Trist was planning to leave for Vegas. These cases are often personal; one parent wanting the child for themselves. And yet, something in me—maybe the mother in me—believes Kate is telling the truth.

But where does that leave Kate? Despite my misgivings about the police, they'd be foolish not to check in with the other women in Tess's life, so for now, I leave that to the side. Of course, there's the possibility this is a ransom plot or some stranger might have taken Tess. It happens. Fame attracts the crazies, and all the paparazzi photos might have drawn the attention of a pedophile. But Kate's right, the public is against her, and so, it seems, are the police. If I'm going to help her, I'm going to need to know more than her alibi.

"You have to stay strong, Kate, for Tess," I say gently. "No matter what the public thinks, they don't get to decide your fate. The courts do. I can help you. But you're going to need to tell me more. I know you like your privacy, but can you tell me about your relationship with Trist?"

Kate fidgets with the cap of the water bottle. "What do you want to know?"

"Let's start with how you and Trist met. It was six or seven years ago, wasn't it?"

Kate nods. "I met Trist at Harrigan's. It's a posh resort up north on Quadra Island. I was working there after graduating university with a degree in music. My parents gave me a hard time about that. They're both from working-class families, and they were nervous I wouldn't be able to get a job with a music degree. Well, they were right. My student loan repayments were about to start, and I needed to find work. I saw an advertisement for a boat tour guide at Harrigan's, taking tourists to see whales and sea lions. I knew all about boats from hanging around with my dad at work. Anyway, I applied and got the job." Her eyes grow wistful. "Best summer of my life."

"Because of Trist?"

"Because of Trist. He was a struggling guitar-for-hire then, but he was as handsome as he is now. The resort brought him in to play in the bar most nights. His voice was mesmerizing. One night, I stayed late and got up the courage to introduce myself. I told him I loved to sing and he insisted I perform a song. There were only a few people in the bar, but I was so nervous. I sang 'Killing Me Softly with His Song,' ironic, because that was what Trist was doing to me every night in the bar." Kate smiles at the memory. "Trist came in with harmony, like backup, and when I was done, he gave me a standing ovation. We started hanging out after that. We harmonized sometimes, and I introduced him to reggae. He started using some of those beats in his tracks. He said I had talent. It wasn't just that we were attracted to one another; he made me feel seen. Still, in the back of my mind, I thought I might be a fling for him. When the summer ended, he asked me if I would go with him on a small tour around the province. He was playing some festivals, and he wanted me to come."

"What did your parents think?" I think I know, but I want to hear Kate's perspective.

"They were less than thrilled. It wasn't about race, like the tabloids would have you believe, although they would have been delighted if I'd married a nice Jamaican boy. They wanted stability for me back then, and Trist was a wandering troubadour, no roots, no family. He had spent years taking every gig he could to get by, and I took part-time jobs here and there, but nothing permanent that might interfere with following his shows. I told him he should write a love song—that's how every musician seems to break out. He wrote 'Goin' Down on Love,' and the rest is history. I remember when he got his record deal, he rushed back to the little one-bedroom we were living in, and he asked me to marry him."

Kate's face is wistful. I swallow, my throat filling. I hear Mike's voice when he finally found himself after years of grief for his parents, *Jilly, I want to marry you.*

"My dad blew up when I told him I was going to marry Trist. Mom and Dad saw Trist and me as a temporary thing—a couple of crazy kids who would get bored with each other and move on. Then I sat in their kitchen and told them Trist had hit the big time, and I was marrying him. When it sunk in I was serious, Dad lost it and told me to get out of the house." She halts, wipes her eyes. "So I did," she whispers. "I just got up and walked out before Mom could talk him out of it. I didn't see them for years. Not until after Trist and I had separated."

"So you married Trist," I say. "How did that go?"

"Great, for a while. We were in love. Trist toured the country, then the continent. And I was by his side."

"What changed?" I prod.

"What do you think? Fame," she says. "The tabloids were relentless. Photographers hounding us all the time. Bloggers digging up everything about me. My falling-out with my parents, my transcripts, my old friends, criticisms about my hair, my weight. Some of them had a hard time with our biracial marriage. I never thought it mattered, but they did. Social media was even worse. My whole life was on display for everyone, and everyone had an opinion. Trist liked the attention because they flattered him, but they called me a gold-digger, and that's the exact opposite of what I am. I loved Trist before the money, before the fame. It felt so unfair, so unnecessary, but I guess it got clicks. So I cried a lot. Trist tried to comfort me. He and his management team—by then he had a whole support staff—assured me it would die down if I were more active, more visible, attended more events with Trist so the public could get to know me better. The choice was mine, but I knew Trist wanted me to try." She sits back and sighs deeply.

"I was in a bad place. Uncomfortable in the spotlight. Skewered on social media. We were trying to have a family at the time, but I kept miscarrying."

I remember now, seeing headlines about their fertility struggles. About photos outside of clinics. "I'm sorry," I say. "That can't have been easy."

She takes a gulp of her water, blinks hard before she speaks again. "I lost three babies," she says. "The last one I miscarried alone. Trist was on tour."

The portrait of an isolated person grieving loss after loss comes into focus for me. What Kate needed was her husband, compassion, and the privacy to grieve, but the world gave her criticism and judgment.

Kate goes back to playing with the cap of her bottle. "It got out we were trying—something Trist said in an interview—and then the press started in. Poor Trist wants a baby, but Kate's infertile, that sort of thing. We tried everything . . ." She trails off, lost in her memories. "And then a miracle happened, and we had Tess." She smiles. "For a while, we lived in bliss. Trist cut back on his appearances, so it was just the three of us basking in the glow of our little family. I felt as though I had my husband back again. It didn't last."

"You mentioned to Detective Kan that you and Trist had different approaches to parenting, particularly how much Tess was in the limelight."

Kate nods. "The media is obsessed with Tess. Even as a baby, she had this quality—star quality, I guess. She'd smile at the cameras at a basketball game, and the world would light up. But I wanted to shelter her from the press and the cameras. I wanted her to have a normal childhood, like me, one where she could get dirty and explore without having to think of the paparazzi. I was worried what the attention would do to her, but also what might happen if the press turned on her, as they had me. The world is not a friendly place to biracial people. Trist felt differently. He doesn't get it. He doesn't see the micro-aggressions. He would take her to publicity events, show her off. It made me so angry—I didn't want Tess growing up that way. We fought a lot about it. It wasn't like the old times when he would tell me I had a choice. Now he said I had to come with them, show the media what a happy family we were. I went along with it for a while; I figured if I was there, I could protect Tess."

I think about the photo of Tess with Trist and Kate from this morning's headline—Trist blithely carefree, Kate focused on protecting Tess from the cameras.

Kate's still talking. "Once, a pap got right in our faces with his camera, and I pushed him back. The tabloids made a huge commotion about that. *Crazy Kate loses it*, they said. *She's so emotional*, they said. I tried to tell Trist it was too much, they were getting too close, but he was livid with me. I told him he cared more about what the public thought of him than what his own family wanted, that he was vain and shallow. We said terrible things to each other. That was the beginning of the end."

"Whose idea was it to separate?" I ask.

"Mine, actually. We went on a family vacation to try to repair things, but the paparazzi followed us, and Trist did nothing to stop it. I couldn't go on like that, and I told Trist so. He said he still loved me, but we were making each other miserable trying to stay together. He was very gentle, very generous. He thanked me for all I'd done, for inspiring him to write 'Goin' Down on Love,' and then he said I could have the house and we could share custody. I'd have Tess when he was on the road, and he'd have her when he was in town. We did that for a year, and then out of the blue, Trist applied for sole custody and got it. I was only allowed to have Tess on weekends."

I wait for her to continue, but she doesn't. What had Edith said this morning? It was quite the battle for custody? Something happened in that courtroom, something Kate doesn't want to talk about.

"Why did the judge give Trist custody?" I ask.

"Because they said I was a bad mother," she says quietly.

"And were you?" I ask gently.

Kate bristles. "Are you on my side or theirs?"

"Your side. But if I'm to help you, I need to know everything about you and Tess."

"I was a good mother. But I wasn't a perfect person."

I wait.

Kate sets her water bottle to the side, meets my eye, and once more I'm reminded of her strength. "After the separation, I went through a depression. The tabloids were calling me names. My marriage was over. I had no career. Oh, Trist provided me with a house of my own and generous alimony, but I had no purpose. I was lost. When I was with Tess, all that faded away, but then whenever Trist would come back from a tour, she'd be gone, and the depression would worsen. It was getting harder and harder to come out of the gloom."

Kate's words hit home. I've been there, too. Fortunately, I had people to help pull me out. Kate was alone.

"I started taking an antidepressant to help," she continues, matter-of-fact. "But it took some time before I got the right dosage, and in that time, I struggled to provide Tess with a structured environment. She pulled away from me. Every time she was with me, she would cry for her dad, for Selma. I couldn't make her happy. That's what the detective was referring to. I thought I had things under control, but Selma thought otherwise. Unbeknownst to me, she went to Trist and told him I was unfit. That's why he filed for sole custody." She pauses. "But I still had weekend access. Pulled myself together and reconciled with Mom and Dad. Mom taught her Jamaican songs and dances. Every Sunday there was a big brunch after church at someone's house, with jerk chicken and escovitch fish. When Monday morning came, Tess would get angry and raise a fuss."

"When Selma picked her up?"

"Yes. Selma used to drop her off Fridays and pick her up Mondays. I was shocked to hear her testimony in court. Some of the things she said were true, but others were exaggerated. But then again, my mind wasn't clear. And my daughter *was* pulling away. It was a very dark time for me." She sighs. "I'll never forget the judge's pronouncement—*Inability to provide a structured environment. Inability to discipline the child and teach her right from wrong. An unhealthy dependence on the child that will undermine the child's ability to achieve independence."*

It's enough to give Trist custody and limit Kate to weekend visits. But Edith said Kate was only allowed to see Tess on supervised visits. There must be more to deny a mother the right to be alone with her child. There's something else Kate hasn't told me.

"Kate, why did they limit you to supervised access?"

"That came later. Like I said, it was a dark time, but I was getting better. I was figuring out my medication. I had patched things up with my parents. And I was working on my relationship with Tess. She was confused at first—she was never happy when she arrived each weekend—but after a while, she seemed to forget about Trist and Selma and remember how much fun we could have together. Each weekend, she was my little girl again. With Grandma and Grandpa we would go for long walks on Jericho Beach, a few blocks from my house, and comb for shells. On cold days, we would put on our coats and boots and splash around in the low tide. We would go for ice cream, and I would read to her at bedtime. But come every Monday, Selma collected her, and my heart broke all over again."

Kate may have been taking an antidepressant, but time with Tess was clearly the best medicine for her. I can see the pain on her face even now. "What happened?" I press.

Kate splays her hands on the table. "One Sunday night, Trist phoned and said he was going on tour with his new girlfriend, Lena, and they would be taking Tess with them. I told him he couldn't do that—the judge said I got Tess every weekend. Trist came back, all cold and icy. 'Read the order, Kate. It gives me the right to take Tess with me if I am going to be

away for more than three weeks. I checked with my lawyer.'
Then he hung up.

"I was out of my mind with grief. We had had such a beautiful weekend, Tess and I, and I couldn't bear the thought of losing her for weeks. I couldn't sleep, so I took a sleeping pill. It must have reacted poorly with my antidepressant because I completely passed out." She looks away now. "When I woke up, Selma was standing over me with Tess in her arms. She said she found Tess on the kitchen counter eating cookies and the cookie jar broken on the floor. Tess was fine, but Selma was shocked. 'You didn't answer the bell. I had to use the key you hid in the flower box to get in.' She kept saying, 'What would have happened if I hadn't arrived when I did, if I hadn't found the key?'

"The rest is history," Kate says bitterly. "Trist went to court the next day asking to have my weekend access revoked. Nothing I said mattered. The judge agreed with Trist I could not be trusted with Tess alone. Maybe she was right." Her eyes meet mine. "But I was never on drugs, like the tabloids said. I never did illegal stuff."

Motherhood is a precarious business. One mistake and they take your child away. I repress an inward shudder. I look at my watch—6:30. Mab and Claire are waiting. I need to wrap this up. But not quite yet; before I go, I need to know one more thing.

"You said you were distraught at the thought of being away from Tess for such a long time. How did you handle the news Trist is planning to move to Vegas with Tess? Tell me the truth, Kate."

"I won't lie to you," she says. "I'm appalled. I am determined to get custody of Tess. But properly. After that horrible day with the sleeping pill, I figured out my medication, created a support system with my parents, followed every guideline of the supervised visits to a T. Last week, my doctor and my social worker told me they would support an application to the court for greater access. I wouldn't have jeopardized that by taking Tess." She pauses. "But now, she's gone. Ms. Truitt, you have to help me get her back."

My tiny daughter's face fills my mind, and the thought of losing her immobilizes me. And then my professional muscle memory kicks in. At times like this, you have to give the client hope.

"We will get Tess back," I say. "You will make your application for custody. I'm on your side. I believe you."

"Thank you," she replies. "Not many people do."

"I'm going to help change that," I say. "But for now, we've done all we can do. I don't think you should be alone tonight. Can you stay with your parents again?"

She nods, then fumbles with her cellphone and sends a text.

We make our way down the long door-lined corridor, through the still-chaotic reception hall. Officer Nathan watches as I approach her booth but offers no greeting. She speaks into her mouthpiece, and within moments, four police escorts are upon us—two for me, two for Kate.

"Thanks, Ms. Truitt," Kate says as she slides into the back of her cruiser. "I appreciate your help, but you must know, all I care about is finding Tess. That's my priority."

"Understood," I say, my hand on the door. Claire's face floods my mind again. "As I said, I'm a mother, too."

Kate's eyes soften. "Then you know."

"I do."

Defence Lawyer Rule Number One: Get the money up front.

Defence Lawyer Rule Number Two: Don't get too close to the client.

My first day back on the job, and I'm breaking both. I close the door and watch the car move away. Above, the clouds darken. The summer sun is gone.

CHAPTER 9

THE CRUISER STOPS IN MY drive. It's past seven p.m. I spot Edith's little car parked down the street. Has something gone wrong? Like a trained chauffeur, the officer in the front passenger seat alights and holds my door open. I slide out, give a small wave.

My heart is pounding, and it's not because I'm running up the steps. My mind has slipped gears. A moment ago, I was immersed in the riddle of where Tess can be and Kate's role in that. Now all I can think of is Claire, Claire, Claire. My baby Claire.

I push open the oak door, enter the dimness of the entry hall. "Edith," I call.

Silence. Then Edith appears, Claire bundled in her arms. "Welcome home," she says cheerily. "Claire, say hello to Mommy."

I rush to them, take Claire into my arms. My daughter waves

her tiny hands and opens her mouth in a gaping, wobbly smile. I plant kisses all over her face. Oh, what a perfect angel I have.

Finally, I look up at Edith. "Where's Mab?"

"I'll fill you in later," Edith says with a nod at Claire. "Right now, we need to get this little lass ready for bed. I've given her a bottle."

I cradle Claire, and we go upstairs. Edith guides the baby bedtime routine with expert efficiency—changing, zipping on Claire's pyjamas, passing her to me for a final good-night buss before snuggling her into the soft cushions of her bassinette. Her eyes grow heavy and finally close. Edith sets the monitor, and silently we steal from her room.

"Have you eaten?" Edith asks as we descend the stairs. "I'm guessing not. Come, I've concocted a meal of sorts from cold cuts and salads I found in the fridge."

I follow behind, but instead of the kitchen, she turns to the dining room. I pause on the threshold. I haven't had a meal in this room for months, preferring the kitchen to the memories of the rare but special dinners I had here with Mike. After, we would move to the sitting room, where Mike's fingers would slide over keys, playing my favourites: "Claire de Lune," "La Fille aux Cheveux de Lin." Now, I see white napkins, wineglasses, and artfully arranged food on porcelain plates. I blink back tears at Edith's gesture. For the first time, the old memories don't sting.

"This is lovely, Edith. And I'm starved." I tuck into my seat as Edith pours Chardonnay into crystal glasses. "Just a little," I say. I haven't had a drink in months.

Once Edith slides into her chair, I pick up my fork and dig into my *salade composée*—rare roast beef, fingerling potatoes, roasted spears of asparagus. The scent of homemade mayonnaise wafts to my nostrils. "Amazing," I murmur. All I've had today is that granola bar.

"So," Edith begins. "You didn't mention you were returning to work when we spoke this morning. What changed?"

I fill her in on Cy's call. "You're looking at the lawyer for Kate Sinclair-Jones," I say. "I'm surprised Mab didn't mention it. Where is she, by the way?"

Edith sighs. "Mab has left," she says simply.

I put down my fork, stunned. "Left? Just like that? Without telling me?"

"So it seems. She called around three p.m. and asked if I could come look after Claire because she had somewhere to be. When I got here, she was standing on the porch. She thanked me for coming, then said she loved Claire, but this wasn't a good fit. She picked up her bags and left. That was it. Oh yes, she left an address where you could send her pay."

I feel shame creeping up my cheeks. "Did she say why it wasn't a good fit?"

"She said she told you she expected Saturday afternoons off."

My heart sinks. "She did mention something about that when she first started. It completely slipped my mind when Cy called."

"Don't blame yourself, dear. She should have reminded you if it was that important. I would have come over to look after Claire."

A wave of sickness sweeps over me. I put my napkin down. "I can't do this."

"What can't you do?"

"The whole mother thing. I can't do it. Right from the beginning, I couldn't do it. I couldn't breastfeed Claire. I couldn't stop her crying those first weeks. I can't ooh and aah and do the baby

67

talk like other mothers." I choke back a sob. "I have to face it, Edith. I can't care for Claire, and I can't keep a nanny to do it for me. This is my third nanny. In three months. It's never a good fit. It never will be. If Mike were here, he would figure something out. But I . . . I—"

Edith is at my side, taking my hand in hers. "Look at me, Jilly."

I look up.

"First, you are a good mother. I see how you are with Claire. She smiles for you, snuggles into your arms. She's not five months yet, but she has body language. And so what if you can't talk baby talk? You never learned. That United Church couple loved you, but they weren't big on cuddling. So of course it doesn't come naturally to you. But you and Claire are working it out fine."

"I—"

She holds up a finger. "Let me finish. Second, you need to get back to your practice. The law is your life. You come alive when you are on a case. You are a brilliant defence lawyer. It's good for you, good for your clients. Your practice is part of you, my dear. You can't give it up. It wouldn't be good for you, wouldn't be good for Claire." Edith tightens her grip on my hand. "So, social worker that I am, I have come up with a plan. While I was waiting for you, I telephoned a friend—Liz is her name—who runs a daycare. Not far, the other side of Granville Street. Usually, you would have to wait for months to get Claire in, but Liz has had a vacancy, and as a special favour will take Claire."

"But she's so little," I object, aghast.

"No, not too little. Liz specializes in the little ones. From three months to five years old, five days a week. Claire will be loved and hugged and will have a great time interacting with the other babies and toddlers. In my opinion, she will better off there than alone here with a nanny."

"But there would be days—lots of them—when I'm in court or a police station and can't pick her up until late." I shake my head. "No, it wouldn't work."

"I've thought of that," says Edith. "I'm enjoying my volunteer work and my rose garden. But I would love to have Claire with me for a few hours now and then. If you can't make it, I'll pick her up, take her home with me." She smiles. "I must admit I'm being selfish. Having Claire with me more will bring me great pleasure. I can be her pretend granny."

I'm standing, pulling Edith to me. She's not thin, but I feel the fragility beneath her strength. I hug this woman who has saved me more times than I can recall and is now doing it again.

"Edith," I breathe through my tears. "You're no pretend granny. You're the real deal."

Edith pats my back. "Now, now." She doesn't like the attention. "You must eat. And tell me about your new case. How is the mother?"

I nod and take my seat, wiping my eyes with my napkin. "Kate is distraught. Everyone at that police station is desperate to find Tess. Of course, as you predicted, they're giving Kate a good grueling. There is a witness of sorts who puts Kate in the picture." I take another bite, thinking about Dante Bocci the photographer. "But I don't think it will hold up."

"Already back in the swing, I see," Edith says, eyes twinkling over her wineglass.

"I told Cy just the interview, but I can't abandon Kate now." I remember my lawyerly duty. "I can't share more detail. All I'll say is Kate told me some of the dirt from the custody battle you mentioned." I swirl my wineglass, take in the butter-lemon scent of Chardonnay. "That woman has been through the wringer, and now this. She's stronger than people think."

"It takes one to know one," Edith replies. "Having you there must have been a comfort to Kate. We can only pray little Tess will be found alive and well."

"I hope so." I can't bear to think what it will do to Kate if Tess isn't found.

Edith changes the topic, and we chitchat as we finish the food, but my mind races over the details of the case. By the time I say goodbye to Edith and climb the stairs, I feel the weight of the day on my shoulders. It's a familiar feeling: weary contentment.

Edith is right. I am a mother, but I am also a lawyer. The law is in my brain and in my blood. For the past three months, I've been afraid I will lose Claire the way I lost Mike. It's a dangerous world, my work. But I can't live that way. Will I worry? Yes. Always. But that's what motherhood brings. I peer over Claire's sleeping form in her bassinette. The best I can do for my little girl is to push beyond the fear, give her an example to follow.

I slide into my bed, resolved. This Monday, I will go back. Back to my little office. Back to the courtroom to do justice. Or try to.

I'm not religious, but I say a silent prayer they will find Tess. Does Kate know where she is? Is she lying when she says she wasn't the woman in the boat? And why was Dante so aggressive—is he afraid of the police? Maybe he was hired to point the finger at Kate? Assuming he's on the up-and-up, how could he identify Kate with such confidence if what he saw was the blur of the photos?

With luck, they'll find Tess, and none of this will matter.

Tomorrow is Sunday. If the rain showers let up, I will bundle Claire in her carrier and take her down to Jericho for a long walk on the beach, like Kate used to do with Tess. We will breathe in the sea air and feel the wind on our faces. We will stop to watch the children splashing in the rising tide and the dogs cavorting in the sand. We will be happy.

CHAPTER 10

THE BOARDROOM IS FULL OF yellow and aqua balloons floating along the ceiling, bobbing in the corners.

Welcome back, Jilly, a modest banner proclaims.

One by one, they greet me, my office family.

My receptionist, Debbie, sports a Hermes scarf—*a gift from a new beau?* I wonder—as she embraces me. Then there's my partner, Jeff Solosky, his new glasses rounder than the last pair, if possible. My faithful associate, Alicia Leung, her long mane now cropped in a pixie cut that suits her fine features. And in the back, with his thumb raised, is my redemption project, Damon Cheskey, not on the official payroll now that he's studying law, but still part of our little firm. I saved Damon's life twice, first when I got him acquitted of murdering a drug dealer he had pumped five bullets into, second when I pulled the plug on his plans to OD himself.

I shake my head, rub a tear from my cheek; I have missed these people.

An hour ago, I was dropping off Claire at Liz's daycare. My heart was tight as I climbed the stairs, Claire in my arms, Edith toting Claire's diaper bag behind me. I was worried Claire wouldn't like it, I wouldn't like it—and that Liz wouldn't like us.

A step inside, and my worries dissipated. Liz, an ample woman with unkempt grey curls flowing to her shoulders, greeted us with a smile and reached out for Claire. She cradled her in her arms while Edith and I watched. This was not about me, I realized, it was about Claire and Liz.

Edith explained Liz grew up in this house, and she turned the first floor and the spacious garden behind into a daycare when she inherited it. "She spent a year-plus wrangling bureaucrats and fighting NIMBY neighbours to hang the rainbow sign between the pillars of her front porch."

I looked around the space with a new appreciation. The once-elegant parlour was lined with bassinettes and changing tables. In the room beyond, parents were kissing tots goodbye. A little girl howled, clinging to her father; a small boy, anxious to get to his toys, waved his mother off. Distant laughter cut the air. Claire smiled up at Liz, and Liz cooed back.

Edith caught my eye. *Didn't I tell you?*

Now, I stand in the boardroom of the fledging firm of Truitt and Solosky, buffeted by my colleagues. In honour of what Debbie announces is my return, a heap of pastries and muffins occupy the centre of the table, and she circulates coffee to everyone—not the usual Starbucks paper cups but real brewed coffee in white art-deco mugs. I raise an eyebrow, spot a slinky new Italian coffee machine on the credenza.

I turn to Jeff. "I go away for a few months and return to find a new coffee machine and real mugs."

Jeff guffaws. "Contrary to Yeats's prognostication, in this little office, the centre continues to hold. Same old criminals, same old tales of winning and woe." He gets serious. "Debbie said we needed to go green. No more paper."

"Expensive, going green," I say.

"We can afford it," Jeff says with a smile.

Debbie appears at my side. "What do you think?"

I put my arm around her. "Long overdue. I can live with it."

She beams and claps her hands. "Photos, we need to see photos of Claire. Now."

I reach for my phone.

"No, no. Too small." Debbie pushes a sleek new iPad toward me and connects the devices. "Much better," she pronounces. She sits and begins to scroll through my photos, oohing and awing as the others gather round. Claire, all forehead and blue eyes with a tuft of black hair. Claire sleeping, Claire in her chair waving her hands at a mobile, Claire with her mouth arranged in what I proudly tell them is a smile.

"You sure?" Jeff asks skeptically.

"Positive," I reply. "She talks in full sentences, too."

Laughter all around.

I will not, I vow, be one of those parents who fills every conversational space with her child's latest feats. Still, this is nice.

The photo show ends. Debbie pushes the iPad aside and we catch up, as friends do. Jeff and Jessica are buying a townhouse in hopes of starting a family. Alicia is devoting all her spare time, which isn't much, to RISE, an NGO helping destitute women get the legal assistance they need. Damon, with characteristic immodesty, announces he's at the top of his class in law school and complains it's too easy. And the money, it seems, has kept rolling in—enough to stave off bankruptcy and buy new office furnishings on the side.

I admit to an unexpected pang. Silly me, I had imagined the Truitt in Truitt and Solosky was indispensable. Everyone got along quite well without me, thank you. In fact, it's me they're concerned about. I can see it in their eyes. They haven't forgotten. The depression I fell into after Mike died. My last case, the one I try not to think about. Jeff's filed an appeal for my client, but we're still waiting for the hearing date.

He surveys me over the rim of his coffee cup. "So, you're back."

More a question than a statement. We have an unwritten rule, Jeff and I. No prevarication, no equivocation. The straight goods, no exceptions. It's kept our partnership going a decade plus.

"I already have a case," I say brightly.

"The disappearance of Trist Jones's kid. You're acting for the mother," Jeff says.

"I held her hand during the police interview Saturday. But I don't know where it's going. Maybe they'll find the little girl. I hope so. Anyway, no body, no crime. No crime, no case."

"Hah," says Jeff. "You forget about all those wrongful convictions."

"Yeah," I say.

Silence descends on the room. I glance at the worried faces around the table; Tess's disappearance has gripped everyone. And everyone is thinking the same thing: Tess disappeared Friday, today is Monday. It's going on four days since she disappeared. With each day, the chance of finding her alive diminishes.

"What's she like?" Alicia asks. "Kate."

"She's devastated. As any mother would be."

Damon pipes up. "Do you think she's involved?"

I shoot him a look.

He shrugs. "That's what they're saying online."

"She denies it. That's all I can say. For now."

They fall silent again, suppressing their suspicions. No one loves Kate, already cast as the bad mother in the ongoing custody battles over little Tess, but they understand the rules binding criminal lawyers, what they can say and what they can't, even to their closest associates.

"Anyway, whatever happens, it's just one case." I try not to let my anxiety show. In the old days, they used to line up at the door to buy my services. Jilly Truitt, hottest defence lawyer in town. But my halo has been knocked askew and I know it.

"You'll get more," says Jeff. "In the meantime, I can use your help. I'm overwhelmed."

I can see he regrets the words the moment he utters them. It used to be the other way around—I fed him the scraps from my table.

The elated mood of the morning has deflated like the balloon sagging over the table. Debbie, sensing the change of atmosphere, claps her hands and announces it's time to get back to work. It dawns on me that if I ever held the baton of authority, it has now shifted to my receptionist. I watch in bemusement as Jeff and Alicia retreat to their respective offices. Damon waves goodbye and announces he has a class to get to.

"Come see what I've done with your office," Debbie commands, and leads me down the hall to my old digs.

CHAPTER 11

I LOOK AROUND MY HOME AWAY from home. Old brick walls, a big window looking out over the lamps and cobbled streets of Gastown two floors down. Nothing has changed, except the desk is cleaner. The shimmering blue of the ocean and the green of the forest in the Gordon Smith painting I love still glow from the wall, and my couch still sits in the alcove beneath the window.

"Turn around," says Debbie.

A giant TV screen stands on a credenza on the wall behind me. How did I miss that?

"Everybody is meeting by video now. I've set you up on all the platforms. And if you find yourself missing your afternoon TV, you can stream it," she teases.

Maybe she thinks in my months at home I've become a fan of soap operas.

Debbie clicks a remote, and the news comes on. Tess's face fills the screen, and the news anchor introduces a clip of the police press conference from earlier this morning. Detective Kan stands at a podium, Tess's picture on the wall behind him, and addresses the crowd of reporters. It's the same message as yesterday morning. *The search continues. We are working on leads.* What leads, Kan doesn't say.

"Within hours of Tess's disappearance on Friday, we launched a massive search," Kan reminds the crowd. "Fifty officers, eighty lay volunteers, and eighty-five retired law officers began combing the hills, forests, and rugged coves of Bowen Island, and they are still hard at it. On the supposition Tess may have been ferried to the mainland, we have extended the searches to Vancouver and its outlying neighbourhoods. Despite all the efforts, we have not yet found Tess."

Nor, it seems, have any suspects been turned up, I think.

Off camera, a reporter asks a question. "The temperature dipped to plus nine Celsius last night. How likely do you think it is the girl is still alive?"

If the child was lost on the island, her chances of survival are zero to nil. Not to mention the bears and the cougars. I repress a shudder, but Kan takes the question in stride.

"At this time, we're still operating under the assumption she's alive," he says calmly, but his grey eyes seem worried. And tired.

The news anchor cuts to an interview with Trist Jones. His handsome face stares at the camera bleakly, every inch the grieving father as a young woman asks him what happened that last day with Tess.

"We went down to beach and walked along the shore, looking for shells," he tells the viewers. He rubs his chin and looks down, and I see he has something clasped in his hand. A shell. He is a performer, and he knows how to work the media. But there's an air about him that rings true. "Tess collected the shells in her little pail, then ran on ahead, shrieking when she found one. We were so happy . . ."

"Take your time, Mr. Jones," the reporter says softly.

"Thank you." He manages to continue. "It was such a sunny day—the last of summer, I remember thinking—so I let her take off the jacket she was wearing over her swimming suit and play in the water. I sat on an old recliner someone had dragged to the beach as she paddled around in the tidal pools at the shore. I told her to be careful, not to go too far. I laid back and watched her play in the sand. She'd dumped her shells and was building something with her pail. And then, and then—" Trist's voice breaks. "I must have fallen asleep. The next thing I knew, I heard a boat and my partner, Lena, calling, *Where's Tess?*" Trist lowers his head for a long moment. "We searched everywhere, but Tess was gone. Her pail and shells discarded on the beach."

"There's no agony greater than the agony of a parent whose child has gone missing," the reporter intones. Trist nods. A tear makes its slow way down his handsome cheek. "What about Tess's mother?"

"We couldn't contact her Friday. I understand the police took her in for questioning Saturday and released her."

"Some say Kate has had difficulties," the reporter persists.

"I can't comment on that," Trist replies.

Fair enough, I think, but the question has done damage. The police have taken her in for questioning. Draw the obvious inference. I've seen enough. I take the remote from Debbie and turn the TV off.

"Poor man," Debbie says.

I sigh. "It's 'poor man' when Trist falls asleep supervising his child, but when Kate does it, she's labeled a bad mother and loses custody. The double standard continues."

Debbie gives me a curious look. "I best get back to my desk, then," she says.

I know Debbie's opinion, but I decide to gauge the public mood for myself. I slide into my chair, open my laptop. It feels good to be back at my desk. I take a moment to savour the feeling before facing the chatter on Facebook and Twitter. I am not disappointed; the screen spews an array of opinions: *Trist shouldn't have left his little girl alone, but then, you can't watch a child every second, can you? The mother must have something to do with this. Everybody knows about the terrible custody battle between Trist and Kate. And why haven't the police come up with anything?* Already people are clamouring for the resignation of the Lower Mainland police chiefs and speculating on the competence of the detective heading up the search, Igor Kan.

Kan could relieve the pressure by informing the public that the police have photos of a woman in the boat with Tess and Dante's positive identification of Kate, but so far, to my relief, he has refrained from doing this. Until he has more, Kan will content himself with keeping close tabs on Kate. Eventually, she'll take him where he wants. But will he wait too long? With each passing hour, Tess's chances diminish.

My phone buzzes. I check the caller ID, recognize what might be the RCMP.

"Jilly Truitt speaking," I answer.

"Detective Kan," says a gravelly voice.

"I saw you on TV this morning. You're looking tired," I say.

Kan doesn't waste words. "We are dealing with a new development, Ms. Truitt. We need to question Ms. Sinclair-Jones again. We can send a cruiser to pick her up, or you can bring her in yourself if you prefer. How do you wish to proceed?"

I feel a chill. This won't be good. "I'd appreciate some detail, Detective."

"You'll get it at the station."

"Very well," I say tersely. "When and where do I appear with my client?"

"Same place. RCMP Headquarters, Richmond. Immediately."

I look at my watch, it's 11:22. I have no idea if Kate is still with her parents in Burnaby or if she's returned to her own house. Either way, I need two hours. "One thirty," I say. "Assuming I can find her right away."

"I can help," says Kan. "She is at her residence in Jericho." He gives me her address on Owen Street.

I curse my stupidity. Of course Kan knows where she is, even if I don't. Every second of every hour of every day.

"One thirty," I say.

"Good," he grunts, and hangs up.

CHAPTER 12

EXCITEMENT VIBRATES OFF THE WALLS of the precinct as Kate and I pull up before the doors. On Saturday, only a few people hovered around the entry as my police escort led me inside, but today it's a different scene. A crowd waving *Find Tess* banners pushes against police barriers, shouting outrage and concern. Abetted by three days of relentless press speculation, public emotion is rising like a high tide, and word something is about to break has gotten out.

I stop the car and look at Kate. She pulls up the hood of her aqua puffy as she turns from the peering eyes of the crowd.

"They hate me, Jilly," she whispers hoarsely.

Kate is rattled. Has been since I picked her up at her house, a modern infill with windows facing the sea. She looked like she hadn't slept in days. The circles under her eyes were purple and her hair was loose. I notice she never wears it pulled back anymore. That was the style when she was with Trist. Now she lets the curls grow naturally.

I glance at my watch. We're early. I've made good on my word to get my client to police headquarters promptly. If Kan is in such a hurry, he owes me valet parking. Besides, I have no desire to make Kate walk the gauntlet of the crowd. I pick up my phone. "Ms. Truitt here. Please send someone round."

A minute later, a man in blue denim and a T-shirt is bending at the window of my car. He flashes a police badge, and I hand him the keys. I lean over to Kate, touch her hand.

As we pass through the precinct doors, I fear the worst—that Tess is dead.

Igor Kan, towering over a phalanx of officers, awaits us in an inner corridor. He steps forward, nods. No *thanks for coming*, no *sorry for the rush*. Just the minimum. "This way, please."

I try reading his voice—same flat gravel—and fail. I look at his face. Grim.

The news, whatever it is, will not be good. I catch Kate's anxious eye, attempt a reassuring smile.

Kan opens the door to a room that looks more like a boardroom than an interrogation room. At the end of a long table, a man sits behind a steno machine, fingers poised to record all that happens. Video cameras beam down from on high. Kan is no longer investigating; he's about to tell us how it is.

He motions Kate and me to chairs on one side of the table, pulls out a chair for himself on the other.

"Please repeat the warning," Kan tells the officer at his side. Sergeant Burr again. Half the group of officers have fallen away; only a privileged few remain behind.

Burr recites Kate's Charter rights. Kate meekly nods. "I understand." She is pale, she is shaking, but so far, she's holding it together.

"Ms. Sinclair-Jones," Kan begins. "This morning, a couple walking on the north end of Bowen Island detected something washed up on a beach. Two items left behind by the tide. They retrieved these items and provided them to the police. Please tell me if you recognize them."

Sergeant Burr steps forward, hands Kan a plastic package.

"Item Number One," Kan intones.

With infinite care, he removes the tag and retrieves the contents. A piece of torn cloth, I think. Kan, holding it delicately between his thumb and index finger, shakes it out, and I realize what it once was: a little girl's swimming suit, pink with butterflies. Tess has just celebrated her fifth birthday. *Is this the size of a five-year-old?* I wonder.

"No, no," Kate moans softly beside me. "No, it can't be."

Kan holds the article up for the cameras to catch. "Do you recognize this article of clothing, Ms. Sinclair-Jones?" he asks, voice low.

Kate nods through a cloud of tears. "It's the swimming suit I bought for Tess before our last visit two weeks ago. She'd just learned how caterpillars become butterflies."

Kan turns to take a second package from Sergeant Burr, but I interrupt him. "Please. This has come as a shock. My client needs a few moments."

Kan nods, and we wait while Kate collects herself. After an interval, she looks up with faltering bravery, nods at a package by Kan's left hand. "Show me the rest," she says.

Kan unzips the second package and pulls out a child's shoe. He holds it up by the ankle strap, and I stare at the tiny pink Croc—

the kind of shoe a little girl might wear on a beach. "This washed up behind a rock, a few yards away from the swimming suit."

Kate is shaking her head. "I've never seen that—shoe. But—" She turns away.

"But what, Ms. Sinclair-Jones?"

"It would fit her." Her voice is a whisper, but the clacking steno machine picks up each word.

"I thank you for your cooperation, Ms. Sinclair-Jones," Kan says. "I should inform you Tess's father and Ms. Lena Rodriguez, the friend who was with him on the island, have also been shown these articles. They identified both items as being the clothing Tess was wearing when she disappeared. Including the shoe, which they purchased only last week." He pauses. "So, it seems clear these items of clothing belong to your daughter, Tess Sinclair-Jones."

He's going to spare us the obvious inference, I think, because Kate is clearly in shock, but he doesn't.

"We have not recovered Tess's body," he states. "But with the discovery of this clothing, we have sufficient evidence to presume she drowned at sea." Kan gives me a bleak stare. "Dead by drowning at sea."

Kate doubles over in grief, and I glare at Kan. "A bathing suit and shoe that anyone could buy don't prove Tess is dead, much less that my client has anything to do with it. These items could belong to any child. They could have been lost by accident or thrown overboard. Or someone could have planted them. The possibilities are endless, Detective."

"I beg to differ. Coupled with the identification of your client as the woman in the boat, they prove a lot," says Kan. "I think you lawyers call it circumstantial evidence. Many strands make a rope, and that rope is proof beyond a reasonable doubt."

"Your identification is worthless—Dante's photos are too blurry to prove anything. And you can't prove death, let alone murder. Your strands are too weak to make a rope, Detective."

Kan looks at me coolly. "We have more than the photos, Ms. Truitt. As you will discover in due course."

Aah. The old police tactic. Don't tell the client's lawyer any more than you have to.

Kate's soft cries cut through my speculation. "But you said this morning you still presumed Tess was alive," she says.

"That was before we received this evidence," Kan replies.

"Tess is not dead," Kate insists, looking around wildly. "I know she is not dead. We need to find her." She stands up, makes for the door. Burr leaps to restrain her, but I head her off, pulling Kate back to her chair.

"Kate," I whisper. "Listen to me. We need to finish this. When we're done here, we'll leave and figure out what to do."

"No," she cries, turning in my arms toward Kan. She strains forward, her words vehement. "It's easy for you, isn't it? Presume the child is dead and you've solved your case. But you are wrong. You're a detective. Your job is to find her."

Kan narrows his eyes. "Then tell us where she is, Ms. Sinclair-Jones. Tell us what you've done with Tess."

"I haven't done anything with Tess," Kate cries, her voice rising. "I told you. I haven't seen Tess for weeks."

Kan scrapes back his chair and slowly stands. He looks down at the tattered swimsuit and the shoe on the table before him, looks up at Kate. His eyes droop in a look of infinite sadness. "Kate Sinclair-Jones. I charge you with the murder of your daughter, Tess Sinclair-Jones." He nods at Burr. "Take her into custody, Sergeant."

CHAPTER 13

TUESDAY MORNING, THE DAY AFTER Kate's arrest, and I am scrambling to get the bail papers together that I hope will spring her from jail.

An hour ago, I waited in the little courtroom for the police to bring Kate up from the cells and formally accuse her of killing her daughter. A frail figure shrouded in orange prison garb, she shot me a frantic look as the clerk charged her with first-degree murder. Kate knew what to say—I had told her.

"I plead not guilty." A tremor in her voice betrayed her fear.

Before they led her back to her cell, we had a quick huddle. "Get me out of here," she whispered.

Now I'm trying. I sit at my computer, pull up the form, and start. I've drafted bail applications a hundred times, but today the words aren't coming. Maybe I've been away too long. Or maybe—*admit it*, I tell myself—I'm too involved. What should be a routine job—finding the right legal words to put before the judge so she can decide—is overwhelmed by my misplaced need to get Kate out.

The law says there's a presumption of release, meaning the Crown must show Kate shouldn't be released because she's a danger to society or might reoffend. Kate's not a danger to society and she's not likely to go on a crime spree if she's released. What worries me is that the Supreme Court says the bail judge can consider community feeling. And whatever Kate did or didn't do, community feeling is running against her like a high spring tide.

The jury of public opinion has filed in behind Kan and concluded this woman who neglected her child in life has now killed her. I read it on Twitter, I feel it in the air.

Jeff steps into my office and plants his long form in front of my new television, which hums with yet another press conference. First up are the chiefs. They take turns reading terse scripts on the progress of the investigation. The child, Tess Jones, is believed to be dead. Her mother, Kate Sinclair-Jones, placed by an eyewitness at the scene, stands charged with her murder.

The chiefs step back, and Detective Igor Kan strides to the podium. If the flashing press cameras bother him, he doesn't let it show.

"My colleagues have given you the basic information." His deep voice is flat, devoid of emotion. "I am here to answer any questions you may have."

The assembled reporters come at him fast and hard.

"Can you tell us what evidence led you to conclude that Tess is dead?" one asks.

"We found clothing she was wearing at the time of the abduction," Kan replies. "A swimsuit and a shoe on the shore. From that, we surmised she was dead. Drowned."

"So you haven't found Tess's body?"

"No." He bows his head, then raises his chin and stares grimly at the press. "But the ocean is a dangerous place and we believe her to be dead."

Remi Smith, a seasoned court reporter who likes putting the police through their paces, shouts from the back of the press pack. "How can you be sure Tess is dead? A couple of scraps of clothing aren't much. Are you continuing the search?"

I lean in, curious. Remi's right. Kan all but closed the case when he arrested Kate yesterday. Early days for that.

"We have no body," Kan admits. "So, yes, we are continuing the search for Tess. We have police officers, retired police officers, and laypeople still searching the island. We are following up on everyone who was on or near Bowen Island and on the ferries to and from. We also have an extensive bank of cellphone data we are continuing to investigate." Kan sucks his breath in, weighing how much to say. "We don't believe the child wandered off, in which case she would probably not be alive at this point, after three and one half days. No ransom demand has been made, making kidnapping for money unlikely. As the charges we have laid make clear, we believe Tess was abducted by her mother."

"In which case, she may still be alive? Isn't it true statistically that abductions by mothers don't usually end in the child's death?"

"Yes," Kan replies tightly.

"Then how can you be sure Kate Sinclair-Jones murdered her daughter? You have no body, so for all you know Tess is still alive."

Kan winces. Remi has found the soft underbelly of his case and made a palpable hit. "We have a swimming suit and a shoe washed up on the beach."

"Which does not prove—"

Kan cuts Remi off. "We also have photographs showing a woman who fits Ms. Sinclair-Jones's description in a boat with the deceased shortly after the abduction." A collective gasp runs through the press assemblage at this new piece of information, but Kan continues. "And the photographer who took that picture has identified Ms. Sinclair-Jones as the person he saw in the boat with the child."

Remi, undeterred, shoves her mike closer to Kan's face. "You're telling us Kate Sinclair-Jones took her daughter for a boat ride—something a parent might innocently do—and from that and a couple of scraps of clothing on a beach you conclude the child was murdered by her mother? Do you call that solving the case?"

Kan's voice betrays his ebbing patience. "At this stage, we can't be one hundred per cent sure. But we don't need to be—proof beyond a *reasonable* doubt is what the law requires. Our job as police is to assess the evidence and determine whether it is sufficient to lay charges and proceed to trial."

"And find the missing child," Remi says, unwilling to let it go.

"If Tess Sinclair-Jones is alive, we will find her. I promise you that. We expect more evidence will be forthcoming. But at this point, we believe we have enough evidence to support the charge of first-degree murder against Ms. Sinclair-Jones."

"It's true, isn't it, Ms. Sinclair-Jones has a history of aberrant behaviour?" a man yells out, thrusting his microphone in Kan's face.

Kan steps back. "No comment."

Cacophony erupts. They sense Kan shutting down, and they want to get their questions in before he disappears.

"Isn't it true a report was filed in the custody proceedings last year to that effect?" someone else shouts.

"No comment." Kan decides he's had enough. "That's all I have to report at this time," he says, moving off stage. The reporters pursue him, yelling queries in his wake, but Kan is gone.

The voice of the newscaster cuts in to announce what we all know: the press conference is over.

I switch off the TV, and Jeff turns to me. "I think it's time you tell me a little more about your case, partner."

CHAPTER 14

"**T**HEY DON'T HAVE A BODY. Hard to get a murder conviction without a body," I tell Jeff after I fill him in on the lineup, the interrogation, and Kate's alibi.

"That old myth," Jeff scoffs. "Bodies go missing all the time. All the prosecution needs to prove death is circumstantial evidence—something to undermine the theory the victim disappeared into thin air. They've got the bathing suit and the shoe. And chances are they'll eventually find the body, or part of it. Every recreational boater and beach bum will be out there looking. Tough case for the defence."

Jeff and I have fallen into our old sparring routine—I put forward our defence, he shoots it down, I come back, if I can, with a rebuttal. In this case, I can't. Jeff is right that lack of a body alone is not going to ruin the Crown's case.

"They don't have a motive," I say, moving on. "Whatever else you may say about Kate, she loves her daughter."

"Perhaps too well," he ruminates. "Remember Othello: *I kissed you ere I killed you.*"

I force a smile. "I've missed your poetic moments. But the truth is, even without the bard, the Crown will have its problems. Let's suppose Kate wants Tess badly enough she's willing to break the law and steal her from Trist. Why this way? And how would Kate know Trist would bring Tess down to the beach and conveniently fall asleep so Kate could snatch her away?"

"Not so easy to kidnap a child in the city. Her nanny would have been with her every second," Jeff observes. "On holiday, things are freer. Don't forget Trist was thinking of relocating to Vegas. Maybe he forced Kate to act. Kate, desperate to see her daughter, could have waited in the bush or around the corner for her opportunity to take her. Besides, it doesn't have to add up. Desperate people do desperate things. And from what I've heard, Kate wasn't a model of rational behaviour. Lashing out at paps. Doing whatever she did to convince a judge she couldn't be trusted alone with Tess."

I nod. He has a point. "We need to get the transcripts of the court proceedings in the custody case, see what's in the affidavits of the nanny, Selma. And Kate's medical records—the Crown will try to use that. I'll ask Alicia to dig the stuff out. Still," I muse, "first-degree murder does seem a tad ambitious. The Crown needs to prove Kate had a plan to kill Tess. That doesn't fit. Kate may have been irrational, but she loved Tess, and would never deliberately harm her."

"That's not what the judge who reduced Kate's access to supervised visits thought," Jeff counters. I wince. He's right, yet again. "Anyway, Jilly, even if you're right about Kate, you know the drill.

If in doubt, charge the suspect with first-degree murder. If the jury buys it, good. If the jury finds reasonable doubt, invite them to convict on second degree or the included charge of manslaughter. What Kate planned to do doesn't matter for manslaughter—recklessness is enough. Or maybe kidnapping."

I return to the draft affidavit on my desk. "I'm wasting time speculating. I have a woman to get out of jail. And I have a problem. The judge will want security."

"She has a nice house," Jeff offers. "That and her passport should be enough."

"I suspect her house is tied up in a trust—that's the way divorce lawyers handle things. And public opinion is not on her side. They want her behind bars, not roaming the streets. The judge may want more."

"What about her family?" Jeff asks.

"Not much money. Dad's a retired boat mechanic. Mom's an about-to-retire ESL teacher. They may own their modest home, for what it's worth. And they'll support Kate morally, promise to keep her in the jurisdiction. That may count for something."

"Why don't you put them in as sureties for now, then get them in to go over the specifics?" Jeff suggests.

"Right," I say, staring at my blank screen.

"Boat mechanic, eh?"

I look over at him. "Are you thinking what I think you're thinking?"

"Yeah. Kate knows about boats, her dad knows about boats. He knows his way around marinas, maybe has access. It fits."

I sigh. "And Kan doubtless knows this. But the photographs are blurry. Sloppy work for a professional photographer."

We sit in silence considering the implications.

"What do you know about Igor Kan?" I ask. It's time I knew more about who I'm dealing with inside the police.

Jeff raises an eyebrow. "The bio or the gossip?"

"Gossip, please. But start with the facts."

"He's originally from Russia. His dad was a diplomat. Did something the regime didn't like and fled Russia and came here in the nineties when Kan was a kid. They dropped the five last syllables of their name and kept the Kan, much good that did them. Fifteen years later, Kan was on a ski trip in Whistler and came home to his parents' bodies. Poison. People think it was Putin. Kan's father was suspected of passing on secrets to the Americans in Cold War days."

I shudder. "Sins of the father."

Jeff nods approvingly. "Exodus," he says. "Or, if you prefer, *Star Trek: The Next Generation*, episode sixty-five. Now, when Kan's not sussing out criminals, he rattles around in the condo his parents left him on Lost Lagoon and works out."

"No doubt reads Tolstoy," I say dryly.

"That, too. Anyway, he's good. Solved four murders in the last year. Quickly developing legend status."

I think of Kate, grieving, unstable, locked up in jail. I have to get her out. "Jeff," I begin. "I want you to do it—the bail hearing. You're our expert."

"I'm in the Court of Appeal in an hour. No time. Besides, this is your case. I'm not going to do it for you." He gives me his here-comes-a-lecture look. "This case is big, Jilly. It's tough. It's high profile. Just your sort of case. The very case to relaunch yourself into the wild world of defending the guilty—and the occasional innocent."

But what if I can't? I think. I'm struggling with the affidavit.

I swallow my pride. "With everything that happened with Mike, then losing the big murder case, I don't know if I can do this. They're saying I'm washed up."

"Who says?"

"Cy."

"But you're not. You're not washed up. You're ready." Jeff pauses. "And Alicia is here if you need her."

No use arguing. "I guess I should call Mr. Sinclair."

"Good luck," Jeff says at the doorway. "You won't need it, though."

I wish I believed him.

CHAPTER 15

SAMMY SINCLAIR IS A BANTAM rooster of a man, small and wiry and possessed of furious energy.

"It's already been a day. Why haven't you gotten her out yet?" he rasps in a high-pitched voice, pacing our little boardroom. So much for my image of a retired egoless boat mechanic. Sammy Sinclair is Sir Galahad, out to right the calumny heaped on his daughter by the press and the state—the daughter he loved so much that he threw her out of the house when she told him she was marrying Trist.

When I asked her to step into this meeting, Alicia didn't hesitate. She's already tapping away on her laptop, filling out the affidavit while Mr. Sinclair agrees to be Kate's surety before we've even asked him.

"Ms. Leung and I are working on the application now, but we

need to discuss a few things with you." I motion to a chair across the table from us. "Please have a seat, Mr. Sinclair."

Reluctantly, he sinks to a chair, unbuttoning his sports coat. His torso remains rigid, and he flexes his gnarled hands into fists on the table, but not before I see his calloused palms and cracked nails. Sammy may be retired, but a lifetime of repairing boats has left its mark. The thought crosses my mind that he may have helped his daughter do what the police say she did. I repress it.

"Let me give you some background," I say. "The default position for bail in Canada is release. It rests on the prosecution to show why Kate needs to be locked up while she awaits trial. First, they need to convince the Justice of the Peace they have a good case against her. On this count, even though Kate denies it was her in the boat, the photos and the lineup identification, along with the bathing suit and shoe, amount to pretty strong evidence."

"So, she stays in jail?"

I shake my head. "No, that's the first step. If the Crown's case looks credible, the next question is whether the Crown can show there's a risk Kate will reoffend or run."

"Reoffend?" His laugh is bitter. "Last time I checked, she only had one kid."

I lean back. Does Kate's father think she's guilty? I push the thought away. "What about fleeing the jurisdiction?" I ask.

Mr. Sinclair sniffs. "Not much chance of that, I'd say. Kate hasn't been out of the province much. We took her and Tess to Hawaii after she left Trist, but that was about it for travelling. We had a good time. Tess loves the beaches, you know." He closes his eyes as he remembers better days. "That was before Trist and that nanny took away Kate's weekend access. That Selma ruined Kate's life."

"What can you tell me about the nanny?" I ask. Selma's report about the shattered cookie jar and Kate passed out in bed had instigated Trist's applications to revoke Kate's weekend access, but Kate never said Selma had ruined her life. More like Selma jerked her out of her stupor and made her get her act together.

Sammy has a different view. "We had a falling-out when she married Trist, so I wasn't in the picture until she left him. The way I see it now, Selma doesn't like Kate. She was against her from the start. They're opposites, that's why. Kate is soft, thinks all a kid needs is love. Selma's religious and knows kids need rules and regulations. But Selma is smart, I'll give her that, she weaseled her way into Trist's good books and convinced him Kate was a bad mother. That it was his duty to demand sole custody."

How do you know all this? I want to ask. *Is this the version Kate gave her father?* I wonder. Or, in his grief, has he manufactured this so he can blame someone else for the tragedy befalling his little family? I make a note to follow up with Kate on Selma and return to the topic at hand—getting Kate out on bail. "Can you assure me that Kate's not a risk of flight?"

"Yes. Anyway, don't they put those leg bracelets on to make sure you can't go anywhere? I saw that on TV with that Huawei woman."

I repress a smile. "You're up on things, I see."

Sammy nods. "Sounds like a slam dunk, then."

"Not quite," I caution.

"Even if we win on the reoffending and absconding points, the law allows the prosecution to raise a final objection—the community fear and outrage test. That means if the crime is so shocking the community would be outraged at Kate's release, there's a chance the JP could decide to keep her locked up."

"I'm sure you're aware Tess's disappearance and Kate's arrest have shocked a lot of people," I add.

"That's bullshit," Mr. Sinclair replies, his brown eyes flickering from me to Alicia and back again. "You'll keep her locked up because someone else has hurt feelings? I thought you lawyers believe in the presumption of innocence. I saw that on TV, too."

I hold up a hand. "We do, and I agree using community outrage to keep a person who is presumed innocent in jail doesn't make much sense, even if the Supreme Court says so. Chances are, the JP will see it the same way, too, but you need to be aware it could happen."

Sammy shakes his head. I can see all this legal talk has upset him. He is used to the nuts and bolts of machinery—either the boat engine works or it doesn't. Without it, you're dead in the water. He sighs. "You're the lawyers. Do what you need to do."

"We need your help, Mr. Sinclair. Are you prepared to be surety? That means swearing an affidavit saying you will make sure your daughter sticks around and behaves if she's released."

He scoffs. "As if I could ever stop Kate from doing anything she wanted to do. I told her to get an education that would guarantee her a career, she studied music. I told her not to take up with Trist, she married him." He scowls. "She's never listened to me. After the divorce, when she lost custody of Tess, she finally decided it might be a good idea to do what Angela told her and take a teacher's course. Now I worry it's all too late." His voice softens and his eyes grow wistful. "I love that baby; she's my only grandchild. When Kate finally started coming round again and introduced us to Tess, it was like a beam of light shone in on our lives, me and Angela. She softened me, Tess did. I prided myself on being a good father to Kate, taking her with me to work when

Angela was teaching and we had no babysitter. But I wanted her with me, wanted to teach her how things worked, how the world worked. I wanted everything to be good for Kate, perfect for her." He swallows. "I was hard on her, though. I see that now. Tess is like a second chance, a chance to be softer, more loving."

I study him. This man cares for his daughter. He might not have supported her decisions, but he loves her. Wants the best for her, especially what he thinks is best.

"Will you tell the judge you'll stop your daughter from running, Mr. Sinclair? Yes or no?"

He sighs heavily. "Sure, if that's what it takes to get her out."

"And you will put up your assets—your house if you own it—to back that up?"

"Of course. Kate is all that matters. And Tess."

Alicia's nails click as she types the promise into her laptop. There's a beat of silence as she tidies up the documents, then they come rolling off the printer in the corner. Copies for him, copies for me.

"Please read this," I say, handing him the affidavit. "I need to call the Crown to see how soon we can get a hearing. In the meantime, you can let Ms. Leung know if you need any changes. If not, sign the affidavit."

In my office, I connect with the bail counter at the Provincial Court Building. There's a long silence when I say I'm acting for Kate Sinclair-Jones. "Let me transfer you," the voice says.

A minute later, the phone crackles. "Edmund Schmidt." I remember Edmund. A bit cocky, but not unintelligent. "I've been expecting your call, Ms. Truitt," he says. "And the answer is no."

"Come on, Edmund, you don't even know what I want."

"You want bail for your client, one Kate Sinclair-Jones, charged with first-degree murder in the death of her daughter, Tess. And the answer's still no."

"Correction, I want to *apply* for bail. Tonight."

"No, no, no. I'm afraid your client will have to linger in Her Majesty's custody a little longer. My instructions are to oppose bail."

I think of how it will be, how it *is*, for Kate inside prison. I can't let her stay there for a third night.

"On what grounds?" I ask.

"On the grounds your client is unstable, and nobody knows what she may do. Only way to ensure she will be here to face her trial is if we keep her in custody."

"How do you propose to prove Ms. Sinclair-Jones is unstable?"

"The nanny's affidavits in the custody fights. I have summaries, but I'm waiting for the originals. I should have them later tonight, but I won't have my material ready until very late. Which is why your application can't go ahead tonight."

My back is up now. Is this one of Kan's moves? Or Cy's? "Since when do we need originals, Edmund? This is a person's constitutionally guaranteed liberty you're talking about."

"You've been out of the game for a while, Jilly," Edmund quips. "Let *me* tell *you* how it will be. You get your papers to me today. I look at them and prepare the Crown's case. When I'm done—tomorrow, maybe the next day—we'll trundle into court and talk to the bail judge. In the meantime, your client stays in jail. With the case we've got against her, chances are she's staying there forever."

"I don't think so," I say evenly, smarting at his assumptions—the assumption a few days' delay doesn't matter, the assumption I'm rusty and can't do anything about his stalling. "*This* is how it will be. I file the papers within the hour. You will have your brief

ready to go at nine a.m. tomorrow. I'll be at the courthouse waiting. I'll read it, and at ten we'll talk to the judge."

After a beat, he replies, "Very well, if you insist. Wouldn't do it
for anyone else, Jilly."

"Thanks," I say.

"Good to have you back," he says.

I hang up and return to the boardroom.

Sammy Sinclair is standing at the end of the table, signing the
final page of the affidavit. "Well?"

"They're fighting bail. Say they need the night to prepare the
Crown's material. I can't say I'm surprised. This is big. Big for
the public. Big for the Crown." I gesture to Alicia. "Can you have
the bail papers run over to the courthouse and served on Edmund
Schmidt?"

She nods, picks up the papers, and exits.

Sammy fixes his brown eyes on mine—nice eyes, dark and shining and round. "One more thing, Ms. Truitt. You're plowing ahead
like there's no tomorrow, but I'm not an idiot. I know lawyers
don't come for free. In fact, I know they charge a lot. Kate has a bit
from Trist. I have some savings from the sale of our house when
we moved into my father's home, but we're running through that
fast. Which leaves us living off my pension, and Angela's when she
retires next year."

I fidget. I know the rule, know what Jeff expects—get the re-
tainer, preferably fat, up front. I look at Sammy, at his worn sports
coat and the frayed collar of his pale blue shirt. Kate doesn't have
anything but her car, a house Alicia has confirmed she can't pledge,
and a monthly maintenance check from Trist. She'll need them if
Tess is alive, if she can get custody again. If, if, if.

I think of what my partner will say when I tell him this one's pro bono. He won't be pleased. But he's the one who wants me to take the case. Then it hits me. The truth is I want to take this case, loser that it is. *Consider it the price of my re-entry to criminal law, Jeff.*

"I guess I get to do this one for nothing," I say brightly.

Mr. Sinclair pauses at the door and turns to me. His weathered face threatens to crumple for a moment, then he regains his composure. "I suppose I should say thanks," he says, overly gruff. Then he leaves.

I hear Debbie sigh in the lobby.

CHAPTER 16

WEDNESDAY MORNING, AND I'M IN bail court. The Justice is crusty. I've miscalculated again. I thought she would at least listen; now I realize she has no time for the lawyer of the woman the press has been vilifying. I pulled up the headlines on my iPhone over morning coffee, and what I read wasn't pretty.

Justice Dhaliwal flips the white tab at her throat. "You want bail? In *this* case?"

And then Edmund, having let her rant at me for five minutes, stands up and stuns us. Rising to his feet, he intones, "The Crown consents to bail."

"Really?" inquires Justice Dhaliwal, eyebrows arched.

"Really," Edmund replies. "On conditions, of course."

"What conditions?"

"The usual—undertaking to stay in the Lower Mainland pending trial. And a surety. I understand the accused's parents live here, and her father is willing to act as a guarantor."

The judge shuffles the papers on her desk. "In other words, exactly the conditions the defence has proposed?"

"Precisely," he says blithely.

I shoot Edmund a dark look. *You could have told me yesterday. Or even this morning.*

He winks. "And oh yes, Your Honour, we'll need an ankle bracelet to make sure the accused doesn't take off."

What I thought would take all morning is wrapped up in a matter of minutes. As we go through the formalities, it dawns on me: Kan got to Edmund last night. Kan wants Kate at large, in case she leads him to Tess, or what's left of Tess.

Sammy Sinclair and his wife, Angela, a thin woman with a worried expression, have been sitting in the front row of the courtroom watching the proceedings. I see Kate in them—her mother's green eyes and fine nose, the defiant set of her father's chin. Angela leans to Sammy and whispers, her grey-black hair pulled up in an elegant chignon. She is every inch the lady in her tasteful dark coat and pearl earrings.

The formal proceedings over, Sammy and Angela follow me to the foyer while we wait for the clerks to lock on Kate's new fashion accessory.

We huddle together.

Wednesday morning in Provincial Court is a zone of semi-controlled chaos. Homeless people sit side by side with the better-kept on benches, both waiting their turn to enter the maw of the justice mill while their loved ones support them. Lawyers bustle, preparing arguments, making deals. Among a gaggle of reporters, I spy a familiar face—Remi Smith. She's staring at Angela. "Let's move," I say, and guide her toward the exit, Sammy at my back.

Outside, the sky has darkened, and the smell of rain sweeps into the lobby of the courthouse. Sammy Sinclair sniffs the disagreeable, dank air.

"What's taking them so long?" Angela asks. "Where's my Kate?"

"She'll be here," I say.

Angela surveys the jostling crowd. "Shall we go outside and wait?"

Better to be away from the media's eyes anyway. The rain is coming down in earnest, but I point the Sinclairs toward an overhang outside the courthouse. "I'll go get her."

Inside, I stand against the wall near the door and avoid the curious stares. At last, Kate's small figure emerges from the huddle of humanity crowding the door to the inner precinct, wearing the aqua puffed jacket and faded blue jeans from Monday when they charged her with the murder of her child. She spots me, and I usher her past the reporters.

"I want to go home, Jilly," she whispers.

"Right away."

Outside, Sammy and Angela wrap their arms around their daughter. I step away, leaving them to their private moment.

Sammy's rising voice brings me back. "You're coming back home with us." He is holding Kate by the arm. "I've put up my house and everything I have to get you out. You leave and it's all gone. I'm going to watch you every second." I give him a look, and his tone softens. "Besides, you shouldn't be alone now."

Angela moves him aside. "Come with us, Kate," she says gently. "You shouldn't be alone."

Kate yanks her arm away. "No, Dad, I need to be alone, alone in my own place. I have to find Tess. I promise I won't run." She looks down. "As if I could, with this thing on my leg."

Sammy leans in. "Kate, you need to prepare yourself."

Kate balls her fists as her eyes fill with tears. "No. We only need to find her," she shouts.

Out of the corner of my eye, I spy a semicircle of reporters crowding closer. Remi is typing furiously into her phone. I can already see the headlines: *Mother charged with murder of her child observed fighting with her father after bail hearing.*

I step between the press and Kate and push back the Sinclairs. "Quiet," I hiss, casting a look over my shoulder at the slowly re-treating press.

"It's the only thing that matters," says Kate, in a softer voice. "I know she is alive. She's out there somewhere."

Grief has stages. The first is shock, the second denial. If this is grief, Kate's in the denial stage, denying Tess is gone, maybe denying she made it happen. If it's not grief, I need to know the reason Kate is convinced Tess is alive.

"Now, here's what we're going to do. Mr. and Mrs. Sinclair, you're going to go home. Kate, we need to talk."

Sammy Sinclair stares at me for a long moment, and I read betrayal in his eyes. He wants to take Kate home. Too bad. I serve the client. Arm around Angela, he turns wordlessly and they walk away, leaving me and Kate alone, the newshounds on guard.

"Come," I say, and take her to my ancient Mercedes under my office a block away. Once Kate is inside, I slam the passenger door a little more roughly than necessary. This isn't how I planned my first case back. Kate is supposed to be in her parents' car, winging away from me. Instead, I'm stuck with her.

CHAPTER 17

"THE FIRST NIGHT WAS THE worst," Kate says, worrying away at her napkin as she stares into the fireplace.

We are in a small log-lined room at the Stanley Park Tea-house, English Breakfast steaming from the cups on the table before us.

How we got here, I'm not sure. Revving my car out of the parking lot of the courthouse, I found Cordova and headed across the isthmus to Stanley Park. Rain hit the windshield as we drove past the Douglas firs. Then, on the other side of the wooded peninsula, a sign for the teahouse appeared through the gloom. The place was deserted on this bleak day; there wasn't a car in the parking lot. A refuge against the storm. And as good a spot to have it out as any.

Outside, breakers hurl against the cliffs and tall cedars crack before the gale, but here, all is warmth and comfort. If only Kate could feel it. She's on edge, still rattled from her two nights in prison.

"When they brought me from police headquarters, they stripped me, took photos of me naked. Like I was some criminal," she says. "They took swabs of my mouth, hair for DNA, and my fingerprints. It took forever to get the ink off." She chokes back a sob. "Then they led me to a tiny room with a cot and a toilet and slammed the door in my face. I was cold, so cold. I have been low, but never low like that."

"Jails are not nice places," I say. I should have warned her that in the eyes of the prison wardens, she is a criminal. The presumption of innocence may apply in court, but it stops at the jailhouse door.

Her eyes glaze over, lost in thought. "The second night, I had a dream. I saw it all. All the bad choices I had made. I understood in the dream why I was where I was, in a stink-hole of a prison. I remember thinking, I must be dying, and that's good. And then it came, so strong I knew it was true: Tess is alive."

I sit back and digest Kate's words. She doesn't have much—correction, she doesn't have *anything*—to prove Tess is alive. No facts, no circumstances, just a gut belief. A mother's intuition. But Kate is onto something. Kan can dismiss the possibility Tess is alive and lay his murder charges, but Kate's best defence is finding Tess alive. The chances decrease by the day. It's six days since Tess disappeared. The more time goes on, the likelier Kan will find a body. We need a backup plan.

I place my hand on hers. "Don't worry. Kan said the police

are still looking for her. They're not going to give up. I won't let them." I pause. "At the same time, we can't forget you're charged with murder. We have to build your defence. In case we don't find Tess—" I falter. "—alive. We don't have to prove who took her. All we need is reasonable doubt you didn't—"

"Kill her?" Kate interrupts, pulling her hand from mine, jostling the table. Amber liquid sloshes onto the tea saucers. "I would never hurt Tess. Aren't you listening? She is alive. You have to find her."

I feel for her. If Claire disappeared, I wouldn't be able to think of anything but getting her back. I decide this is not the time to give Kate the technical truth, to tell her I'm not a detective but a lawyer, and that my job—my only job—is to provide her with the best defence the law allows. An idea comes to me. Maybe I can be both.

I lean forward. "Okay, Kate. Let's assume you're right, and Tess is alive. The best hope we have of finding her is figuring out who kidnapped her."

Kate's eyes brighten a little. "Yes, exactly. How do we do that?"

"We talk to everyone who knew Tess, everyone who saw her in the days and weeks before she disappeared. You say you were not the woman in the boat. The question then is, who was she? Who would have wanted Tess?"

"It could have been anybody," Kate says. "Her picture was all over the tabloids, Trist made sure of that. The country was obsessed with her. It could be a stalker, a crazy fan, or—" She shivers and wraps her sweater more tightly around her thin shoulders. "Some child predator who wanted her for his own. That's my nightmare."

I knew something would happen, she had said back in the interrogation room the first day I met her.

I chew my cheek. "Given Tess's celebrity, it's possible, though ransom and child predator cases are about ten per cent of child abduction cases. If it was ransom, we would have gotten a demand by now. As for a child predator, those databases aren't public. The police have files of known child predators, and they should be tracking down every one of them—if they aren't, we'll make them."

"What about the other ninety per cent?" Kate asks. I have her attention now.

"Statistics vary, but generally, almost fifty per cent of child abductions are by one of the parents."

"Trist wouldn't. He's got no reason to."

"I agree, but I'd still like to speak to him." *If he'll talk to me,* I think. He hasn't said anything directly negative about Kate in the press. Despite all they've been through, maybe there is still love there. I'm going to have to count on it.

I fish in my purse for a pen and paper but come up empty on the latter. I grab a napkin, push it toward Kate, and hand her the pen. Her hand is unsteady, but she writes down a telephone number and a West Vancouver address.

"The other forty-something per cent of the cases are by people well-known to the child—close family members, friends, and acquaintances. For the purposes of our investigation, we'll concentrate our efforts on this group." I gesture to the napkin with Trist's information on it. "I want you to draw up a list of all the people who came into contact with Tess—relatives, nannies, babysitters, the teachers at her preschool. Names and addresses, if possible."

Kate nods, then pulls out her phone and starts going through the contact list, jotting down the pertinent information.

"Does Trist have family in the area?" I ask.

Kate shakes her head. "He's an only child, like me. We used to talk about that. Trist said we'd make sure we had more than one child. Except we didn't." Her voice trails off before she hauls it back. "His parents both passed away years ago."

"What about his management team? Any staff?"

"His manager is still the same, I think—Rex something—but others might have changed."

"List what you can. I'll confirm with Trist."

"How do we do follow up on all these people?" she asks as she scribbles.

"I have a detective I use."

I make a mental note to call Richard Beauvais, my go-to private investigator. Richard migrated west from Quebec two decades ago and settled up-valley, where he lives with his wife, Donna, and their twins. He's crazy busy, but he always makes time for me. At least he used to.

"I can't pay you," Kate says. "Trist's lawyers tied up the house is a trust. I only have my car."

"Don't worry. I know about the house; I discussed it with your father. If you can help, fine. Otherwise, we'll do what we lawyers call pro bono. He cares for you, Kate. You know that, don't you?"

She cups her tea. "Yeah. I used to think he didn't love me. He was so tough on me, dragging me around the marinas with him, barking at me to hand him tools and paint trim. He didn't believe in my music, didn't like Trist either. But after Trist and I separated, when I reached out to my parents, he had changed.

Watching him with Tess, seeing how much he loves her, I realize my dad always loved me, too. He only ever wanted me to be safe and happy." She laughs without mirth. "But we all know how that turned out."

"Your mom and dad don't want you to be alone right now. I think they're right." I pause, watching her face. "Will you let me take you to their house now, Kate?"

Her answer is a long time coming. "Yes. But I won't stay for long. I need to find my bearings."

She hands me the napkin, and I fold it and tuck it away in my purse. Only after I've dropped her in Burnaby do I retrieve it. Inside the car, I scan the names. Some I expected—Lena, Selma. Some I don't—preschool teachers, social workers. There are two noticeable absences though: Sammy and Angela Sinclair. Kate wouldn't suspect her parents, but the oversight makes me hesitate. The grandparents had only recently had Tess in their lives. They loved her. And Sammy knows boats— as does Kate. I think about the woman in the photo. Tess was looking up at her with love. What are the chances it's Angela? Yet Kan hasn't so much as bothered to search Sammy and Angela's house. Or has he? I worry about tunnel vision—once the police get a suspect in their sights, they forget about all the other possibilities.

I shake the thoughts from my mind. I need to understand what's happened here, but I've gone too far and let my imagination run wild. I check the clock: two p.m. Maybe I can get Claire early and get started on this list from home. Make some calls from the den. Or maybe I won't. You can lose a child in an instant like Kate, or you can lose her minute by minute, hour by hour. I need to see my daughter, need to hold her.

I tuck the napkin away and slip the car into drive. Kate's trauma fills my brain and morphs with my own trauma of losing Mike. The date is etched in my mind, never far from the surface— thirteen months tomorrow. The initial shock of grief has ebbed but the dull pain deep in my body will always be with me. I wonder if it will be the same for Kate.

CHAPTER 18

THE CALL I'VE BEEN EXPECTING comes at precisely 9:10 Friday morning.
Cy. The man who pulled me into this case and back to the job
within a day.

I had planned a gentle reimmersion into practice—working
from home three days a week, but Kate's case has scuttled that
plan. Apart from taking Wednesday afternoon off, I've worked
four straight days in the office. For the first time in months, I've
spent whole hours thinking about something other than Claire.
It's been hard—my mind keeps slipping from the case I'm reading
back to her—but it's felt good, too. From her first uterine kicks,
she has been my constant preoccupation, my only love. My heart
ached as I relinquished her to Liz's arms this morning. I longed
to take her back, say, "On second thought, I can look after my
daughter today." And then I thought of Tess, missing for exactly

one week, and Kate, her anguished mother. I pasted a smile on for Liz and said I'd see her at five.

I try not to think about how it's going to be as we ramp up for trial five or six months from now when Claire will be starting to babble, maybe even crawling. Someone else will witness her milestones while I'm stuck in a courtroom waiting for the jury's verdict. Would Mike have wanted this for Claire and me? Do I want it?

My mind goes back to the night Mike died. I see him lying on the floor in the front hall, blood seeping from the hole in his forehead onto the carpet. I feel his body beneath mine as my ear searches for the trace of a heartbeat. Thirteen months to the day since he died, and I feel the pain like yesterday. He wanted a child, and I told him no, not now. Now I have the child. Will I make the same mistake with her?

A week ago, I wouldn't have been asking this question. Thanks to Cy, now I am.

He gets right to the point. "Nice to see you're on the case. Got time for lunch today?"

In the old days, I would have scanned into the next week for a free luncheon spot. Now my calendar sits empty. No point pretending I'm busy. "Delighted," I say. "Where and when?"

"Where else, Jilly? Our old haunt Bacchus."

At precisely 12:30, I stride into the lobby. I'm wearing a dark dress loose enough to disguise what's left of my baby bump and a bomber jacket of creamy beige leather Edith found in the closet when she came to clean house before Claire was born. I've had a much-needed haircut and tell myself I don't look half bad for a new mother.

Looking around, I smile. Bacchus hasn't changed. Couches

to drown in, flowers everywhere. I breathe in the lingering scent of Old English furniture polish oozing from the wood panelling. Bacchus is a civilized oasis where warring lawyers retreat during ceasefires to lick their wounds and plan future forays. I haven't been here for months. In fact, I haven't been to lunch with anyone for months. I've missed it. I brush aside my earlier equivocations and put my identity crisis on hold.

I find Cy at our usual booth in the back room. Privacy times two. If anyone wants to find us, they'll need a warrant and a search party.

He struggles to rise when he sees me. I wave him down, but he insists. Leaning on his crutch, he pulls me to him with his free arm. "Jilly, you look splendid."

"Good to see you too, Cy," I reply, and slide into the bench opposite. It's then I notice how much Cy has aged since I last saw him five months ago. A polio survivor with partial paralysis, life has long been difficult for him, but the waxy cast of his skin today takes me aback. For the first time, it dawns on me that Cy, my mentor and adversary, is mortal.

James, every lawyer's special waiter, emerges to take our order.

"James's Special," I say. I half-expect him to say that was last year, but no, he smiles.

"Poached halibut and slaw, no sides, no fries. Good to see you back, Ms. Truitt."

James turns to Cy, but he's looking deep into the single malt he's nursing. "Don't feel like much," he says. "Bring me a club sandwich."

James nods and retreats.

"I meant it," I say. "About it being good to see you."

"That's big, coming from you, Jilly."

I shrug. "Maybe I'm mellowing."

Cy smiles. "Not bloody likely."

I allow myself a small smile. I've missed sparring with Cy, in court and out. Our battles have taught us everything there is to know about each other. We have an understanding—just the truth, no bullshit—and we hold each other to it.

James brings food and I take a bite. I've forgotten how good steamed halibut tastes. I allow myself a long moment to savour the sea before I swallow and get down to business.

"This is the first time in our decade-long acquaintance you've invited me to lunch, Cy. What's the occasion?"

He studies his sandwich, pushes it aside. "It seems I'm lead prosecutor on *The Crown v. Kate Sinclair-Jones.* So, I thought we should meet—kick things around, talk about how it will go."

My fork hits my plate with a clunk. Cy's slippery hand has been moving the pieces behind the scenes. He knew from the beginning he was going to tell the police to charge Kate when they asked him if they had enough evidence. And he called me to hold her hand to make sure he'd get the opponent he wanted—a weakened, out-of-shape woman who they say has lost her edge. I feel my bile rising. Once again, Cy's outsnookered me.

Heat rises in my cheeks, but I offer Cy a tight smile. "And how sweet of you to choose me as defence counsel."

"Jilly, I had no idea—"

"Whatever your game is, I'm going to fight as hard as I can for Ms. Sinclair-Jones." I serve him a cold look. "Frankly, I find it appalling you've charged her with murder. You don't even know Tess is dead. You should be devoting all your effort to finding her."

Cy reels back at my barrage. "Hold on, Jilly. You're way off base."

"Yeah, I've lost it again," I quip bitterly.

"If you want the truth, I called you to hold Kate's hand because I wanted to get you out of your slump and back to the world you love, no other reason."

Once again, he's turned the tables on me. I'm on an illogical rant, and he's the adult in the room. "Out of my slump, Cy? My partner is dead and I've got a five-month-old, you fucking idiot." I suck in my breath. "I don't need your help. I'm doing fine on my own."

Cy raises a pale hand. "Peace. Let's get back to what matters—the case."

"Yes, the case," I echo, as I throttle my temper and move on. "Last I heard you don't have a body. Hard to get a murder conviction without proof of death."

Cy bites his sandwich, chews. "We have all the proof we need with the bathing suit and the shoe. No rational person believes Tess is still alive, not after eight frigid nights. And no one will believe it six months from now when we get to trial. The child, my dear Jilly, is gone, as in D-E-A-D. Her body will probably wash up in the November storms."

I swallow a forkful of slaw and clear my throat. "You have a few strands of equivocal evidence that, at best, suggest Tess was taken from the beach. It doesn't prove death."

He waves me off like I'm a bothersome fly. "We have enough."

Is he going to call off the search? I wonder. "If it turns out the child is alive and the police have stopped looking, there will be hell to pay."

"They're still on it. It would be nice to have a body for the trial. In the meantime, we're going for a direct indictment."

I sit back in genuine shock. *It would be nice to have a body?*

Is he serious? And is Cy passing up on the opportunity to give his case a dry run before testing it on the jury at trial? "In a case as flimsy as this, you don't want a preliminary inquiry?"

"We're confident in our case. We know the evidence estab-lishes Ms. Sinclair-Jones is guilty as hell beyond reasonable doubt. So why waste time and the taxpayers' money on a preliminary inquiry? We'll be filing the direct indictment next week."

I lean forward, eyes locked on Cy's. "It's called justice. You don't put a person through a murder trial without assuring the system and the public you have a prima facie case." I don't mean it as an insult, but Cy takes it that way.

"If you think a preliminary judge would throw out the charges because we can't produce a body, motherhood has addled your brain," he retorts.

I bristle. "I'm trying to warn you off a precipitous decision. I'd hate to see you embarrass yourself, Cy. But it's your choice and I can't stop you." I fold my hands. "So, tell me about the trial you're proposing—time, place, and date."

Cy pushes his plate aside and takes a deep draught of scotch. "It's a simple trial, not much prep. We're into October now. So even with the delays you will doubtless try to pull off, the trial should take place as the daffodils are blooming mid-March." He glances at me. "Unless you need more time for some complicated defence, the existence of which I cannot imagine."

I could tell him what I'm thinking, but I prefer to keep it to myself. His case is full of holes. Without a body, we can argue the child is alive. And Dante's identification of Kate as the woman in the boat is based on blurred photos we can run a truck through on cross-examination. Even if we don't call a witness, we have our reasonable doubt.

"Nothing complicated," I say. "Simple. And true."

Cy laughs. "I know you better than that, Jilly. As a prosecutor who likes to win, I should never have called you to help Kate at the police station. I should have remembered you have a way of pulling rabbits from hats at the last minute. Like the Vera Quentin trial." I smile. I'd manoeuvred the accused's husband into taking the rap for his befuddled wife. "But this case is different," Cy continued. "There's nothing in the hat. I'm too wise to push you, but I suspect you have nothing. When the time comes, you'll throw Kate on the mercy of the jurors and hope for the best."

"If you say so, Cy."

Weariness creeps into his voice. "I need to get this trial done soon. Not because the public is clamouring for justice for Tess. For me."

I study his face and see sallow skin, dark circles under his eyes, and folds where there used to be flesh. "Is everything alright, Cy?"

"My heart isn't what it once was. Job stress isn't helping. I'll take this trial and then gracefully bow out."

"As in retire?"

"As in retire. This will be my last trial."

I sit back and digest his announcement. In my mind, Cy would go on forever. Weak of step but never faint of heart, my eternal adversary. No wonder he's rushing the case through.

"I'm sorry about your heart," I say. "Are you sure you should take this trial?"

"I'm sure. It's a simple trial, and one that matters. Particularly to me. A child's life is precious, irreplaceable."

Cy stares into his glass. I know what he's remembering: the infant son he and Lois buried all those decades ago. They never had another. I think of Cy's life now. With Lois gone, all he has is the job. And even that is coming to an end. Maybe there was some truth to why he asked me to take on this case. Maybe he didn't want to see me lose the very thing he'd do anything to keep—his career.

Just when I think Cy is softening, he flicks back into form. "This is the very trial to cap my prosecutorial career. I can go out on a win, secure in the knowledge justice has been done. The perfect trial."

"If there is to be a trial, let it be a fair trial with an impartial jury," I say as Cy summons James for the bill. "For that, you need to put a muzzle on Trist Jones's freedom of expression. I drive to work, and there's his voice on the radio, bleating about how he's lost Tess. I plop on my couch after dinner and there's his fucking face on the screen pleading for justice. He's everywhere. Yesterday, I turned on the TV to his sobbing voice saying the sooner the trial is over the better. I.e., Kate should be behind bars. His fans out there in Lalaland are filling in the dots."

"I take your point," Cy says, surprising me. "Consider it done."

He pays, and we rise from the table.

At the door, Cy turns to me. "Oh, I almost forgot, Jilly. I would be remiss if I did not pass on greetings from Detective Igor Kan."

"Tell Kan to stuff his greetings, Cy," I say bitterly. "I detest the man. The way he treated Kate at the police station—she was terrified, in shock at the news Tess was gone. Did he care? No, he pushed on with his cockamamie theory she had killed her child. Any decent man would have given her a few hours to pull herself together. What he did was inhumane." I stare at Cy. "Kan is not a man, he is a cold, calculating automaton who is concerned with one thing—putting notches in his belt of convictions until he clinches the rank of commissioner. Spare a thought for a suffering mother? For the child who may still be out there somewhere? No way. He's racing for conviction, the truth be damned. No, Detective Kan has no time for me, and I have none for him."

Cy's cab pulls up. He lurches toward it and yanks the back door open. He offers an ambiguous smile as he settles into the seat. "Don't be too hasty to condemn, Jilly. It's a fault you have. Maybe he's just doing his job. Maybe he likes you."

I shake my head. "No way, Cy." I grab the handle and slam the door shut. Cy waves back to me, still smiling as the cab pulls away.

I stare after the departing car. Greetings from Detective Kan, indeed. Cy's up to something, something I don't get yet.

I have no time for games. If the trial is for March, I have work to do. Time to muster the forces.

CHAPTER 19

BACK AT THE OFFICE, I find Jeff. I know he won't help me on Kate's case, but I still need to tell him we'll be footing the bill. I perch myself on the edge of the credenza in his office and deliver the news. Oh, and Cy is prosecuting and we're in for a fight.

"There's always legal aid," he says, frowning.

"True. But you know as well as I do legal aid won't cover much more than our basic expenses, if that, even on a case as prominent as this. Plus, they'll look at Kate's house and say no. It's tied up in a trust, but that won't impress them. Another thing, this file has two prongs. The most important is continuing our efforts to find Tess. I'd love to leave that to the police, but I don't think I can. Cy says they'll keep up the effort, but he's already concluded Tess is dead. I've left a message for Richard. He's buried in a fraud case but is going to call me next week. This could get expensive . . .

You're my partner and you should know." I halt. "And approve. I won't do this without your backing."

Jeff pushes his round glasses up his nose and eyes me directly. "So, you want to find Tess. Have you considered if you find her dead, you'll lose your one big defence? That the Crown doesn't have a body and thus can't prove death."

I swallow. "You are one hundred per cent right. But if I find her alive, I win. And the client's instructions are to find Tess, above all else."

Jeff sighs. I can tell he's going to say no, so I cut him off.

"Hear me out," I say, rising and pacing the room. "We investigate who could have taken Tess, and in doing so, establish alternate suspects. That's how we build Kate's defence—and honour her wishes."

"And how do you propose we do that?" Jeff asks, patient.

"First, we keep riding the police. They have resources we can only dream about—CCTV camera data from all over the Lower Mainland, access to the Sex Offender Registry, and border crossing data. They have a duty to find Tess if there is even the slightest chance she's alive."

Jeff takes off his glasses, rubs the bridge of his nose. "Jilly, have you forgotten the police, having laid murder charges, are invested in the theory Tess is dead? They are not going to work to prove they are wrong." He shifts in his chair, changing tack. "Let me be blunt. Last time I checked, our business was law, not investigation. Continuing the investigation could conflict with your duty to get your client an acquittal."

"You know we always investigate—that's how we win."

"Sure, we investigate to bring out evidence the police haven't dug up or won't dig up. But we don't investigate to find evidence that will blow a legal hole right through our case."

"If we find Tess alive, the case will be over," I argue. "The best defence of all."

"Maybe, maybe not. Depending on the facts, they might still charge Kate with kidnapping." He pauses. "Leave the investigation to the police, Jilly. Focus your efforts on building a defence and beating the charges. That's what you can do, what you should do. Otherwise, you risk charges of professional negligence."

"I know." I slump into the chair opposite his desk. It's been on my mind since I dropped off Kate at her parents' Wednesday afternoon. My voice drops. "But a child is missing, Jeff."

I watch his face soften. He doesn't have a child—he and Jessica have been trying—but he can imagine.

"Okay, go ahead and bring Richard in," he says. "On one condition. He can use his contacts in the force to monitor how things are going. But he can't send people out searching, can't get actively involved in interviewing and investigating beyond what you need to build a defence. Bottom line, we're lawyers, and we stick to the law. Our job is to do everything in our power to secure our client's acquittal. Deal?"

I consider Jeff's proposal. Much as I'd like to give Richard Kate's contacts list and let him go wherever his instincts take him, whatever the cost, Jeff is right—my duty is to build Kate a defence. Something in me knows Kate is telling the truth, something in me believes she's right when she says Tess is alive. But finding Tess is Kan's job, not mine.

"Deal," I say, rising from my chair.

CHAPTER 20

IWALK DOWN THE HALL TO Alicia's office and am greeted by stacks of files covering every surface. Even in this age, when so much is stored on the cloud, lawyers still like hard copies.

I slip into the chair opposite Alicia, search for her face between the stacks, and finally find it, dark brows, clear eyes, black spiked hair. "Looks like you're busy, Alicia."

"Not at all," she says, offering me a smile. I know her life is lonely. Her parents have gone back to Hong Kong, and now she lives alone in her apartment in Metrotown with her cat Puff, whose photo stands behind her on the windowsill. For fun, she works. "How is Kate's case going?"

I fill her in on my lunch with Cy.

Alicia knows Cy's reputation. "That's not good news. Cy doesn't fight fair. And no preliminary? That doesn't give you much time."

I nod. "It will be an uphill battle. We can't do much, we're a law firm. But I want to investigate everyone who knew Tess. Come up with a list of alternate suspects. Richard will help, but . . ." I trail off.

She leans back. "You want me to be your second."

"Yes." I feel guilty asking her. "I won't need much time—an hour here and there. Jeff has made it clear he won't step in. I've learned the hard way I need a partner on this kind of job, someone to discuss my approach, tell me when I'm off track." I remember my last court case, how it ended in disaster. I clear my throat. "Flying solo is not an option. And you're a fantastic lawyer."

Alicia sits silent for a moment. "You know I won't say no, Jilly. Not to you. Not to this case. But I need help." She gestures to the files around her. "I'm snowed under."

"I understand." I survey her office and it hits me: Alicia is no longer my assistant; she is managing hefty files on her own. A lot has changed since Jeff and I hired her over five years ago. "You've taken on a lot for the firm. In addition to your own cases, you've helped hold down the fort while I've been away. I know that. I think it's time we brought in a junior lawyer to help with the more routine things."

Her face brightens. "That would be great."

"Good, I'll talk to Jeff about it. By the way, have you had a chance to get those documents I asked you for—the transcripts of the custody hearings and Kate's medical records?"

Alicia swivels in her chair, reaches for her credenza, and pulls out three inches of paper wedged deep in a stack. How does she know where everything is? "Here are the transcripts. Nothing on the medical front; you know how slow doctors are."

I thumb through the documents, find the transcripts, and skim through the double-spaced print—I'll save the close reading for later. I find what I'm looking for near the bottom—an affidavit signed by one Selma Beams. So that's her last name, I think. I dig deeper and find another, this one from the hearing to end Kate's weekend custody.

Selma starts with her qualifications to give an opinion. The style is stiff legalise, but her voice comes through.

I, Selma Beams, have been the principal caretaker of Tess Sinclair-Jones, daughter of Trist Jones and Kate Sinclair-Jones, for the past three and a half years. My time with the Jones household both before the parents separated and thereafter has allowed me to form an opinion of the parenting skills of each parent, and in particular of the child's mother, Kate Sinclair-Jones.

I skip down to what matters. Selma describes arriving at Kate's house on Monday morning to pick up Tess after her weekend with Kate. She rang the bell, but no one answered. Alarmed, she scrabbled for a spare key in a planter and opened the door. She heard Tess crying in the kitchen and ran to her. Tess was sitting on the counter, wailing amidst a mess of cookies and broken crockery. Somehow she had managed to crawl onto the counter but had no idea how to get down. After rescuing Tess and calming her, Selma went upstairs where she found Kate in a deep sleep.

And then the verdict.

It is my firm opinion based on this incident and other examples of neglect I have observed that Kate Sinclair-Jones lacks the mental stability and judgment to maintain a safe environment for her daughter, Tess Sinclair-Jones. In my opinion, the best interests of the child require that the weekend access granted to Kate Sinclair-Jones by this honourable court be revoked.

I put the affidavit down and look at Alicia. My face must say it all. "Not good?"

"Not good, but not unexpected," I reply. "Pretty much what Kate told me. Except for the aftermath—the incident and losing weekend access shocked Kate into doing something about her depression and anxiety. She sought treatment and had recovered to the point she was going to apply for reinstatement of joint custody."

"The doctors and treatment people she was seeing were prepared to support her?"

"So Kate says. But we need to see the medical records to be sure. Forget the early records, Alicia, focus on her recent treatment under Dr. Etherton, I think that's the name. If he won't give you what we need, let me know and I'll talk to him."

My phone buzzes. Claire's daycare. "Sorry, Alicia, I need to take this." I step out of her office and answer. I hear crying in the background, and my heart skips a beat.

"Everything okay?" I ask.

"Yes," Liz says. "But Claire's caught the cold that's been passing through, and she's feeling a little warm. I'm afraid I have to ask you to take her home until her fever drops."

Edith had warned me about this—one day the daycare will call to say Claire is sick and you must take her home—but guilt fills my chest. Would Claire have gotten sick if I'd stayed home, postponing my return to work? I quickly gather my things. Logic tells me Claire will be fine, but my heart skips a beat as my imagination runs wild. *She will be fine. She will be fine*, I repeat to myself. I hurry out of the office to my baby.

CHAPTER 21

I POP AN ASPIRIN AND WASH it down with water. Claire blows bubbles in her chair on the counter. *The little germ machine*, I think, but I'm grateful she's well again. It's Monday morning, and the fever plaguing Claire all weekend now has my immune system in its grip. It probably didn't help that I haven't slept properly in three nights, worrying over Claire as she fussed.

And when I wasn't worrying over Claire, I was worrying over Tess. It's now been eleven days since she went missing. The police ruled out a ransom kidnapping when no demand was made within seventy-two hours after Tess's disappearance, I've learned. That possibility eliminated, they moved to arrest Kate. I have been harbouring a hope they were wrong, but now, a week and a half since Tess disappeared, I've struck the kidnapping theory from my list of possibilities, too. My mind thrums with conjecture, keeps coming back to Kate's list on the napkin. Fever or no, if I'm to mount her defence, I need more information.

I pick up my phone and dial Kate's number as I rock Claire's carrier.

Kate answers on the first ring. "I'm back in my own house," she informs me. Her voice is calm, no trace of her nervous pitch at the Tea House.

"You're feeling better then?"

"Still frantic but intermittently rational. Jamaican food and family is a powerful curative." She pauses. "Any news on Tess?"

"Not yet," I say. True to Cy's word, police searches have continued, but now they are sporadic, more for show than real. The helicopters that once hovered over Bowen Island are gone, and only a few searchers remain. Occasional police announcements reveal nothing. The absence of news grows more ominous with each day.

"Nothing at the beach where Tess disappeared?" Kate asks.

"No. Just the groove in the sand where a boat pulled up, but the tides have pretty much washed that away." I could tell her about the flowers on the beach, in case she hasn't seen them on TV, but I don't. "I have my investigator on the case. He's good. We'll know the minute the police know something."

I'd called Richard yesterday and filled him in on the case.

Kate's disappointment comes down through the phone. Followed by anger. "We're tired of waiting for the police. We're taking over."

"Who is taking over?" I ask, confused.

"My dad and I. We're going to search for Tess ourselves."

Last I saw Sammy Sinclair outside the courthouse, he wanted Kate to accept that Tess might be gone, wanted her to fight for herself. Now he's agreed to search? Maybe he's realized this is the only way he can love his daughter. After being so hard on her for so long, maybe he's finally listening to what Kate wants, what Kate thinks is best.

"We have a plan," Kate is saying. "I'm going to drive around a different part of the Lower Mainland every day, and he's going back to the island to comb every inch in case the police missed something."

It's hopeless, I want to tell her. If someone took Tess, they won't be hanging around shopping malls with her. Nor are they likely to have kept her on Bowen Island. I look at Claire, brush the dark hair at her forehead with my fingers, and reconsider. I would do the same in Kate's position. She can't sit alone in her house, all day every day. Driving around will give her something to do. And it will keep Kan's boys and girls busy as they try to tail her. I imagine Sammy Sinclair, pushing his bulky torso up the island's hills, and hope his heart is good.

"Good plan," I say, keeping my skepticism to myself. "Our best hope is to find Tess. You'll have your daughter. And they'll drop the murder charge."

Kate hesitates. "Are you sure? I don't trust the police, I don't trust the courts. The system has been against me ever since Trist and I split. They'll find something else; they'll keep persecuting me. Have you read the papers? I try not to, but Dad tells me they say this will be the trial of the decade, if not the century."

She has every reason to be paranoid. Her bail hearing coverage over the weekend was brutal. Kate, the feckless mother, looking stunned and belligerent as she glared at the cameras from under her aqua hood. Kate, who should be in jail and not out on bail free to walk the streets. Kate, who did not care for her child in life, and now has ended it. To lose a child is a terrible thing. To lose a child and be unjustly blamed for her death is unfathomable.

I try to comfort her. "If Tess is found alive and well, the only charge they could conceivably bring would be kidnapping—and then only if they can connect you to the disappearance."

Her voice rises. "They can't, I wasn't at the island. I wasn't in the boat. How many times do I have to tell you that, Jilly?"

Jeff's observation about Kate stealing the boat comes back to me. I think I know the answer, but I have to ask the question anyway. "Kate, do you know how to operate a boat?"

She huffs. "So you don't believe me when I say I was never in that boat."

"It's not a matter of believing. It's what the prosecution can use against you."

"Yeah, I can operate a boat. My dad used to take me with him when he worked weekends. He's the best boat mechanic in Vancouver. All the marinas wanted him. For Dad, being able to handle a boat is a basic life skill. He made sure I learned how."

My heart sinks. Another strand in the rope of circumstantial evidence Kan hopes will connect Kate to the woman in the boat.

"It's one of the things we were planning on teaching Tess together," Kate says quietly. "Dad borrowed a cruiser last year when I still had Tess on the weekends. We took her up Deep Cove. We pulled up on a deserted beach and lit a campfire and roasted marshmallows to make s'mores. Dad let her take the rudder on the way home—just pretend, but she thought it was real. She shrieked when he gave the engine a spurt—" When Kate resumes, her voice is a whisper. "I used to think if anything happened to Tess, I would kill myself. Now it has, and I keep on living. Hope, that's what keeps me going. The hope of seeing Tess again."

In the silence, Claire lets out a small cry.

"Was that Claire?" Kate asks.

I pick Claire up and rock her in my right arm, cradling the phone against my neck. "Yeah, she's getting over a cold. Me too, so we're both at home today."

"You're so lucky," Kate breathes. "I'd give anything to share Tess's next cold. Are you looking after Claire yourself? Don't you have a nanny?"

"Nope. My last nanny quit. Now it's me and the daycare and my friend Edith. I wasn't lucky with nannies."

A long pause. "I wasn't either, as it turns out. Selma stole Tess from me."

I shift Claire in my arms, lower her back to her carrier. "Tell me about Selma, Kate."

"It was all my doing," Kate says. "Hiring her, I mean. Looking back, I was so protective. At first I wanted to do everything for Tess myself. But Trist convinced me it was too much for me, we needed a nanny. Finally, I relented. We interviewed about forty, but I always found something wrong with them. Trist finally lost his patience, and we had a big fight. I was sitting in the park with Tess, crying my eyes out, when this young woman slid onto the bench beside me. 'I recognize you,' she said, 'You're Kate Jones, Trist's wife. And this is little Tess.' I remember how she looked at Tess, lying in her pram. 'May I touch her?' she whispered. Something made me trust her, so I said yes. We talked for a while and she went away. But I saw her again in the park, and then again. I liked her, we got to chatting. It turned out she was a nanny who had recently moved to Vancouver and was looking for a new position. We checked her out. She had a great résumé. So we hired her. And we weren't disappointed. Selma is wonderful with Tess— loving and playful yet structured in a way I'm not. And she was so good around the house. She was a wonderful cook. Trist and

I both loved her." Kate halts. "I didn't know then she would turn against me."

"How did that start?"

"She thought I was lax with Tess. I was used to going with the flow, letting her eat when she wanted, go to bed when she wanted, that sort of thing. Selma thinks routine is essential for a child. I know now she is right."

I try to imagine this ménage-à-trois of Trist, Kate, and Selma. Kate told me that she and Trist had been having difficulties then. How had that played into the situation?

"Forgive me for asking, Kate, but I need to know. Trist and Selma. Did you ever wonder? I mean, did you ever think they might be involved with each other?"

Kate bristles. "What makes you think that?"

"Well, the way things turned out, it was Trist and Selma together and you shunted out of the picture."

"No way. There was never anything like that between Trist and Selma. Selma is very proper, very religious. It would be against her principles. No. Never.

"It's true when we separated, she took Trist's side, signed the affidavit giving him custody. It came as a shock, the things she said about me. I thought she liked me. But there's nothing between Trist and Selma. Their relationship is very professional."

Something in Kate's tone sounds too defensive. I consider probing, decide to let it go. "You told me earlier Selma helped you get your stuff together, something like that."

"Yeah, I learned a lot from her. I see now Selma only ever wanted the best for Tess—but for her, *best* meant *perfect*. I'm not perfect, but I tried to do better, especially after Trist got custody. That time when I took the sleeping pill and Selma found Tess on the kitchen counter was a total fluke. I was trying hard to get better, hoping I would eventually be able to get shared custody."

Kate's voice turns bitter. "I know I'm not perfect, but Selma knows I love Tess more than anything in the world. Sometimes people write you off anyway."

I move to my desk and stare at the blurry photos of the woman in the boat. Tess is looking up at her, laughing, like she trusts her.

After our lunch, Cy sent me the photos, in an uncharacteristically early disclosure. I thumb through them; it will take more than a few blurry photos to get me to tell Kate to take a guilty plea.

"Could the woman in the boat be Selma?"

"I suppose it's possible," Kate replies after a thoughtful moment. "But I doubt it. Why would Selma want to steal Tess? She was with her all day, every day."

I pull out the napkin on which Kate wrote the names of people who knew Tess and cross Selma off the list. "What about Lena, Trist's girlfriend?"

"Don't know her. Don't care to. Met her a few times, but that's it. It's not about her being with Trist—it's about Tess. Tess doesn't like Lena. Even Selma doesn't like Lena, and that's saying something."

I look over at Claire, sleeping now. What makes a child turn against a person who wants to love her? Could it happen to Claire and me?

"Why doesn't Tess like Lena?" I ask.

"I don't know. Whenever I ask Tess about Lena, a dark cloud comes over her face. She shakes her head and clams up. Once, Lena came to pick her up from a supervised visit, and Tess cried and clung to me. I got her calmed down, but she wouldn't take

Lena's hand, wouldn't look at her." Kate's voice drops. "She sobbed all the way to the car. It broke my heart."

Claire stirs, her little fist stabs toward her reddened nose and she mewls.

"I have to go, Kate. Claire needs me. I'll think about what you told me."

I pick Claire up, pull her to my chest. Her forehead is still hotter than I would like—relapse? I touch mine, it's hot, too. I mull over the morning's revelations. Love your child, but not too much. Be spontaneous but insist on routine and order. Above all, avoid the grenades threatening to explode in your face at any moment—illness, alienation, abduction. I hug Claire closer.

The doorbell rings, not a question but an announcement. Edith fills the doorway to the den. She lays a basket on my paper-cluttered desk and starts emptying the contents. Cough syrups, baby and adult. Pain killer. A panier of fruit and the piece de resistance—a pot of chicken soup. She lifts the lid, and the steam assaults my nostrils.

"Vitals," Edith pronounces, scanning me critically. "You look terrible, Jilly. Up to bed for a nap. I'll bring you a bowl before you drift off." She takes Claire from my arms. "As for this little one, it will be my pleasure to take charge."

I want to stay, want to make notes on what I've learned from Kate, but I know better than to argue with Edith. "Okay, okay," I grumble as I head for the stairs. "But kindly remove your chicken soup from my documents."

I lie in my bed and pull the covers to my chin. I am exhausted. A chill sweeps over me, and I long for Mike beside me to warm my aching bones. For now, chicken soup will have to do.

I hear Edith's steps on the stairs, sit up to take the broth. When

I've done my duty, Edith tiptoes out, finger to her lips to tell me Claire is once more sleeping.

I lie back against the pillows and drift toward sleep. Random thoughts sift idly through my brain. Selma is not the woman in the boat; Lena is the one to investigate. A frontal attack will not do; I must plot my course carefully. Trist. Trist is the key. I will go to see Trist.

CHAPTER 22

"LEAVE THE PREMISES. NOW."

The guard looms over me. He pats his sidearm to make sure I get the message.

It's Wednesday, and I'm outside Trist's North Shore mansion. Plan A was to call the number Kate gave me; I stuck with it to the ninth ring, then I switched to Plan B and drove across the Lions Gate Bridge. After half an hour lost in the maze of winding streets they call the British Properties, I found the address Kate had scribbled below the phone number. There was no number on the gate, but I knew this was it.

My fever only abated yesterday, but I stand my ground before the glowering guard, a burly man in navy rain gear and a dark red turban. Hardeep Singh, his name tag says. "No entry," he says, scowling.

I didn't leave Claire with Edith to come all this way and be turned away. "I need to talk to Mr. Jones about his daughter, Tess. I'm a lawyer. I'm acting for Mr. Jones's wife. Ex-wife." I pause. "Please, tell him I'm here."

The guard looks down his prominent nose at me. "Show me your card."

I pull a card from my coat pocket. He holds it close to his face for several moments. "Wait here," he says, then heads inside, leaving me on the front step.

The sun is out but I'm shivering. I stomp my feet, reminding myself why I am here. I need to learn everything I can about the hours and minutes before Tess disappeared. I know what Trist has told the press about what happened—playing in the sand with Tess, falling asleep in the sunshine, waking to Lena's scream, "*Where's Tess?*"

But I need to know more. Like, where was Lena and what was she doing as the day unfolded? Somewhere in the minutiae might lie the clue that leads me to the person who took her.

I check my watch. It's been ten minutes since the guard left. I'm too cold to wait any longer. As I lift the antique brass knocker, the door opens and the guard steps out. He gestures inside. Trist is letting me in.

A woman in a black top and pants leads me through the foyer to a room at the back of the house overlooking a terraced pool, brimming limpidly despite the October chill. Beyond the pool, green lawns spread to a fringe of tall conifers. I wonder what Lena thinks of this place. Not Vegas but not bad either. "Coffee?" the woman asks before waving me in. I decide to take it as a sign Trist will talk, nod *yes, please.*

Plush couches line the room, and three TVs are stacked in a

column, filling an entire wall. An earnest newscaster talking about Tess beams from the highest screen. Below it, frenetic figures follow a puck.

From the couch nearest the TV wall, a man unfolds his long limbs and reluctantly rises. Trist in a jogging suit. He turns to the screens, flicks them off. The local Canuck game is the last to go. He drops the remote, which hits the low table with a careless clunk.

"Good morning," he says, pushing his long blond hair back with one hand while shoving the other in my direction. He looks exactly as he did in that TV interview: strong chin, hooded eyes, green and luminous, with that hint of vulnerability that drives the young girls wild. And his voice, even in speech, is the voice I remember from "Goin' Down on Love"—a clear tenor.

"So, you're Kate's lawyer," he says.

"Jilly Truitt. Thanks for seeing me."

What he says next surprises me. "How is she? Kate, I mean."

"How you would expect. She's distraught. Scared for Tess." I take a closer look at him. Deep lines etch his face, and his jogging suit hangs on his long form. "Suffering. Like you are."

He gives me an appraising look, nods.

"The media—and the law, for that matter—seems convinced Kate, not you, is to blame," I offer. "What's your opinion?"

Trist hesitates. "At first I thought it was a ransom case. The police, too—they moved in and set up a command post in the house to trace all incoming calls and social media. They kept it up even after that jerk came in with the pictures of the woman and child in a boat. Maybe that was part of the kidnapping, they thought. But after they found the torn swimming suit, they changed gears and pulled their crew out. I keep hoping we'll get a demand—I would pay anything to get Tess back—but I'm giving up on that, too."

"What about Kate?" I prompt.

"Kate has had her difficulties. I would be the first to say she's not always been the perfect parent, but neither have I. She wouldn't have done this. It rips me that she's been arrested."

His belief Kate is innocent will make no difference to the law, but after all the anti-Kate flack from the police and the press, it's welcome.

"Hardeep said you wanted to talk about Tess?"

"Yes, I do. I want to find Tess, and I need to build a defence for Kate. Neither of us believe Kate abducted Tess, but the police do. For them, the case is solved. So it's up to us." I pause to let my words sink in. "I need to know what happened to Tess. Help me, Mr. Jones."

He tilts his head and gives a mocking laugh. "Me? How can I help you? I'm the guy who fell asleep while someone stole my child. Remember?"

"You can help a lot, Mr. Jones. To find the truth, I need to understand what happened the day Tess disappeared. Everything. I know you've probably been over this with the police countless times already, but can you go over it one more time with me?"

The woman in black arrives with two coffees and a smile. Trist watches her leave before turning back to me.

"Be my guest. Can't make things worse." He gestures to the couch behind the coffee table and sinks into it. I take a seat opposite.

"Thank you, Mr. Jones. Do you mind if I record this?" I gesture to my phone.

"Why?" he bristles.

"I don't want to miss anything—or worse, misconstrue something you say."

"Alright. But this is confidential, okay? Nobody else sees the tape unless I say so."

"Absolutely confidential, Mr. Jones."

"You might as well call me Trist. Everybody else does. Even the bloody police."

"Let's start with you and Kate."

"What's to say? We fell in love. We married and had a kid. It worked until it didn't. So we divorced. I still love Kate—she was with me through all the tough times—but I can't live with her."

"What did you fight about?"

"Hah, what didn't we fight about? Tess, for one thing. Kate wanted to keep Tess away from the press—she hated the attention and wanted to protect her. I disagreed. I have a public, and I want them to know me as I am—a family man with a gorgeous daughter. Besides, Tess doesn't mind the photo shoots. She likes to play up to the cameras." He pauses. "We also had different parenting styles. We were both laid back but Kate much more than me. And then Kate started to get depressed and anxious and—well, the rest is history."

Trist's version fits with what Kate has told me. I decide to move on.

"Why Bowen Island?"

He stares at me, elbows on his knees, angular face cradled in his long-fingered hands. He takes his time.

"I'd come off a long tour. I needed a rest. I got this idea we needed to get out of the city, do some wilderness. A long time ago, when I was starting out, I did a gig at a resort on Quadra Island. I loved the ocean, the solitude . . ." He trails off. "I talked to Lena, my girlfriend, about it. It seemed perfect, just us three alone in the solitude of a beautiful island, bonding, resting, getting back to basics. She wasn't sure, but we went online and found the place on Bowen. Looked perfect. Late September, too late for sunbathing, but you never know, you can get a stretch of summer weather if you're lucky. And if we didn't, we could take walks on the beach and sit around the fire in the evening."

"You said Lena wasn't sure. She didn't want to go?"

His lip twists. "Lena's a Vegas girl, a dancer. The great outdoors is not exactly her thing, but I convinced her the quiet would be good. She said she was actually looking forward to it."

I study his face, wondering why Lena changed her mind.

"When did Lena tell you that?"

"Oh, let me think. A few days before we left."

"Did she say why she changed her mind?"

"No. Turns out Selma couldn't come with us—something about having to take her grandfather to the doctor. I remember Lena saying it would be nice to be alone, the three of us."

I settle back and consider the possibilities. Lena had a plan that made going to an island wilderness with a five-year-old who didn't like her tolerable. She wanted Trist to move to Vegas with her, and for that she had to convince him she was wifey material: loyal lover, game companion, would-be mother to his child. And not having Selma around was a plus.

"Can you walk me through the day Tess disappeared, Trist? How did it start?"

"It started like any other day that week. Tess got up early and I got up with her, gave her some cereal. I got her dressed, and she watched cartoons on her iPad for an hour or so. By then, Lena was up and offered to amuse Tess while I answered emails and had a call with my agent. Then she surprised me with lunch, which turned out to be a disaster."

"How so?"

"Lena made an omelette, but Tess didn't like it and threw it on the floor. I told Tess to get the garbage can and help me clean it up. When we were finished I said, *Tell Lena you're sorry.* Tess pouted but finally apologized. I said it might be best if she went to her room for a while."

I think of Claire, wonder if she will throw my food on the floor in a tantrum some day and how I will feel. "Was Lena upset?"

"Yeah, you could say that. No one had much of an appetite after that. Lena threw all the food into the garbage, scraped the plates, and filled the dishwasher. I tried to help, but she shooed me away. I could see she was crying. She was frustrated. Tess can be a handful. *Take the boat out for a spin,* I said. She had learned to operate the boat and was quite proud of herself. I told her to pick up some stuff for supper. That the fresh air would do her good. I started cleaning up and turned around and there she was—smiling and offering me a big glass of red wine. She called it a peace offering. She slung her bag over her shoulder and headed out the door."

I think about Trist falling asleep on the beach. Had Lena put something in the wine?

"And then?"

"It's my fault," he says simply, without preamble. "I dozed off. The sun was so warm, I was so relaxed. I remember thinking: just a few minutes. I must have slept for more than an hour." His fists clench. "And now I've lost my child and will carry the guilt as long as I live. I can never forgive myself."

His openness takes me aback. In an age of assumed guises and dissimulation, Trist is guileless. People respond to it, his fans love him for it. I study his face. Can this openness itself be a guise? I test the waters.

"You mentioned Lena was trying her best to deal with Tess. How do Lena and Tess get along?"

He takes a while to answer. "It was a work in progress." He gives a short laugh. "Actually, more work than progress. Lena put effort in. Read her stories, took her to the park, did her hair. Sometimes Tess was okay, but sometimes Tess rebuffed her, sulked and pouted. Or worse, like throwing an omelette on the floor. With me, with everybody else, Tess is happy, agreeable. With Lena, she's a little monster."

I can guess at the explanation, but I ask the question anyway. "Why do you think Tess rejects Lena?"

"Tess is smart, and despite all Kate's lapses, Tess loves Kate. She sees Lena taking over Kate's role, and she doesn't like it. And Lena has never been around children, so she is definitely not the maternal type. Maybe Tess picked up the false vibe."

He leans forward, elbows on knees. "Lena cried a lot about how Tess treated her. I tried to reassure her. We had a great thing going, Lena and me, and she was trying to make it work."

"You say 'had.' Aren't you and Lena serious?"

He gives a harsh laugh. "Yeah, we were talking about getting married." He pauses, clunks his coffee mug on the table with more force than necessary. "But it's over."

"How so?"

"She left for Vegas two days after Tess went missing. I mean, I can't blame her. Police crawling all over the house, paps outside snapping pics every time you poked your nose out. And then my manager said we shouldn't be photographed together anymore with Tess gone and all, which didn't go over well with Lena. So she decided to leave. I understand that. But I can't forgive her for the way she left. She didn't discuss it with me, didn't even leave a note. I came home from an interview with the police and she was gone. Her stuff, too—closets completely emptied. And then, when I went online, I found out she had cleaned out our joint account—two hundred K. Gone. Just like that." He flicks his finger in the air.

"Wow," I say.

"Yeah. Wow." He leans back against the cushions.

My gaze slips to the shelves flanking a faux fireplace, where photos stand. I see Tess, beaming up at the camera from a small red wagon. The sun catches the halo of her hair, her face radiating joy. Better times. My eye skips to a silver-framed portrait of a woman with dusky skin and black hair and a soulful smile that makes you want to love her. "Lena?"

Trist follows my eye. "Yeah, Lena. Some days I hate her, some days I still love her. God." He shakes his messy mane and gives a short laugh. "Life is crazy. I have a gig coming up in Vegas if I can pull myself together. Who knows? Maybe we'll hook up again."

Crazy indeed, I think. "How did Lena react to Tess's disappearance?"

"Well, like me, she was frantic when we realized Tess was missing. But she handled it better. I was a basket case, so Lena took over. She called 9-1-1. Talked to the police, showed them the beach, Tess's room, gave them food and soft drinks. Held my hand when they put us in the cruiser and took us into town for questioning."

There is so much I do not know. I am still waiting for disclosure. "Did the police question Lena?"

"Yes. First they questioned me. They put me in a room, went over everything. Then they did the same with her. Questions about our movements that morning, about anyone she'd noticed on the island, about how Tess was behaving that morning. About when she arrived back to find me dozing on the beach and Tess missing. They finished with her and had her take me home. I was such a mess, I think they were grateful to have an adult in the room."

I loop back to the day Tess disappeared.

"After Lena left in the boat, what happened?"

"I went upstairs and got Tess. The day had turned bright, and she said she wanted to go swimming. I found her bathing suit—the one that later washed up on the beach—and helped her put it on. We walked down to the beach to see if we could see some whales. I'd read Tess a story about whales the night before, and all she could talk about were the orcas. It was so good, after all the travelling, all the time away from Tess, just to be by the ocean holding her hand.

"We had such a beautiful time that afternoon, Tess and me," Trist says wistfully. "We ran down to the sea, and when she screamed the water was cold, I picked her up, swung her around, and carried her to shore. She was still pretending to be a breaching dolphin when I settled on an old chaise they had down there and closed my eyes. The next thing I felt was something wet and cold on my chest. Tess had dumped her sand pail on me. She was laughing."

"And then?"

Trist conjures the memory. "The rest is like a dream," he says at last. "I remember feeling the sun, feeling sleepy, lying back on the recliner. I remember Tess standing over me and closing my eyes with her little fingers, like I used to close hers when I put her to bed." He chokes back a sob.

"The next thing I remember is hearing the roar of a boat motor and Lena screaming, *Where's Tess? Where's Tess?* I panicked. We searched the beach, we searched the house and the grounds around it, no sign. I was wild, out of it with fear. I couldn't believe Tess was missing. Lena grabbed her phone and started dialing. *What are you doing?* I remember asking her. I will never forget the look she gave me—a look of total, utter contempt. *Your child is missing. I am calling the police.*"

Trist bows his head.

CHAPTER 23

WE SIT IN SILENCE. TRIST'S head is between his knees and his hands hang limply to the floor. He is tired, he is broken. I have ripped the scabs off the wounds that were starting to heal, and he is bleeding again. I should put my arm around him, thank him, and leave him to his grieving. But there are still questions I need to ask.

"Who do you think could have taken Tess?"

He shakes his head. "I don't know. I know about the photos. They say it's Kate. Kate can handle a boat, Kate probably wanted to see Tess desperately. But I don't think she would have done this. Unless—"

"Unless what?"

"I read the other day about a mother who had been denied

custody who abducted her children with her father's help and took them over the border to the States with forged identities. Kate could have done something like that. Run the boat south to Bellingham and turned Tess over to someone there."

He halts. He's holding something back.

"What is it, Trist?"

He shifts uncomfortably. "Well, like I said, I don't think Kate took Tess. But she found out Lena and I were talking about getting married and had put a down payment on a place in Vegas. I don't know how she found out, maybe Tess said something, but after a supervised visit, Kate phoned me, mad as hell, and said I couldn't do this, couldn't take Tess away from her to a foreign country. She would tear my eyes out before she would let me move to Vegas. I mean, she was wild. I tried to calm her down, but I told her I wouldn't make any promises—if Lena and I decided to move, we would move and take Tess with us and there was nothing she could do about it."

I take it in, trying to hide my shock. I've been gloating the Crown has no motive, and now that illusion has been shattered. Kate had downplayed the Vegas move, hadn't said anything about Trist buying a house there. Cy will call Trist to tell the jury what he's told me—Kate knew Trist had bought a home in Vegas, knew Tess would be lost to her, and threatened violence. All her dreams, all her plans to get joint custody would come to nothing. So, she decided to steal Tess away while she could.

I feel anger welling up. I asked Kate to tell me everything, *trusted* Kate to tell me everything, but she's been holding back on me. Never told me in all our chats that Trist and Lena had bought a place in Vegas and were already planning the move.

I swallow my anger and move on. "If Kate didn't take Tess, who did?"

"A kidnapper, maybe, though no ransom demand has been made. Maybe something went wrong and they had to abandon the plan." Trist sits back, closes his eyes. I know what he's thinking: Tess was killed when things didn't work out. "No, not that," he breathes.

"Were there any strangers—or family members or associates— who seemed overly interested in Tess?"

"Everyone loves Tess. Even my crusty Vegas agent, Rex Wiseman, dotes on her, brings her presents every time he comes to Vancouver. Tess is beautiful and funny and loving." He allows himself a crooked smile. "And sometimes a little ragamuffin."

"I mean someone who took an unnatural interest," I say, making a mental note to check out Rex.

"You mean a pedophile," Trist hisses, leaning forward. "Tess's face is all over the web, all over the tabloids. That was my choice, and I have to wear it, but some pervert stealing her away? No, no, never that."

I change the subject. "We need to identify the woman in the boat. She's dark-haired and slender, but we have little else. So far, I see three women in Tess's life who could fit that description— Kate, Selma, and Lena. We've talked about Kate and a little about Lena. Tell me about Selma."

Trist considers. "Selma is a great nanny, organized, intelligent, devoted to Tess. When Kate became sick, Selma saved us. She identified what was happening, brought in a doctor for Kate. And she took over. When I was away, which was a lot, Selma looked after Tess single-handedly."

"How does Tess relate to Selma?"

"Tess loves Selma, and Selma loves Tess. It's that simple."

"Selma played a role in the custody applications you brought against Kate?"

"Yes, thank God. When Kate and I separated, I assumed we would share custody—Kate would have Tess when I was touring, and I would take over when I was back home. It worked for a while. But then Kate started to get sick. She went to a dark place. I wasn't seeing her much, so I didn't know how dark. But Selma did. Without Selma, I would never have understood Kate's depression and anxiety meant she couldn't properly parent Tess. Selma persuaded me to apply for sole custody with weekends with Kate. That seemed to work for a while, but every time Selma went to pick Tess up after a weekend visit, there were issues— Tess outside in the cold without a jacket, Tess sick with a runny nose and nothing being done about it. Once, when she went to pick up Tess after a weekend visit, she found her playing in the street, with the door open and Kate upstairs. Kate made light of it, said she'd just run upstairs for a minute, but it started Selma worrying about Tess's safety when Kate was looking after her. Then when Selma found Tess in the kitchen one morning wailing on the counter while Kate was comatose from sleeping pills upstairs, she decided to do something. I hated to reduce Kate to supervised visits; it killed me to do that. But Selma was right, we had to put Tess's well-being first. When Kate got better, she could start parenting Tess again."

So there wasn't one incident of neglect but many. Another thing Kate hasn't told me. I picture Selma telling Trist these things in the evening after Tess had been put to bed, crying a little, Trist putting his arm around her to comfort her, telling her he'll do whatever she wants.

"You and Selma were close?"

Trist rears his head, cuts me off. "Only when it came to Tess.

Our relationship was strictly professional." His words fit with what Kate has told me, and I decide to let it go. So far, Selma is checking out. "How does Selma feel about Kate?"

"She likes her, I think. It was Kate who found her, hired her. Until Kate became sick, everything was fine."

"And Lena? Does Selma like Lena?"

A short laugh. "Well, I can't say Selma thinks highly of Lena."

"What do you mean?"

"You have to understand. Selma was brought up religious, born again with some crazy twists I still don't understand. No drinking, no smoking, no cards or dancing. Lena, on the other hand, likes the odd joint. I don't let her do it around Tess, but Selma knows; she can catch a whiff of weed from a country mile. And Selma can tell Tess doesn't like Lena, and that's a bad mark against Lena, too. Selma never says much, but Lena feels her disapproval like a wet blanket. Like I say, Selma staying behind was a plus for the Bowen Island trip." His lip twists. "Getting away from Selma for a few days was not entirely without appeal."

I smile, remembering how I sometimes flinched under Mab's disapproval. "I can imagine."

Trist looks up. "You have a kid?"

"A little girl, Claire. Five months old."

"Lucky you." He rubs the corner of his eye with his fist.

I get back to business. "Was Selma invited to move with you to Vegas?"

Trist hesitates. "We hadn't worked that out yet. I wanted Selma to come but Lena was against it, kept talking about finding a nice nanny in Vegas who was mixed race like Tess. She hadn't given us an answer—she has family here—but she knew we wanted her to come with us."

"Have you seen Selma since Tess disappeared?"

Trist shakes his head. "She called me when the news broke. I'm afraid I didn't deal with her well, in the state I was in. She must have been grieving, too. I remember her saying Kate did this."

Probably a reflection of her fear, I think, but I will need to check this out.

"I told my manager to lay Selma off while Tess is missing, with enough money to tide her over until we know more."

"Let's talk about Lena," I say.

"We already did."

"A few more questions," I say with a smile. "It seems Lena may have been frustrated with the fact Tess didn't seem to like her, especially because she was planning to marry you. I'm sorry to have to ask you this, but do you think part of her wanted Tess out of the way?" I don't add what keeps nagging at me—that Lena took a boat out knowing Tess would be on the beach, having given Trist a big glass of red wine that may or may not have been spiked.

He sucks in his breath, looks at the ceiling and sits down. "No," he says. "The idea is ludicrous. Lena loves Tess. And before Tess went missing, she was trying to make it work."

Trist stands. "I'm afraid I have an appointment. I have to end this."

As if on cue, the woman in black appears. Trist stands. "Please show Ms. Truitt out," he says.

I wave absently to the guard as I make my way down the walk to my car, my mind working to organize this new information. One woman in the boat, three candidates.

Kate failed to tell me she knew Trist had bought a place in

Vegas and the move was happening. That's motive. No motive for Selma; the decision to take her to Vegas hadn't been made yet. Lena, the future wife saddled with a child who rejected her, had motive and opportunity.

Richard, pack your bag for Vegas.

CHAPTER 24

I PULL AWAY FROM TRIST'S HOUSE and head home.

It's only early afternoon, and I should go into the office, but I veer south toward Shaughnessy. I need to relieve Edith, need to be home with Claire.

Edith greets me in the hall, her index finger pressed to her lip. She points upstairs. "Sleeping," she whispers. "I think she'll be okay to go to daycare tomorrow."

"Thanks, Edith."

"Get some rest if you can. You look tired."

"Yeah. I knew being a working mother would not be easy, but I didn't count on feeling so stretched—I never seem able to give what I want, either to Claire or to my case."

Edith shoots me a knowing look. "You need to give yourself more credit, Jilly."

I wave her away. "I'll take over from here."

Edith fetches her coat and purse, heads out. I'm checking the monitor is on—hear Claire's snuffles—when my cell rings. Richard.

"Update already?" I ask. It's only been a few days since I put him on the case.

It is Richard's wont to open a conversation with a light-hearted *bonjour, madam,* but today he is all business. "The police are making an announcement this evening," he says tersely. "You're going to want to prepare Kate."

My stomach wrenches. I brace myself for bad news.

"They've found the boat," he says.

"The boat," I echo woodenly.

"The boat in Dante's photograph. The boat with Tess and Kate in it."

"Which remains to be proven," I remind him. "Where was it found?"

"Washed up in a cove near Britannia Beach. Battered, in bad shape. Probably tossed up by the storm last week. Nobody goes there, there's no road in. A boater spotted it, thought it might be related to the disappearance, and called the police."

It's not so bad, I tell myself. Sooner or later the boat was bound to turn up. But it's not good either. Not good that it looks like the same boat, not good that it's washed up in a mainland cove where the winds could have driven a boat abandoned off Bowen Island. I ask the obvious question. "Lots of boats get washed up in storms. How do they know it's the same one?"

"I couldn't find that out, but they seem very confident it's the one Dante Bocci photographed. And they've checked to see whether the boat matches any boats reported missing recently."

"And?"

"Two similar boats have been reported missing. One was taken from the Vancouver Yacht Club, where Kate's father was employed."

My heart sinks to my stomach. Another strand in the rope of circumstantial evidence Cy will weave. "He worked at several clubs," I say.

"Hey, I'm not the prosecutor, Jilly," Richard rebuffs. "I'm on your side. I'm just telling you what I know. It will take a while to complete the investigation and get the details, but the police are going to announce the discovery tonight. They wouldn't do that unless they were sure. Kan is no fool."

I could call up Cy, get the details now. Part of me, the pent-up frustrated part, wants to look at the boat pronto. But the sensible part says I should wait for the police report so I know what I'm looking for.

"Thanks, Richard. I appreciate the heads-up." My mind goes back to my visit with Trist. "I need you to clear a few days for me."

"Right now?"

"Yes, if you can." I know he's busy. "It's important," I add.

"*Pas possible*," Richard reverts to French when he's testy.

I move on, undeterred. "I had a long chat with Trist today. It seems he and Lena were planning to get married. They'd already bought a place in Vegas. With Tess."

Richard inhales sharply. "Merde. If Kate knew, that gives her a motive to steal Tess."

"You got it," I say. "And she knew."

"And didn't tell you," says Richard.

"Got it again. I keep forgetting how smart you are, Richard."

"So what do you want me to do about it?"

"I want you to go to Vegas and check out Lena." Jeff's face, telling me to keep Richard on a short leash, fills my mind. I'm going too far, but I have no choice.

"She's in Vegas?" Richard sounds surprised.

"Yes. Took off two days after Tess disappeared. Here's the thing, Richard. Lena is dark and slender; she could be the woman in the boat. She desperately wanted to marry Trist but Tess was in the way—Tess didn't like Lena. So Lena decides to take Tess out. Maybe she had it planned before she went to the island, maybe it was a reaction to Tess acting out that day. Anyway, she had learned how to handle the boat. She offered Trist a big glass of wine, maybe spiked to make him sleep, told him to take Tess to the beach and left in the boat. She circled around for a while until she was sure Trist was out, came back, plucked Tess off the beach, and took her around the point. Where she was photographed by Dante Bocci. She disposed of Tess and returned to give the hue and cry to the police."

"And the bathing suit and shoe?"

"She threw them into the water near the beach where they were found before heading back to the lodge."

"And how does this theory fit with the boat that washed up?"

My head is spinning. "I don't know, Richard." I wait for a response but none comes. "Well, what do you think?"

"I think it won't wash. Lena leaves Trist on the beach and steals the kid from under his nose? Crazy."

"Yeah, I know it's a long shot. But the more I think about this case, the more I think we're dealing with someone a bit crazy. Someone driven by irrational grievances or desires. We can't look for the normal. We need to look for crazy."

"I hate to tell you this, Jilly, but it won't fly. It's pure speculation, improbable speculation at that. Without something concrete to tie Lena to the woman in the boat that's washed up, the judge won't let you put it to the jury." He pauses. "Fuck, Jilly, you're the lawyer, you know that."

"That's where you come in, Richard. I want you to fly down to Vegas. Find out where she's staying, who she sees, what she does. Kate, Selma, and Lena are the only candidates we have for the woman in the boat. Lena left the country right after Tess disappeared, the other two are still here. We need to suss out Lena. Now. Watch her, find a way to talk to her."

"You think she's stupid enough to tell a stranger she knocked off her lover's child?"

I sigh. "Probably not, Richard. All I know is we've got to check it out. Look for some fact that substantiates the theory. If I have to, I'll go down myself. It's only a two-hour flight."

"No way." Richard's voice ratchets up a notch. My ploy is working. He won't let me go down myself. Not now, with Claire in my life.

"I have to finish a report on a casino fraud. It will take me two days. This is crazy, Jilly, but I'll find a way to get down to Vegas before the weekend if you insist."

"Thank you, Richard," I breathe. "And thanks for heads-up about the boat."

The phone goes dead. I stare at the black screen in my hand. Watching brief only, Jeff said. Now, in my insane desperation to get Kate off, I'm sending Richard to Vegas to investigate Lena. I'm in this case too deep. I've crossed the line.

I lean back in my chair. My fatigued mind switches from Lena back to the boat. Why are the police so certain that the boat that washed up is the same boat Tess was in? Is it more tunnel vision—

if a boat like the one in the photograph washed up in the vicinity, it must be the same one—or do they have more?

They haven't connected Kate to the boat yet—all they have is a connection between the boat and Dante's photograph. But the boat could change that. A hair in a crack, a fingerprint on a gunwale, can set her free. Or sink her. And the boat being washed up doesn't fit with my theory on Lena. The boat Lena took that day was the boat that came with the lodge, which hasn't gone missing—the police found it tied to the dock when they arrived. Could Lena somehow have switched boats? Unlikely, and anyway, why would she do that?

Nothing fits, nothing makes sense. But it doesn't look good for Kate. Kate, who hasn't come clean with me. Kate, who had motive and opportunity.

The monitor is emitting static. Claire is waking. I need to tell Kate the police will announce they found the boat before she hears it. I punch in Kate's number as I climb the stairs to Claire's room.

"Kate," I say. "They've found the boat."

PART II

CHAPTER 25

IT'S OCTOBER 13. CANADIAN THANKSGIVING weekend is over—three entire days with Claire.

Yesterday, Edith appeared in a swirl of crisp autumn winds and blowing leaves with a small turkey and the fixings. We spent the afternoon puttering in the kitchen and catching up. "Claire is flourishing in Liz's daycare," I told Edith, "and despite my misgivings, I am content to be back at work.

"Your first Thanksgiving," I cooed encouragingly at Claire as I offered her a dab of pureed potato and turkey. She bubbled out the first bite and howled. I looked at the mess on the spoon and her chin and put turkey on my mental list of acquired tastes.

Last year, alone and pregnant, I could not bring myself to give thanks. But time has passed. The absence of Mike is still a hole in my heart, but now I have my child, and for the first time since

Mike's death, I feel grateful. Grateful for Claire. Grateful for Edith. Grateful to be alive. The bullet should have got me, not Mike. But I cannot change what happened.

After Edith left, I bundled Claire up in her snuggly and took us for a walk in the park. The cold wind cut through my jacket, but Claire dozed contentedly. I spared a thought for Kate and Trist, alone in their separate griefs.

Now it's Tuesday. I've dropped Claire at Liz's daycare and I'm back in the office. Things are not going well here. Not for lack of trying.

I push open the door. Debbie greets me with a bright smile. "Wait a minute," she calls as I breeze by with a wave. "Files for you. New cases." I double back and take the proffered folders from her hand. My idea of returning to work is to focus on Kate's case and ease in gradually. Debbie has a different plan. If experience is a guide, Debbie will win this battle.

I slip into the chair behind my desk, sip my latte, and survey my new files. I take one, open it, and look at the top page. Eight months ago, a forty-seven-year-old woman struck and killed a cyclist with her car and is now charged with manslaughter. She claims the sun was in her eyes, but she blew .08 on the breathalyzer, just over the legal limit. No other offences. Maybe the sun *was* in her eyes. I look at what the Crown is offering—two years to be served at home. We can do better. But not until we get the junior I promised Alicia. Jeff was quick to agree to it, even suggested he'd conduct the interviews. With any luck, we'll have someone by next week.

I pick up a second file. One Ryan Coyne has a sexual assault conviction. As per the law, he's been placed on the registry of sex offenders. He wants his name removed and thinks I'm the to person to help him do it. Fat chance on both counts.

But the file makes me think about Kate's case. The Sex Offender Registry is confidential, but maybe there's some way in. I need to see for myself.

I turn to my computer, search for the site, read how a member of the public can access the names in the registry. The only way is to get the commissioner of the RCMP to release them. In principle, I'm all for protecting privacy, but now I curse it. No way Madam Commissioner will hand over her lists of pedophiles to a defence lawyer.

I pull Kate's file from the briefcase at my side and fish out the photos of the woman in the boat. I stare at the top one, willing myself to see what I have missed. And then I do. The photo isn't about the woman—it's about the child. The way the child looks up at the woman, the way the sun catches her hair like a halo. I've been so obsessed with the woman I failed to realize Tess was the focal point. Maybe *Dante* is a pedophile. Or takes pictures for pedophiles.

I pick up my phone and dial Richard.

"It's Kate's case again," I say when he answers. "I know you're off to Vegas tomorrow to check out Lena. But if you get a minute between checking in and landing, could you start thinking about the photographer?

"Dante Bocci," I continue. "The guy who took the photos of the woman and child in the boat. Crown witness number one. I need to know his background. Employer, financial situation, legal run-ins. The whole shebang."

"Good idea. Sure. But I can't do it while I'm flying."

"When you can." I take a deep breath. "Another thing. I need to know if anyone on Bowen Island that day is on the Sex Offender Registry. I need to know if Dante Bocci is on it."

I wait for his response. "Richard?"

His voice when he finally answers is gruff. "You know I can't go there. The Sex Offender Registry is confidential."

I think of the complaint in Ryan's file. His name on the registry closed doors and returned job applications. "Some people can."

"Jilly, be serious. I could get two years in jail if I used information from the registry, even if I could somehow get my hands on it. This is not like the States. We don't have Megan's Law giving anyone access to sexual offenders' whereabouts. If you want that info, you'll have to persuade the police. They're the only ones that can access it."

I lower my voice. "I wouldn't want you to put yourself in jeopardy, Richard. But info, even confidential info, can be leaked. If you hear anything, let me know."

There's a long pause before Richard sighs. "I'll ferret around. But if it's any comfort, I'm sure the police have been all over the sex registry files trying to connect them with anyone on or near the island from the moment Tess was reported missing."

I picture Kan's dour face. "We know how they work," I say. "The moment they lay charges, the investigation is over. Assuming they *started* combing the Sex Offender Registry, they shut it down when they charged Kate. They think they've solved the case."

"Yeah. If I find anything, I'll let you know."

"Good luck in Vegas," I say and hang up.

I hear Jeff's step outside, hear the front door open and close— he's off to court. Sooner or later, I must tell him I've put Richard on active investigation. I don't relish his reaction.

I double down on the file before me; it's time to assess where we stand.

Cy, true to his word, filed a direct indictment against Kate last week. I pick up the list of people to interview that Alicia and I drew up last week. Lena, if Richard can find her when he flies to Vegas on Wednesday; Selma the nanny; Winnifred, Trist's housekeeper—is she the woman in black who offered me coffee at Trist's house? I curse myself for ignoring her on my visit. Dante, a riddle, wrapped in a mystery, inside an enigma.

I slide the list away and scan Richard's notes about police activity. Kan has pulled everyone off the island except two semi-retired beat cops. The police have talked to everyone on the island, and no one saw a woman and child on a boat on Friday, September 25, the day Tess disappeared. A ninety-year-old retiree says he saw a strange metal-hulled boat in the neighbouring cove a few days before the abduction; the police noted it but failed to follow up. Not that I blame them. Boats come and go all the time, and some sit in this cove or that for a few days. On the mainland front, Richard's inside informants tell him Kan has reduced the staff checking out CCTV film to two—not enough to monitor a shopping mall on Christmas Eve.

We still don't know if Tess is dead or alive. Each day, my hope she may be found grows weaker. The police haven't found a trace, nor have the thousands of online citizens who say they are looking for her. Kate's dad came back from five days trekking up and down mountains on the island, exhausted and discouraged. Kate's been driving around the Lower Mainland, a different suburb every day, with no luck. She thinks she's being followed. A small green car, she says. Probably undercover police, I tell her, although I'm not ruling out a pap.

Not only have we failed to find Tess, we haven't advanced an inch on the legal front. The Crown claims Kate had opportunity, and without a credible alibi, we can't refute that. Richard's assistant has grilled the students in Kate's morning class and no one remembers her that day. Kate has nothing but her word to show where she was the day Tess disappeared and the long night that followed. Kate's knowledge Trist was planning to move Tess to Vegas before she could bring her motion has given her a plausible motive. Summary: Kate's trial is drawing closer, and we still don't have a theory for the defence.

I write *Defence* at the top of the blank paper and print two names under it. My gut tells me if there is a defence—a big if—it will lie with Dante or Lena. Both were on the island the day Tess disappeared. Both had the opportunity to take her from the beach while Trist snored. Something's not right with Dante's identification—the vibe he gives off, scared but overeager. Is he covering for someone? Or is he afraid for himself? And Lena—no need to rehearse the case against her. She needed Tess gone and made sure Trist was sleeping so she could snatch her. A Google check reveals her name on Vegas marquees. It's not clear where she grew up or what she did before Vegas, but chances are she had to do some clawing to get where she got. Lena is tough. She gets what she wants.

I write a third name in smaller print below: Selma. Selma needs to be checked out, too, to make sure we've covered every base. I've asked Richard to talk to her. But not much will come of that, I suspect. Selma has no motive, no presence on the island, and is scared stiff of boats. And her self-description in the affidavits she filed in the custody proceedings mesh perfectly with the description of her Kate and Trist have provided—Selma, the devoted nanny, straight as an arrow. No social media presence I can find. An ordinary young woman who likes looking after children.

I sit back and survey my sheet. And then I reconsider. All we have is speculation; speculation won't raise a reasonable doubt.

I pick up the photo of the woman in the boat and stare at it. Who is she? Kate, Lena, Selma? Richard will suss out Lena this week, but the report I asked him for on Selma will have to wait. I feel impatience rise. I want it all now, always have.

Learn to wait, Jilly, Mike used to chide me. Lord, do I need him now.

CHAPTER 26

"**W**HAT THE HELL WERE YOU doing, Jilly?"

It's Wednesday morning, and I'm in Jeff's office. Jeff is pacing the floor, up one wall and down the other, while I stand in the corner.

I start to answer, but he cuts me off. "We had a deal, Jilly. Richard will keep an eye on the police but no active investigation. Now Debbie tells me he's winging his way to Vegas to check out that two-bit dancer Trist hooked up with. Whose idea was that? I suspected something was up—thank God I investigated."

He swivels his torso and leans over me, hands on hips, glowering. "I thought I could trust you. I thought we were partners."

"You can and we are," I say as evenly as I can manage. "And I owe you an apology. I was planning to tell you. Things have been moving so fast . . ."

Is this the best I can do? Pathetic.

"Who's paying for these wild goose chases?" Jeff demands.

"Looks like I am." I suck in my breath. "Lower your voice, Jeff. Our new junior is sitting in the outside office waiting to meet us. Unless she's heard the ruckus and fled."

Jeff's eyes roll behind his round glasses, but he lowers his voice. "So what do we do now?"

"In the short term? We go out there, all smiles, and show Shanni this is a lovely, civilized place to work. In the longer term, we carry on, with changes. I thought I could do this case without investigating every lead, but I can't. Kan has pointed the finger at Kate, and he's grinding the investigation to a halt as we speak. For him the case is solved. But Kate is facing life in prison, and there's no proof Tess is dead. She may still be out there somewhere—" I break off. "No one is looking but us. Help me, Jeff."

Jeff eyes me coldly. "That's not good enough, Jilly."

"I promise from now on I will keep you in the loop. We will have weekly meetings Fridays at four thirty p.m., when court is done." I halt, thinking of Claire, how I look forward to seeing her each afternoon at five. I grit my teeth. Now, Edith will have to pick her up on Fridays. "I don't like staying late on Friday any better than you do, Jeff, but there's no alternative. For the next few months, our weekends will start a few hours late."

"Meetings," Jeff says bitterly. "Useless. I'll tell you to stop, and you'll carry on anyway."

"No, Jeff. I know it's not something I'm used to doing, but I promise to listen. We'll talk things over and decide together."

He shakes his head. "Decide together? I'll believe it when I see it." He's still angry, but he's cooling down. "Let's go out and greet our new associate," he says gruffly.

"I'm sure you chose well," I say smoothly.

Jeff grunts and pushes the door open. To his credit, he pastes on a plausible smile.

"Shanni, let me introduce my partner, Ms. Jilly Truitt."

Shanni Patel rises to greet us. She is tall and slender and wears her thick dark hair twisted into a bun. Her deep-set eyes shine with intelligence, which doesn't surprise me—Jeff's memo said she was in the top ten per cent in her criminal law courses. I supress a pang of pity. *Why do you want to spend the rest of your life doing this crazy job?* I muster a smile and grip her proffered hand in my two.

"Ms. Truitt," she gushes, "this is such an honour. I admire you so much."

I nod as she goes on with how she's followed my career and wants to walk in my footsteps. When the palaver winds down, I tell her how much I'm looking forward to working with her, and excuse myself, leaving Jeff to settle the details. I hope he doesn't mention the hours.

I head for my office. As I pass, the entry door opens.

"What are you doing here, Richard? I thought you were on your way to Vegas."

"I am." Richard looks at his big Fitbit. "Flight leaves in exactly ninety-three minutes. I dropped by to tell you I had coffee with Selma yesterday afternoon."

"Once again, you surpass my expectations." I nod toward my room. "Five minutes?"

Inside, we flop into our chairs. Richard starts talking, no time to waste.

"Bottom line: Selma is everybody's dream nanny. Loves kids, adores Tess. I got the impression she feels she loves Tess more than Tess's parents and is a little angry about being treated like a mere ex-employee, i.e., ignored. Oh, the police talked to her, twenty minutes pro forma. Not that she has much to add. She had a good reason for not going to the island with Trist and Lena: her grandfather had health problems, and she needed to drive him to specialists that week."

"Fits with what Trist said," I say.

Richard nods. "When I asked her who might have taken Tess, she clammed up. 'No idea, but it wasn't me.'"

"I can understand her feeling overlooked," I say. "Did she say anything about Kate?"

"That she would never forgive her. I didn't know what to make of that. Forgive her for what? For being an inadequate parent? For something she did to Selma?"

"Or perhaps for killing Tess?" I finish.

Richard nods. "*Aucune idee.* I tried to follow up but she refused to say more."

"Anything else stand out?"

"Maybe it was grieving for Tess, or dislike of Kate, or discomfort with being interviewed, but she seemed edgy. Weighing every word before she uttered it. After fifteen minutes, she got up and left. No explanation. 'Sorry, I've got to go.' And then she turned and said, 'Don't call me again.'" Richard shrugs and stands to go. "That was it."

I struggle to hide my disappointment. I hadn't expected much to come from talking to Selma, but still, it feels like another door slamming shut.

"I'll look at the report," I say. I round my desk and give Richard a big hug. "Bon voyage, *mon ami.*"

CHAPTER 27

"WE HAVE DISCLOSURE," ALICIA SAYS, excitement in her voice as she bursts in my door. It's Thursday morning, and I'm settling into the day's work with my café latte.

"Yeah? You sure? Way too soon for Cy to be disclosing." We both know Cy discloses the Crown's documents late in the day, if at all.

"Well, perhaps not full disclosure. A few witness statements."

"Like the cops who searched the beach and found nothing, telling us they searched the beach and found nothing?"

"Yes, some of those, but I think you'll want to see this one: Dante Bocci's statement to the police the night Tess disappeared." She proffers a sheet of paper.

My heart picks up a beat. This *is* interesting. "Let me see."

I reach for it. "Have a seat," I say, motioning to the chair on the other side of my desk. "This may take a while."

I scan the page. This is not the usual police-dictated *here's what we think you told us, sign on the dotted line* report. It's a transcript of what Dante told the officer, and it sings with his voice—self-importance with an undercurrent of anxiety.

Dante begins with his regimen on the island. He rises at ten-ish and prepares a leisurely breakfast. A big breakfast. He takes it out to the porch and sits down at the wooden table. He sips his coffee slowly. When he's done, he cleans up and takes the path down to the ocean, where he does his yoga stretches. Back up at the cabin, he checks out his email and settles on the porch to read. Lunch is one thirty, followed by a post-prandial nap. By the time he wakes, it's three thirty, time for another walk.

The officer patiently nudges Dante back to the present.

"Today, ah yes, today. Today was particularly fine, so I decided to take my camera with me. I thought I might get lucky, see a pod of orcas. I took the trail down to the beach and followed the path winding around the shore to the north. I must have walked for twenty minutes when I looked up and saw a small boat, about three hundred feet offshore. A boat with a small child in it, and a woman I assumed must be her mother. A wave of ocean mist enveloped them, giving the scene an ethereal cast. A lovely scene, so I photographed it. I wanted atmosphere, not precision, so I didn't put my telephoto lens on." I hear Dante sighing through the words on the page. "If I had known they what I know now, I would have done differently.

"I put my camera back in my pack and continued my walk," Dante continues. I forgot all about the boat with the woman and child. I remember I stopped for a while and sat on a log, staring out at the ocean. After a while, I got up and moved on. I came around a wooded point, and then I saw it again—the boat. This time it was closer. The woman looked up—maybe she heard my footsteps—and I saw her face, saw it clearly, a tawny face with high cheekbones and full lips, a beautiful face framed by black flowing hair. An unforgettable face. And then, suddenly, the woman broke her gaze, hit the engine stick, and gunned the boat away. I watched it recede. Then I turned and took a shortcut back to the cabin. I didn't think any more of it until police knocked on my door that evening. I showed them my photos. You know the rest."

We have more, Kan had replied when I told him his blurred photo was worthless. This is the more, and the more is devastating. Silly me, assuming the only view Dante got of the woman was the view through his camera lens. This man, who never forgets a face, saw the woman in the boat up close and clearly. The next night, he picked that face out of a photo lineup and again selected it in the physical lineup that followed. The identification I bragged I could knock out of court five minutes into cross-examination is rock solid. Kan has his case.

Alicia reads my thoughts, nods sympathetically. "Bad," she says.

"Yeah, not good," I say.

My stomach twists. I didn't admit it to myself, but the truth is in my reaction. I believed Kate when she told me she was not the woman in the boat, that she was never near the island. Now I have proof she was. Irrefutable proof, unless Dante is lying. But why would Dante lie? My instinct tells me Dante is afraid, and because he's afraid, he's trying to please the police. The paper flutters as I hand it back to Alicia.

"He's lying," I say.

"If he's not, this isn't the first time Kate has failed to tell you the truth," Alicia responds.

"You have a point." A sudden weariness sweeps over me. I recall lecturing Alicia when I was teaching her the ropes: *You need to take the case as it is.* I keep giving Kate the benefit of the doubt, even when the facts rear up and smack me between the eyes.

But we're not there yet. Dante may yet be lying. I pick up the phone and dial Kate.

CHAPTER 28

ﾠIT'S MONDAY AFTERNOON, AND MY team is gathered in the boardroom of Truitt and Solosky to strategize on *The Crown v. Kate Sinclair-Jones.* The weekly Friday meeting I promised Jeff has been rescheduled for Monday to allow Richard to brief us on his trip to Vegas. "Whatever you say, Jilly," Jeff said, giving me a skeptical look.

ﾠI cast my eye around the table. Despite Shanni's addition and Richard's return, it doesn't take long. As teams go, this one is pathetic. Jeff, sharp lawyer but advisory brief only; Alicia, three years under her belt and overwhelmed with other files; Shanni, called to the bar a total of three months; and Richard, our in-house detective. Rounded out by me, Jilly Truitt, former go-to defence lawyer that the street says is all washed up. I sigh. This is our team, for what the press is dubbing the trial of the decade. David and Goliath all over again.

ﾠFor the occasion, I've set up a whiteboard. I stand beside it, marker poised. Everyone else is huddled around the table awaiting my revelations. Which will be underwhelming.

"I observe we are at last entering the twentieth century," Jeff quips with a nod to the whiteboard.

I ignore him.

"Let me begin by sharing where we are," I open. "We have a murder trial coming up. For today, I'd like to stop thinking about how we find Tess and start thinking how we're going to get an acquittal for Kate. Whether Tess is alive or dead, whether Kate cares or doesn't care about the charge against her, it's our job to do everything we can to help Kate beat it." I pause. "So, this is why I asked you to this meeting. I want to dissect the case. Look at the legal angles. Brainstorm how we can best develop our defence." I look at Jeff to make sure he hears the next part. "Don't hold back, say what you think. You may not believe it, but I promise to listen. This is a tough case—perhaps the toughest we've ever faced—and we need everyone's views."

Down the table, Richard shakes his head. *Oh ye of little faith*, I think. I'm dying to hear what happened in Vegas, but I want to start with the anatomy of the case.

At the top of the whiteboard, I've written the charge—first-degree murder—with included charges in a series of dropdowns: second-degree murder, manslaughter. Out to the side, kidnapping.

"Let's begin with first-degree murder," I say.

I list the elements the Crown must prove below the heading. *Homicide*, to wit, a killing. *Actus reus*, an act done by the accused leading to the homicide. *Intention*, the accused planned to kill the victim, and did so deliberately with malice aforethought, to use the elegant language of the law.

Second-degree murder follows. Like first, except the intention can be formed on the spur of the moment—no deliberate plan to kill is necessary.

Manslaughter. Unintentional homicide. Recklessness or criminal negligence supplies the necessary criminal intent.

"The Crown will attempt to satisfy the first element, homicide, through the bathing suit and single shoe recovered on the shore after Tess's disappearance. It's weak—usually they have a body—but it may be enough to convince the jury. If they can't show homicide, we're home free. But if they can, we need to move on."

"Don't have to show homicide for kidnapping," Alicia puts in, pointing to my side drop-down.

"We'll leave that for later. What about the act—the *actus reus*—connecting Kate to Tess's hypothetical death?"

"The Crown says Dante's identification establishes Kate was the person in the boat with Tess. Tess is dead, ergo Kate must have killed her," Jeff supplies.

Everybody nods.

"Moving on," I say, "what about the deliberate intention, a plan to kill, necessary to convict of murder? The Crown will rely on motive."

Shanni raises her hand. This is her first full day on the job. She's wearing the female lawyer uniform, a black pants suit with a crisp white shirt. If she lacks confidence, it doesn't show. *Good*, I think.

"I've spent the weekend boning up on the case," Shanni says. "The evidence is weak. Kate may not have always been a good mother, but she loved her daughter. Why would she kill the daughter she loved?"

Jeff is swift to counter the argument. "Number one, Kate is unstable and doesn't think like other people. Number two, Kate, rightly or wrongly, believes Trist, with his travelling and girlfriends, is destroying Tess. Number three, the relationship between Kate and Tess had broken down. Tess was throwing tantrums and screaming when the nanny dropped her off for weekend custody with Kate—it's all there in the nanny's affidavit on the motion to remove Kate's weekend custody."

I frown. Selma's second affidavit did mention an incident when Tess had cried when Selma dropped her off, and Kate told me Tess was acting out on weekend visits. Driven by what I now see is my positive bias toward Kate, I overlooked the implications of Tess's behavior toward Kate. Maybe Jeff is right.

Jeff carries on. "Sure, now Kate says her plan was to present a cleaned-up version of herself to the court and apply for joint custody. Doesn't cost her anything to say that now, and we know she has nothing to back it up—not even an appointment with a family lawyer to discuss her chances of success. And now we learn she knew Trist and Lena were planning to marry and take Tess to Vegas with them, putting her out of Kate's reach. Put it all together, and you have Kate in her crazy mind deciding Tess is being destroyed. In her mind—and remember, we have to think what Kate would do, not what we would do—the only option was to end her torment by ending Tess's." Jeff casts his eyes to the ceiling. "I see it all now, a final hug, a tender kiss, as Tess slips over the gunwale and into the water . . ."

The room sits in uncomfortable silence. I want to tell him he's wrong but can't find the words.

"Hold on a minute," Alicia says at last, and I want to jump up and hug her. "You paint a vivid picture, Jeff. But I can't buy the final bit, Kate deliberately casting the daughter she loves into the sea and to her death. Neither will the jury."

Shanni nods vigorously. Richard sits cradling his chin in his hand. "Depending on how crazy they paint Kate and how closely they connect her to the boat they've found, Jeff might be right," Richard offers. "It goes against instinct to think a mother would kill her child. Without more, the jury wouldn't buy it. But if you add up Kate being crazy and a link to physical evidence, a jury might be convinced."

I start to disagree, reconsider. I promised to listen. Cy will paint the same picture Jeff has. "Richard may be right," I say. "And we must not underestimate Cy's power to cast a spell on the jury. An essential element of what Jeff has said is that Kate is unstable. We need to refute that if we can. She says her psychiatrist believed she had recovered from her depression and anxiety and was prepared to support her application for joint custody. We need to build that case and put it to the jury if we can."

Jeff is nodding. Maybe I'm making progress.

We move on through the Crown's alternate scenarios. If the Crown can't prove deliberate killing, they will try to prove spur-of-the moment killing. If the jury doesn't buy that, they move down the chain to manslaughter. The Crown will say Tess is dead, and she was last seen in the boat with Kate. This leaves only two possibilities. Either Kate killed her deliberately or she killed her by doing something reckless and criminally negligent.

"So," Jeff says, moving to sum up, "the Crown has a small chance at proving first-degree murder, a better but still slim chance of proving second-degree murder, and a pretty good chance of establishing manslaughter, provided they can convince the jury Kate was in the boat and Tess is dead."

"Right," I say. "Which means Kate faces a small chance of twenty-five years in prison, a better chance of ten years in prison, and a pretty good chance of five to ten for manslaughter."

"That probably sums up how the Crown sees it," says Jeff. I nod, careful not to let my elation show. Jeff is slowly moving from angry skeptic to helpful advisor.

I turn and rub the whiteboard clean. "Now, we come to the interesting part," I say. "Our defences. First, the Crown has not proved homicide—that is, a criminal death. Tess's body has not been found. There may be other explanations for the swimsuit and shoe washed up on the beach."

"Good luck," groans Alicia.

"For your penance, you get to look up all the cases where Courts of Appeal have thrown out convictions because the prosecution has failed to produce a body," I say. "Shanni can help," I add with a smile in her direction. "*Second*, the Crown cannot show a connection between Kate's conduct and Tess's presumed death. The photos of the boat are indistinct, but Dante's identification worries me—we now know he says he got a second and much clearer view of the woman in the boat. We'll have to attack that in cross-examination."

"It will be hard to shake Dante's claim," Jeff says.

"Agreed," I say. "It will be a challenging cross-examination. Shanni, make a note to find out whether Dante Bocci has any visual impairments. Chances are he doesn't, but we need to check it out if we can. Also, we need meteorological data for the weather and position of the sun." Shanni nods as she taps the requests into her laptop.

"The other thing we need to do is look into other women who fit the description and might have been on the island at the time," I say. "We have three candidates at the moment—Kate, Selma, and Lena. For the moment, I think we can take Selma off the list—too many things don't fit, and it appears she has an alibi—she was in

Surrey with her ailing grandfather when Tess disappeared. So let's focus on Lena. Richard, what did you learn in Vegas?"

Richard opens his laptop. "Nothing damning but nothing exonerating her either. I swung by the house Trist was supposed to be buying—I thought I might find Lena there. I found it. A swanky place, with one of those gilt-edged for-sale signs peeking discreetly from the hedge. I called the number, and the agent told me Trist had cancelled the sale and walked away from his deposit. I hit the road again. It took a while, but I eventually located Lena in a cheap hotel on the outskirts of downtown, living off fumes and room service. She had tried staying with a friend, but the paparazzi discovered where she was and camped out across the street, followed her everywhere she went. Her friend couldn't take it, so she moved to the hotel."

He pauses. "I knew this was a big story—Trist's daughter disappearing—but I didn't realize how big. They love Trist in Vegas, and there's speculation online about what happened to Tess, including posts focusing on Lena, the wicked would-be stepmother. All this, despite the fact Kate has been charged. The Vegas media are still all over the story. If Lena wanted to get away, she shouldn't have picked Vegas."

"Same in Vancouver," I say, "except here the focus is on Kate the wicked mother."

"I'll spare you the details of how I enticed Lena to lunch—it involved pretending I was a scout from France looking to engage her in a new show in Paris."

Smiles move around the table; this is Richard at his creative best.

"The Paris part interested her, I think. She'd love to leave Vegas for a while. Still, she said no. I persuaded her the paps wouldn't notice her slipping into the back booth of the restaurant in the Best Western where she's staying. So she finally agreed."

"How did she look?" Shanni breathes.

"Pretty good, actually. Lena would look good in rags, if you get my drift. She was wearing a loose black shift, dark glasses, and a mask left over from COVID. But she still looked good. And when she pulled off the mask to take a sip of wine—ooh la la, mon dieu." Richard feigns a swoon, and even Jeff laughs despite himself.

"We talked about the theatre scene in Paris for a while, and then I found a way to raise Trist and Tess's disappearance. Maybe she hoped to get back together with Trist and wouldn't want to go to Europe, given he was scheduled to do a show in Vegas in a few months? She laughed and waved her cigarette—we were into after-lunch drinks by then—and said hell no, she wouldn't mind, but with all the paps and media attention there was zilch chance. She and Trist would have to wait until the goddamned mother was convicted before that could happen."

Trist's words come back to me, *Maybe we'll hook up again.* I wonder if they've been in touch all along.

"So she thinks she and Trist will get back together again," Shanni says.

"Yeah, and 'this time without that fucking kid.' Those were the words she used."

"Did she say anything else about Tess?" I ask.

"Tess was a terror. She took a drag on her cigarette and laughed. 'I understand why her mother might have offed her—I was ready to kill her myself on more than one occasion.'"

Alicia's jaw drops. "Those were her words?"

Richard holds up a small recorder. "You can check them out yourself. Got them right here."

"Don't get excited," Jeff says. "People say they want to kill kids—their own or others'—all the time. Very few follow through."

Jeff is right. In fact, if Lena did off Tess, it's unlikely she would now talk about wanting to kill her. Still, she clearly dislikes Tess. Perhaps we can make something of that at trial. Which twigs a new thought. Cy will need to call Lena as a witness, if only to establish the background facts. Calling witnesses from out of the country can be difficult. Maybe that's why Lena fled to Vegas, why she finds Paris even more appealing. I'll ask Shanni to look up the law on out-of-country witnesses.

"Did Lena say anything about coming back to Vancouver to testify at the trial?" I ask.

Richard shakes his head. "No. We didn't get there. The waiter who'd been serving us all those drinks started looking at her, and she suddenly slammed her bag shut and told me to call her if the job came through."

We sit in silence, digesting what Richard has told us about Lena.

"Great work, Richard," I say. I see Jeff nodding. If I am not yet forgiven for sending Richard to Vegas, I soon will be.

"Richard has also had a conversation with Selma," I say.

Richard takes up the invitation and recounts what he told me last week about his encounter with Selma.

"I agree, not much there," Jeff says.

"Then let's move on to Dante," Richard says.

My eyes widen. When did Richard have time to look into Dante?

"I need to do more work, but I dug out some preliminary facts. Dante Bocci is forty-seven years old, and lives in a lovely old house halfway up the cliff with a gallery attached for his art, as he calls his photographs. He drives a high-end Porshe, vacations in Europe in the summer and Palm Springs, where he owns a second house, in the winter. And, as we know, takes occasional vacations elsewhere."

Richard looks up from the screen he's reading from. "How does he do all that on a photographer's salary, you're asking. I don't know. He does have a reputation as a portrait photographer, makes money from it, but not enough to support his lifestyle. I intend to dig into his finances, if you agree."

My heart sings. My instinct about Dante wasn't off the mark. "Great, Richard," I say. I shoot an anxious glace at Jeff.

Jeff looks at Richard. "I endorse further investigation of Dante's finances," he says, and offers me a tight smile.

CHAPTER 29

Monday Morning, the second day of November.

I park myself on my office couch and stare at the screen. After weeks of total silence on the Tess case, the task force has announced a press conference for ten o'clock.

The screen shifts to an undisclosed room at the force's headquarters. Kan's square face fills the screen, and I lean forward. While other officers report from time to time—even Sergeant Burr was allowed a cameo role at last week's press conference—Kan has become the ex officio face of the team.

Kan looks blandly bored as he launches into his update, probably not what they advise at public relations police training, but it's what he's going with today.

"Today marks thirty-eight days since Tess Sinclair-Jones disappeared," he intones. "Although the police believe Tess to be deceased and have laid charges against the suspected perpetrator, we have continued to search for the child in the hope she is still alive."

Kan looks up. "Today, the task force has concluded there is no realistic possibility the child is still alive. Accordingly, it is bringing the intensive phase of the search effort to a close. Kidnapping has been ruled out, as has death by natural causes. While we cannot conclusively say precisely how the child died, finding further evidence is extremely unlikely. The police will continue to monitor airports and border crossings and welcome any relevant information from the public. We thank the public for its support throughout this ordeal and express our deepest sympathy to the family."

Kan stares out from the screen bleakly for a long moment. "That is all I have to say. Absent the unlikely event more relevant evidence comes to light, there will be no further press conferences on this matter. Our efforts will be focused on bringing the person we believe responsible for Tess's death to trial and to justice. Thank you."

Kan waves the reporters off, turns, and exits. I flick off the TV.

There's only one thing on my mind: talk to Kan.

Technically, I should be talking to Cy. But Cy can't give me what I want—Tess.

I wait fifteen minutes to give him time to get from wherever he was to his office and dial the number Debbie gives me. A bright voice tells me Detective Kan is not available. Can she take a number? I give her my name, tell her it's urgent, and settle back at my desk.

I need to convince Kan to renew the search for Tess. A decade and a half in the law has taught me not to trust cops. But Kan is in his own class—more sensitive and urbane than the average cop and wilier by half. I need to appeal to the sensitive side.

While I wait for Kan to return my call, I turn my attention to Ryan's case. My fingers find my keyboard, and I bring up the Sex Offender Information Registration Act. I find what I'm searching for—the section giving law officers the discretion to share information on the registry with mere mortals, where the interests of justice require it. I push the print button and run off a copy. I've instructed Shanni try her hand at drafting the petition we need to start Ryan's constitutional challenge in Federal Court. One way or another, I'll need to memorize the legislation's every word.

I'm deep into the provisions of the act when my phone rings.

"Detective Kan here," says the voice I recognize, sandpaper rough.

"Thanks for returning my call, Detective."

I consider how to put my request. Either he'll take it as me telling him how to do his job or me telling him how to help me do mine. Not an easy sell either way for a man as prickly as Kan.

"Detective, Tess disappeared more than a month ago. You have charged Ms. Sinclair-Jones, but she maintains she knows nothing about what happened to her daughter. My client believes Tess is out there somewhere. If she's alive, we must find her. If she's no longer alive, we need to know that, too, so her parents can grieve her properly and justice can be done. That's the reality, Detective. I know you care, must care about the missing child. Yet this morning, you told us the search is winding down. No more helicopters, no more search parties." I take a deep breath. "Detective, my client is overwrought with anxiety and grief. She needs closure. You must find the child."

Or at least the body, I think, and bite my tongue. Tess's body would take away our best defence. I imagine Kan's face softening, but I'm disappointed. "Only your client knows precisely what has happened to Tess," he says coldly. "But we know enough. We know that she was thrown into the ocean. And we know that all that is left of her is a tattered bathing suit and a shoe. It's a savage place, the Salish Sea—a piece of flesh doesn't last long."

I feel myself gagging. My fingers weaken and my phone slides to the desktop. I want to ask him how an ocean predator would swallow the body but cough up the swimsuit, but I don't. "On your theory of the case," I say, recovering. "But there are other possible theories. Your duty is to continue to search for the child until there is no possibility she is alive. And we are not yet at that point, Detective."

I change tactics. "You are an experienced police officer, Detective Kan. You know that if Tess turns up molested or dead because you called off the search you will wear that failure forever. You also know that tunnel vision—investigating to confirm your theory of the crime to the exclusion of all other possibilities—is dangerous."

Kan is unimpressed. "The definition of human stupidity is repeating the same hopeless act over and over, Ms. Truitt. We have kept this search open much longer than justified. Our officers have searched Bowen Island thoroughly—tree by tree, beach by beach, house by house—and combed the Lower Mainland. We have found nothing, nothing but the sad conclusion that your client took her daughter's life. There is no point repeating fruitless investigations."

"I understand, Detective Kan. But may I ask you this: Do you have any leads, any details I might not know of?"

"None we haven't shared with you."

"I assume you have checked the Sex Offender Registry to ascertain whether anyone on the island that day is listed?"

"Yes."

"And may I ask—"

He cuts me off. "I am not at liberty to share information regarding who is or is not on the registry. The criminal code doesn't give me the authority. Surely you know that, Ms. Truitt."

"The act—section thirteen, I believe—provides the commissioner of the RCMP may authorize persons to consult the database. You could ask the commissioner."

"What are you getting at?"

I can't mention Dante—and if Dante were on the registry, Kan would have investigated him—so all I can do is suggest that we might be able to do something he can't if we could see the list. That, and appeal to fairness. "In some countries, the defence would know what names are on the registry. Here, I have to work blind, unless you help me. I'm asking you to allow the defence to consult the database to ascertain whether any registered sex offenders were on or in the vicinity of Bowen Island at the time of the offence. This is relevant and material information for the defence and should be disclosed. I promise confidentiality."

"Section thirteen is intended to let the commissioner allow access to researchers and such," he barks, falling back on legal formalism and eschewing fairness. "It was never intended to allow access to defence lawyers. You must know that. To make the RCMP disclose local sex offenders to any defence lawyer who thinks it might have some bearing on their case would shoot a cannonball through the privacy protections of the registry."

Give up, Jilly, I tell myself. *You've met your match. Kan is superbly informed and has the better side of this argument.*

"I have your answer," I say stiffly. "We will apply to the court."

"Now it's my turn to tell you your business, Ms. Truitt. I suggest you discuss that with Mr. Kenge."

"I will," I say harshly, and give it one more shot. "We don't know Tess is dead, Detective. You haven't produced a body. A bathing suit and shoe are far from conclusive. There is a good chance she is alive. Don't let your race to a conviction blind you to your primary duty—to find the missing child."

"Do not lecture me on my duty, Ms. Truitt," Kan says in his gravelly voice.

I register my quickening heartbeat but persist. "If you won't give us access to the Sex Offender Registry, Detective, use it yourself. Until we know Tess is dead, you have a duty to keep searching for her."

"We have done the registry search. We found nothing of interest. Satisfied?"

No, I'm about to say, but the phone goes dead.

CHAPTER 30

*N*OTHING OF INTEREST, KAN'S VOICE rings in my head. I'll be the judge of that. If he won't do his job, I will. It's Saturday morning, and I decide not to spend the weekend nursing my frustrations.

The media has responded with a big yawn to Kan's decision to call off the search. Consensus seems to be there isn't much chance of finding the child alive, and anyhow Kate is guilty and will be brought to justice in due course. Only Remi, pointing to the Casey Anthony case from Florida, maintains that too much is unknown and the search must continue. Casey Anthony's toddler went missing July 15, and the remains weren't found until December 11, almost five months later.

Everyone still loves Trist though. He hasn't been talking since I told Cy to muzzle him, but he feeds the media frenzy with paparazzi shots that send the hate tweets against Kate surging. Just yesterday, the cameras caught him opening the front gate of his West Vancouver mansion, bending to retrieve the flowers that mourners had left overnight. He gave the paps a sad wave before he retreated.

I watch the reruns Shanni provides each day with increasing bitterness. Trist may not have killed Tess, but he's playing games. Defending Lena to me, while implying she drugged him with red wine to make him sleep through the abduction. Telling me he hasn't spoken to Lena since she left, while she tells Richard they'll hook up again when the trial is over. Telling me he doesn't believe Kate could have taken Tess, while feeding the police stories of her craziness that make the accusation plausible.

I did a quick run to Bowen Island to view the lodge and the beach two days after Kan arrested Kate. I saw the flowers, in-spected the gouge in the sand where the police said the abduct-ing boat pulled in—before an officer ordered me off the property. Now the police are gone. I decide to spend my Saturday viewing the crime scene. If I am to defend this case at trial, I need to know every detail of the shore where Tess disappeared and the paths Dante wandered that afternoon. I ring Edith and propose a drive.

"We won't go far," I say. "Over to the North Shore, a ferry ride to Bowen Island. It's a lovely day. We'll see forests and ocean, and if we are lucky, two or three whales."

Edith, who is no fool, snorts. "This is not about whales, Jilly. This is about your case. Your own white whale." Still, she agrees to come.

Two hours later, I am easing Mike's old car—my Mercedes con-vertible won't hold the three of us—down the ferry ramp onto Bowen Island, Edith in the passenger seat. I sneak a glance back at Claire dozing in her car seat.

We take the narrow road bisecting the island, a dark journey through a medieval forest, except where the trees part to make way for miniscule meadows and gardened cottages lit up by sunshine. On the west side of the island, we park our car, bundle up Claire, and walk down to the docks. Edith was right to warn me to dress warm—the north wind bites our faces and buffets our backs. Claire, game until now, begins to mewl. I scan the horizon, a dim mist of frozen grey. If there are whales out there, we would never see them.

Edith's eyes are scrunched tight against the wind; Claire sobs.

"Okay, okay," I say. "Let's go."

We pick up two hot chocolates in the little store and get back in the car. I backtrack on the trail that brought us here and take an abrupt left.

"Where are we going?" Edith asks.

"To the northwest side of the island. More precisely, to the place where Tess disappeared."

I take a right and another left, too many twists to count. The road is a track.

"We may be lost," I murmur.

"There," says Edith. I follow her finger and I see it, the peak roof I recognize from the photographs.

I push the car through the trees and downward on a barely marked trail and pull up before the house. The roof thrusts up like a cathedral, flanked by low wings on either side. Broad sheets of glass glint in the midday sun like mirrors. I scan for lights, see none. A gust of winter wind rocks the car, and I feel a frisson of fear. We are alone here, Edith and Claire and me. We still don't know what happened to Tess—maybe the person who took her is out there, watching us. I curse my foolhardy stupidity. Why did I bring Claire and Edith into this? Why expose my infant daughter to danger?

And then I see it. A glint of glass through the trees at the side of the house. I make out a vehicle's contours. Someone else is here. I look back at Claire, look at Edith. I suppress a pang of fear.

Leaving the car running, I get out. "Stay here with Claire," I tell Edith. "I'll only be a minute."

I take the boardwalk leading from the gravelled parking pad toward the house. I turn and look west. Below me, faded grass gives way to a low stone wall, and beyond that, the beach stretches to the water. I suck in my breath. The wind and waves are wicked today, battering a bouquet that has survived the storms. I try to imagine how it was the idyllic September afternoon as Trist lay on his chaise while Tess played in the sand. At the beach's edge stands a dock. I see the boat, see Trist and Tess on the beach, see Lena waving goodbye and revving the motor as she sets off for her jaunt to the store. I see Trist settling into the recliner, dozing in the sunshine. I imagine another boat, or maybe the same one, slipping silently to where the sand meets the water and scooping Tess up.

A sudden crash interrupts my reverie. I look up and make out an indistinct figure emerging from the bush. My heart lurches. Maybe the police are still monitoring the place, even though Kan says the island search is off. Or maybe this is someone else.

The figure gives a shout. "Hullo there."

He's bearing down on me from the slope behind the house, a middle-aged man, shoulders broad beneath his shabby down jacket, half running, half sliding. Sammy Sinclair is descending on me, arms churning like broken windmills as he struggles to keep his balance on the slippery slope.

"Ms. Truitt," he shouts as he nears me. "Ms. Truitt, I've found it!"

My heart picks up a beat. "What have you found?"

"Pink Croc. The other shoe."

CHAPTER 31

I FOLLOW SAMMY UP THE SCRABBLY cliff, pushing vegetation from my eyes and grabbing at jutting boulders to steady myself. The path is an old deer trail, zigzagging up the slope. *How did you ever find this trail?* I want to scream, but I don't have breath to waste on words.

Sammy stops when we reach a clearing. I look down at where we've come from. Far below, the metal roof of the house gleams in the mist, like the wings of a broken bird. He picks up a walking stick he must have abandoned and points it at a leaf pile. He flicks a leaf with the point of the stick, and I catch a glimpse of pink.

I bend for a closer look. The heel of a child's Croc pokes up from a bed of mud and debris. Not much, but enough to tell me it's the mate to the shoe found on the beach after Tess disappeared.

I straighten, my mind awhirl. How did the shoe get up here? And what does this do the Crown's theory Tess died at sea? I grab my phone. "Hold up the leaf, Mr. Sinclair. I want to photograph this."

"I took a photo myself," he says, but he complies.

"Did you touch the shoe, disturb it?" I ask.

He shakes his head. "I'm not that dumb. Don't want my fingerprints on it. They'd probably say I planted it there. I lifted the leaf with my stick and there it was. Then I heard an engine and a car door slam below and ran down and saw you."

"Good work, good thinking." I take a deep breath. There are rules about what defence lawyers must do when they find new evidence. If it incriminates their client, they must hand it over to the police. But this shoe runs a truck through the Crown's case against Kate. Still, my gut tells me it's too important to keep to ourselves. I don't know where it may lead—perhaps even back to Kate.

"I'm calling the police," I say.

"No," says Sammy, grabbing my arm. "The police will bury this. The defence doesn't have to disclose its evidence, I looked it up on my phone. So we keep this to ourselves. At trial, you call me, and I tell the jury how I found it, how it shows someone else took Tess."

I stare at him. It's like he had this rehearsed.

"It's not that simple," I say. "Besides, this may help them find Tess. If we don't share this, and they fail to find her as a result, we would never forgive ourselves. I've got to call Kan."

"No," Sammy shouts, but I wrench away. I pull my phone from my pocket and start to dial. It takes five minutes fighting with operators, but I finally hear his gravelly voice. "Kan here."

"Detective, it's Jilly Truitt. I am on Bowen Island, at the top of a cliff behind the property where Tess disappeared. We have found the mate to the pink shoe washed up on the beach. You need to come and look at it."

There is a long silence. When I think he's going to hang up, I hear his voice. "Have you touched the—the article?"

"No. Mr. Sinclair found it under leaf debris—he's been searching the island since Tess disappeared." *Found what you missed,* I want to say, but decide this is not the time to gloat. "Nothing has been touched, nothing has been moved."

Another silence as Kan calculates the time it will take him to get here. "I'll be there in two hours. I'll phone you when I get close. And don't touch anything, not the object, not anything in the surrounding area. Understood?"

"Understood." I stow my phone.

I nod to Sammy. He's still scowling, but he follows me down the trail. I return to my car.

"You're back," Edith breathes as I slide into my seat. "I was beginning to worry."

I glance rearward; Claire is sleeping.

"You found something," Edith says.

"Kate's father found the other shoe. The other little pink Croc. Not where it should be, on the Crown's theory, washed up on some beach, but near this clearing on the top of the slope." I wave to my left.

"What does it mean?" Edith asks.

"I don't know. But I intend to find out."

CHAPTER 32

I STAND AT THE SIDE OF the trail and wave Kan's black police limo onto the clearing where Sammy and I wait.

I have spent the hour and three-quarters it took Kan to arrive cataloguing the lay of the land. The shoe is about three feet from the cliff, at the edge of a flat grassy area big enough to park three or four cars. A track concealed by grass leads from the main road to the small clearing. Sammy had driven his SUV up to the clearing while we waited. At my suggestion, he pulled it back to the edge of the main trail. The police, when they get here, will want to scour every inch.

I peer down at the pink heel peeking from the debris. The shoe washed up on the beach was for the right foot. This one is the same size for the left.

One thing is clear—the shoe in the clearing raises more questions than answers. Questions that might give us the reasonable doubt we need.

"Turn in after the parked blue Toyota SUV," I tell Kan when he phones. "You'll see me."

Kan parks at the edge of the clearing and pulls his lanky form from the car, slamming the door behind him. "Hello," he says.

He contemplates the snuggly on my chest where Claire is dozing. Edith, off to the village to get some lunch, offered to take Claire, but something about this place makes me want to keep her close.

"I heard you had a child," Kan says.

"Claire, my daughter," I say, bouncing her gently.

Kan nods and walks to my side to glimpse Claire's face. He probably knows I lost Mike, too. It was a big police story, how they were supposed to be protecting me, how they arrived too late. I think of Kan's murdered parents. He has had his losses, too. We exchange glances, briefly lost in our separate memories.

Sammy Sinclair walks up.

"I think you know Sammy Sinclair?" I offer.

"Haven't met formally. Other officers interviewed Mr. Sinclair."

Sammy puffs out his chest and scowls, but four decades of dealing with crusty yacht owners has taught him it's wise to do the polite minimum, and he takes the gloved hand Kan offers.

"Let's see what you've found, Mr. Sinclair."

Sammy leads him to the spot and points his stick.

Kan bends. "Ah," he says. "Looks like the heel of a pink shoe."

"It's been here the whole time," Sammy can't resist gloating. "And you guys missed it."

Kan does not reply. He takes a knee and studies the piece of pink plastic. "We'll wait for the site team," he says. "They should be here any minute."

His complacence shocks me. "Is that all you can say?"

He gives me a bland look that says it better than words: *What do you expect?*

I turn away from him, my mittened hands cradling Claire's bottom, and stare out to the roiling waves far below. A dark cloud bank is rolling in, momentarily blocking the sun. The temperature plummets.

I have nothing more to say to this man, who after weeks of accusing my client of drowning her child at sea and dragging his heels on the search for Tess, can only say *we'll wait* when new evidence blows a hole through his case. A deep anger drags at my innards. The discovery of the second shoe in a clearing where a car could have waited to abduct a child demands reckoning and consternation. Now. But Kan is content to push his hands in his pockets and admire the trees. How can he be so sanguine, faced with this investigative failure? So much for his minions combing every inch of the island.

A wind gust batters my back. I look up at a black sky that could erupt any moment. I pull Claire's cap closer.

Kan moves back beside me. "Mr. Sinclair must stay, but you don't need to wait, Ms. Truitt." He nods across the clearing.

I look up, make out Mike's sedan through the trees. Edith is back.

I eye Kan stonily. "I will wait."

The approach of vehicles interrupts my words. Two police cars and a forensic van pass Edith and move into the clearing. Kan raises a warning hand. He doesn't want them messing up the site before they have a chance to examine and photograph every square inch.

Kan walks over to the side of the clearing to talk to the police officers. I can't hear what he's saying, but I see their eyes follow his hand to the place near the shoe, where Sammy and I are waiting. They nod and return to their vehicles for gear.

Kan waves us back as officers armed with measuring tapes, shovels, and cameras descend. They photograph the leaves, they photograph the leaves being lifted, they photograph the pink shoe. They check their photos and do it all again. Time passes, the sky darkens, I feel the first few drops of rain. Claire stirs. I glance across the clearing. Edith has sensibly decided to wait in the car. Leaves removed and bagged, the officers mark a square on the ground and cut into the soil. A flat shovel moves beneath the soil, and the marked area is lifted and placed into a box, where it is once again photographed before the box is lidded and marked. The shoe remains embedded in the earth. We won't have the pleasure of seeing the entire shoe revealed.

Kan lets his eye rove the site, and then, as though we're an afterthought, settles on the place Sammy and I are standing.

"We'll take this to the city for further examination," he says. "We'll let you know what we find."

Across the clearing, the officers who took the evidence are packing up their vehicles. The van and two officers will remain to map and photograph the clearing. It will take the rest of the day and a big chunk of tomorrow.

Kan scans the trees at the edge of the clearing, oblivious to the sleet. His eyes come back to rest on Sammy. "Mr. Sinclair, you will have to come with us back to the city, so we can take your statement. I'll take you in my car. If you give me the keys to your vehicle, one of the officers will follow with it."

Sammy digs in his pocket and hands over the keys.

"I would like to be present when the statement is taken," I announce.

"Certainly, Ms. Truitt." Kan glances at Claire. "But you must understand, we can't delay."

As if a child's presence delays anything. "My car is waiting below," I say stiffly. "I will follow you to headquarters."

I find the car and Edith, buckle Claire in her seat, and slide in. Edith hands me a sandwich as I accelerate out. I thank her for waiting and fill her in.

"I'll drop you and Claire at home and carry on to the police station," I say. "Do you mind? I'm so sorry. They're taking Sammy's statement. I have to be there."

Edith treats me to an enigmatic smile. "It's taken a while, Jilly, but you are back. Definitely back."

CHAPTER 33

THE STATEMENT DOESN'T TAKE LONG.

Kan sits on one side of the table, flanked by multiple officers while Sammy and I sit alone on the other side. He nods and an assistant starts recording.

Kan leans back in his chair. "Tell us everything, Mr. Sinclair. Why you were on the island, how you found the shoe."

Sammy tells Kan how he's been searching for weeks without finding anything, until today, when after climbing the cliff behind the house, he found himself in a clearing he hadn't visited before. His walking stick poked through leaves and struck something solid. He lifted the leaves with the tip, and there it was—the heel of a pink shoe, like the one the police found on a beach on Bowen Island after Tess disappeared. He'd watched enough detective shows to know he shouldn't touch the shoe or disturb the site.

But he got out his phone and took a picture. At this point he heard a car below and skidded down the cliff to see who it was. Me.

"Ms. Truitt called you, Detective. You know the rest."

"We are grateful for your help," Kan says. "And for your persistence in the search."

I sigh. It's the closest to gratitude we're going to get.

"You have to find Tess," Sammy says, his eyes wet. "Now we have proof she didn't drown in the ocean like you said. Someone took her. Brought her to that clearing and drove her away. We need to find that person, we need to find Tess."

Kan gives him a look close to sympathy before his face hardens. "We're a long way from knowing any such thing, Mr. Sinclair. All this shoe does—if indeed it is the other shoe—is raise more questions."

Sammy strains forward. "Enough questions that you need to rev up the search, Detective," he booms.

"Mr. Sinclair, I sympathize with your loss, and I wish I shared your belief that Tess is alive. But sadly—" he breaks off. Kan is all kindness. He's following the police manual—treat the addled witness with dignity. "Again, thank you for helping with this investigation. I can assure you we will investigate this discovery thoroughly and take whatever action is appropriate."

Kan stands. The interview is over. Sammy looks at me for direction. I nod. There is nothing more he can do here.

I watch as Sammy's bantam chest sinks, deflating with defeat. Even though he's found the vital clue—a clue Kan and all his men failed to uncover—nothing has changed. He struggles to his feet and allows the officer who grabs his elbow to guide him toward the door. He turns his head back to me before the door closes, and I see tears on his cheek.

An awkward silence fills the room.

A quiet black anger settles on my shoulders. I stare at Kan through narrowed eyes. "Sit down, Detective," I order. "We need to talk."

Kan gives me a surprised look, then sinks to his chair. We stare at each other across the table.

I look to the door through which Sammy has disappeared. "You see a broken man," I say.

Kan has the grace to nod.

"I am not going to argue with you, Detective, about whether this shoe is the mate to the one you say was found on the beach. Nor, assuming it is, am I going to argue about what it does to your theory the child was drowned at sea. But I will say this: If there are two shoes in two different places, there are two possible ways the child disappeared. One by land, the other by sea. As long as there are two viable theories, the police have an obligation to continue to search for her."

"We have our photos. And our identification."

"From a witness who may be compromised. Yes, you have blurred photos and your so-called identification, but you know as well as I, Detective, the frailties of identification evidence. You had two pieces of solid evidence: a child's shoe washed up on a beach and a bathing suit. But now things have changed. We have another shoe atop the cliff at the end of a path connecting the house to a clearing with vehicle access. Someone may have taken Tess from the beach and up the path to their vehicle parked there." I lower my voice. "One shoe was lost in the struggle on the hill. Maybe the other was planted on the beach along with the swimming suit, to mislead the police."

Kan's enormous hands move to the table and grip it. "Your

imagination is impressive, Ms. Truitt. But it doesn't change what we know. Second shoe or no shoe, the only conclusion that makes sense is your client took the child that day and drowned her."

I shake my head. "So blindly pig-headed," I say. "So sad."

"Don't patronize me," Kan snaps.

"Never," I retort.

We stare stonily at each other.

I survey Kan and his phalanx across the table. "Gentlemen, let us reserve our debates about guilt and innocence for the jury. But two facts—*facts*, I say—are now clear beyond doubt. One, I have delivered a critical piece of evidence to you, evidence your vast resources and intensive searches were unable to find. Two, the discovery of this evidence changes your situation. You cannot confidently rule out the possibility Tess was taken in a car that day, and may still be alive." I fix my gaze on Kan. "Detective, with the greatest respect, you must renew your search for the missing child."

"We shall see," says Kan.

"Detective, I could have kept this evidence and produced it at trial to rout your theory Tess drowned. The law does not require defence disclosure unless the evidence clearly implicates the accused. The chances of you proving drowning beyond a reasonable doubt after I showed the jury the second shoe would have been zilch. But I brought you this evidence to persuade you to continue your search. A child's life is at stake."

I take a deep breath to let the point sink. "You now have the shoe, thanks to me. But I have photos of the heel of the shoe and the place where it was found. And I have Sammy's evidence. If you refuse to renew the search for Tess, I will go to the press. I will show them the photos, and Sammy Sinclair will tell his story. The public will lap it up. *David against Goliath* always plays well. The police, with all their resources, combed Bowen Island for weeks and found nothing. The child's grandfather, however, refused to give up and found the shoe. Found it a few hundred feet from where the child was last seen. Now all he and his daughter ask is that you do what justice and compassion require—renew the search."

Kan casts his gaze to the ceiling, mulling his options. At long last, he looks at me again.

"Very well, Ms. Truitt. You leave me no choice. If this discovery checks out, I will issue a press release stating new evidence has appeared, thanks to Mr. Sinclair's diligence, and that we are grateful to him for bringing it to the attention of the police."

Kan glares at me. He doesn't like being forced. Especially by a woman.

"Thank you, Detective," I say.

"Anything else, Ms. Truitt?" he asks tightly.

"Yes. You will tell the press that in view of the new evidence, you are renewing your search for the missing child."

Kan looks at the ceiling, mulling it over. "Agreed," he says, standing and stiffly offering me his hand. "One qualification on the matter of the search for the child," Kan says, and I feel his other hand on the small of my back. "We will continue the search for the child, based on what we know now. But new evidence may emerge that changes the situation, making further search futile. You and your client must understand and accept that."

A premonition seizes me. Kan expects more, maybe has more already. Evidence he hasn't revealed.

CHAPTER 34

Sammy's discovery of the other shoe has sent Kate into crisis mode as she imagines how it ended up at the top of the ridge and what might have happened to Tess thereafter. I spent Sunday afternoon trying to console her. I'm not sure she understands the police have resumed their search because of his discovery. Or maybe she understands but knows it won't succeed.

In contrast, I floated my way through Sunday on a cloud of elation. The second shoe has kicked a hole in Kan's theory of the crime and upped the chance of convincing the judge to dismiss the Crown's flawed case before we so much as call a witness.

On Monday afternoon, after planning how to tell the jury that the second shoe blows a hole through Cy's case against Kate, I zipper up my bag and head for home. Or more accurately, for Liz's daycare.

I push open Liz's front door and stop dead in my tracks. Balloons bounce from the walls, garlands hang from the ceiling. Liz waves and deftly weaves her way through a gaggle of little bodies toward me, with Claire in her arms. Claire sees me and reaches out to me.

I pull Claire into my arms and plant my kiss. Juggling her on my hip, I look around the room. "What's all this?" I ask, batting away an itinerant balloon with my free hand.

Liz stops dead, her smile frozen on her face. "You mean you don't know?"

I stare at her, bewildered. "What? What should I know?" I stammer.

Shock mingles with gentle pity in Liz's face. "It's Claire's birthday," she says.

I stare, not understanding. "Claire is only six months old." Then it hits me. Six months is a milestone on the daycare calendar. And today, November 9, marks six months from my daughter's birth. "I mean, I know, I just didn't think about it. I've been so busy—"

I stop mid-sentence. Liz's stare tells me this excuse is not acceptable.

"We always celebrate our six-month birthdays, don't we, sweetie?" Liz says, leaning to buss Claire on the cheek. "Even if Claire is too young for cake, the older children enjoy a little piece."

A chorus of knee-high toddlers shout "Cake!" and squeal around my feet.

I feel my face reddening. There is a word for what I am feeling—shame. Or maybe that other word—guilt.

"We thought you knew," says Liz. "Now that you're here, sit down and have a piece of Claire's cake."

Liz pulls up a stool, and I sit, grateful, still cradling Claire. Liz leaves the room and returns with a gooey slice, pink marbled incongruously with yellow, which she places on the tiny table before me. I shift Claire to my left knee, clutch the fork Liz proffers, and attack the mess. I roll the icing around on my tongue. "Delicious," I pronounce.

The children gather round me, laughing as they watch me struggle to convey morsels from the table to my mouth. At one point, Claire reaches up for the interception. My fork balances perilously, then twists, sending a mound of cake hurtling to the leg of my pantsuit and to the floor.

"Score!" I say. Claire shrieks her delight from my knee.

"No problem," says Liz. "Claire is such a communicator." Liz beams. "Sometimes I think she's talking. I mean words, real words."

I take this as praise and bend to kiss Claire's forehead. She pushes at my fork again, and I salvage the last morsel.

Parents flock to pick up their children, gusts of rain in their wake. There are shrieks, howls, and children running everywhere, some toward their parents, others gleefully away.

I stand and begin to gather up Claire's paraphernalia, bouncing her on my hip as I move from living room to kitchen and back again, stuffing the baby bag hanging from my shoulder with bottles and boots and diapers. Claire grabs for a balloon as I reach for her favourite teddy on the playroom shelf and howls when it evades her grasp. I grab it for her and feel myself swaying. I totter, and Liz appears and rights me again.

Somehow, I bundle Claire into her coat, wave goodbye, and

close the door, shouts of "Happy birthday, Claire" following us. Outside, I strap Claire into her seat.

The windshield wipers beat against the storm, and I strain to see the pavement ahead. Dear Lord, I pray, get us home. Parenthood makes the firmest agnostic a believer. Beside me, Claire senses my stress and begins to sob.

"Just a minute, darling," I say as I turn into a strip mall. I unbuckle Claire and, clutching her to me, race through the rain into the steaming heat of Millie's bakery.

The elderly lady waiting at the counter looks at us with alarm. "You go first," she says and steps aside.

"A cake," I tell the waif who takes my order. "With six candles." She looks at me, she looks at Claire. She shakes her head. "Whatever you say, lady."

Ten minutes later, we are opening the front door of the house.

I turn on the kitchen lights, unzip Claire's coat, and tuck her into her little recliner. I remove the cake from its box, marvel that it is only slightly battered, and place it on the breakfast counter. I insert six candles, arranging them just so. Even if Claire is too young for cake, she'll enjoy the light show. I look at my beautiful child, and suddenly, I see Mike in the tilt of her chin. My throat closes, and tears cloud my eyes. He should be here.

I swallow and pick up the phone. "Edith, can you come? . . . Yes, right now . . . No, nothing's wrong, we're celebrating . . . Yes, six months today."

Twenty minutes later, Edith arrives, clapping her hands, offering Claire a tiny wrapped box. "A little locket," she says. "I meant to bring it over sooner."

I retrieve a bottle of Mike's Veuve Cliquot from the wine fridge he had installed in the pantry before he died, pop the cork, and fill two tall glasses. We raise our glasses—*to Claire*—and Claire beams back. I light the candles and together, Edith and I blow. The flames flicker and die.

"That means good luck," Edith whispers, smiling up at me.

Holding our glasses high in our right hands, we hug each other.

CHAPTER 35

KAN CALLS ME TUESDAY MORNING.

"The tests are in. The shoe you found Saturday appears to be the mate of the shoe found on the beach. One never knows for sure, but the materials analysis puts the chance of it not being the match at less than one point five per cent. I will be announcing this at one p.m. today."

I start to say thank you, but the line goes dead. Kan doesn't want to hear *I told you so*.

I ring Kate and tell her about Kan's press conference. She swallows a sob and rings off. I stare into the middle distance, trying to gauge Kate's state. A week ago, she was in hyper mode, combing Vancouver's suburbs in the frantic belief she would find Tess if she only drove around enough. Now, when the discovery of the second shoe and Kan's promise to continue to investigate should be giving her hope, she seems to be slipping back into grief and depression.

I shouldn't be surprised; Selma in her affidavits talked about Kate's swings between manic activity and depressive lows. And it's not just the mood swings—behind my growing apprehension lurks the suspicion that while Kate may not be consciously holding back information, mental distress is colouring what she tells me and what she omits. I imagine Kate on the stand and worry. I'm a lawyer, not a psychiatrist, but it is becoming clear I need to find a way to manage Kate's stability.

I call Sammy. His gruff voice tells me he's given up hope, too. "I don't care what that man says," he says. "Nothing will come of it. They will never investigate; we will never find Tess."

Jeff, Alicia, Shanni, and I meet in the boardroom to watch Kan's one p.m. press conference. Debbie has ordered sandwiches, and we pour ourselves coffee from the machine. Alicia pushes a button, and Kan's square face fills the screen, his big hands on the podium.

"I'm here to bring you an update on a recent development in the investigation into the disappearance of Tess Sinclair-Jones," Kan intones. "Last Saturday, a small pink shoe was found buried under leaves in a clearing above the residence where the child was staying with her family. Testing has established that in all probability this shoe is the mate of the child's shoe found on a beach on Bowen Island shortly after her disappearance. This discovery does not change our view that Tess drowned at sea at the hands of her mother on September twenty-fifth. However, we will continue to investigate this latest discovery and continue our search for the child, out of an abundance of caution and respect for Tess's anguished family." Kan pauses, looks out over his audience. True to his word, he gives Sammy credit. "The task force is grateful to Sammy Sinclair, the missing child's grandfather, for his part in discovering the shoe. I would be happy to take any questions you may have."

Reporters push forward, their faces obscured in a psychedelic swirl of mikes. Still grasping the sides of the lectern, Kan reels back when Remi thrusts her mike in Kan's face. "Does finding this shoe mean it's possible a pedophile or kidnapper could have taken the child up the hill and smuggled her away by car?" she yells.

"That is a possible hypothesis," Kan responds crisply. "But as I said, we are still of the view Tess was drowned at sea by her mother on September twenty-fifth. We have the photos of Tess and a woman identified as her mother in a boat, an eyewitness, the bathing suit, and a shoe. There may be other explanations for how the mate of the shoe came to be in the clearing at the top of the cliff behind the lodge, but that does not detract from the strength of the evidence we have to support our theory of the crime. Still, we are treating this new discovery seriously."

"So, when you say you are investigating the new discovery, you're saying you are investigating whether someone else—a pedophile or kidnapper, say—took her?" Remi persists.

"We're looking at any scenarios to explain how the second shoe got to where it was found," Kan replies.

"Including suspects other than the child's mother," she shouts triumphantly.

"I did not say that," Kan snaps.

Kan's gaze circles the room, looking for a more merciful interrogator, but Remi won't let him go. "The police combed the island for weeks. How do you explain how Tess's grandfather could find the shoe when all your officers failed?"

Kan's lips press into a thin line, and annoyance flicks across his usually impassive face. "I cannot answer that question. The shoe was partially buried in the mud and covered with leaf debris. It would not have been visible to the naked eye." He pauses. "Other explanations might come to light in the fullness of time."

"Like the second shoe might be a plant?" shouts a pap.

"Precisely," says Kan. I inwardly curse.

"Have you called in new resources, increased the number of people in the search team as a result of this development?" Remi asks.

"We have engaged all the resources we think necessary," Kan replies.

"That's what you said before," a voice yells from the back of the room.

"No further questions," Kan says and stalks off.

The host comes on with her take-away. *"New evidence has surfaced in the Tess Sinclair-Jones story. The mate to the pink shoe found on the beach days after Tess's disappearance was discovered by the missing girl's grandfather on Saturday near the house where Tess was staying with her father, Trist Jones. However, police continue to believe the five-year-old died by drowning at the hand of her mother. Now, on to other news . . ."*

Alicia flicks off the TV.

Jeff turns to me. "Do you think Sammy planted the shoe?"

I stare at him. "Why would Sammy do that?" I remember his excitement as he ran toward me, arms waving like windmills. "If he did, he's a better actor than I think he is. He was so excited, flustered almost. And how would he get the other shoe?"

"Ah-ha," Jeff says. "Your assumption that Kate is innocent is blocking your thinking." His gentle tone sends a chill down my spine—he's about to skewer me. "Assume the Crown is right, and

Kate stole Tess from the beach," Jeff continues. "Assume further, her dad was aiding and abetting her. Kate steals Tess, and Sammy backs her up with logistics—a getaway car. Somehow one of Tess's shoes comes off in the boat. Tess, with one shoe on, drowns. That shoe later washes up on the beach. Kate grabs the other shoe from the boat and takes it with her to meet her father. Maybe the car is in the clearing and they lose the shoe there. Or maybe Sammy keeps it and later claims he found it in the clearing in a bid to destroy the Crown's case against Kate."

Jeff's scenario stuns me. "Are you suggesting Kate and Sammy agreed to kill Tess?"

"Not necessarily. More likely they wanted to get her away from Trist before he took her to Vegas, planning to keep her somewhere safe until the furor died down. Maybe something went wrong and Tess drowned, or maybe she's been hidden somewhere." Jeff shrugs. "Lots of things could have happened. The point is, Sammy's discovery doesn't mean Kate is off the hook."

We all stare at Jeff. *Like the second shoe could be a plant*, the pap said, and Kan agreed. Come the trial, Cy will tell the jury the second shoe proves nothing more than Kate and her father were colluding, and the jury will buy it. I curse my stupid trusting nature.

"What do you do now?" Jeff asks. Pity has replaced his adversarial tone, and I hate him for it. I also note the pronoun *you*. It's still *my* case, not his.

I put on a brave face. "We push the police on the third-party angle. Kan can't discount it."

"Ha," says Jeff.

I stare at the screen, black now. My heart contracts when I think of Kate, doubling over when I told her about her father find-

ing the other shoe, then hanging up when I told her Kan was calling a press conference. She knows something I don't.

I pull myself together. "Thank you, Jeff, for your reality check.
We can take nothing for granted. But my gut tells me the police
know something we don't. Something important. We need to find
out what it is."

CHAPTER 36

WE NEED TO FIND OUT *what it is.* The words reverberate in my mind like an incessant meme. But to find out, we need to know what we're looking for. And I don't have a clue.

When in doubt, call Richard. He answers on the first ring.

"Where are you, Richard?"

"East Hastings. Investigating a massive welfare fraud."

"Can you pop by the office for a minute?"

"Anything to get away from these government accountants. I'll be there in fifteen."

Richard is in casual Canadian mode, denims and a red plaid shirt hanging loose over a black tee. He takes the chair opposite my desk and crosses his legs.

"We found the second shoe," I say.

"I heard. It's all over the press."

"Finding the shoe may turn out to be good news, but it also complicates things. Assuming it wasn't planted, how did it get to the clifftop behind the lodge? Maybe someone was taking Tess out that way—there's road access—and the shoe got lost in the process? But we haven't a clue who or how."

"What about the boat, the photo? What about the shoe and swimming suit on the shore? How do they jive with this development?"

"I don't know. Maybe the photo is a ruse, maybe the shoe is a ruse. Maybe the shoe on the beach is a plant or maybe the shoe in the clearing is a plant. The permutations and combinations make my head spin."

I scan Richard's face; he's listening.

"Somewhere, beneath this mess of conflicting facts, lies the truth—the single explanation consistent with all the contradictory facts. We need to find it."

"Even if it indicts our client?"

I sigh. "I've finished agonizing over the theories, Richard. Let's find the truth." I lean forward. "The truth about the missing child whose face haunts me night and day. I'll defend my client as best I can. But based on the truth."

"Don't let the Law Society hear you say that."

"On this case, my gut tells me the truth is the only way forward. I'll take my chances with the Law Society."

I can tell he likes this idea. "So what do we do, boss?"

"Keep our minds open to all possibilities. That's why I called you. But let me start by throwing out some ideas."

"Fire away."

"Number one, Kan knows something we don't, although I don't have any proof. We have to find it.

"Second, we follow up on the Dante angle. Kan says he's not on the Sex Offender Registry, but we need to find out if he has ever had anything to do with child pornography or offences against children. He could have taken Tess, then cocked up the blurry photo and made the false identification to draw attention away from himself."

"Good point. I think we believe Kan on this one—if Dante were on the registry he'd be behind bars. Looking for a known sexual predator is always the cops' first recourse. But that doesn't mean there's not something else on Dante that explains everything—something Kan doesn't know. I got a whiff from a source that there was police interest in Dante Bocci at some point, but my source went cold. I tried to verify. Dante's record is clean. All traces have vanished."

"Or been covered up," I murmur, half to myself. "Something is off with Dante. I think you are telling me it's the same with you."

"Oui, madam," Richard sighs and rises. "Gotta go. I'll keep working on the rumour. Maybe I'll get lucky and find something."

He exits with a discouraged wave.

I swivel in my chair and contemplate the scene on the street below my window. Gastown's lights are already gleaming, and it's only four p.m. We're heading into the dark time of the year. When all is shadow and chimera, and nothing is clear.

Richard will devil his way through the opaque layers of police inspection and detection. He's a student of the clandestine relationships and deals that determine who gets pursued and who gets off, who gets a second chance and who gets none, what goes public and what gets buried. The law is the law, clear and precise, but how it is enforced is opaque. Except, perhaps, to someone who knows as much as Richard.

Once, I searched for a single theory of the defence; now I am resolved to search and let the facts emerge as they will. Like finding diamonds in a pan of sand, the challenge is to extract them from the circumstance in which they are embedded.

I start with what we know, or think we know. A photo of a child who must be Tess in a boat in a cove near the lodge Trist had rented. A child who was not seen thereafter. She could have been drowned, as the police propose. She could have been abducted and taken elsewhere. Leave out the swimming suit and shoes, found in different places for now—there may be various explanations for these.

Maybe, as the police say, Kate took Tess. Maybe Lena took Tess. Maybe it was Dante.

Dante's motive: pedophilia. He had become infatuated with the beautiful angel-child with tawny hair and opalescent eyes the media paraded before him and wanted her for himself. Or maybe he wanted to take pornographic pictures of her to sell on the dark web. Either way, evil.

The rumour about Dante's past is probably the idle imagining of a cop to stoke his self-esteem. But Richard is right to keep poking around. Something will emerge. But I need more. I need someone to rove the dark web for Dante's spore. And then it hits me.

Damon Cheskey.

Damon is a genius on the web, dark and otherwise. And he's finishing third-year law and could use some spare cash.

It takes three tries to get him. He returns my call during a ten-minute break between classes. I explain my need to find traces of Dante Bocci on the dark web. He doesn't promise to help, but he doesn't say no either. "I'll think about it."

"And another thing," I say.

"Yeah?"

"I've been thinking about CCTV cameras, Damon. The kind they put up on street corners and in shopping malls. If someone took Tess, presumably they're keeping her somewhere. There could be photos of her out there somewhere."

Damon snorts.

"We need to get our hands on surveillance video," I continue. "Shopping malls, parks, schools, streets, intersections—they're all equipped with cameras. Millions of CCTVs. Sooner or later, if Tess is alive, she's bound to show up in the databases they generate. Whoever has Tess can't keep her locked up in a basement indefinitely."

"You see *Room*? That's exactly what happens."

"Maybe, maybe not. If Tess is alive, her image may be up there in the cloud. Or soon will be. We need to find it and get it down."

Damon laughs. "Impossible. You think you can find the bit you want, a bit that probably doesn't exist, out of all the billions of bits out there in the datasphere? Without a clue where to go? Not to mention you don't have a warrant." He halts. "The police are doing this, right? It's their job to monitor the CCTV data."

"I have reason to believe they aren't effectively monitoring the data coming in. I heard they only have two people on it."

"I can't go there, Jilly. You'd have to get me access. And if you asked, they'd laugh you off the phone."

"Let's see what I can do, Damon. In the meantime, let's start combing the dark web for signs of Dante."

CHAPTER 37

Cy DELAYS DISCLOSURE. HIS UNEXPECTEDLY swift release of Dante's statement was an aberration, calculated to send the message that I don't have a chance. Now Cy's back to his old form, dragging his feet on document production.

It's Sunday evening. We have developed a routine, Edith and I, of sharing Sunday supper. Sometimes she invites us to her condo, sometimes she comes to my house. We do simple, comforting food and dote on Claire and her latest accomplishments. Tonight, it was her newfound ability to pull herself up from a crawl to stand against the sofa. Edith and I oohed and aahed and laughed and cried at her faltering efforts to stay upright. For a few hours, I forgot about Kate and Tess.

But now Claire is abed and Edith has returned home, and I am in the den alone. My mind goes where it always does in idle moments: *The Crown v. Kate Sinclair-Jones.*

It's mid-November, and where do we stand? I pull my laptop to my lap, open it, and count the days in my electronic calendar.

Well over a month ago, Richard phoned to tell me about the boat, and I demanded the police report on it as soon as possible.

A month ago, Cy sent me a paltry few witness statements, Dante's among them.

Two weeks ago, give or take a day, we discovered the second shoe, and Kan promised the world a renewed search for Tess.

Nothing has come from any of this. *We have more*, Kan keeps saying. I need to see it.

"Cy delaying disclosure? Why are you surprised?" Jeff snorted when I complained to him Friday. "It's to his advantage to delay. He knows that until he gives us his evidence, we're spinning our wheels."

It's not like I've been wasting time. I've interviewed Trist. Richard has checked out Lena. I've made repeated calls to Kan to inquire as to progress in the search for Tess. "We are still looking," he tells me politely.

The thought of Kan brings a bitter taste to my mouth. Sammy was right. I could have held the discovery back, pulled it out at trial like a rabbit from a hat and shaken the stunned jury into an acquittal. Instead, I foolishly called Kan in, and congratulated myself when he promised to reopen the investigation on Tess. Kan has done nothing, and we are back to square one.

Richard has been going over flight logs, searching for children who have flown out of YVR since Tess disappeared. Impossible work, since accompanied tots do not have passports, ergo no photos in the records. Right up there with trying to get into CCTV logs. Bottom line: we need more.

I decide to do what lawyers always do when they can't think

of anything else: file a motion, this time for Crown disclosure. I touch the cellphone beside me to check on my latest emails. And there it is. Big, bold, popping up high on the page. Message from Cy. I click on it. Correction, not a message, a document dump, a blizzard of electronic data bytes. We have disclosure. En masse. Cy—or more likely one of his minions down at the Crown office—has been working all weekend.

Electronic bundles, guarded by a maze of passwords, are pouring into our system. Tomorrow I will have Debbie print them out, but tonight, I'm stuck with electronic grazing.

I scroll down the index whoever compiled this has helpfully provided: investigation reports, transcripts of Kan's interviews of Kate, the prison record of Kate's brief stay in custody. I open the last one; a stark photo of Kate's face in profile, pale and anguished, comes up, and I click back out. A duplicate statement from Dante Bocci, swearing Kate is the woman he saw in the boat and later in the lineup, along with photos. Photos and more photos—the lodge, the beach, the gouge in the sand where the mysterious boat pulled up. And then, most devastating of all, graphic images of the tiny torn swimming suit and pink shoe the police say Tess was wearing when she disappeared. Except we now know there is another pink shoe—a shoe no one can explain.

I scrutinize the police report accompanying Dante Bocci's statement—something Cy neglected to send with the statement last month. Interesting. Dante's statement paints a picture of his cooperating with the police. But the police report reveals otherwise. According to the officers, they banged on Dante's door. Then, hearing no response, pushed it open and found Dante in the throes of packing his possessions. Asked where he was going, he told them he needed to get back to the mainland and needed to catch the next ferry. Asked whether he had seen anything relating to a missing child, he said no. In a stroke of prescient police work, the female officer asked, *Take any pictures this afternoon?*

A few, Dante had admitted.

Mind if we have a look at your camera? the officer asked. She picked up the camera, scrolled back on the day's photos. *I think this might be interesting,* she announced as she viewed the photos of the woman and child on the boat. *If you don't mind, Mr. Bocci, we'll be taking you back with us to police headquarters. And for now, we'll keep your camera.*

What other photos did Dante take that day? I wonder. I make a note to demand production of everything found on Dante's camera.

I move on. Documents, so many documents. Expert reports, laboratory analyses. Photos, photos, and more photos, graphs and bar charts, appendices and summaries. Weather reports, marine boating reports, statistics on child abduction. Reams of reports telling us what the photos and the factoids mean. Or may not mean.

I close my eyes. I am overwhelmed. Where will we start? How will we get through it all? I think of our puny team. Whatever made us think we could handle the complexities of a modern murder trial? We'll lean more on Richard and Damon to help. I could bring in another lawyer, but who will pay for her? Not legal aid. My mind reels. Maybe I will prevail on Jeff to bail me out of the mess I've landed us in?

Enough. I decide to close down and tackle this in the morning, when I'm fresh. I'm moving to exit when I see the file I need to see, the file I've been waiting for all these weeks: police reports on the boat found near Britannia Beach. If Kan's *more* exists, I will find it here. I open the file.

I study the top photo. The boat, Cy told me, is a wreck, destroyed by the waves that swamped it and flung it against the shoreline rocks. It sits on its side, a dented piece of metal twisted in an ell. The bow is crushed. The shaft of a broken tiller announces the place where the engine once sat. I leaf through the other documents. Closeups of the damaged underside. Good background, but nothing will turn on it.

I close the photos and pull out the police reports summarizing how the boat was found and brought to the shed in Britannia Beach. Two days after Tess went missing, a girl hiking on the rocks above the cove beach noticed it, thought it might be connected to the missing little girl, and phoned 911. Local police made a preliminary confirmation of the wreck. Hours later, Detective Igor Kan arrived. Having made a preliminary inspection of the boat, he ordered it secured and transported to a government shed in Britannia Bay, where it would be held under lock and key. All of which transpired with meticulous care, if the report is to be believed.

I flip to the next report, recounting the more detailed examination of the wreck after it was taken to the storage shed. Photos detail a forensic team in hazmat suits and gloves poring over every inch of the wreck to determine how it was destroyed and what it can tell us about how Tess disappeared. The boat did not run out of gas—there was still plenty in its intact tank. Ergo, it was abandoned, whether at sea or on land is impossible to say.

Supplementary reports follow. A meteorological analysis details strong winds in the gulf two days after Tess disappeared, which could have carried the boat from Bowen Island to the cove where it was found. An identification report seeking to determine but unable to conclude the boat's owner. The wreck reveals no licence, no number, no name—no way to connect the boat to a person.

I move to a more detailed report. Inquiries reveal that a boat of the same description was noted as missing from the marina of the Vancouver Yacht Club five days before Tess disappeared. Ah, yes, I recall, Cy told me about this, insinuating it established a connection with Kate. The missing boat's owner, Ian Adey, attended at the storage facility to inspect the wreck. He confirmed it appeared to be his boat—a simple aluminum Lund shell. The report notes that hundreds of such boats were manufactured, and without more precise identification, like an engine serial number, conclusive identification is unlikely. Bottom line: the boat could have been the boat taken from the Yacht Club shortly before the abduction, but we cannot know for sure.

Not terrible, but not great. Sammy Sinclair used to work as a mechanic at the Vancouver Yacht Club, and he used to take Kate with him on weekend calls. Kate knew her way around the club, would know where to find a small boat and how to take it out. It's a fragile strand in the rope the prosecution will need to braid.

I scan down to the technical reports. I look for a fingerprint report, find none. Strange, the forensic team wouldn't have missed that. I'll have to send a request for further inquiries.

And then I see it: *Hair Analysis.* Dated last Thursday. Perhaps this was what they were waiting for. I click on the file and open it.

A photo. The cracked wooden seat of the boat. A screw. And caught beneath the screw, a long dark hair. I read the accompanying text.

The identified hair found was sent for laboratory testing. Colour black, Afro characteristics. DNA tests confirmed the hair matched the hair taken from Kate Sinclair-Jones's head on her arrest. See accompanying laboratory report.

I rock back in my seat. Kan has known about the hair ever since the boat washed up. Maybe not the final lab confirmation, but a long black hair confirming Dante's identification. He let me rail at him about the inadequacy of Dante's photos and identification, all the time knowing he had irrefutable evidence that Kate was in the boat—Kate's ebony hair caught in a screw in the tiller seat.

And Kate has known. Known that she was the woman in boat. Known and lied to me.

CHAPTER 38

I AM FURIOUS, I AM SEETHING.

I have been duped by Kan, Cy, and Kate.

Kate has sworn to me, over and over, she was never on the boat. I trusted her denial even in the face of Dante's assertion he had seen the face of the woman in the boat clearly and it was Kate. Trusted her and took her case. Now her hair has been found wedged on the seat in the boat, and I am stuck.

It's Monday morning, and I'm standing on her stoop. I bang my fist on the door. It swings open. I sweep in, stride to the living room, and throw my coat on a chair.

"You lied to me, Kate."

She looks at me with wide eyes. "What do you mean? I never lied to you."

I force myself to calm down. This is not how a lawyer should address a client. "Sit down, Kate," I say. "We need to talk."

"Sure." She slumps to a hassock.

"The police found a hair in the boat. A hair analysis says it matches the hair they took from you at the jail."

She sits back and her mouth opens. Shock, I think. And then it's gone. Kate the actress is back.

I speak into her silence. "They took a hair sample from you when you were arrested. They did DNA tests. The DNA of the hair in the boat is identical to the DNA of the hair the police took from you when you were arrested. Do you get it, Kate?"

I watch the blood drain from her face. "It can't be my hair. I've told you, Jilly, I was never in that boat. There's been a mistake."

I stare at her in silence.

"Maybe someone planted it, to make it look like it was me in the boat," she says in a small voice. "Maybe they made a mistake in the testing. All I know is I was not the woman in the boat that day."

I shake my head. "Who would have planted your hair in that boat, Kate? Why? And how could they get your hair? You live alone. Not easy to get a strand of your hair."

Kate's fists ball, and she looks at me through angry tears. "How should I know? I'm losing my mind, Jilly. It's like there's some giant conspiracy against me. Lies, each one more ridiculous than the last. I'm an unfit mother. I stole my daughter away in a boat right under my former husband's eyes. And now my hair is in the boat. I can't explain it. It doesn't make sense." She breaks off in a wild sob.

Sympathy wells up in me; I stifle it. Kate hasn't come clean with me from the start, and now, when all the lies have been confounded by irrefutable evidence, she claims a giant conspiracy to destroy her.

"You need help, Kate," I say.

She straightens. I stare at her lovely tear-stained face. She had everything—talent, a famous and rich husband, a beautiful child—and she managed to lose it all. Now she claims to have turned herself around. I don't believe it.

"What do you mean, I need help?" she asks in a scared whisper.

"Psychiatric help. I want to help you, but I can't run this case when I can't believe what you're telling me. I trusted you, Kate, and when I realized you had been holding back on me, I continued to give you the benefit of the doubt. But now this—your DNA in the boat with Tess—I can't trust you anymore, Kate. I need to know what I'm dealing with."

"You're dealing with a heartbroken woman, Jilly. I never held back, and I'm telling you the truth now—whether that hair is mine or not—I was not in the boat that day."

"Maybe, maybe not," I say, my anger ebbing into weary resignation. "I'm not going to argue with you, Kate. I know you have your own psychiatrist, the one who says you're better now, but I need you to talk to mine."

"I don't need a psychiatrist, Jilly. I need my little girl . . ."

I ignore her plea. "If you want me to continue to represent you, you will see Dr. Pinsky. As soon as I can arrange it—tomorrow, I hope. I need to know where you're coming from, Kate." I pause. "I need to know if I can put you on the stand at trial."

Kate rocks back in shock. "You *will* put me on the stand. I have the right to tell the world it wasn't me in the boat."

I shake my head. "It's not for me to decide whether you are guilty or innocent, Kate. But as a lawyer, I can't allow a witness I know to be lying take the stand. Or a witness who is fabricating, making it up as she goes along, whether deliberately or because of the way her mind works." I pause. "I won't be a party to deceiving the court, Kate. I need you to see Dr. Pinsky."

Kate stares at me. She turns and reaches for the water glass on the table nearby. Her trembling hand grasps it, lets it fall back. Kate has assumed many guises in our short relationship, but this is the first time I have seen her coming apart. Or pretending to.

I pick up my bag. I survey my client, a shaking figure of pathos huddled on a hassock. For the second time, I stifle my pity.

I hear my voice, hard and cold. "Don't go anywhere, don't do anything. Dr. Pinsky will come to see you. Wait for my call."

I turn and leave.

CHAPTER 39

THE DAY IS BRIGHT AND the sea is calm. Richard and I are cruising north on the Sea to Sky Highway, the ribbon of road connecting Vancouver to the ski village of Whistler on our way to Britannia Bay.

To see the boat.

My mind goes to Kate, who in ten minutes will be sitting down with Dr. Pinsky. She will try to manipulate him, but my faith is in Pinsky. He will not be deceived.

A few houses and sheds are scattered on the outskirts of what was once the largest copper mine in the world, or so they say. There's a little museum attesting to past glories. But spent mines are sad spaces, and people tend not to linger or put down roots.

"Some background before we go in," I say as I motion Richard to a museum parking place. I pull out my reports on the boat, hand them to him to look at. "You don't need to read the reports,"

I say, noting the time. "Two things to be aware of. One, the police do not appear to have fingerprinted the boat—at least, there is no mention in the report. Two, they found a black hair under a screw on the tiller seat that analysis says matches the one they took from Kate at the jail."

Richard looks up.

"Just so you know," I say.

He puts the truck in gear, and we follow Google to the boat shed.

A police cruiser idles nearby, and a uniformed officer heaves out of the passenger seat and approaches. "Ethyl Gzowski," she growls. We show her our ID. The scowl on her square face tells us she doesn't like defence counsel checking out the evidence. She gives us a curt nod, and we follow her to the door.

The shed's locked up tight. Before we can enter, she must cut the security tape and make numerous entries in her black book. She opens the lock and slides the door back on its creaking rails.

The boat sits inside, still propped on the metal trailer used to tow it here. An aluminum shell. Or wreck of a shell.

Richard and I walk around and inspect the remains.

"Pretty beat up," Richard observes.

"It capsized and got banged around on the rocks before being washed up in the cove," Gzowski offers.

"I would tend to agree," says Richard wryly as he circles the wreck, noting numbers and dents.

My mind turns to speculation as I watch. Did Kate, on the Crown's theory she's the woman in the boat, wreck it and lose Tess, then swim to shore? Or did she kill Tess, then abandon the boat and swim to shore, leaving the wind to finish off the boat? Or did she pull it up in some cove on Bowen Island and hike back to the ferry to the mainland? If the former, is she a good enough swimmer to have reached shore? If the latter, why hasn't anyone come forward to say they saw Kate on the ferry?

I push a thought I've been repressing to the fore: Who tore Tess's bathing suit from her body? Kan says a denizen of the deep scooped Tess up, consumed the body, and spit out the bathing suit. I think back on the ocean shows I've watched. Seals and sharks and killer whales might swallow a child, but would they take the trouble to spit out the scrap of cloth that she was wearing? I can see the headline: *The Case of the Fastidious Carnivore.* Perhaps I can use this with the jury. Or did some human predator tear it from her fragile body?

I feel ill, stop the thought before I complete it. All this speculation leads nowhere. We need to do a search of the ferry logs to and from Bowen Island and the Mainland—not only for the day Tess disappeared, but for the days before and after. They don't take names, but sometimes people make reservations. And someone may have noticed someone behaving strangely. I catch my breath. Maybe even noticed the famous little Tess. The logs won't be enough; we need to interview the staff on the ferry. Surprisingly, Cy's disclosure does not contain ferry records. Could Kan have overlooked this? He's too good for that. But if he's investigated the ferry angle, where are the records?

I pull myself back to the present. "Can you show us where they found the hair?"

Constable Gzowski flips open her iPad and shows me a photo of the place where the first slat of the tiller seat meets a metal strut. Caught in the screw holding the slat to the steel strut attached to the shell is a barely discernable thread, long and wavy.

"Here," says Gzowski, rounding the back of the boat and

pointing to a spot where someone has attached a tape bearing a specimen number. I study the spot. Not much, a screw and a piece of wood. My imagination supplies the hair that once was there, and I suppress a shiver. Cy will haul this wreck of a boat into the courtroom for the jury to see and point to the spot where the hair was found. The jurors will follow in rapt attention. Demonstrative evidence, we lawyers call it. One demonstrative is worth a thousand words.

If Richard is worried, he doesn't show it. He is still circling the boat, inspecting and re-inspecting Gzowski's photo and the tape and the place in the boat where the screw meets the wooden slat. I can see how a hair could get caught in the crack between the slat and the screw. The screw wasn't screwed in properly, leaving a small crack between the two surfaces. Richard takes a photo.

Richard shines his flashlight on the underside of the broken piece of metal that was once attached to the boat's engine. I know what he's looking for: fingerprinting residue. We exchange glances.

Richard takes some final photos, checks his notes, and straightens. "That about wraps it up."

She locks the door after us and notes our departure time in her little black book.

"Thank you, Constable Gzowski," I say, but she's already heading to her car.

"Even with the photos, I hadn't expected the boat would be so banged up," I say when we're back on the highway heading south to the city.

"Yeah. Whoever was in it abandoned it at sea to the waves to finish it off."

"They must have had help," I say. "Someone in another boat who picked them up."

Richard considers. "Unless the police are right: Kate killed Tess, abandoned the boat near the rocks, and swam to shore. Went to the car she had hidden nearby, got in and drove home. Or rather, to her parents', where she spent the night. Easy."

"Which might explain the second shoe in the clearing. She took it with her as a keepsake and lost it."

Richard gives me a strange look. "Some keepsake."

I stare ahead glumly, watching the pavement disappear beneath the hood of Richard's truck.

Richard breaks the silence. "The grease on the broken tiller interests me. Looks old and gummy, which suggests the police forgot to test it for fingerprints. A part of the boat you'd expect the driver to touch. Careless police work, maybe."

"We might be able to make something of it in cross-examination, suggest the police didn't do their job. Leaving the possibility an unknown person was steering the boat."

"I agree. That's why I took so many photos of the tiller. You should be able to make some miles with it in cross-examination."

"Or we could ask the police to fingerprint the shaft."

Richard scowls. "Chances are they'd find Kate's fingerprint. Don't go there, Jilly."

"Or it could lead us to finding who took Tess," I say. "To fingerprint or not fingerprint; therein lies the conundrum. This could be another ploy to dupe me into strengthening the prosecution. Or it could lead me to the truth."

Silence descends as we ponder the implications.

CHAPTER 40

THE GREASY TILLER ON THE boat obsesses me.

Someone's print is on the boat, someone who is not Kate. A print that will provide the solution to Kate's case. I have no evidence for this. Not even a groundless suspicion. But the idea obsesses me.

"Don't go there," says Jeff. "Chances are, what you'll find will be Kate's print."

I am wearing out the floor around our boardroom table.

"Richard says the same. But how much worse can it get? They already have her hair in the boat."

"For God's sake, sit down, Jilly. As you keep reminding me, maybe you'll be able to explain the hair, although I don't see how. Anyway, we have to wait to see what our expert will say. Either way, Kate's fingerprint on the tiller won't help."

I slump into a chair. "I feel it in my bones, Jeff. It was someone else in the boat. If only there was a way of fingerprinting the rudder without the Crown knowing."

"No way. They have the boat under lock and key. I'll do a lot to win a case, but breaking and entering police premises is in my personal no-go zone. Our best hope is to introduce viable suspects when we get before the jury. We can't prove any of them took Tess, but we talk about a reasonable doubt."

"Reality check," I say. "We have a few alternate suspects, but none beyond the stage of preliminary speculation. We think Dante may have a police file, but it's a rumour. Lena would have been happy to have Tess out of the way, but Richard found no support for that in Vegas. No pedophiles in the area. No kidnappers. So far, no one close to Tess who would have gone to all the trouble to steal her off a beach."

"We dig deeper," says Jeff. "Talk to everyone we can who knew Tess or got near her. Trist. Lena. Selma. The housekeeper. Hope something will turn up."

"We're working on it," I say. "Richard's working on a list of everyone who had anything to do with Tess, complete with background, criminal record checks, the lot. I've talked to Trist. We're trying to crack Dante's police file. Richard's talked to the nanny, Selma. A model nanny who's pissed off no one pays any attention to her and thinks Kate took Tess. She won't help us if she can help it."

I give Jeff a bleak look. "In the meantime, we have a decision to make about the tiller—do we ask the police to fingerprint or not?"

Jeff starts to answer, but the door opens. Debbie pokes her head in. "A Jeremy Essex is here. Wants to see you."

Jeff raises an inquiring eyebrow.

"The guy I retained to look at the Crown's hair evidence," I say. "I expected a report, not a visit. Show him in, Debbie."

Jeremy Essex is a thin man of myopic stoop who wears wire-rimmed glasses. I motion him to the chair at the head of the table.

"Mr. Essex, this is my partner, Jeff Solosky. Have you found anything interesting?"

"Well, yes and no," says Essex in a high, reedy voice. "I'll put it in the report. But something's puzzling me. I thought I should run it by you first."

"Fire away."

"My analysis verifies the Crown's—the black hair found on the boat belongs to your client."

I expected this, but still, my heart sinks. "That's all?" I bite my tongue. *You could have just sent your report.*

"It's the other hair, the one they say belongs to the child."

"The Crown didn't test that hair."

"No, but I did."

"And?"

"The DNA profile doesn't match your client's. In fact, I can say with a high degree of certainty the person with pale hair is not genetically related to your client."

I lean back in my chair. "You mean the hair is not Tess's?"

"I didn't say that. I said there's no genetic relationship."

I look at Jeff, Jeff looks at me. "Thank you, Mr. Essex," Jeff says. "This is helpful. You were right to bring it to our attention immediately."

Jeff rises and ushers him out the door.

"I think we need to talk to our client," Jeff says.

CHAPTER 41

KATE SITS IN THE CHAIR Jeremy Essex occupied only an hour before.

She's wearing a black jacket emphasizing her fragility over a tee and jeans. She looks frightened. I'm dying to know how the interview with Dr. Pinsky went, but the discovery that the other hair on the boat—the hair we thought belonged to Tess—is not genetically related to Kate's hair takes precedence.

"Why did you ask me to come?" she whispers.

"Because we've learned something we don't understand, something we need you to clear up," I say. "By the way, this is Mr. Solosky, my partner."

"Not on the case," says Jeff. "Just advising."

I shoot him a dark look. As if Kate cares.

"We hired an expert called Jeremy Essex to look at the hair evidence the Crown disclosed," I say.

"Yes?"

"He confirms the dark hair on the seat near the tiller is yours—a perfect match for the hair they took from you in the jail."

"Someone must have planted it, I told you."

"It's not that hair that concerns us, Kate. Mr. Essex also performed an analysis on the lighter hair the police say belonged to Tess. His analysis shows the person with light hair bears no genetic relationship to you. In other words, she's not Tess. Or if she is—"

We watch the colour drain from Kate's face. "I—I can explain," she whispers.

"Please do," I say.

"Trist and I adopted Tess."

"But you said—"

"I told you after many failed efforts, we had Tess. I did not tell you how we got her, Ms. Truitt."

"You should have told me, Kate. It could be important."

"Trist and I vowed never to tell anyone. It was our secret. I *couldn't* tell you." She stares at Jeff and me, fear in her eyes. "And now I have. You must never tell anyone—"

"But people would have known, there would have been records," I persist.

Kate shakes her head. "It was a private adoption. What they call a closed adoption. No one knew. Trist and I were away for the six months before her birth—an extended trip to Europe. We came back with our baby. No one knew she wasn't our biological child."

I sit back, flabbergasted.

"I don't know why this matters," Kate says, cross. "We love her as much as if she had been born to us—maybe more." She swallows. "And losing her hurts just as much."

I exchange glances with Jeff. He is leaning forward, his mind working. "It could be important in this way," he says. "We need to check out the biological parents. It's possible one might have regretted the decision to adopt out, decided to get their daughter back."

Kate holds up both palms. "We can't. We're not allowed to know. Even Trist and I don't know. Like I said, it was a blind adoption. Trist made it happen through intermediaries—layers of agents—so no one would ever know. No names, all records destroyed. We wanted it that way. Even we can never find out."

Kate looks at me, looks at Jeff. "Can I go now?"

Jeff and I exchange glances. "Not yet," I reply. "What if someone did find out?"

"You think they'd take her?"

"Kate, *someone* took her. You should have told me she was adopted. You should have told the police! Enough with the secrets. How can I defend you if you won't tell me the truth?"

Kate's eyes well with tears. "I'm sorry. I didn't think—but please, don't tell the police unless you must."

"From now on, think, Kate. And please. No more secrets."

Kate nods. Stands up to leave.

"Thanks for coming in," I add, in a belated attempt at good manners.

"What the hell do we do with this?" Jeff asks when Kate is gone.

"Nothing. Nothing we can do, if Kate is right about the blind adoption. Why would we try? Even if we could find Tess's natural parents, the chance they're involved because they're genetically related to her is nil to zero."

"Except they have a motive. To rescue the child from a broken home."

I give Jeff a level look. "One thing is clear, Mr. Advisor. There are too many moving parts in this case, too many things that don't fit. And my client keeps lying to me by omission. I am going to go with my gut and ask Cy to have the police to finger-print the tiller."

"Be it on your head," says Jeff, and exits the room.

CHAPTER 42

IT'S TAKEN TWELVE DAYS TO organize the visit to the shed in Britannia Bay where the boat is stored. I called Cy after learning Tess was adopted. I explained the grease on the tiller and the apparent lack of fingerprinting. "If Kan didn't fingerprint, then there weren't any fingerprints to be had," he huffed. "Kan will never agree to this." It took a few more calls, but yesterday Cy called me to tell me today is the day.

I grab a coffee, blow a kiss at my sleeping child—Edith will be taking her to daycare this morning—and head for the office in sleeting rain. The time 7:10 on my dash startles me; what happened to the woman who, three months ago, didn't rise before ten? I stand at the door of Truitt and Solosky in the semi-darkness and grope for my keys. The woman who, two months ago, wouldn't come near the office now can't stay away. I need to fix this obsession with Tess, but I don't know how.

I turn the lights on and park myself behind my desk. I check my emails. Right at the top, Richard's message leaps out at me. His buddy in the CCTV section checked Damon out and sees no reason not to let him look at as much footage as Damon's boredom threshold can tolerate. Good news; if there is anything to ferret out, Damon will do it.

My iPhone pings. Eight o'clock: time to get moving if I'm going to make it to Britannia Beach by nine. My stomach clenches. Jeff is right, Richard is right, I am foolish to ask for a fingerprint that may convict my client. I find my car in the parking lot and head west.

Cold rain sheets the windshield all the way.

I pull up in the parking lot outside the shed. To judge from the covey of vehicles, I'm late. I recognize Richard's pickup, note the presence of three police cars and a forensics van.

I find my umbrella and step out, my Sorels splashing in a car-size pool of water. I pull my down-filled coat tighter against the driving rain and move toward the police officers huddled under an overhang by the door. No one greets me.

I flip my umbrella shut and look up. Officer Constable, the woman who supervised the first search, glares at me from narrow ice blue slits. Two other cops—presumably the forensic team—stand heads bowed and shivering against the rain, unable to manage even a nod. Even Richard looks glum as he greets me. It's clear they all would rather be somewhere else than at this bleak shed on this bleak shore, huddled in the pelting rain.

Behind us, I hear an engine and turn to see who has arrived even later than me. A black car, no markings. The door opens, and the long form of Detective Kan unfolds itself from the driver's seat. He slams the door behind him and hunches toward the assembled group, hands in his pockets, bare head slanted against the torrent. Impeccable as always, white shirt and blue tie beneath his open trench coat.

He gives me a nod. "Ms. Truitt."

I wave Richard up and introduce him. "Richard Beauvais, helping me on the defence."

The assembled group waits while Officer Gzowski makes a note in the book where she records all vital things, enters the date, time, and second on the security sheet, cuts the plastic ribbon around the lock and, inserting her key, gives a shoulder push to the steel door.

I step inside toward the battered boat, a sepulchral shadow in the gloom of the shed. What am I doing here? They will find what they find. I look at Kan, hunched over the boat. Now I've picked up on the tiller, he wants to check it out for himself.

Kan motions to the broken tiller, and the team in hazmat suits and gloves start their work. Photos. The application of sprays and mysterious substances. Translating whatever they see to iPads. The team works efficiently, but it takes time. After an eon, they step back and start packing their kit.

I move to the side of the boat, peer down at the slatted seat. Kan hovers two feet behind to make sure I don't touch anything.

"That's where you found the hair?" I ask, pointing to the circle that marks the spot where the hair was found.

"Yes."

"I would like them to fingerprint the area around the circle," I say. "The top surface, the edges, and the bottom."

"They checked it the first time," Kan says.

"In case they missed something."

Kan shrugs, motions the team back. They're half-packed, but if they resent the new order, they don't let it show.

"We'll let you know what we find. It will take the lab a couple of days." He looks at me from hooded eyes, his lip twists down. "Contact me if you find any more holes in my police work."

"You can count on it, Detective," I say brightly, as we step outside. "As a matter of fact, there is one thing I've been wondering about. Three boats were reported missing. You say this is the one from the Yacht Club. I assume you've followed up on the other two?"

"We have," says Kan. "We brought the owners of all three boats to have a look at this." He nods at the wreck. "The owners of other two said this boat was not theirs."

"Have you positively identified this boat as the one that went missing from the Yacht Club?"

Kan's eyes narrow. "The owner says it appears to be the same boat. Unfortunately, neither the boat that went missing from the Club or this one have identification numbers. We have a number on the engine but the owner's records didn't give us anything. The owner—name is Vince Stoddard—gave a statement. It's in the Crown's disclosure, when you get around to looking at it."

"When Cy gets around to sending it," I snap back.

"Not my problem," says Kan. He slides into the seat of his car and slams the door.

Richard walks me to my car. "Why the hell did you ask them to print the seat?" he growls.

"A hunch."

CHAPTER 43

MONDAY, DECEMBER 7, AND I'M back at Kate's house.

Once, she called me every day; now she's silent. I haven't heard from her since Jeff and I hauled her into the office to explain the results of Tess's hair analysis. When I call her, no one picks up. Kate's continued silence nags at me. I don't know yet if I'll put her on the stand, but I want to be able to if necessary.

Yesterday I received Dr. Pinsky's report on Kate's mental status. Like every other psychiatrist in this town, he's up to his ears in life-and-death cases and puts his legal files on the back burner unless they're urgent. Sussing out Kate's complicated mental state for a trial months away didn't make the grade until recently.

I've worked with Pinsky for years; he's bailed me out in more than one trial. I imagined his long face and rimless glasses as I perused his report summary. *History of anxiety depressive illness;*

now stable on suitable medication. Mildly paranoid, tends not to trust people. Some evidence of compulsive behaviours. Appreciates the consequences of her acts and has a clear sense of right and wrong, although scores high on the deception scale, i.e. definitely capable of lying if so motivated. And then a note in brackets: *[Subject has been under enormous stress due to recent events, namely the disappearance of her daughter and the charges she faces. Her ability to cope and aid her own defence is a testimony to her strength of character.]*

So Kate is sane and functioning within the normal range. Which doesn't mean she's not deceiving me. Maybe she's holding back on me intentionally, maybe it's a symptom of the inability to trust Pinsky mentioned.

I decided to make a house call.

Half an hour later, I was pulling up before Kate's house and pushing through a wet gust of wind to her door. I hit the bell. While I wait, I cast my eye around the small forecourt. No lurkers, no people waving placards. The web surfers who hate her haven't found her house yet, thank God.

The door opens a crack, the chain secure. The green-brown iris of Kate's eye surveys me. She hesitates, like she's not sure she should let me in, then disengages the chain and pulls the door open.

"Why are you here?" she asks. Her bitter voice has an undercurrent of apathy.

I step in and shut the door behind me. "I came to fill you in on developments about the case." It's nagging at me that I made the decision to go for the fingerprint on the tiller without consulting her. It's a choice that could convict her, and I should have put it to her, but in my pig-headedness, I pushed through. They could haul me before the Law Society for this, maybe disbar me. Too late to tell her now; all I can do is hope for the best. Another reason to pray the fingerprint they find doesn't belong to Kate.

"I've told you, I don't care about the case. Only Tess." She stares at me. "Let's be frank. When you told me you didn't believe me, insisted I see your Dr. Pinsky, I realized you are not my friend. I thought you believed me, thought you were on my side. But you are not my friend."

"How did you get on with Dr. Pinsky?" I ask. I'm interested in her take on his visit.

Kate shrugs. "I've seen a few shrinks in my life. He fits the mold. Caring on the outside, all the while scheming how to throw you under the bus. My current guy is the only one who ever wanted to help me."

"Perhaps I should talk to him," I say.

Kate's lips press into a thin line. "Perhaps you should."

I nod. Kate is upset with me, and it's my fault. I took her case on like my own. I bled for her, swore to find her child for her. I over-promised, and now I'm pulling back to what I should have been from the beginning—her lawyer. *Don't get too close to your client*, rule number two.

"Let's go upstairs and talk," I say, nodding to the glass stairs behind her.

Kate turns listlessly and starts up.

We settle in our usual chairs. Her face is a blank mask.

I decide to confront her hostility head-on. "You are right, Kate. I am not your friend. I am your lawyer. I am working for you. I am working to keep you out of prison for the rest of your life. To do this, I need to ask questions, dig up things you would rather keep private." I pause. "I have to take an objective view of where we are. Maybe you haven't lied to me, but you have been withholding information—about Trist moving Tess to Vegas, about the true lows of your mental illness, about Tess's parentage. And your hair on the boat—well, we'll see how that turns out. The point is, my job is to do what's best for your case, not what you want."

She makes no reply.

"And another thing. You need to tell me everything, Kate, even if you don't think it's important. I'll be the judge."

She sits silent, considering.

"Can you do that?"

"I'll try." Her face is bleak.

"I know this is hard for you. How are you?"

"I'm scared," she says in a small voice.

"Why are you scared?"

She turns her head away, surveying me from the corner of her eye. "Why should I tell you? You'll say I'm paranoid. But if you had the media on your back for years, if you had to live with all the evil things they've said, you might understand. It was bad enough before Tess disappeared, but now, since they charged me, it's unbearable.

"I try to ignore it, block it out," she goes on. "But one evening I went on social media. I know you told me not to, but I thought it couldn't be worse than what I'd already heard." She swallows. "But it was. Way worse. It was—obscene. I shut it down within ten minutes, but what I saw was enough. Too much. Now it's in my mind all the time. The things they say I did—" She breaks off, shaking her head. A tear steals down her cheek.

"Maybe I'm crazy, but sometimes I think they're after me. I watch for cars following me, and sometimes I think I see them. I'm afraid to pick up the phone, so I don't." She halts. "Some of the tweets—there was a whole conversation saying I'm evil for not pleading guilty. They say I'll get off on a technicality like that Casey girl in Florida did." She halts. "I keep thinking about her. The jury acquitted her, and the public outcry was crazy. She had to take a new identity. Even if you get me off by some miracle, Jilly, what future do I have?"

She looks at me bleakly. "Some of what they say on the web is so evil, I can't help but think they'd lynch me if they had the chance. And Jilly, I don't know how to say this, but some of the tweets were about you, even mentioned your little Claire."

I feel a stone where my stomach should be. I lost Mike to a criminal who thought I had crossed him. Will I lose Claire for defending Kate?

"These people are evil, Jilly."

I nod. "You mentioned you're afraid to pick up the phone. Why is that?"

"Once when I answered, I heard a man's heavy breathing. He wouldn't speak. The next day, it happened again. It freaked me out. I don't know who it was, how he got my number. And then, last night, there was a message, *You are evil. End this and plead guilty.* There was more, but I didn't listen to it all."

"Did you erase the message?"

"No, but I should." She points to the phone on the desk. "It's still there."

"Don't erase it," I say. "I'll report it, have the police investigate it."

Kate nods, bows her head in silence. Maybe she's paranoid, maybe she's scared to tell me everything. Maybe I would be the same in her shoes.

I think of Dr. Pinsky's final footnote. "You are strong, Kate.

I know that by now. Just to get through your days, your nights, would be something most people could not manage. But you are managing. You are hanging on."

"Tess keeps me going. I tell myself she's still alive; I tell myself I will find her. If I keep sane, if I keep on the good pills and off the bad ones, I'll find her." Her eyes slip to the keyboard. "I spend my afternoons practising a song I will sing to her. Brahms' Lullaby."

She crosses to the keyboard, sits down behind it. She plays a few chords, and her voice floats out, tremulous, but clear.

Lullaby and goodnight
With roses bedite
With lilies o're spread
Is baby's wee bed.

Kate's fingers slip from keyboard, and she gives me a small smile. "It needs more work."

"It was lovely."

Kate's gaze moves off and out the window. "Tess is alive. I will see her and sing this song for her."

I pick up my bag and head down the stairs, scrunching my eyes against the tears.

CHAPTER 44

BACK AT THE OFFICE, I call Cy.

"Cy, the web is full of hate talk against Kate, and now she's receiving threatening phone calls. She needs protection immediately."

"What's this all about?"

I tell him enough to make him sit up in his chair across town. "I can't do this, Jilly—I'm a prosecutor. We'll have to bring Kan in. I'll have him come to your office."

I hang up and phone Liz's daycare. Liz seems surprised; I'm not one of those parents who calls in every half hour. "Just wanted to see how Claire is," I say.

Liz chuckles. "Something up, Jilly? I can assure you Claire is fine, although I'm having difficulty keeping her from trying to climb onto the tabletop."

I laugh and sign off. I think of Mike, bloody on the floor the night he died. *If anything were to happen to Claire . . .* I push the thought from my mind.

An hour later, Kan pushes through the double glass doors. His eyes scan our modest outer office—*Is this what defence digs look like?* Maybe he thought I spend my days in one of the glossy glass towers uptown. Debbie, who seldom gets to see a cop, much less a real detective, ushers him into my office with aplomb. "Have a seat. Coffee coming right up." Then, with a glance to me, "Message for you when you're free."

Kan folds his frame awkwardly into my Eames client chair, his bulk rising over its delicate arms. His face is impassive. "What is this about, Ms. Truitt?"

I tell him about Kate's telephone message. No, I didn't listen to it, but I think his people should. Do an assessment. Perhaps they can trace it. And the web, they should monitor it as well. He takes it in, jotting notes in a small book as I proceed.

"One more thing," I say. "Some of the online talk mentioned me, my daughter. Claire."

Kan makes another note in his mysterious book.

I wait. He's going to say he doesn't see any danger, this is another defence ploy to divert him from what matters. A ditzy accusation by an over-excited female lawyer. Still, I can't be making this all up. The web is what it is, and I'm asking him to check out a real message on Kate's phone.

He looks up. "I'll send someone over to check the message and see if we can trace it. And for the rest—you must know we're monitoring Kate."

The minimum, I think. Not even an offer to put a guard on the house. "You disappoint me, Detective. Let me put it this way. It's fashionable for lawyers these days to talk about the precautionary principle," I say. "The idea is that if something bad *could* happen, you don't let it. They're usually talking about the environment, but let's apply the principle to this case. Assume someone is tailing Kate. Assume someone is leaving threatening phone calls. Assume public outrage is running high against her. What precautions should we take?"

He looks at me stonily. "Nothing," he says. "Do nothing."

I don't hide my anger. "Really, Detective?"

"If we applied the precautionary principle to the internet, free speech would be over, Ms. Truitt. We live in a mean world, but we also live in a free country. We can't shut this stuff down. The police can't even monitor most of it. Privacy protection. But let's get to your real concern. Does the hateful internet chatter mean your client's in danger? The answer is no. The messages are nothing but the usual bilge and vitriol, people spewing out their frustration and anger and concern. They're just words. They won't touch Kate—or you."

He leans back. "As for the phone message, we will check it out." He gives a wry smile. "And as for Ms. Sinclair-Jones's fear someone may be following her, I can assure you she is right. We are keeping tabs on her everywhere she goes."

"Make sure she stays safe," I say. "Neither of us wants anything to happen to Kate."

Kan shifts, drills his eyes into mine. "Ms. Truitt, I know there was a plot to kill you last year, and I know they shot your partner instead. I can understand how this experience might make you worry something terrible will happen again."

"Allow me to translate," I say, aware of my voice's caustic edge. "Jilly Truitt, lady lawyer, is acting irrationally. Let's humour her little fears."

Kan raises his hands. "You put words in my mouth, Ms. Truitt.

I might accuse you of many things, but irrationality? Never." He smiles and lowers his hands. "All reasonable precautions will be taken to ensure your and your client's safety." He looks me in the eyes. "You have my word."

He unfolds himself from the chair and rises.

Debbie almost collides with him as she arrives with the coffee. He glances at her but moves on without a word.

Debbie's eyes follow him. "That didn't take long," she says as the doors swing shut behind him.

"No. It didn't," I say.

"Damon called. He said to meet you at the stream at four tomorrow."

"The stream?"

"He said you would know it."

"Sure," I say, picking up my phone to google Vancouver's beaches. Then I pause. Damon is not trusting information to the air waves. Maybe I shouldn't either.

CHAPTER 45

JERICHO BEACH IS THE MOST westerly of the beaches lining the south shore of English Bay. I drive across the Burrard Bridge and take a right on Cornwall, pushing west. I pull in at the last parking area but one before the hill leading to the University of British Columbia.

It's blustery here, gusts of wind pushing out the rain that's been falling for the last four days. I pull my coat tighter and cross the grass median to the place where the salmon stream debouches into the Pacific.

Deep in the night, it came to me, what Damon meant by *the stream*. Long ago, he took me to a small stream flowing across the beach to the ocean to show me how the salmon were once more running to their breeding waters inland. A small step to restore an ancient landscape.

I find Damon on the wooden footbridge spanning the narrow stream, staring into the trickle of water below. He senses me and turns.

He is still my beautiful boy, the boy I rescued from a murder charge, the boy I saved from a fatal overdose. I am wary of the arrogance of do-good interventions, but he is here because of me.

He turns back to the stream. "Look," he says. "Two dead salmon. This is excellent news."

"Really?"

"Yes. Once, this stream ran red with spawning salmon. Then new roads, sewers, and houses destroyed the stream, and the salmon couldn't navigate upward. They disappeared. But people who cared built culverts, dredged blockages. No one believed the salmon would come back; it just seemed the right thing to do. But this year, they came back. They swam up the stream, made their egg nests, and died." He points to the dead fish below. "In the spring, the young salmon will swim out to the sea. The cycle will be restored."

"Good to know," I say. "Is that why you brought me out here?"

"No. I didn't know the salmon were back." He turns, his blond mane floating back in the wind. He nods at the beach stretching westward around the point. "Let's walk.

"I'm still trolling through the CCTV data," he says when we reach the water's edge. "It's driving me mad. People milling by shopping malls, restaurants, gas stations, hour after hour, day after day. And there have been a lot of days since Tess disappeared."

"You're telling me the task is impossible," I say.

He shrugs. "I've listed my indices, concocted my algorithms. I'm not looking for any kid, I'm looking for a five-year-old with an Afro." He allows a grim smile. "When I find a possible match, I record it, blow it up. Most times the quality is so bad it would be impossible to identify the child. But I keep working. I've got my photos of Tess on the desk beside me, and I keep looking for one like her." He laughs. "In fact, I'm getting into it. I feel I know Tess, that I'll recognize her when I see her." He pauses. "If I see her."

"Yeah," I say. "I know it's a long shot. But it's all we have right now."

"Kate still thinks Tess is alive?"

I remember the words Kate used yesterday. "She used to say she knew, now she says she believes."

We walk on, damp sand tugging at our steps. We're almost at the end of the beach where the great logs thrown up by autumn storms lie in heaps like giant matchsticks. The tide is coming in; time to turn back.

Damon turns to face me. "I found the file, Jilly. I found the file on Dante."

CHAPTER 46

IT'S SATURDAY, HALFWAY INTO DECEMBER, and we're preparing for Claire's first Christmas. Edith has dragged in a tree—not perfect, but the best the Vancouver markets had to offer—and I have purchased two giant bags of decorations and lights. Now we're decorating the tree together. More accurately, I am standing on a ladder, attempting to follow Edith's instructions. From her playpen in the corner of the living room, Claire shouts her delight.

"I know what to do. I did this for my mother in Ireland," Edith says. "She had a grand tree."

"Much bigger than ours," I murmur.

"Oh, much bigger," says Edith, who has retreated to her social worker persona for this occasion. "Please place that ornament an inch higher, Jilly. Everything must be symmetrical."

When we're done, Edith proclaims the tree acceptable, if still a "puny wee thing." It has been a long process, which included sending me back to Canadian Tire twice to replace ornaments that "didn't match." But now Edith is satisfied, and the tree is finished. I breathe a sigh of relief.

Despite my daughter's joy at the proceedings, my heart is shadowed by the fact someone out there may be plotting to kill Kate. Or me. Or worst of all, Claire. To bring a child into the world is to pledge yourself to care for her, to defend her. I have brought Claire into the world, but I fear I cannot protect her. Now, as I descend the ladder and return her innocent smile, I feel my heart break.

I've explained to Edith why a police car is sitting in the lane near the house twenty-four hours a day. She shook her head—she wishes I had chosen a less-complicated life—but is kind enough not to remonstrate. Kan called me last night with an update. The police have been unable to trace the threatening calls—the caller must have used a burner, Kan says. The good news is they've been talking to Kate every day, and there have been no further calls, and Kan has put a watch on my house and Liz's daycare. I called Kate last night, and she seemed less anxious.

We sit down to a late lunch of hamburgers and air-fried chips. Claire is in her highchair, messing with the baby food Edith has made for her. Then I called Jeff about Dante and left a message.

I'm on my first bite when my cellphone rings. Jeff's name comes up.

"Excuse me," I say, pushing away from the table and making for the den. "Hope this is work, Jeff," I quip into the phone on the way.

"Just got in from the airport." Jeff has been in Calgary, something to do with a biker gang. "What's up?"

"Dante Bocci," I say.

"Do tell."

"Damon has found something." I remind myself of Damon's unease with cellphones. "Can you come by?"

"Sure. Jessica's out Christmas shopping. I'm all yours."

Half an hour later, Jeff bangs on the door and lets himself in. He goes straight to the kitchen and the baby chair on the table. He bends toward Claire, smiling. She looks startled, and I think she's going to cry, but his nonsense words reassure her, and she smiles.

"She hasn't seen many men," I say, marking another deficiency in my parenting profile. "And by the way, when did you learn baby talk?"

"I've been practising with my sister's baby."

I smile. Jeff and Jessica have been hoping for a baby, so far without luck. My heart does a positive uptick. I need Jeff by my side on this case, but so far he's been clinging to his advisor-only role. But he's been thinking about kids and how precious they are. His sister's baby. Kate's Tess. My Claire. And now he's here on a Saturday afternoon. Put it all together, and he might be softening his stance on the case.

Edith scoops Claire up and starts zipping her into her snow suit. "Off to visit my niece. Her kids are a little older, but Claire will enjoy them."

"Edith believes in giving babies as many diverse experiences as possible," I tell Jeff. "Says it develops their social skills."

Edith makes a moue, hefts Claire in her arms, and exits. Jeff and I push the machine buttons for coffees and settle into the den.

"What's with the police presence?" Jeff asks before I manage my first sip.

I wince. "I was hoping you wouldn't notice."

"They may be plain cars, but they have police written all over

297

them. They watched me climbing the steps. Presumably, I passed muster."

"I wasn't going to tell you, Jeff. With this guy, the fewer who know the better. Or that's what we think."

Jeff's brows beetle. "You are my partner. I need to know."

I sigh. "Okay, but keep it to yourself. Someone has been phoning Kate from untraceable burners telling her to plead guilty or he'll kill her. And if she told me, he'll kill Claire and me. I told Cy, and he brought Kan in. Now we're all under police protection."

"This is serious," Jeff breathes. He looks at the door where Edith exited with Claire, looks back at me. "You can't deal with this alone, live with the threat, and run this case. It's too much."

I put on a brave smile. "You do what you have to do."

"I'm trying to tell you I have your back, Jilly. Maybe I'm just an advisor, but I can do more."

I reach over and touch his hand. "Thanks, Jeff."

"What's the scoop on Dante?"

"As you know, Damon's been going through the police CCTV data, looking for Tess. He's not having much luck, but he found something else. A file on Dante."

"How the hell did he do that?"

"I didn't ask." I look Jeff in the eye. "And I don't want to know."

"Ah-ha." Jeff sighs. "We enter the murky waters of undercover investigation. Whatever happened to warrants?"

"Need reasonable and probable grounds. As you well know. In this case—"

"So what's in the file?"

"Dante was investigated for making intimate photos of little girls. Child pornography. Some were graphic. Little girls, no clothes on, privates visible."

"Ah-ha." Jeff's voice turns down in disgust.

"But for some reason, the police didn't pursue charges. As we already knew, Dante Bocci has no criminal record. Clean as a whistle."

"Why didn't the police lay charges?"

"Seems Dante brought in a big gun from Toronto. The TO lawyer talked big, ran all over the investigator. Dante's work was art, not porn. If they dared to prosecute, he would go to the press and accuse the police of harassment of an innocent artist. Who knows what happened? But the police stopped digging, and a year later the file was closed."

"Did Dante sell the stuff online?"

"The police had been looking into that, but they stopped. Not clear why."

"Do the police know Damon found the file?"

"Damon doesn't think so. He's good. Knows how to get in and out of a file with no trace." I pause. "The police file would explain why Dante was so scared that day on the island, why he was trying to get away before the police came calling and found the photos. He didn't want anything to do with the investigation into Tess's disappearance. It was too late to avoid that—the police had his camera with the photos of the woman and child in the boat—but he made good by identifying Kate, shifting any blame away from himself."

Jeff stands, stretches his long arms. I feel a pronouncement coming on.

"We need to pay Mr. Bocci a visit. Now. Where does he live?"

"Richard reports Dante has a gallery in White Rock. Attached to his house."

"So we pay him a call."

"He will recognize me, Jeff. No way he'll invite us in."

Jeff scratches his chin. "He doesn't know me. Even if he googled me, which he probably has, he wouldn't recognize me with this beard. We drive out there and park in a discreet spot. Maybe I'm in the art business and want to buy some of his stuff. I'll figure it out, get my foot in the door."

"And me?"

"Hmm. The gallery is open to the public—selling stuff on a Saturday this close to Christmas. You can go into the gallery and look around. Buy something for Edith."

The afternoon stretches before me. We probably won't learn much, but who knows? A little Christmas shopping may be just the thing.

CHAPTER 47

WE CLIMB INTO MY VOLVO and head for White Rock, a picturesque seaside town where Canada meets the American border.

The morning rain has blown through, and the beaches on the far side of the tracks sparkle under soft grey skies. They used to run tourist trains from Vancouver to Seattle through here. Now, trains seldom pass.

Shops, restaurants, and art galleries line the esplanade that fronts the sea. We make our way up the slope into an old residential area. Glassy two-story houses intersperse with postwar bungalows vying for the best view of the Pacific below. Everywhere, gardens spread. It's too late for flowers, but the dampened foliage shimmers grey green in the afternoon light.

The lady in Google Maps tells us we have arrived. I backtrack and park under an overhanging willow tree, and we get out. I look up and see the sign protruding from a hedge with an arrow pointing down the street—so discreet you'd miss it if you weren't looking—Bocci Gallery and Photography Studio.

"I'll go into the gallery," I say. "You come along a couple of minutes later and ring the bell on the house."

"Sounds like a plan."

I pass a gap in the hedge revealing a narrow walk leading to an old-fashioned porch. The house is mock Victorian, yellow brick obscured by a wall of ivy, bay window to our left; straight ahead, an entry foyer jutting out from the façade. A few steps farther, wide pavers lead to modern windows and a glass door. *Bocci Gallery*, a sign announces.

The room is a recent addition, with floor and walls of weathered cedar. Light seeps from clerestory windows, illuminating the walls and photographs in black and white, punctuated by the colour slash of oil paintings. The scent of wood and sweet oil fills the air. I breathe deeply; I like this space.

I am not alone. Two women are looking at hand-crafted ceramics of grey and blue on tables in the near corner. At the back of the spacious room, a man stoops, leafing through mounted photographs hanging on a display rack. A young woman with red hair pulled back into a bun stands behind a small counter, ready to ring up purchases or offer assistance.

"I'm looking for a gift for a friend," I say as she approaches. I move toward a shelf displaying ceramic picture frames, motion to a frame of pale ivory overlaid with a delicate floral motif. I could have a photo of Claire blown up and placed in it; Edith would treasure it.

"This is lovely," I say. The assistant nods and removes the frame from the shelf. "If you don't mind, I'll look around and see if I want anything else."

"Dante does a bit of everything," she says, waving around the room. "But it's portraits, mostly of women, he's best known for."

I tour the room, scanning the portraits. A former premier of the province, chippy feistiness shining through her celluloid smile. A noted television journalist, as lovely in maturity as she was five decades ago. A lieutenant-governor, a renowned sommelier. A collection of the who's who among the women of British Columbia.

"No lawyers," I quip.

The assistant gives a tight smile. "Quite right. No lawyers."

I spend some time taking in the exhibits. I am particularly taken with the bust of an elderly woman, an erect African goddess. Dante dabbles in sculpture, too.

Sensing I've overstayed my welcome, I wander to a stack of matted photos in a corner, partially covered by a plastic garbage bag. I pull the bag off and start flipping through it. More women, unknown, photos of trans people. And then, beneath my fingertip, a face I know, a face etched in my mind.

Tess.

"A few odds and ends, ready for the dustbin," the clerk says as she crosses to where I stand. She leans over my shoulder, sees where my finger has paused. I turn my head to her, eyebrows arched.

"And this?"

"You like it?" the assistant asks.

"He's really going to throw it out?"

"I could ask." She gives me a look. "I'm not authorized to give it away, if that's what you're wondering."

"Oh, no. But I like it," I say. "There's a word for this."

She laughs. "Such as?" She gazes around and spots a cobweb.

While she goes back to the desk to grab a duster, I snap a photo of the portrait with my phone. "Ethereal."

Hair like a halo. Small pointed chin. Kate's eyes.

I let the photo fall back into the stack and scan the portraits lining the walls. "Does Dante do many child portraits? I have a daughter . . ."

The clerk shrugs. "I wouldn't say he specializes in children—as you see, most of these are of adults. Mr. Bocci likes the challenge of catching the character behind the façade. Josef Karsh is his hero."

"Ah, yes," I say. "The famous Winston Churchill photo. Churchill was presenting the bland façade of the great man. Karsh wanted more, he wanted the great man's snarl of belligerence. He snatched his cigar from his hand and clicked the shutter in the same instant."

"Mr. Bocci would probably say it is difficult to achieve such artistry with children. They are what they are. Unformed. No façade, no secrets to extract. No character."

"I could argue." I smile, thinking of Claire's shifts from stubborn will to sunny exuberance. Then I think of Tess's response to no more weekends with her mother. "But I know what you mean."

She hesitates. "If you are interested, I could ask Mr. Bocci if he would do a portrait of your daughter." She glances at my worn Burberry, quality, but faded. "As you would expect, Mr. Bocci's fees are rather elevated. These days he prefers to spend his time on personal creative passions."

I am standing at the counter, paying for my picture frame, when I hear the sound of a latch. I look up. A door is opening—the door connecting the gallery to the house. Jeff crosses into the gallery, Dante close behind him.

"Here you can see some of my work," Dante is telling Jeff, as he waves to the portrait-lined walls. "If we were to do a show, I would need to bring in new pieces. I'm not a fan of retrospectives. I like my art to be fresh—"

Dante's voice cracks and fades as he sees me standing at the counter. The colour drains from his face.

I look at Jeff, nod toward the street. As I swivel to leave, the door to the house opens again.

A girl stands in the doorway, her pale shape stark against the dark of the passage beyond. A young girl, perhaps ten or eleven. Her eyes are huge, her lips parted, as if she wants to speak. Do I imagine it, or does she look frightened?

Dante whirls. "Emily," he rasps. The girl turns and retreats into the darkness.

Dante turns, all smiles again. The women, clutching their ceramics, are staring at him with open mouths. "Sorry, ladies, just my niece."

Jeff nudges my elbow, and we leave.

CHAPTER 48

THE BRIEF CALM IS SHATTERED by a sudden shower; the windshield wipers take up their beat against the windshield.

We're on the highway, putting as much distance between my car and White Rock as we can, as quickly as we can. Jeff and I sit silent, encased in our solitary bubbles of shock.

"So much for our attempts at amateur sleuthing," I say, breaking the tension with a laugh. "I think we should stick to lawyering."

"I was doing pretty well until you entered the picture," says Jeff. "Recently hired artistic director of the Audain Gallery in Whistler, looking to mount a new exhibition—portraits of British Columbia notables. Dante swallowed it, hook, line, and sinker. Until he saw you."

"What, if anything, did you learn?"

"Let me think. Dante lives alone, except for a disturbed niece he looks after. Emily, you saw her in the door as we were leaving. I learned his mother, who is eighty-four and has a pacemaker, lives down the hill from him in a bungalow. I was working my way around to Bowen Island last September when he got up and said we should take a look at his work in the gallery. And you? What did you learn, Sherlock Truitt?"

"I learned he has a large, matted photograph of Tess amongst a stack of photos covered by a black plastic bag slated for next week's garbage."

"Wow! Stop the car!" Jeff yells. I move to brake, but he holds up his hand. "Kidding."

"It's a lovely photo, Jeff. Grainy, slightly out of focus. But it's perfect. The child is looking straight at the camera. She is talking to the camera."

"Are you saying Dante had access to Tess? Maybe has access to Tess even now?"

"I'm not saying anything. I'm asking questions. He wouldn't keep her at the house, but she could be with someone he knows. His mother lives nearby. I'll ask Richard to check her out."

I downshift to join the lineup waiting to enter the Massey Tunnel.

"Another thing," I say.

"Yeah?"

"The girl. Emily. The niece. I think there's more to the story. Sure, she's disturbed. But the question is, who disturbed her? Present tense, who is disturbing her? Did you see how she scuttled away when Dante spoke to her? And her face. Like she was going to speak. Like she wanted us to rescue her." I lower my voice. "Don't forget, Jeff. This is a man suspected of producing child pornography.

"It all fits," I say. "Dante steals Tess off the beach while Trist is sleeping and puts her in his car, which is parked in the clearing at the top of the hill. He drugs Tess so she's out of it. He drives back to his cabin, stopping to undress Tess and toss her bathing suit and shoe into the ocean on the way. He's upset there's only one shoe, but he has no time to go back. He goes into the cabin to collect his stuff, leaving Tess in the vehicle. The police come knocking, find his camera and the photos of the woman and child in the boat. He agrees to go back to the city and give them a statement, scared stiff the police will search his vehicle and find Tess. But they don't. He gives his statement and identifies Kate as the woman in the boat, goes back to his car."

"Doesn't fit with him taking a photo of Tess with the woman in the boat."

I sigh. "In this case, nothing fits. Maybe he photoshopped Tess and Kate? Or maybe he photographed Tess with Lena in her boat?"

"Too farfetched for reasonable doubt."

I nod. He's right. "But I do know this: something is off with Dante."

We emerge from the tunnel, ride in silence through the south city suburbs. Saturday evening is coming on. The bars along Granville are bringing out the glasses, the restaurants polishing their cutlery. Christmas lights glow everywhere. The holiday is upon us.

I pull up at my front door behind Jeff's parked van. "Looks good," he says with a nod to the house.

I nod, too. Edith has strung lights across the entry porch and hung a pine wreath with red ribbon on the front door. Light glows from within.

"Come in for a drink?" I ask.

He shakes his head. "No. Jessica will be back from shopping. We've got a party to go to later."

"Sure," I say, thinking of the empty evening stretching before me. Not empty. Claire and firelight are enough for me.

My hand is on the door; I open it. On impulse, I turn back to Jeff.

"Can I ask you one thing?"

"Anything."

"Tell me the truth, Jeff. What did you make of Dante?"

"Under the façade?" he asks with a smile.

"Yeah. The unrevealed character."

He shifts, his eyes gleam in the darkness. *"There speaks a devil who is sick of sin."*

He sees my inquiring stare.

"Dante has sinned, Jilly. He hates the sinning, but he will sin again. And again. A devil may regret, but he cannot change. Therein lies the tragedy."

PART III

CHAPTER 49

MONDAY MORNING AND I'M BEHIND my desk.

I open my emails, and there they are. The police reports on the greasy tiller. It's been more than two weeks since the police took prints from the boat. Last week, I sent a warning message to Cy—get us the reports or I'll go to court to get them. Now, at long last, they have arrived.

I open the email, feel my stomach tighten. Chances are this is not good news. Before I can dive in, I sense a presence—Jeff, leaning on my doorframe with his morning latte.

"The print report from the boat tiller," I say.

He slumps into the chair opposite mine. "Let's have it."

I scroll down to the summary. "Number one: they found prints on the tiller."

"And?"

"Number two: three prints, which match Ms. Sinclair-Jones's prints in size and shape and several of the whorls."

"Jilly, don't make me drag this out of you."

"Sorry, Jeff. Time for our case summit. Boardroom."

It's time to face facts: we've been floundering on Kate's case. But things have happened since our last board huddle. Our visit to Dante, what we've learned from Trist and Selma, and the now-inconclusive fingerprint report. There are a couple things I won't raise today—Tess's adoption and the death threats against Kate, Claire, and me. Keep it simple, keep it to what we need to talk about to move ahead with our defence. We face not one line of inquiry, but several. Diverse threads of evidence, all inconclusive, but each strengthening the rope Cy will try to braid to establish Kate's guilt. It's time to inventory what we have and pull the strings together. Or try to.

Our diminutive boardroom wears festive garlands today. Debbie spent the weekend—still no new man in her life—decorating the office. Holiday garlands frame the coffee counter, and holly encircles the lights. Mistletoe surmounts the door in case someone feels the urge to steal a kiss. The scent of pine hangs heavy in the air.

I used to think holiday frippery was foolish, but now that I have Claire, I get it. Liz's daycare is awash in Christmas and Hannukah regalia. The children's eyes light up as they place candles or reach for special sweets. Festivals bring joy and offer a reprieve from everyday cares. I look around the table and survey the mound of papers dwarfing the poinsettia centrepiece. I think of the unmarked cruisers parked across the street. We have many cares, we have need of this.

Every chair around the table in the small boardroom of Truitt and Solosky is filled. Richard, Damon, and the legal team—Jeff, Alicia, Shanni, and me.

"There have been several developments on the case since we met in October. I'd like to run over them, brainstorm with you about the implications. The first one you all know about—the discovery of a second pink shoe in a clearing above the lodge Trist was renting. After testing, the police concluded it's the mate to the shoe found washed up on the beach the day after Tess disappeared, and they appear to accept that it was not a plant. So, this opens a second line of inquiry: Did someone steal Tess while Trist slept and take her up the hill to a vehicle parked in the clearing? If we can plant this suggestion with the jury, we may persuade them there is reasonable doubt on the Crown's allegation Kate took Tess."

"This presupposes they reject Dante's photo and eyewitness identification. Not to mention Kate's hair in the boat," Jeff notes.

I nod. "Or if not rejecting that evidence, at least have a doubt about it. We'll get to Dante and the hair, but I agree getting the jury to give credit to the alternate hypothesis that Tess was taken by land will require us to show the weaknesses of the Crown's evidence. If the jury is convinced by the Crown's evidence, they are unlikely to give the alternate hypothesis much credit."

"Who would take Tess away by land, and why?" Alicia asks.

"We don't know. There are various possibilities. A pedophile, maybe."

"Ninety per cent of child disappearances involve relatives or someone who knew the child," Richard puts in.

"True, but we can't ignore the ten per cent that don't. I take your point, though. We'll get to the people who knew Tess in a minute. But for the moment, perhaps we should talk about Dante Bocci."

I pause. All eyes are on me now. "There are several elements here. Number one: Damon found a police file from 2018 showing the police were investigating Dante for production and distribution of child pornography. For reasons that remain unclear but involve a hotshot lawyer from Toronto convincing the police he would put up a tough fight based on freedom of expression and artistic merit, the investigation was dropped in 2019. No charges were ever laid."

Alicia sits back. "So, Dante is interested in little girls. Maybe interested in Tess?"

"Not so fast," I caution. "But yes. Perhaps."

"Can we get the file so we can cross-examine him on it?" Alicia asks.

Damon shakes his head. "I can't find it anymore. Like someone knew I was poking around and erased it. I have my notes; I suppose I could testify to what I found, if necessary."

Does Kan have his team following Damon in his excursions into the dark web, I wonder?

"We'll see," I muse. "Perhaps there is another way to show he was into porn? Like finding he was flogging it on the dark web?"

Damon nods. "We could try."

"Element number two," I say. "Jeff and I went to Dante's gallery last Saturday. In the gallery, amongst a stash of photos slated for the trash, I found a photo of Tess. I took a quick pic on my phone."

I flash my photo of the photo onto the monitor on the console. "The photo I took isn't great—the assistant was giving me the eye—but you can make out Tess's face and hair. It's a beautiful portrait. But how did it come to be taken? Is it a blow-up from the photos he took of the woman in the boat? The definition and pose suggest otherwise. Did Dante have access to Tess at some other time? Before Tess was taken or after?" The group falls silent, considering the implications. "Jeff spoke with Dante, pretending to be a gallery owner interested in showing his stuff." I look across the table. "Jeff?"

"My ruse didn't get me far," Jeff says wryly. "I tried to work in his link to the case: wasn't he the man who took the photos of the woman in the boat sort of thing. But he wasn't biting. Gave me a bland smile."

Richard shakes his head. "Stick to the law, Jeff. Leave the detective work to me."

"Right," says Jeff, and we all smile.

"But we need to think of all possible scenarios, even if they seem far-fetched," I say. "The police report says Dante was packed and ready to go and seemed anxious to be on his way. It's possible—far-fetched but possible—that he could have taken Tess to the clearing and transported her to his cabin, sedating her and hiding her in his SUV. He could have undressed her and thrown the swimming suit and shoe into the ocean on his way back to his cabin. He would have discovered she had lost a shoe but had no time to go back and look for it. When the police came, he was forced to show them the photos, which pointed away from him to Kate as the abductor. The photos could have been doctored . . ." I trail off. "I know there are a lot of *could've*s, *would've*s, but I think we need to consider the possibility."

"Were the photos time-stamped?" asks Shanni.

"Regrettably, yes," I reply. "Ruling out the possibility he took them on another occasion."

"We should look into whether he might have doctored the date," says Richard. "But assuming this could have happened, where is Tess now?" Richard asks.

"Good question. We saw a girl at Dante's, ten or eleven. Dante said she was a niece. But no sign of Tess."

"If he took her, he wouldn't be stupid enough to keep her at his house," says Richard.

"He mentioned his mother lives nearby," Jeff says thoughtfully.

Richard shakes his head. "Still too close."

"Damon is working on CCTV camera data, looking for someone like Tess."

"With nothing to show for it," says Damon, shaking his head.

"So that's the Dante angle," I say. "If you come up with any ideas, let me know. But now, let's take a break. When we come back, we'll talk about other suspects."

CHAPTER 50

WHEN WE REASSEMBLE OVER COFFEE and Christmas cookies, I say, "Time to look at other suspects."

I glance around the table to see how this is going down. Nods all around. So far, so good.

"We've been looking at everyone who knew Tess, had anything to do with her," I continue. "However unlikely a suspect they may seem."

"Here's a partial list," Richard offers. "Lena, Trist's partner. Selma, Tess's nanny. Winnifred, the housekeeper, who I will interview later this week. Trist's Vegas agent, Rex, who was fond of Tess, brought her treats and fussed over her. I've checked him out. Doting grandfather. Happily married for thirty-six years. No record, no sign of crime or deviance, aside from a gambling habit that keeps him working into his sixties. In fact, he was buying chips in a casino at the time Tess was taken."

"What about Trist?" asks Alicia.

I shake my head. "I talked to him. I don't think he took Tess. He had her, why would he take her? Lena is interesting, however. Lena wanted to marry Trist. Tess did not like Lena and made her life difficult. Lena told Richard as much when he went to Vegas to talk to her. She admitted she said she would kill her."

Richard barks with laughter. "Parents say such things in the heat of the moment. I know, I have twins."

I nod. "I should add a few additional facts. Tess disappeared shortly after Tess threw the lunch Lena prepared for her all over the floor. Lena was upset and took the boat out to the store. Before leaving, she gave Trist a big glass of merlot. She did not share that drink. Then at the beach, Trist falls asleep. Uncharacteristically, he says." I survey my audience. "You get the picture."

"So Lena's back in Vegas?" asks Damon.

"Yes. Two days after Tess disappeared, she cleaned out the joint account and jumped on a plane. Trist was upset but hinted they might get back together when he's down there for a gig in a few months. Lena hinted the same thing to Richard when he talked to her in Vegas."

"Which raises the possibility Trist and Lena may have cooked up her departure to get her out of the jurisdiction while the police were focused on Kate," Shanni muses.

I give our new associate an appreciative look. She never misses a trick.

"And Trist and Lena live happily ever after in Vegas, with no Tess to mar the blissful picture," says Alicia.

"Not so fast," Shanni says. "Richard went to Vegas and watched her a few days, found no trace of Tess. And as Jilly pointed out, it's hard to believe Trist would be party to killing his child."

Jeff and I exchange glances. Would Trist care less about an adopted child than a natural child?

"Plus, Richard spent three days poking around Vegas, but discovered nothing incriminating. Lena's story holds—fed up with cops and paps and longing for warmer climes, she took off for Vegas."

Jeff shakes his head; another far-fetched theory. "I don't think we have enough on Lena to get us beyond speculation. Maybe something will turn up, but on what we have, the judge wouldn't put the possibility to the jury. What about the nanny, Selma or whatever?"

"Richard met with her a couple of weeks ago." I look down to the end of the table. "Richard?"

Richard slides a file across the table to me. "Here's the full report.

"I started with a background investigation," Richard says, reading from his own copy. "Selma Beams grew up mainly on a small farm in east Surrey owned by her grandfather. Her parents were fundamentalist Christians, moved around a lot, from revival to revival. Selma was bright but underachieved at school. Her parents died in a car crash coming back from a religious meeting when she was seventeen. Must have thrown her for a loop—there's a blank between age eighteen and twenty—seems she got caught up with a cult and went under for a while. Then she straightened up and started looking after people's kids. That led to vocational training as a childcare provider, where she led her class. She got a job, which ended when the family moved, and then went to work with Trist and Kate as a nanny to Tess, who was about a year old at the time. Both Trist and Kate speak highly of her. She looked after Tess until Tess disappeared from Bowen Island."

"She wasn't there when Tess disappeared, right?" Jeff asks.

"Right. She took a week off to look after her grandfather, who was ailing, according to her police statement."

"That's it?"

"Yeah. Except to reinforce that she appears to have been an excellent nanny. Good grades at vocational school. Excellent references. One thing is clear. Although Kate respected Selma, Selma had a low opinion of Kate's parenting ability. Selma was behind Trist's applications for custody against Kate."

"What about your visit with Selma?" I prompt. I think back to the brief account Richard gave me at the time. "Fill in all the details, Richard."

"I had a hard time finding her—finally ran her down through the Surrey address on her government card. She hemmed and hawed but agreed to meet me for coffee at Tim Horton's on 126th Avenue. Medium height, short dark hair, brown eyes. She slammed her bag on the table and said, 'What do you want to know?' Then, before I could answer, she went into a monologue of grievance. She was angry and edgy. She was upset that apart from a brief police interview, no one had talked to her about Tess, even Trist. 'After four years of service, he just sent my check,' she said. 'Correction, had his agent send my check.' No questions, no concern for her. She said she loved Tess more than anyone. I inferred she was grieving her loss. She also seemed to agree with the Crown theory that Kate had taken Tess and killed her. It was pretty much a rant for fifteen minutes. And then she grabbed her purse off the table and said she had to go. That was it."

"Was Selma aware Trist and Lena were planning on taking Tess to Vegas?"

"I think so. Trist wanted to take Selma to Vegas but Lena was against it."

"Keep an eye on her," Jeff says. "A lot of emotion, from what you say. Maybe something's going on underneath."

"She sounds worth talking to. I'll follow up myself."

Jeff rolls his eyes upward. "Thought you were spending Christmas week in Whistler with Martha and the family."

I sigh. Jeff is right. We won't get to Selma until the holiday is over.

"One thing I will do, before the break: I will talk to Trist again."

I look around the table. Everyone is fatigued. We've been through a lot, and we haven't made discernible progress in unravelling the tangled mystery of the sunny day Tess was abducted or how we can mount a credible defence for Kate.

I clap my hands. "That's it for today."

As if on cue, Debbie enters with a tray bearing glasses of mulled wine. "Christmas cheer," she calls out. We take our glasses and relax. The gloom dissipates into laughter and chatter about holiday plans.

I try to pick up the mood but fail. I sip my drink at my end of the table and brood. For us, it's holiday cheer. For Kate, not so much. And Tess, if by some miracle she's out there somewhere? Five years old. Terrified. Missing her mom and dad.

I raise my glass. *Merry Christmas, Tess.*

CHAPTER 51

TRIST WON'T ANSWER MY CALLS.

Tomorrow, I leave for Whistler. Today is my last chance to talk to him before the holiday. I decide to pay him an in-person visit.

This time, I find the house easily, the hole in the hedge, the long walk. I have my story ready for security, but the guard is gone. The house is dark. Perhaps Trist has left for Vegas. Why not? Not much to hold him here.

I step up to the door and ring the bell. I hear brisk footfalls from within, and the door swings open. It's the woman from my last visit.

"I'm Jilly Truitt. I was here a while back. I'd appreciate a few minutes with Mr. Jones."

"Mr. Jones is not seeing visitors."

From deep within, I hear a growl. "Who is it?" And then, "Tell her to go away."

"Mr. Jones is unwell," the woman whispers.

"I won't be long," I say in a voice loud enough to penetrate the inner sanctum, and stride past her. The lounge where we spoke on my last visit is empty. I turn down a hall, bedrooms on either side. I halt at the open door at the end of the corridor.

Trist is lying on a couch. Beyond a partial wall, I see tangled bedclothes. He eyes me as he flicks the TV sound off. "No," he moans. "Not today. Had a bad night."

"Yeah, I can see that."

Trist's face is grey. Dark circles rim his eyes. He glances at the lit spliff in his right hand.

"What's going on, Trist?"

"Nightmares, no sleep. At three a.m., I took a pill. I want to sleep until this nightmare ends. But I can't."

"I'm so sorry," I say. "Forgive my intrusion. Now that I'm here, can I have a few minutes?" I soften my voice. "It's about Tess."

He stubs his reefer into an ashtray on the glass table at his side. "I didn't used to do this stuff. Now I do it too much."

His voice today sounds deeper than I remember. But he's a master of vocal gymnastics. Could the deep voice threatening Kate on the phone be his?

"I want all this over," he is saying. "I used to think Kate had nothing to do with Tess's disappearance, but now I'm not so sure. A lawyer for the Crown came to see me a while back." He looks up bleakly. "Jilly, they have an airtight case. Tess is gone, and Kate's going to prison. Kate needs to plead guilty and end this whole miserable saga, let us all get on with our grieving. But you defence lawyers are dragging it out." His voice grows rough. "It's cruel and inhumane."

I feel my back go up. Maybe Trist has been feeding on the social media posts that want Kate locked up pronto without a trial. I hear it all the time: finish this, plead your client guilty. End the misery for everyone and save the taxpayers money while you're at it. "Kate says she's not guilty. She's entitled to a trial before her peers. And I intend to give it to her. Contrary to what you believe, the Crown's case is weak. The Crown cannot even prove the first element of homicide—that Tess is dead. So don't lecture me about throwing in the towel, Trist. We are going on."

He stares at me and gives a bitter laugh. "You're not a bad person, Jilly Truitt. But you think you can change reality. Deluded." He reaches for the spliff and lights it again. "What is it you want, then? I'll tell you if I can. Then you can go and leave me in peace." He takes a deep drag; the acrid smoke curls upward.

"We've found a portrait of Tess," I say. "A photo taken by Dante Bocci."

"Is that the guy who identified Kate and Tess in the boat?"

I bristle at the *identified*, but I know it's not the time to quibble. "Yes, the very same."

"So maybe he took a shot of Tess at the same time as the other one."

"No, this photo is different. It's a posed studio photo, a portrait."

Trist stares. I'm onto something, my gut tells me. Dante comes to photograph Trist, notices Tess, becomes obsessed.

"We need to know when Mr. Bocci took the photo—before Tess was abducted or after. Can you help me, Trist?"

Trist looks out the window at drifting snowflakes. "Maybe. A lot of people photograph me. Part of the business. I can't recall them all. But it's possible this Bocci guy was one of them. The name seems familiar, but maybe I remember it because he was there that day on the island and the police mentioned him." He rolls his eyes to the ceiling. "Yeah, Bocci. It rings a bell."

"When he came to photograph you?"

"If he came to photograph me."

"Yes. If this Bocci came to photograph you, is it possible he would have seen Tess?"

"I guess he could have. I mean, people are coming and going. They tell me where to sit and I sit, where to stand and I stand, how to pose and I pose. Sometimes they wait because I'm busy. I suppose if Bocci was one of them, he could have run into Tess while he was waiting. She would have been with Selma. Yeah, Selma. You'd have to ask Selma."

"By the way, have you seen Selma since Tess disappeared?"

He shakes his head. "I told you last time—"

"Do you have a copy of the photo Mr. Bocci took of you?"

"The photo it's *possible* he took of me?"

"I stand corrected."

Trist sits up straight. Suddenly he is angry. "Look, you're telling me some photographer came here and took a picture of my daughter without my permission and that he was on the island the day Tess disappeared? The one who took the photo of Kate and Tess in the boat. And now he's showing that portrait? That pisses me off. I can't give you names, but the guy who handles my publicity would know. Tell Tony to find the bugger and get the photo back. Tell Tony to sue him."

I stare at Trist. A pedophile stealing his daughter isn't enough to make him angry. But a photographer showing her portrait without his permission sends him off the wall?

Trist's anger resolves into pain. "Would you please leave now?" he moans. "I have a headache." He shakes his mane as if to dislodge his suffering. "So much *stuff*. I try to get away from it, but I can't. I cancelled the house deal in Vegas, but they keep badgering me about the gig. I can't do a gig now, maybe ever." He balls his fists and leans toward me. "I want to stop the world and get off," he hisses.

He looks up at the TV, the screen now filled with a huge muted Santa. "Christmas is the worst," he whispers, tears welling. "Tess loved Christmas."

I bend down, touch his shoulder. "I need your man's name and number."

"Winnifred," he yells. The woman appears. "Give Ms. Truitt Tony's contacts." A bitter laugh. "Ms. Truitt thinks she can change the world. Let's not stand in her way." He halts. "Oh yeah, and get that photo back. The asshole . . ."

Five minutes later, I'm wheeling across the bridge, Tony Kinsella's card tucked in my pocket. The radio blares a Noel carol, "Merry Christmas." Merry Christmas, indeed.

CHAPTER 52

JANUARY 1, AND I'M IN the library watching the year-end news round-up.

My Christmas vacation has come and gone. An idyllic week in the chalet with my foster family—Martha, Brock, stepbrothers, spouses, grandchildren, and pets. Long evenings before the fire. Good food, good laughs. Even a day on the slopes. Skiing has never been my thing, but Martha, desirous of an afternoon alone with Claire, shooed me out. For hours at a stretch, I did not think of Kate and her missing daughter. I tried to repress my awareness of the unmarked police car around the corner under the pines, but no one else seemed to notice.

Now, with the holiday over and the new year upon us, I sit in my chair before the TV and contemplate what lies ahead. Dank rain has replaced crisp snow, and Mike's old house exudes a chill, which I have laid a fire to fend off. Edith, on the sofa, watches

Claire navigate the room on two feet with hands braced against the furniture. She falls, picks herself up with Edith's help. I see determination in the set of her tiny chin. She looks at me and gives a triumphant shout.

"Claire will be walking soon," Edith pronounces.

"Not quite," I say, but I smile.

"The holiday spirit is making you mushy," Jeff told me as I wished him well the last day at the office, bouncing Claire on my hip. "It's just business as usual."

"Wait till you have a little one," I say. "It changes your perspective. A bit of mushy is good."

I look back at my empty life after Mike passed, the difficult time after Claire was born, when all I had was the hope my "maternal instinct"—if I indeed possessed it—would carry me through to a better place. And now it is happening. My life is full. Claire, Edith, my work. My heart breaks for Kate and Trist; this will be a difficult holiday for them without their little one. I imagine Tess's face lit up by Christmas tree lights.

Before hitting Highway 1 and the route to Whistler, I detoured to Kate's house on impulse. Standing on the stoop with Claire in my arms, I rang the bell, no answer. Then, at last, the door creaked open, and Kate's wan face appeared. Her eyes opened wide with wonder as she took in Claire's presence, her pink cheeks, rosebud mouth open in a toothless grin, and wispy dark hair. Kate's thin hand reached tentatively to touch Claire's cheek.

"Your Claire is beautiful," she whispered, and let me in.

We sat in her living room—modern white walls, a lot of glass. A few artfully chosen landscapes.

I told her about Dante. "I found a portrait of Tess," I say. I pulled out my phone, blew up the photo I took of the portrait. Kate's breath caught, the beginning of a sob.

"He went to the house to photograph Trist. It's possible he met Tess and photographed her before the day on Bowen Island." I paused. "Or maybe after. We're looking into it."

Kate's lips parted. "Do you think—"

"I don't know what to think, Kate, but we're working on it."

Her fists balled, tears filled her eyes. "Don't tell me any more about the case, Jilly. It makes no sense, and when I try, I drive myself crazy. This terrible Dante monster—" She broke off. "The only thing I know is what I believe. Tess is alive."

"Like I say, we're still at it. We can't give up."

Kate made no response. Her eyes moved to Claire, sleeping in my tummy pouch on my knee. "Can I hold her?" she whispered.

I froze in terror. The allegations in Selma's affidavit flooded my mind. *Kate is dangerous. Kate cannot be trusted with a child.* I looked at Kate and saw the yearning in her eyes. I told myself my fear was ridiculous.

I unstrapped the pouch and passed my precious child to her.

Kate's long fingers touched Claire's face, then bent to kiss her cheek. "Here," she whispered, and handed her back. I breathed deeply and pressed her to me.

The television blares on. I am weary of the old year's woeful news. Disease, war, dictators, criminals, floods, and fires. I curl up and open Kate's file.

The newscaster says a name that breaks through my concentration: Tess. I slam my computer lid and look up.

"In late September, Tess Sinclair-Jones, five-year-old daughter of pop singer Trist, was abducted from a Bowen Island home where the family was vacationing," the announcer intones. "An extensive search of the island and Lower Mainland revealed no trace of the missing girl. Her mother, Kate Sinclair-Jones, has been charged with her murder, but some retain hope that Tess is still alive. Tonight, we talk to the little girl's nanny, Selma Beams."

A young woman's face shines out at me. At last, I meet Selma.

I don't know what Selma looks like at home on the farm, but tonight she looks good. Her dark hair is cut in a stylish bob. Her pale skin glows through a thin layer of makeup, emphasizing her dark eyes. She is wearing a short-sleeved tee over dark slacks. I try to make out the tattoo on her neck but fail.

I hold my breath as I wait to hear what Selma has to say.

The announcer goes on. "Selma, you were little Tess's nanny for over four years. How are you dealing with her disappearance?"

Selma bows her head, raises it again. "It's been difficult. You see, I loved Tess," she says. "People think nannies do their job like robots, that they're machines who wipe noses and feed formula and change nappies. But it's not like that at all. We nannies come to love our babies. Sometimes more than the parents."

Selma has thrown the bait; the interviewer, a young woman in a tight dress and high heels, takes it. "So you felt Tess's parents didn't care for her as parents should?"

Selma halts, considering her words. Her lips purse. "I'm sure they loved Tess." I cringe at the implication. "But Trist is on tour a lot. He's in the public eye."

"What about Tess's mother, Kate Sinclair-Jones, who is now charged with her murder?" the host asks.

Selma hesitates, looks down as if she wants to avoid the question. "I shouldn't say."

"But you signed an affidavit supporting Trist's custody application, in which you suggested Kate wasn't an adequate mother," the host persists.

"I did," Selma says, looking straight at the camera. Her angry eyes say she meant it.

"And after she lost custody, you would take Tess to her mother's house for her weekend access?"

"Yeah, before the courts took that away." Selma pauses. "To be frank, I dreaded the weekends. I hated to say goodbye to Tess. I hated to leave her in that woman's care."

"And why was that?"

Selma's lips purse. "Ms. Sinclair-Jones was unwell after the separation. Unstable."

The host's voice softens. "You say you were worried about leaving Tess with Kate when you took her to her mother's for the weekends?"

"Yes."

"Did you share your concern with Trist?"

"I did." Selma's voice thickens.

"And what happened then?"

"Trist went back to court and asked that Ms. Sinclair-Jones's access to Tess be cancelled. The judge compromised. He didn't cancel Ms. Sinclair-Jones's access entirely. But he cut it back to supervised visits." She pauses. "I hated taking Tess to those supervised visits. She would cry when I dropped her off, but at least I knew she would be safe."

"You weren't with the family on Bowen Island the day Tess disappeared, were you?"

Selma shakes her head. "I wish I had been. Tess would never have been taken."

The host is wrapping up. "Now that Tess is gone, what are your days like, Selma?"

Selma sucks in her breath. "Empty. Horrible. The light has

gone from my life. You can't imagine what it's like to lose a pure, sweet, angelic child. I'm drowning in a sea of misery."

A pain stabs my chest. If I lost Claire, I would not survive. Or if I somehow did, I, too, would be wallowing in an endless sea of misery.

"Tell me, Selma, do you believe Tess is alive?"

Selma hesitates, and her eyes fill with tears. "I would like to think so, but—" She breaks down, unable to speak.

"Thank you, Selma. I'm sure our viewers appreciate your candour. And thanks for what you tried to do for little Tess."

I push the mute button. This is terrible. The host did not ask whether Selma thinks Kate killed Tess, but she didn't need to. The picture Selma has painted leaves no other inference.

Selma offers a tearful nod, and the commercials come on.

Why is Selma doing this? After months of silence, why has she suddenly taken to the air waves? Maybe with the police announcement of the discovery of the other shoe, she fears Kate is going to get off after all? So she's decided to step in to ensure Kate's conviction, like she stepped in to challenge Kate's custody?

I flick the TV off, reach for my cellphone, and dial Cy.

CHAPTER 53

Cy PICKS UP RIGHT AWAY.

"What are you doing, Cy?"

"Watching TV, Jilly."

"Global local, by any chance?"

"Yeah."

"Then you know you've blown any chance of getting Kate an unbiased jury," I say. *I will not raise my voice.*

"Selma said nothing that we didn't all know. It's in the affidavit she filed to support the application to end Kate's visitation rights."

"But nobody knew about that, Cy. Nobody goes digging in old court archives. Now the false supposition Kate was erratic and a danger to Tess has been broadcast across the province. With no one to contradict what she's saying or cross-examine her on why she's saying it."

"Look, I had no idea Ms. Beams was going to do this."

"She's on your witness list, no? And you just happened to tune in?"

"Yeah, like you did. I was flipping channels and there she was. I am as astounded as you are. But look, you're over-dramatizing this. This little show won't prevent you from getting an impartial jury. And if you're worried about the jury, you can always go for a judge alone."

"Yeah, sure." *Just what you'd love.* My *strength* is with juries. Cajoling them, wooing them, pulling them to my side with a last-minute surprise if I can conjure one up. I know Cy knows that.

I start to hang up, but Cy's voice brings the phone back to my ear. "You of all people should know, Jilly, that I have no control over what Ms. Beams or anyone else says. The justice system, like other systems, is reeling under the impact of the digital revolution. We can't control what people say online, like we can't manage what they say to the media. The old days when you could get a jury that hasn't heard biased views about a case are gone. Maybe the jury trial, too. You can rail about Ms. Beams's interview, but it's the new norm."

"The demise of the jury trial," I say. "Is anyone mourning it but defence lawyers?"

Cy doesn't answer.

"That's what I thought. Rein in your witnesses, Cy," I say, and hang up.

Somewhere in the middle of my call to Cy, Edith cradled Claire to her breast and left the room. I take a deep breath, count to ten, and do a few yoga stretches on the carpet.

Jury trials are gone. Oh, we'll still carry on like before, but if Cy is right, the juror with an open mind is a relic. Just as I'm getting back to my job, I find I've been displaced by the digital revolution. I am out of touch; I've been left behind. The world is spinning too fast. Five years back is ancient history, five years ahead terra incognita. And the world my daughter will inhabit? Beyond contemplation. I do another back stretch and let my breath out. *Find your inner calm, Jilly.*

Back in my chair, I ponder Selma and what makes her tick.

CHAPTER 54

I AM BACK IN THE OFFICE on the Tuesday after New Year's.

Jeff is in Whistler, having vowed this is the year he perfects his skiing technique. Alicia and Shanni, who are getting along famously, are off for two weeks on Maui. Debbie is nowhere to be found. The note she pasted on my desk informs me she is AWOL with someone she met at a New Year's party. Let's hope a crime wave doesn't wash over the city in the next three days, with only me to beat miscreants from our doors.

I wonder how Claire is liking daycare after a long break and think of Kate. For some reason, Tess's portrait floats through my mind. I finger my jacket pocket, find the card Winnifred gave me when I visited Trist before Christmas. Now is as good a time as any.

I pick up my phone and ring Kinsella and Associates. I tell the young man who answers I would like to speak to Mr. Kinsella.

"Mr. Kinsella is unavailable. May I take your name and number?"

"My name is Jilly Truitt—T-R-U-I-T-T. Trist Jones has referred me to Mr. Kinsella regarding a matter he's concerned about." A stretch to say Trist is concerned, but he should be. So I do what I need to do.

"Just a moment, Ms. Truitt. I may be able to find him." I hear the muffled sound when a hand covers the audio. "You're in luck," the voice says. "Mr. Kinsella will be a moment."

What does a singer's publicity agent do? I wonder while I wait. In Mr. Kinsella's case, it involved firing Trist's nanny and booking photo shoots. Trist is not into the details; Tony Kinsella is. Maybe when Trist wakes up from his grief, he'll find all his money is gone, like Leonard Cohen.

There's only one word for the voice that comes on the line— *mellifluous*. It waves and undulates and carries me along like a leaf on a stream. I could like this guy, I could even believe him, if I chose to.

"So nice to talk to you, Ms. Truitt. How do you know Trist?"

"Business," I say, as close to the truth as I care to get. "I've visited him a couple times recently."

"Terrible thing, Tess's disappearance."

"Yes. He's devastated. As anyone would be."

"It's the way it's dragging out. No closure, no end in sight. But what's done is done. Tess is gone, and Kate needs to plead guilty. Better for her, better for Trist." A pause.

My mind scrambles for an approach that won't have Tony hanging up within thirty seconds. "This is confidential, Mr. Kinsella. I'll get right to the point. A photograph of Tess has appeared that Trist has no recollection of. Not just any photo—it's a portrait: beautiful, evocative. Trist is upset it was taken and that it's out there without his knowledge or permission. He's trying to figure out who took it and where it came from. And he'd like to get it back. He doesn't like the idea of strangers owning a piece of Tess." Although when he had her, he didn't mind sharing her with the world.

"I understand how he might feel. How can I help?"

"We think the photographer might have been Dante Bocci. Trist remembers some photo shoots over the summer but can't remember the photographers' names. He thought you would know because you booked them. He gave me your number and said I should call you and ask if Dante Bocci had a photo session with him this summer."

"So that Trist can contact Mr. Bocci?" Tony's voice has gone flat, like this isn't sitting right with him. "Trist could have called me himself. I could have fixed this up for him."

"Yes. That's what he should have done. But he's not thinking straight."

"Tell me about it. He's booked for a gig in Vegas in April, but I'm worried he won't be in shape. This tragedy has been good for publicity—the fans are rabid to see him—but he's got to get to the place where he can deliver the goods."

I hear a phone ring in the background, a feminine voice, "Mr. Kinsella . . ."

"Just a minute," I hear him shout to the woman, before he brings the receiver back. "What the hell, here you go. Dante Bocci photographs faces, great at capturing attitude. I hired him to help with a new record cover for Trist in late August. Shot it at Trist's house. He produced some great shots, and I paid him. That's all I know."

"Thanks, Mr. Kinsella. This is helpful."

I lean back in my chair. Dante met Tess when he went to photograph Trist at the house a couple of months before Tess vanished. In my Dante-the-pedophile scenario, he fixated on her and decided to abduct her. But did he take the photo in Trist's house last August? Or after Tess disappeared? If Tess survived the abduction she might still be alive.

Which leaves one question: How do I find out when the portrait was taken? Trist's words come back to me. *Selma would know, Selma was always with Tess.* Richard talked to Selma and got zilch. Maybe I can do better.

CHAPTER 55

I PULL UP RICHARD'S FILE ON Selma Beams, check out her address. File and computer stowed in my bag, I tell Debbie, who showed up this morning looking the worse for wear, to take the rest of the day off.

I've profited from three days of uninterrupted solitude to go through Cy's disclosure. I may not have learned much new, but I know the file, as lawyers say. If an issue arises, I know every document bearing on it. I can pull it off the electronic file and produce it to the witness. *You said what? Let me show you this document in which you assert the contrary.* Every barrister's dream moment.

But today is Friday, and I'm weary of staring at my computer screen. Outside in the park, frost coats the grass, and the January sun is shining. I decide to pay Selma Beams a visit.

If Jeff were here, he'd be asking the question that matters: *What do you hope to accomplish by calling on Selma Beams?* And I would answer: *I don't have a clue.* And then I would think again and say, *I want to know what she is hiding.* Because the facts I know—excellent nanny who loved Tess and is grieving her like everybody else—don't sync with her actions.

She tells Richard she won't meet him, then agrees to have coffee with him. She says she will try to answer his questions, then sabotages his chance to ask them by launching into a vitriolic tirade and flouncing away after fifteen minutes. She avoids the press who are clamouring to interview her for three months, only to show up on New Year's Day, groomed, poised, and ready to tell all. She is the consummate childcare professional sworn to confidentiality, but she tells the world her former employer was an unfit mother. I can't make sense of Selma, and my instincts tell me I need to try. Maybe I'll get lucky, and she'll tell me whether Dante photographed Tess in August.

One thing I know: a direct approach won't work. If Selma wouldn't talk to Richard, she won't talk to me. I don't like it, it's not what lawyers should do, but I'll have to use a ruse if I'm going to get my foot in the door.

Google Maps takes me down Highway 1 and over the Fraser River's north arm to Central Surrey. Fastest growing suburb in the Lower Mainland, I read somewhere. Now I understand. Sleek new apartment buildings loom on every side, high-rises, mid-rises, and townhouses. And then, abruptly, I find myself in a neighbourhood of crumbling postwar bungalows.

I make sure no one is following me.

Selma's fifties bungalow is like its neighbours, except shabbier. Small windows flank a peeling door. I make my way up the steps and ring the bell. The door opens, and a face peers out. The face that dissed Kate on television on New Year's Day.

"May I come in?" I ask. "I saw your interview on television. It took some doing to track you down, but here we are. I'm so happy to meet you, Selma."

She regards me warily, half shuts the door. "Whatever you're selling, I'm not interested."

"Don't," I plead. "Let me at least tell you why I wanted to meet you, after I've come all this way. I'm a single mom with a little girl, eight months old. I'm looking for a nanny. I was so amazed by your interview on TV, the way you cared, your professionalism. I thought, if there's any chance in the world I could get this woman to nanny my little girl, I want to follow up."

Selma doesn't open the door, but she doesn't shut it either. The flattery has softened her a little.

"I'm not interested in a new job," she says. "I still believe Tess is alive." She corrects herself. "May be alive."

"I understand," I say. "But in case you are ever interested, I'd appreciate a chance to talk to you. My child is little, we'll be needing a nanny for a long time. Stability and continuity. So important, don't you think? Right now she's in daycare, and I'm managing with a friend's help, but it's difficult." I look her in the eye. "Frankly, I don't know where to turn. I don't want just anyone looking after my baby. I want someone who cares. Like you."

Selma relents, pulls the door open. "A minute, then."

I follow her into the living room. The sofa slumps, and the twin chairs flanking it are faded. Paper flowers sit next to a black Bible on the coffee table. No television, no art, no clutter. A large crucifix above the couch dominates the room. The floors gleam, and lemon polish hangs in the air.

Selma is *clean.*

Selma motions to the sofa and takes the nearest chair. She is wearing jeans and a loose long-sleeved shirt. A cross hangs at her neck, and I make out her tattoo above the worn collar. A cross set against a rising, multi-rayed sun. Richard said that before becoming a nanny, Selma was involved with some cult. The tattoo must be a remnant.

I look around the room. "Nice house."

"It belonged to my parents. They died in an accident in 2017, and I've been here ever since. Mostly weekends, when I'm working for a family. Now, with Tess gone, I'm here more."

"What made you decide to become a nanny?"

"I love children. I prayed to the Lord for guidance. He told me what to do."

I feign ignorance. "Was looking after Tess Jones your first job?"

"No, after I graduated from the course, I did a stint with a family, looking after their little boy. But they moved to California after a year or so, and I found myself looking for a new posting. The Jones job came up, and I wanted it. It was my dream to look after that little girl." Her gaze shifts to the middle distance. "I could feel the Lord's hand guiding me. I saw Tess's picture in a magazine, and I knew what I had to do. I introduced myself to Ms. Sinclair-Jones, and she hired me. It was the Lord's will, what He meant for me."

"I got the impression from the TV interview that you had concerns about the parents, especially Ms. Sinclair-Jones."

Selma bristles. "What has that got to do with you wanting to hire me? I don't discuss my clients."

"Oh, sorry, you seemed to imply—"

"I said what everyone knows. Ms. Sinclair-Jones was not well. There were troubles with her marriage, her husband gone so much.

She became more distant and distracted, so I took over with Tess. Frankly, I thought it best for the child. At one point, the doctors diagnosed Ms. Sinclair-Jones with clinical depression."

She stops, covers her mouth with her hands. "Keep that to yourself, it's confidential."

I think about how it must have been for Kate—her marriage failing, her connection with Tess diminishing. The twin roles she had built her life around were vanishing beneath her feet, and she had nowhere to go but inside herself. I had had my own struggles with depression after Mike died and Claire was born, when the nannies shut me out of her life. I think about Kate, and I understand.

"How did Tess react to her mother's gradual withdrawal?"

Selma looks at me suspiciously. "Does it matter? I thought you were interested in me, not Tess."

"Well, how you felt about the situation that was developing with Tess and her mother, that tells me a lot about you. I promise, it's between you and me, and if you'd rather not—"

Selma considers. She is torn. She is not supposed to talk about what happened in her employers' homes, all the training says so. On the other hand, she is lonely. She needs to talk. Correction, she needs to talk about the little girl she loved.

"I think it confused her," she says at last. "At that age, children think the world revolves around them, so Tess worried she'd made her mommy unhappy. She continued to love her mother—I made sure Tess spent time with her mother every day—but I became her *real* mother for practical purposes. I imposed discipline. Kate—pardon me, Ms. Sinclair-Jones—was incapable. I established the daily routines. I bathed Tess and dressed her and took her to the park and later to playschool." She pauses. "In the last years, after the courts cancelled Kate's custody, I did everything for Tess."

349

I look up. "Thank God you were there."

"Yes, I thank God I was there."

I decide to bring the conversation back to my need for a nanny. "I live a pretty straightforward life," I say. "But I sense I may not be as structured as you were with Tess. Can I ask you this: Were there incidents when your childrearing views conflicted with Trist's or Kate's, and if so, how did you handle that?"

"Oh, many, just between us. Trist used to use marijuana occasionally, and he and his wife drank sometimes. I explained they shouldn't do this around Tess. And there were other issues. Trist and his agent used to take Tess out for what I thought were exploitive purposes, the press fawning and the cameras clicking—I didn't think it was good for Tess. Kate agreed with me. She valued Tess's privacy. But Kate was becoming careless. The doctors were giving her pills that seemed to space her out. I could rhyme off incidents where she left Tess on her own, took her someplace not dressed properly, or interfered with my discipline, but let's just say I started to fear for Tess's welfare. When Kate moved out, my concern grew. Kate and Trist had agreed on joint custody, which meant when Kate had her at her house, it was the two of them alone. I observed alarming lapses in judgment, and I became frantic with worry every time I dropped her off. I had no choice but to tell Trist he must apply for sole custody.

"But even when he got that, the judge let Kate have Tess on weekends. One Monday morning, I came to get her and Kate didn't answer the door. Thank God I found a key in the planter and got in. Tess was on the kitchen counter—she'd managed to get up by using a chair—but couldn't come down." Selma shudders. "Anything could have happened. I got her down and calmed her, then went looking for Kate. I found her upstairs, passed out—" Selma breaks off, reliving the moment. "Tess could have been hurt. We had no choice but to take Kate's weekend access away." She swallows. "Thank goodness the judge agreed, or I don't know what would have happened to Tess."

I look at her. "But something *did* happen to Tess."

Selma gives me a side look. *Be careful*, I remind myself.

"Yes, that's the irony. Something happened. Kate found a way," she whispers.

"It must have been hard for you," I say.

"Yes, but I'm comforted knowing I acted correctly. Nannies sometimes must make hard decisions. They teach you that in school. You can't impose your own values on the parents. You can't criticize. But at the same time, when parental conduct is harming the child, you can't stand by and let it continue." Her voice hardens. "I did what I had to do."

"Did you think about calling the Child Welfare authorities for advice or help?"

Her lips turn down. "I handled it on my own by talking to Trist. I didn't need to bring them in."

Didn't want *to bring them in?* I wonder.

Selma's body has tensed. Her fists are clenched in her lap. She's having doubts. She's going to end this conversation. I must tread carefully.

"I can't help but asking, Selma. Don't answer if you don't want to—it's not relevant to your competence—but was there anything you noticed, anything that happened in the months leading up to Tess's disappearance that might give a clue as to what happened to her?"

Selma's eyes go wide. "No. As you know, I wasn't there when

it happened. I had taken a week off to deal with family issues. My grandfather wasn't well."

"I mean before that week. Say, in the month or so before Tess disappeared?"

Selma's hands unclench and her shoulders go back. Her eyes blaze with sudden anger. "Why are you asking me these questions?" She leans forward. "Who are you?"

She has me cornered; lawyers aren't allowed to misrepresent who they are.

"I'll be frank, Ms. Beams. I *am* interested in nannies—I've had a few. But I am also a lawyer. I'm representing Kate Sinclair-Jones. The truth is, we want to find Tess, or failing that, find out what happened. Ms. Sinclair-Jones believes Tess is still alive. The police say she drowned but haven't explained how. If there is any chance Tess is alive—which we believe there is—we need to find her. I came to see you because you might be able to help."

I push on. "A photographer named Dante Bocci took a photo of Tess. We need to pin down when. Do you recall Mr. Bocci coming to photograph Trist and photographing Tess while he was there?"

Selma is standing, eyes flashing, her voice rising. "Get out of my house."

I gather my coat and pick up my bag and make for the door. As I reach for the knob, I sense her presence and look up. She has followed me, and now she is leaning into me, so close I can feel her breath. I step back, shocked at her proximity. "Give your client this message," she hisses. "She needs to plead guilty now and end this agony for everyone." Selma's angry eyes drill the words home, the same words the man used in his threatening phone calls.

As she reaches behind me to open the door, my eye catches a flash of light on glass over a small hall table. A picture. It's black and white, and the glare on the glass occludes the image, but I catch a halo of hair. At the bottom, on the mat, I make out three numbers: 777.

I turn and run down the steps, the slam of Selma's door echoing in my ears.

CHAPTER 56

IT'S MID-JANUARY, AND I'M STALLED.

I have been helping Jeff with his factum on his biker appeal, and I've prepped for an upcoming presentation at a bar meeting. Much to my surprise, I have been asked to be on a panel on work-life balance. Maybe my reputation is improving, maybe I'm the only mother crazy enough to practice criminal law with an infant at home.

Edith is in Hawaii for three weeks with a friend, and I'm struggling with a severe case of single-parent syndrome. I used to think the office was hectic; now I regard it as an oasis from an unending routine of shopping, bathing, diapering, feeding, and sharing "quality time" with my eight-month-old daughter, who is crawling the floors and climbing the furniture. My den is a mess, my kitchen a horror. This morning, as I breezed out the door with Claire on my hip, Dennis, the guy who comes to bring order from chaos twice a week, rang to say he couldn't make it. "No," I cried.

Sensing my desperation, my cleaning man sought to calm me. "Tomorrow for sure. Promise, Jilly."

I lean back in my chair, sip my latte. My morning mission is to draw up a list of odds and ends on the file that occupies all my idle moments: *The Crown v. Kate Sinclair-Jones*. The quiet is preternatural. I know it can't last.

Jeff enters and slaps the brief I edited for him last week on my desk. "Thanks. Some useful amendments." He looks at the blank notepad in front of me. "What are you working on?"

I make a face and shake my head. I know what he's thinking: I don't have enough to do; I could use another file.

"I have a new rule—don't put anything down on paper unless you're sure it's useful."

"Hah! Hence the pristine pad. You're thinking about Kate's case."

"I am. However, now that you're here, let me run a few probably non-useful thoughts by you."

He slumps into the chair opposite me, rolls his eyes to the ceiling. "Sure, I've got nothing but time. Give me what you got." I've been looking for signs he's willing to move from advisor to partner on Kate's case since he told me he had my back. His frown tells me this is not the day.

"Number one," I say, "get Richard to follow up on Lena in Vegas. What's she been doing since his last visit? Maybe check out Rex again, too, you never know."

"Not likely useful, but spend our money on it anyway."

I wince at the reminder that we are footing most of the bills on this case. "I'll cover it."

"Like hell you will."

I drop my pen. This is unexpected.

Jeff shrugs. "Number two?"

"Find matches for the hair on the boat they say came from Tess and the partial fingerprint."

Jeff cocks his head. "Marginally useful, perhaps, if you could do it. Which you probably can't."

"Number three," I say, "follow up on the adoption, find Tess's natural parents."

"I thought we decided we weren't going down that road? Tess's natural parents didn't want her, didn't want to ever see her again. That's why they agreed to a closed adoption."

"True, but it's a loose end, and it's been niggling at me. What if they changed their minds?"

"Niggling but useless. What's more, impossible. A closed adoption is a closed adoption. The original birth record is destroyed. The adopting parents aren't given any information about the natural parents and vice versa. I know this, Jilly, because I looked into it."

Ah. He and Jessica have been exploring all options. "Then you know that in 1995, British Columbia became the first province in Canada to allow an adopted person to find her natural parents."

Jeff guffaws. "Nice try. An adopted person over the age of nineteen? That leaves Tess out. Even overlooking the minor problem of we can't find her."

"I suppose we could ask Richard to snoop around. Tess is no ordinary child—one parent White, one parent Black. That narrows down the adoptions in the year she was born."

"Jilly, are you serious? How many babies are born in BC each year?"

"In the year Tess was born? About forty thousand."

"And they don't list them by race! Anyway, her birth certificate was destroyed." He looks me in the eye. "No, Jilly. Spend not a penny on this wild goose chase."

I sigh. "I thought you might say that."

"While we're talking about what's useless, how did your interview with Selma go?"

"She answered my questions when she thought I was in the market for a nanny, but when I told her I was Kate's lawyer, she got mad and kicked me out. She's carrying stress; I can't figure out why. Too much for simple grieving. Perhaps she blames herself for Tess's disappearance. If she had been on the island, Tess would never have gone missing." I pause. "It's clear she loved Tess, perhaps too much."

"What do you mean?"

"She didn't have the professional distance you'd expect in a trained nanny. She took over all responsibility. Made all the decisions and figuratively stepped into Kate's shoes." I pause. "Like she was the mom."

"That's the mother in you talking, Jilly. Well-known fact: mothers get jealous of possessive nannies. With Kate unwell and Trist away most of the time, Selma had no choice but to step in."

"This is different, Jeff. Selma talked like she was Tess's mom, like it was fact. Oh, yes. I forgot to mention. She had Dante's photo of Tess over a table in her front hall. She must have asked him to send her a copy when he took the photo? I guess that means he took it in August. Still, it's strange. Even Trist doesn't have one."

Jeff shakes his head. "That does seem a bit obsessive. Let's keep an eye on Selma."

CHAPTER 57

"**I**'VE GOT SOMETHING," DAMON WHISPERS.

We are warming ourselves with lattes in the coffee shop across the street from my office as late January rain pummels the windows. Before we settled in, Damon gave the place a good eye-sweep. Deeming it suitable, he pointed to the farthest booth. His side gig with the police is making him paranoid. Or maybe he knows things I don't. He looks around again. We keep our voices low.

He pulls an iPad from his satchel, types in a command, and turns it to face me.

I take a deep breath.

A mall somewhere, a 7-Eleven. In front of the store, an apron of grey concrete, covered by a skiff of snow. The doors open. A man emerges. I put him in his sixties. I can't see the lines on his face, but the camera catches a shock of white hair and a worn dark coat. The man looks anxiously about him, then looks down. Down at the child whose hand he is gripping. My breath catches. A child who could be Tess.

Her hair is shorter than in the photos I have seen, but the rest is the same. Tight golden-brown curls. Tess's face, maybe Tess's eyes if I could see them. Wearing a puffy pink coat against the cold. The child pulls her hand from the man's, opens her mouth in what must be a cry, and starts to run. The man shouts something and runs after her. My breath sucks in; I know a child's cry of fear when I see it. They disappear off the edge of the screen.

My heart lurches. A man has Tess, a pedophile has Tess.

"Is there more?"

"No, they ran out of range of the camera."

"It could be Tess," I whisper. "Which would mean she's alive."

"Could be," says Damon, but there's doubt in his voice.

"But the little girl was trying to run away."

"Maybe, or maybe it was just a game they were playing."

"She looked scared," I say. "Like she was trying to run away."

Damon shrugs again. "Maybe, maybe not. Maybe you're reading that into it because you want to."

I fight the fear that is rising in my throat. Damon is right. We mustn't jump to conclusions. But one thing is clear: we need to follow up.

"Where was this taken, Damon?"

"A mall in southeast Surrey, on Highway 10."

"What's around there?"

"Just farms and hills. Quite desolate."

"So, we can assume the man and child are located somewhere nearby?"

Damon shakes his head. "More likely travelling through."

My heart sinks. "When was the footage taken?"

"November 29. First snow of the winter that day."

"Two months after Tess disappeared."

"Almost to the day."

"Which would mean that the man, whoever he is, didn't take her out of the country." I breathe deeply.

"Not as of November 29. And assuming it's Tess, a big if. But we're in late January now. A lot of things may have happened since then."

My heart is still riding low in the pit of my stomach. If this is Tess, it is terrible. If it's some other little girl, it could be terrible, too. The police need to investigate.

"Thanks, Damon, great work."

"Sure." Then he turns and does something he's never done before—he places his hands on my shoulders and looks me in the eye. "You're the adult in the room, I'm the kid—that's how it will always be with us. But Jilly, I have to say this. Grandfathers take their grandkids out for drives all the time, and sometimes the kids run away from them. Ninety-nine per cent probability, that's all this is."

I push his arms away. "I'm banking on the one per cent. I'm going to Kan."

He shrugs and turns away. "Your call, Jilly."

We part on the street. "Keep looking," I say to his departing back.

I pull my coat around me and head for the office, pondering how I will tell Kate the news without breaking her heart again.

CHAPTER 58

I SPEND THE DAY AFTER DAMON'S revelation dealing with the fallout.

First things first, I think. Despite Damon's caution, this could be Tess, and the police need to know. I phone Kan.

"We have evidence that Tess may be alive," I say.

Kan takes the news like I'm telling him spring is coming. He is unmoved and nonplussed. His equanimity galls; I bite my tongue to suppress a smart retort.

"A contact I have named Damon Cheskey has been working with the CCTV crews. It's all up-and-up, he's worked for the police before. Damon has found a CCTV picture of a little girl who looks like Tess. Taken in east Surrey on November 29. I think you should have a look at it."

Silence. "Lots of kids out there look like Tess. And November 29 is a long time ago. But send it along."

My voice goes cold. "I trust you will investigate this video, Detective. Immediately. When you see it, you will observe that the child appears to run away from the man. She yanks her hand from his and runs off." I hear the edge in my voice. "Detective, whoever the child was, the man may have been abusing her."

"You're a parent and I'm not. Nevertheless, allow me to point out that children pull their hands from their caregivers and bolt all the time. But don't fret—we'll look at the video and take appropriate action. I must warn you, though. It may not take us far. You know as well as I that the police can't barge into peoples' homes to see their kids without a warrant. To have a realistic chance of finding the child on camera, whoever she may be, we would need a lot more than a CCTV picture."

"Put your people on it, Detective. Last time I checked, this was still a missing child case. If this was just any child, I'd say it doesn't mean anything. But Tess was unique, not many kids like her out there."

"More than you realize, Ms. Truitt. But you never know. We don't want to overlook anything. Send Mr. Cheskey in to see me."

His casual nonchalance has set my blood boiling. Through gritted teeth, I manage a faint thank-you and hang up.

I tell myself that I shouldn't be upset, but I am. Damon tried to warn me that the CCTV sighting probably amounts to nothing, and that's exactly how Kan reacted. I take a few minutes to decide how to break this news to Kate, who ricochets between hope and despair. I am legally obliged to inform her of the CCTV photo, but I don't want to fuel false hope. And even if the child were Tess, what if her captor is a pedophile? I shudder. The mix may be more than Kate's fragile psyche can handle.

I take a walk around my desk to clear my head, stride past Debbie's station to the boardroom, and pour myself a coffee. Alicia strolls in. I'm finding her new look oddly attractive— black boots, black tights, oversize black jacket, sloppy but chic; big hoop earrings, and spiked hair sprayed with streaks of green. Three years ago, when we hired her, Alicia was prim and proper. Now she's found herself. Our clients, the streetwise ones, seem to like it.

Alicia looks at me and reads my frustration. "What's up, Jilly?"

I tell her about the CCTV footage Damon found and follow up with a five-minute tirade about Kan's response.

"He's not stupid, Jilly. And Damon's right, chances are this won't amount to anything. But it could, that's the point. Kan's investigation has been awful. But he cares about his reputation. He can't risk not looking into this in case something comes out later." She pours herself a coffee. "By the way, Richard wants to see you. Said he'd come by around four."

I finish my coffee, swallowing my frustration with Kan. Alicia is right. Kan will take at least a perfunctory look at Damon's video clip. I realize that despite my resolution to keep my professional distance, I've succumbed again to my need to find Tess alive. This is just one more factoid which may or may not be relevant.

Back at my desk, I take a deep breath. I pick up my phone and call Kate.

"We have CCTV video of a child who looks like Tess," I say. "A long time ago, November 29. The hair is shorter, and she's with an older man. The quality isn't great, so we can't say for sure. It's probably some other child."

Kate ignores my caution. "She's alive! How did she look? Was she well?" Her words tumble out in an excited rush, shutting down the rest of my carefully planned speech. If she heard the part about the man, it hasn't registered.

"She looked fine." I decide not to tell her that Tess cried and ran away from the man.

"Oh my God, I know it was Tess, I feel it. I've been telling everyone Tess is alive. They don't believe me, but now we know."

"We don't *know*, Kate. There are many children out there who look like the figure on the footage. But we're turning it over to Detective Kan, and he has promised to follow up. You should know, their chances of finding this child are not high."

"It's Tess. I feel it in my bones."

I don't argue. I feel it, too, the surge of certainty that somewhere out there, Tess is alive, waiting to be found. Although now the hope is darkened by fear of who may have her.

"Any more threats, Kate?" I ask, changing the subject. Kan's failing me on this front, too. His so-called investigation into the threats has gone nowhere.

"Yes. He called again." Her voice drops to a whisper. "I was expecting a call from Dad and was stupid enough to answer. When I heard his voice, I screamed and threw the phone across the room. I could hear his words *Plead guilty, plead guilty now* coming out from the pile of magazines where it landed." Her voice is suddenly clogged with tears.

"Steady, Kate. Hang in there," I say.

"I'm trying," she whispers. "But the trial is coming up, and I'm in such a state, I haven't slept properly for weeks."

She is at the breaking point. "Call your doctor, Kate. Tell him how you feel. He will give you something so you get a good night's sleep. We will get you through this."

"I'm not taking that medicine, not ever, now that I know Tess may be alive. Find Tess, Jilly," she says through her sobs. "That's the only thing that matters. We have to find her."

CHAPTER 59

MY DESK PHONE LIGHTS UP. "Richard is here."

"Bring him in."

Richard slides into the chair across from my desk. He's looking good in a dark jacket over a sweater and jeans, his travelling outfit.

"Just got back from Vegas," he says.

"That was fast."

"We need to be fast," he replies tersely. "In case you haven't noticed, the trial is coming up. I checked on Lena, but my main interest this time was Rex, Trist's Vegas agent. I told you he wasn't a person of interest. I was wrong."

I steeple my fingers. "Pray tell."

"On the surface, everything looks fine. A competent agent, on the up-and-up. He's done a great job building and maintaining Trist's career in Vegas. Has a few other good performers in his stable. Married for twenty years to a woman named Leonora Gem who helped him build up his business, but now he's divorced. He has a nice house in south Vegas. Full of photos of his grandchildren. No criminal record."

"So, what's his problem?"

"After talking to people who know him and foraging into unsavoury sites on the web, I discovered that Rex Wiseman rubs shoulders with shady characters. Three years back, he was charged with possession of child pornography. He was never convicted; the charges were dropped. In fact, they were removed from the public record so no one would ever know they had been laid."

"Let me guess. That was shortly before his marriage broke up."

"Correct. Old story. Wife is shocked and disbelieving. The relationship is over. A few months later, they quietly split."

A chill runs down my spine. "What does he look like, this Rex?"

"Caucasian, middle-aged, tire around his middle."

"A shock of white hair?"

"Yeah, now that you mention it. What's up, Jilly?"

"A CCTV camera shows a child who looks like Tess in the company of a man meeting that description in a Surrey mall on November 29."

"Interesting. But a lot of men meet that description."

I ignore his caution. "See if you can find out if Rex has an alibi for November 29. Now we know of two possible child pornographers who know and adore Tess. I think I'm going to be sick. What kind of world is this for a child to live in?"

"It's much more common than you think, Jilly. But don't get ahead of yourself. In Rex's case, there's nothing to suggest that he was more than a consumer of kiddie porn. Big stretch to abduct a child. And the police didn't pursue the case, so there may have been nothing there. Even though it wrecked his marriage."

I sigh. "Next steps on Rex?"

"I have a contact in the FBI. He's checking out whether they have anything on him. And I hired a DI in Vegas to check out where he was on September 25. If he was home in Vegas, that's probably the end of that lead."

I consider that. "Richard, wherever Rex was on the material dates, the fact he was into child porn may be useful at trial. I'll call you to testify as to what you found. It may be enough to raise reasonable doubt." I change tack. "What about Lena?"

"You remember I pretended I was an agent when I went to see her in the fall? So, I followed up in the same guise this time. She was still staying in the same heartbreak hotel. I told her the Paris gig didn't work out, but she just laughed. She's landed a job dancing in a review, some take on a Broadway show. *Hamilton*, I think." Richard grins.

It's late in an exhausting day, so I hurry Richard along. "Did you pick up anything interesting from her?"

"This time, even though I'm just a showbiz agent as far as she knows, I got her talking about the case. It was late, she was unwinding from the performance. It was like she needed to dump on somebody's shoulder and mine was convenient. She started talking about this trial up in Canada she's got to go to, and had I heard of Trist? Of course. How she'd got involved with him, loved him, was going to marry him, but the kid disappearing ruined it all."

"So, Cy's going to call her," I say. "Not surprised."

"She talked to a lawyer who said it would look bad if she refused to go. Then she moved on to the gig Trist has in Vegas after the trial. Trist has been talking about cancelling, and she's furious about that. So is Rex, by the way. With all the publicity about Tess disappearing, the fans are clamouring for Trist, but it looks like it's not going to happen. That was her big dream, that he would come to Vegas, and they would get together again. But it seems he's still too broken up to perform."

"What did Lena say about Tess?"

"Just that she was so sorry it happened. She mentioned the wine, said she should never have given it to him, that that's why he probably fell asleep on the beach. 'We're conspirators in guilt, Trist and me. It's killing us both, but it binds us together.'"

I arch my eyebrows. Richard's a good read of character, but I can't share his sympathy for the lovely Lena. She's a showgirl and a mistress of maneuvers; she knows how to get her man. Cross your beautiful gams, Lena, lean forward over your drink and shed a tear or two. Even the seasoned Richard will buy whatever you're selling.

"Big thoughts for a Vegas dancer," I say.

"Lena is a smart girl, don't sell her short," Richard snaps. "And she cares. I can see why Trist hooked up with her."

"You don't think she had anything to do with Tess's disappearance?"

"I'd bet my last dollar against it. Lena is up front, no side. 'I liked Tess,' she said, 'but Tess didn't like me. Would I hurt Tess, take her out? What a laugh. As if I ever could. No, my dream was intact. I didn't need Tess out of the way. I figured we'd get married, Trist and me, and eventually things with Tess would work out.' She wiped her eye. 'I never liked my mom much either.'"

I laugh. "She really was dumping on you. I can't believe she'd share her most intimate dreams with a booking agent. You sure she wasn't on to you?"

Richard blinks. "No, she's just lonely. And like I said, I was there."

I smile again, amused by Richard's wholehearted belief in Lena's goodness. "What's she going to do if Trist doesn't go to Vegas?"

Richard shrugs. "Nurse him through the trial—that's the real reason she's not fighting the subpoena—and get back together with him."

I shake my head. "And live happily ever after."

"No doubt." Richard smiles.

I stand up. "You may be right that Lena had nothing to do with taking Tess, Richard. But you should know, when she takes that witness stand, I'm going to cross-examine the hell out of her."

CHAPTER 60

ICHECK OUT TRIST ON TWITTER when I need a break from trial preparation.

Social media is abuzz about the cancellation of his Vegas gig. Half the views are negative—a real entertainer would go on with the show no matter what—the other half sympathetic—how could anyone who has just lost a child get up on stage to perform?

Our fingerprint expert came in with his second report yesterday. The small prints on the tiller could belong to any one of ten thousand people—good news for us—although Cy will argue they should go in to corroborate the hair. As for the thumbprint on the slat of the seat—no matches mean no inferences. I'm all for the right to privacy, but moments like this make me wish everyone's fingerprints were taken and stored when they first get their driver's licence.

Despite all our efforts, we still don't know who took Tess or whether she is alive or dead. Jeff tells me I've got to stop treating Kate's case like a detective novel and start thinking of it as a criminal trial. Bone up on the evidence. Bone up on the law. Let the jury decide and move on. Jeff is right. But it's easier said than done. Every time I focus on the case, the old man holding Tess's hand in the CCTV footage floods my mind. I need to find him. I need to find Tess.

Kan, true to form, has come up with nothing—or nothing he chooses to share with me. *Write him off*, I think bitterly. Over and over, I have badgered him to follow leads I've dug up; over and over he has done nothing. But I refuse to give up. The missing piece that will connect it all and make sense of what happened to Tess is out there. I need to find it.

I remember Dante mentioning his mother lived in his neighbourhood. Maybe she's connected to the man in the CCTV scan. I call Richard, ask him to investigate it. A long shot, but maybe we will get lucky. Maybe, maybe, maybe. I'm tired to death of maybes.

"By the way," Richard says, "I just got the report of the investigator I hired to check out the whereabouts of Rex the Agent on September 25 and November 29."

My heart picks up a beat. "And?"

"I'm afraid we're out of luck on the first date. I confirmed he was in Vegas at a meeting that day."

"He could have had Dante or someone else pick Tess up," I say. "What about November 29?"

"He *was* in the Vancouver area on that date. He flew up to see Trist on the twenty-eighth, returned on the thirtieth. We don't have details of his precise moves—just that he was staying with Trist, probably trying to buck him up and save the Vegas gig. Without talking to Trist, I can't go much further. I tried to reach him, but he won't return my calls."

I consider. "Let's wait. I'll try to get Rex's past in through cross-examination of Trist. Perhaps I can ask Trist about Rex being with him on the twenty-ninth, which connects to the CCTV sighting. The pieces are starting to come together, Richard."

Richard shakes his head like I'm crazy and waves goodbye. Recharged, I return to my trial prep. I have sections in my trial book for each witness, and I flip to the biggest section—Kate. Kate is doing her part, which at this point, weeks before the trial, is reduced to holding herself together. She is working with her doctors and manages a few hours of sleep from time to time. The plead-guilty-or-else calls have halted. Perhaps with the trial just weeks away, the caller has lost hope.

Oblivious to the police detail that follows her everywhere, Kate spends her days on the side roads off Highway 10, tooling through suburbs, haunting shops, sipping coffee she doesn't want in down-market dives. I pity the officers tasked with tracking her movements, but at least I don't have to worry whether Kate has done something drastic.

These days, Kate calls every evening. Cuddling Claire in one arm, I hold the phone in the other and listen to her daily report. Nothing to show for her day of driving. Not a sign. Gallingly, not even any policemen roaming the territory, except the team that stopped her in a mall to warn her against loitering. "But Tess is alive," Kate affirms. "I know Tess is alive. Tomorrow, I'll head south toward the border. You never know."

Hope, as they say, springs eternal.

My presentation to the bar on work-life balance is this Saturday. I put the final touches on my remarks.

My to-do lists checked off, I have one last crack at Cy to persuade him to call off the trial. "Another lunch," I say, "this time on me. Tomorrow."

Once again, we meet at Bacchus. I settle into my wingback chair and survey my one-time mentor and eternal adversary. His face is more drawn than I remember, and his jacket hangs loosely on his shrunken frame. His pallor frightens me.

Cy, who sees everything, acknowledges my unstated observations. "Yes, Jilly, I'm getting old."

I reach across the table to cover his hand. "You don't have to do this case, Cy."

He withdraws his hand. "Jilly, I will do this case."

"I don't have to disclose defence details, Cy, and I won't. But we have evidence that Tess did not die that day on the boat. We have facts that will blow Dante's identification out of the water and discredit him." I think of how Cy went out of his way to get me back to the law. I lower my voice to a whisper. "You don't want to go out this way, Cy. Drop the charges. It's not too late."

"Ha," he says harshly. "As always, you are wildly overconfident, my dear Jilly. I have everything I need. And I have Kate's hair in the boat. Try as you will, the hair cannot be explained away. Kate was there that day with Tess. Tess's clothing washed up on the beach. Tess died, and Kate must be brought to justice."

"Don't forget the other shoe, Cy."

"Any number of explanations for that. Anyway, the jury will have enough. Enough to put Ms. Sinclair-Jones behind bars for a long time." He leans forward. "Where she belongs. She was a terrible mother, Jilly, from the beginning to when she finally threw her baby over the side of that boat. She did drugs. She was spaced out half the time. If it hadn't been for the nanny, the child would have perished."

"What are you talking about, Cy? Have you been trolling through those gossip sites? That is not who Kate is." *Do not judge,* I want to say. There is another side to the story. A mother struggling with a failing marriage, a mother finding herself increasingly isolated and finally excluded and replaced. A mother succumbing to the mental illness that made all the losses feel plausible and deserved.

Cy's face has settled into deep lines. Anger? Old age and the unravelling of judgment? Or could it be that Cy harbours subconscious racist biases?

Cy leans forward, his great forehead close enough for me to see the anguish in his eyes. "A child is the most precious thing one can have in this life. That a parent would abuse that great gift is beyond my comprehension." I get it. Cy is remembering the baby boy he and Lois lost decades ago. His son was less than a year old when he died. "To see a woman like Kate do what she did to her child—" Cy breaks off, overcome. He leans back into his chair.

"I despise those who mistreat their children. The only tool I have is the law, and I will use it." He returns to me, his eyes burning into mine. "I will see Kate Sinclair-Jones behind bars if it's the last thing I do."

"Whoa, back, Cy. It's not your place to judge. Plus, you know the police botched this investigation from the beginning. They've only ever focused on Kate, and they've missed crucial evidence. Your case is not as strong as you think it is. Your personal feelings are clouding your judgment, my friend."

Cy shifts his torso. Sitting in one place is hard on his twisted spine. I expect him to counter with a robust defence of the police effort to find Tess, but he surprises me. "Thanks for the reminder, Jilly. I'm just a prosecutor. My job is to present the evidence the law has dug up and let the jury decide on guilt or innocence. And that's what I will do at the trial, whatever my personal feelings about your client. Just as you, my dear Jilly, will defend your client despite any feelings you may have. Your job is to find the soft underbelly of the Crown's case if you can and get your client acquitted. That's how the system operates. A funny way to find the truth, but it works." He pauses. His eyes are tired and his smile is wan. "Most of the time."

I think about the wrongful convictions I have witnessed, born of vengeance and nurtured by sloppy police work. "Yeah, Cy, most of the time."

We look at each other, pondering the mysteries of the criminal law. Cy breaks the silence.

"Do you remember when you started in criminal law, Jilly? A skinny kid who couldn't afford a proper gown? I could see you had suffered, too, and I mentored you. I taught you to be tough and wily, although you never learned that lesson as well as I would have liked. And when you were ready, I took you on in the trenches. We have fought many battles, Jilly. Tough battles. You thought I was your enemy, but you were wrong. I always was teaching you; I always had your back."

He drains the last of his scotch. "When you lost Mike, I cried for you. And when I learned you were pregnant, I grieved. I didn't want you to go through what I had gone through. And then, after Claire was born, I saw you foundering. You'd lost your way, Jilly. I had to get you back on track. When Tess disappeared, I saw the way. I pulled the strings and got you involved. And it's worked, Jilly. Look at you now."

"Come on, Cy," I say with a soft laugh. "I concede you got me started, mentored me, made me the lawyer I am. But you calling me in on this case just to help me out of a hole? I don't buy it, Cy, I know you too well."

James's approach heads off Cy's rejoinder, but he has the grace to offer me an acknowledging wink. "Your car is here, Mr. Kenge," he says, bending over our table.

Cy, lost in his musings, appears not to hear.

I cover his hand with mine. "Time to go, old friend, time to go."

CHAPTER 61

I'T'S THE LAST SATURDAY IN February. I should be behind my desk preparing for Kate's trial, which begins the week after next. Instead, I'm in a room of the downtown Hyatt expounding on work-life balance before fifty-three tired lawyers here to get credits for continuing legal education.

The organizers have structured the morning around themes. Work and relationships, work and health, work and culture. I'm work and children. Each panellist gives a short spiel, then takes questions. I listen intently to the presenters who precede me. Slick, confident, buoyed by quotations from books and lectures.

I am thoroughly shaken by the time my turn comes. I try to pull myself together as I walk to the podium.

"What I've heard has left me convinced that work is a toxic activity that should be avoided at all costs—it will destroy your relationship, your health, and confine you to a solitary bubble." I catch a titter of nervous laughs. "But I have a confession to make. Work has saved my life."

I look out over the audience. Some are smiling, a few are nodding. I think of what Cy said, and the notes on my iPad suddenly seem irrelevant; I decide to wing it. "I'm here to talk about work and children. I have a daughter—a wee one named Claire, who will soon be ten months of age. She is the centre of my life. She makes me a better person, and therefore, a better lawyer. When she was born, I considered not working, or not working until she was older. But now I know that while that is right for some parents, it would have been wrong for me. The truth is: the law is in me. The courts are part of me. I am less than I should be, than I want to be, when I deny the lawyer in me." I pause. "I love my daughter, but I also need my work. So, I balance, I organize, I prioritize. I sit at the computer at night with Claire in my arms. Claire is happy, and I am content. How will it work out? I can't say. But no one can ever know how it will work out. Parenting is an uncertain business. All we can do is our best."

I fold my iPad; I don't have any more to say. Then I think of all the ways Jeff has helped me, finding the right words to settle me, the right times to step in and take the pressure off.

"I have a good law partner, and good colleagues who believe in what we do. They tell me when I've invested too much time in my work and when I haven't invested enough, and they respect my need to be with Claire. We can't do everything in isolation; we have less control than we think we do. We need to reach out, ask for help when we need it, ask for perspective when we know we've lost it." I take a step back and invite questions.

A woman in the front row stands and waves urgently for the floor mike.

"You're defending Kate Sinclair-Jones, a woman who is accused of killing her baby. How can you defend such a woman?"

"Shame on you, Jilly Truitt," a man shouts from the back of the room.

I reel back, shocked. I've heard this before, but never from a group of professional lawyers.

The room is stirring with murmurs. Some people nod, others are looking at me expectantly. *What can you say to that, Ms. Truitt?*

I feel their outrage. I know all the standard answers, know defending Kate is right. But I fear nothing I say will convince these doubters.

"I am a lawyer, sworn to uphold the law and use the law to protect the rights of those who need legal help. One of those rights is the right to a defence when charged with a crime. I am providing Kate Sinclair-Jones with the defence to which the law entitles her. The jury, in due course, will judge her guilt or innocence. My duty is not to judge, but to provide a defence."

The woman who asked the question shakes her head, unconvinced. I could go on, talk about how the rule of law and the best traditions of the law require barristers to take on unpopular causes, but the moderator, sensing things are running off the rails, thanks the speakers and brings the session to a close.

I slip my iPad into my briefcase, leave the podium, and weave through the clusters of people preparing to go. A young man catches my eye and gives me a thumbs-up; the woman who questioned me stares after me, glowering. I feel utterly alone. Why did I ever agree to do this when I could be home with Claire, practising real work-life balance?

In the corridor, near the deserted registration table, I spy a tall, gangly figure in a rumpled black raincoat. He looks up and I recognize him.

"What are you doing here, Jeff?"

"Learning about work-life balance, what else?" He turns serious. "I told you that day we drove to Dante's, Jilly, I have your back. I suspected Elissa Moreau would hit you with the how-can-you-defend-a-criminal question. It's her latest campaign, and I wanted to be here for you."

I want to hug him, but people are watching, so I just put my hand on his arm and look up at him. His eyes are warm behind his round glasses, and he is smiling. "You did well, Jilly."

I start to remove my hand when he covers it with his. "One more thing, Jilly. I'm with you on this trial. At your side. All the way."

CHAPTER 62

IT'S TUESDAY, FEBRUARY 28, AND we are gathered in the boardroom for a final strategy session on *The Crown v. Kate Sinclair-Jones*, which is set to open March 6.

The last two weeks have been a blur of pre-trial activity—witness lists, pre-trial conferences, the business of cross-examination strategy and witness preparation. Not that we have many witnesses. Our case rests on Kate and the slender hope that the jury will believe her protestations of innocence. That and the suite of pedos haunting Tess's penumbra.

We have come to know our judge, Wilfred Tesik, through a series of pre-trial conferences. Tesik is a slender man with red hair and a sharp nose, who spent the bulk of his career arguing appellate cases for the Crown. He is earnest and struggles to be fair. But he appraises every piece of evidence, every legal argument through the eye of a veteran prosecutor. We start with one hand tied behind our backs.

Now I look around the table at Alicia, Richard, and Jeff. I beam at Jeff in gratitude; I would never have got through the past week of trial prep and motions without him. In the background, Shanni runs around filling coffee cups, lowering the blinds to keep out the late winter sun, and generally making herself useful. Damon can't make it today, says he's too deep into whatever things he's into to pull out now.

"Thanks for being here," I say. "The trial starts Monday. Today, we'll run through how we think it might play out, step by step, witness by witness, and what our strategy is at each stage." I catch Jeff's skeptical look. "Of course, trials are notoriously unpredictable. We must be prepared for anything to happen. But we have to start somewhere."

DAY ONE, I write on my whiteboard. I make three notations under the heading—JURY SELECTION, JUDGES' INSTRUCTIONS, and CROWN OPENING.

"Let's talk about jury selection," I say.

"What's to talk about?" says Jeff.

"For starts, we want some ethnic diversity—preferably two or three people who identify as Black. They'll sympathize with Kate, how she's been treated by Trist and the media, how difficult it's been for her, the only Black girl in his White world.

"But the bigger problem is the press circus that's surrounded this case from day one," I go on. "How we can get an impartial jury in a case like this where people have already made up their minds? When they've had their opinions repeatedly confirmed by social media and the press? Richard canvassed passersby and found that eighty-two per cent believed Kate was guilty." At the end of the table, Richard nods.

"We'll have to play it by ear," Jeff says. "The jurors will be asked if they know about the case and have formed conclusions they might not be able to put aside. If we get fourteen—twelve and two spares—who say they can be impartial, we'll have our jury."

"And if we don't?" asks Alicia.

"We have the judge bring in more people and keep trying."

"Or we apply to have the trial with judge alone."

I think of Justice Tesik's sharp nose and prosecutorial bent. "Not with this judge."

"So, we hope for fourteen people of diverse ethnicity who will swear to listen to the evidence and give an unbiased verdict, based on that evidence alone."

"And, if we're lucky, a few liberal-minded people who understand mental illness and won't write Kate off as an evil ditz," Jeff adds.

I nod. "Moving on, the judge's initial instructions to the jury. Not much we can do about that. He'll outline the various possible verdicts, first-degree murder, second-degree murder, dropping to manslaughter if they don't find intentional killing beyond a reasonable doubt."

"Tesik will be clinically fair," says Jeff.

"Three—Cy's opening. We can't do anything about that either, but it will be tough to listen to. Cy is passionate about securing a conviction, and he'll use every ounce of his eloquence to paint Kate as an irresponsible parent prepared to do anything to get her child out of the hands of Trist and Lena. He may cross the line between fact and embellishment. We need to be prepared to object, keep him in check."

"Without giving the jury any hint that we are worried or outraged. Poker faces, everybody," counsels Jeff.

I erase the whiteboard, write CROWN WITNESSES. Beneath, I write the first name on the list Cy has produced: TRIST.

"Trist will describe the events leading up to Tess's disappearance. Including how he fell asleep. Cy will also take him through the custody saga and how Kate's behaviour made it necessary to remove even weekend access. In cross-examination, we'll try to establish that Kate was a good parent before she started to get sick after the separation.

"There's something a little off, exaggerated, about the Crown's contention that Kate's parenting was so bad it put Tess in danger. Lots of general noise, only a few specific incidents—taking Tess out without proper clothing, letting her play unsupervised in the front yard, and the final incident of Tess howling on the kitchen counter while Kate was passed out upstairs. All from Selma—meaning Trist only knew what she told him. So we'll go hard on that angle. Also, we'll bring out that Tess continued to love Kate, even at the end when they dragged her away from supervised visits, crying and protesting."

"Trist won't know much about that. Selma picked Tess up," Shanni puts in.

I nod. "We'll be walking a fine line in cross-examining Trist. On the one hand, we want to show that Kate isn't a bad mother. On the other, we want the jury to think that he—maybe Lena—had something to do with Tess's disappearance. To do that, I need to attack him—he was content to leave everything to Selma, was careless about the paparazzi around his child. Was he smoking weed on the day Tess vanished, was he drinking, was Tess throwing Lena's omelette on the floor the last straw? Same with Lena. In chief, she'll say she loved Tess, but in cross we need to bring out how she resented her, wanted her out of the way."

"Not to mention the red wine she gave Trist and the fact she was operating a boat like the one in Dante's photo," Alicia adds.

"That red wine story is just too pat," Shanni muses. "Maybe

the truth is he was smoking weed or something worse. Tess wandered away while Trist was high, went too far out, and drowned. Which would make Trist guilty of manslaughter."

"But the gouge in the sand shows a small boat came up on the beach," Alicia puts in.

"No problem," Shanni replies. "Lena comes home, finds Tess missing. She's petrified that the police will charge Trist, so they go down and run the boat up to make the mark. They had time before the police arrived."

I consider Shanni's words. I've played with the idea of Trist's involvement many times, only to reject it, but Shanni has made it sound believable. "Good thinking, Shanni. We can play up these points in cross-examination. It might trouble the jury enough to make them think convicting Kate is unsafe."

"Assuming you knock out the identification of Kate and her hair in the boat," Jeff grumbles. "And don't underestimate Trist. Trist is smart and he's a performer. My bet is he will be on for this show, sober and persuasive. The grieving father. One eye on the jury, the other on his fans."

"Moving on to Lena," I say. "Our goal is to establish that Lena might have been the woman in the boat and that she had motive and opportunity."

I write DANTE on the board, followed by SELMA. "I know Lena will testify, but Dante and Selma are the big ones. Let's take Selma first. The nanny. This is an important witness for Cy. He needs her to paint the picture of Kate as an inadequate parent who repeatedly endangered her child and was crazy enough to find a boat, steal Tess, and drown her. We have Selma's witness statement; she doesn't talk about Kate ever saying she would kill Tess. We'll see what she says on the stand."

"The crazy piece is critical for the prosecution's case," Jeff says thoughtfully. "Without Selma's testimony that Kate was irrational, the jury won't buy that Kate had malice aforethought to kill her daughter, which leaves Cy with manslaughter at best. He has to portray Kate as totally mixed up, narcissistic, and ready—in her crazy mind—to do anything to end her pain and the pain she believed Tess was suffering. The jury will have trouble believing any parent could kill their child. To make its theory work, the Crown must show Kate was the rare exception, and to make that work, they need Selma's evidence."

I nod. "The question is how far Selma will go. Will she be content talking about incidents where Kate endangered Tess? Or will she go further and suggest Kate was acting irrationally where Tess was concerned? If she does, the Crown's psychiatrist will complete the picture with his expert evidence that Kate could have decided the only way out was to end Tess's life. That's Cy's plan.

"Cross-examination is all about understanding the witness," I say. "I wish I had a better handle on Selma. In the TV interview, she set Kate up as the abductor. But talking to her, I didn't get the impression that she hated Kate. Sure, she thought Kate was a bad mother, thought she couldn't be trusted with Tess. But does she want to see Kate behind bars? Perhaps. She said as much to me when she threw me out of her house. I can't figure out what's driving her. I like to have a better handle on a witness before I cross-examine them, so with Richard's help"—I glance across the table—"I'll keep working on it."

"That leaves Dante," says Jeff. "What to do with Dante? That is the question."

"First, we cross-examine to undercut his identification of Kate and the convenient fact that the photo is too blurry to be sure who was in the boat. Second, we bring out his past file—if the judge lets us—to suggest he is interested in little girls. Third, we get him to admit he saw Tess at Trist's house and took her photo, showing he was interested in her. Fourth, we establish he could have done it—he was on the island with a vehicle, he could have picked up Tess and then taken her away in the vehicle, losing the pink shoe and planting the beach evidence on the way. The photos of the woman in the boat were designed to clear him. He could have photoshopped them. It may just be enough for reasonable doubt."

I sigh and make a new heading: POLICE AND EXPERT REPORTS. A collective groan goes around the table.

"Okay, okay, we'll skip through this one. The Crown will call a psychiatrist to give an opinion on Kate's state of mind based on what Trist and Selma say about her behaviour. We'll discredit it in cross on the basis he's never talked to Kate, and call Kate's psychiatrist for the defence to blow it out of the water. Or try to."

I scan the room, decide to ignore the dubious glances. "Unfortunately, we lost our motion to keep out the partial fingerprints. But we'll call our expert, Dr. Essex, to show that the partials could have belonged to any one of thousands of people and are of no value." I look up at Richard. "Still no match for the mystery fingerprint on the seat?"

"No. I've tried, but without more clues, it's impossible to close in on identification."

We move on to the final and critical group in the Crown's case. The police.

"Kan will outline the investigation; other cops will come in to fill in the details. We'll cross-examine them all on the parts that don't fit, like the other pink shoe in the clearing behind Trist's lodge."

Alicia snorts. "Hammer them, Jilly. Detective Kan and his

whole investigation have been a fucking disaster from day one. You need to hit Kan hard, destroy his credibility."

"Alicia, I go to sleep every night counting the boats this investigation has missed—and the mythical one it's fixated on. One, believing Dante despite blurry photos and an undisclosed involvement with kiddie porn. Two, botching the island search. Three, failing to fingerprint the boat rudder. Four, failing to follow up on the second shoe and the CCTV camera sighting, blah, blah, blah. I've been honing an approach to humiliate Kan on the stand."

"Way to go," says Alicia.

"But it could backfire," I say cautiously. "Kan has an enormous reputation, which makes me fear he's cleverer than we think. He has a tragic backstory, which Cy may find a way to make known to the jury. And he has an infuriating way of making every error seem like a stroke of genius, or at least eminently rational."

Alicia gives me a look. "Are you losing your balls, Jilly, or are you into this creep?"

I stifle a smart retort.

Jeff interrupts. "Jilly is right. Kan is good and wily. We have to handle him with care, play it by ear. Subtle insinuation may go further with the jury on this one than a hammer to the head. That doesn't mean we won't be ready with a shopping list of his failings."

I sit down. "That's it. That's our strategy. Sloppy policework and a plausible alternate suspect. If we've poked enough holes in Cy's case or established a reasonable alternative hypothesis, we will ask for a directed verdict of acquittal at the end of the Crown's case." I glance at Jeff, who is rolling his eyes playfully at the ceiling. "If we haven't, we call Kate to say she didn't do it, plus a few doctors and experts, and throw ourselves at the jury's mercy."

CHAPTER 63

JEFF HAS ORDERED ME TO let the adoption go, but it keeps nagging at me. On impulse, I decide to call Kate. I catch her at 8:30 Wednesday morning, before she heads out for the back roads of Surrey.

"I need to ask you some questions, Kate."

"Sure." I can tell by her voice that this is a tired day. But she's up and about, still hanging in, which is the good news.

"You said you and Trist adopted Tess through a closed adoption. Can you walk me through exactly what steps you took, how it came about?"

"Jilly, this can't matter." She is exasperated.

"Humour me, Kate. I need to know. This goes no further. I'm your lawyer."

She sighs, relenting. "We tried everything to have a child. Even surrogacy. Trist didn't like the idea of another woman carrying our baby. Plus the surrogate could come back with demands for more money to keep her involvement secret. So the only thing left was adoption.

"Trist's agent contacted an adoption lawyer who explained the possibilities. Trist and I agreed that the child would have to look like our biological child. If they didn't, we knew the press would start trying to identify the biological parents. We didn't care if it was a girl or a boy, but the child would have to be part White, part Black. The lawyer told us that finding such a child would be difficult, but he had deep connections and could try. If such a child were found, he assured us that the matter could be kept absolutely secret. We would never know the biological parents, and they would never know us. He did mention that when the child was nineteen, they could apply to find out who their biological parents were under a new law. I remember Trist laughing, 'By that time, I won't care.'

"About six months later, the agent phoned us while we were in London. He wouldn't give us details, but he said a healthy, intelligent young Caucasian woman had given birth to a biracial child and was willing to adopt it to a good family. A little girl, healthy and beautiful, not far away, in some Fraser Valley town. We were overjoyed. We had been in Europe for a few months, so I wasn't worried about speculation that the baby wasn't our biological child. We flew back to Vancouver. The lawyer and nurse arrived at our house and handed us Tess. I'll never forget the joy I felt, Jilly. A few days later, we announced the arrival of our child."

"Do you remember the lawyer's name?"

"No. But he assured us he would never divulge any details and that all his files would be destroyed. All I know is that the government issued a birth certificate identifying me as Tess's mother and

Trist as her father, complete with date and place of birth: Vancouver." Kate lowers her voice. "For all I know, this man wasn't even a real lawyer, just a guy who specialized in clandestine adoptions for people like us." Her voice breaks. "Trist paid him a lot of money."

I suppress a shudder. How casually human beings are bought and sold. Just when I think I've encountered every evil in the world, I discover a new one. I feel a pang for Tess, the pawn in this particular scheme. No doubt the pseudo-lawyer thought he was finding a good home for her. Sadly, that is not how it turned out. Trist's casual selfishness twists my stomach. Sure, he wanted a baby to please Kate. But he was neither blind to the boost a baby would give his career, nor above exploiting his child for the paps. I look for a way to tell Kate it's alright, but I don't find it.

"Thanks, Kate," I say.

I return the phone to its cradle. Jeff was right. No way to go down this rabbit hole, no point either. Still, my mind is working. One phrase keeps coming back. *In some Fraser Valley town.* I pick up the phone again, leave a message for Richard.

CHAPTER 64

"**I**'VE GOT SOMETHING," DAMON SAYS, bursting into my office unannounced.

"Yes," I say, feeling my stomach flip. Maybe this is it, the piece that has been eluding us. "Okay to talk here?"

He considers. "Sure. If a law office isn't off-limits to the spies, we're all sunk."

I knock on Jeff's door on the way to the boardroom, and the three of us settle around the table.

"Want to see it on the big screen?" Damon asks.

He taps keys, and his iPad lights up the video monitor. We stare in silence.

The same Shell gas station as in the first video. A battered van pulls up to a gas pump off Highway 10, and a man with white hair and a paunch beneath his parka gets out. He puts his credit card in the pump and prepays, then picks up the nozzle. He places the nozzle in the side of the van and stands, holding it as the tank fills. When the nozzle clicks off, the man places it back on the pump and returns to the driver's seat.

"Look at the window," says Damon.

The rear window is half open, revealing what appears to be a child. The image is indistinct, but I make out a halo of hair. The man gets in the driver's seat and moves the van away.

"Wait," I say. "The licence plate. Can you play that back? Great. Stop."

Damon freezes the image. We stare at the licence plate on the rear of the retreating van. "It's not clear," Damon says. "The first part of the plate is obscured by dirt. Then it looks like what could be a five, can't make out the next number, followed by an *M*."

"Five-something-*M*," Damon says.

The screen goes black.

We look at each other. "When was this filmed?"

"Two days ago."

"Tess is alive," I breathe.

"Not so fast," says Damon. "*May* be alive. The image of the child is blurry and partial. Chances are, it's some other child."

I nod. When it comes to Tess, my imagination overtakes reality.

"What do we do now?" Jeff asks.

"Good question," I reply bitterly. "I would say we show this to Kan and get him to follow up on the man with the van. Except I've grown weary of handing Kan leads he ignores."

Jeff nods. "We know what happened last time we tried that. Damon gave him the video, and we've heard nothing since."

"But now we have a partial licence plate number. I think we have to show it to Kan; we don't have a choice." I consider. "But at the same time, we should get Richard on this." I push myself up, pacing the floor. "Who is this man? And who is the child? We need to know."

"No harm trying," Jeff says mildly.

Damon gets up to go. "Got a paper due tomorrow."

"Thanks, Damon. Amazing work. And can you leave your iPad and access code? We may need to look at this again."

Alone with Jeff, I speed-dial Kan. Cy probably has him in a backroom somewhere, grilling him for his testimony next week. Doesn't matter. We have no choice. I pray that this time he will come on the line instead of his voicemail.

Miraculously, he does. "Detective Kan."

"I'm so glad you answered."

"Ms. Truitt, you shouldn't be talking to me." His voice is brusque. "As you well know, I'm testifying for the Crown at the trial next week."

"This isn't about your testimony, Detective. It's about finding Tess. We have a second CCTV sighting of the man and child. Plus, a vehicle—a white van—and a partial licence plate number."

I wait while Kan considers. He's going to say it doesn't matter— a partial license plate will lead us nowhere, and anyway the chances the child is Tess are zilch to zero. The silence breaks.

"Send me the partial plate and the video," Kan says. He gives me an email address he says is secure. "I'll have a look right away."

I hang up. "He says he'll look into it right away."

"We'll see," says Jeff.

"Yeah," I say. "He won't do a damn thing." I pick up my phone and punch in a new number. "I'm calling Richard."

CHAPTER 65

THURSDAY, MARCH 2, HAS BEEN a trying day.

Yesterday, Kan promised to get right on Damon's latest CCTV scan. Richard, too. Silence. I've tried reaching them, but I hit a blank leave-a-message wall each time.

Now it's Thursday night, and I'm home nursing my frustration and keeping my daughter company in the den. Or more accurately, Claire is keeping me company, chattering nonstop in her private language. I try to respond and smile, but my mind keeps slipping away. *Quality time,* say the patenting experts. *Be in the moment with your child.* I pick up Claire, scoop her into my lap, kiss her sweet-smelling cheek. We've reached an understanding, Claire and I—sometimes I drift away, but she doesn't mind. She knows I always come back.

My cellphone rings and I pick it up. I skip a breath—Richard at last.

"What news?" I ask.

"I haven't been able to get a read on the licence plate, I'm sorry to say. Maybe the police could, but to ordinary mortals like me, the Motor Vehicle Registry is locked tighter than the Kremlin. No way I can get near a readout on all the plates in the province ending with five-something-*M*."

"Anything else?"

"I found Selma's grandfather. Remember you mentioned him for a follow-up a while ago? I wasn't able to talk to him, but I confirmed where he lives. Bill Beams, widower, fifty-nine years old. Lives alone on a farm that's been in the family for generations. House a hundred years old, falling-down outbuildings. I tried to get in, but the property is fenced and the gate is padlocked. No lights, no sign of anyone at home. I talked to the neighbouring farmers. They say he's a nice old man, a bit simple, though. They've met Selma, says she shows up occasionally on the weekend. They haven't seen the old man for a week or two, not that they'd notice, since you can't see the Beams property from their place."

"No sign of a child?"

"No."

"No white van?"

"Not that I could see, although who knows what might be in those outbuildings."

"Richard, we need to find out. I wrote Selma off, but I'm re-thinking. Just too many things about her don't fit. She's hiding something. I don't know what, but I know we need to find it before the trial begins."

"What more I can do, short of breaking into the barn?"

"Go back Saturday. Maybe he'll be home. Maybe Selma will show up. Didn't the neighbours say she sometimes comes on the weekends?"

"Good idea. Leave it with me."

I shuffle a dozing Claire in my left arm and find a pen with my right hand. "Just for the record, can you give me the address of the farm?"

Richard reads it out, and I write it down. "Not easy to find," he says. "Not on Google Maps."

"Another thing, Richard. Could you email anything you have on that religious compound where Selma spent two years?"

"Sure thing." A pause. I wait for the lecture. "Don't go there, Jilly. That compound was abandoned years ago. And long before that, Selma had left and moved on."

I sigh. "You're right. I admit it, I've become obsessed."

"A tad irrational?"

"Just a tad." I laugh. "Indulge me. I'm a mother now."

"Speaking of," says Richard. "You asked me to check out Dante's mother. I pulled up something there. She has a relative who comes to visit. Lives in a trailer near the border. In his sixties, Caucasian with white hair. Could be your man in the video."

My heart quickens. "What does he drive?"

"A small red Toyota. I'm keeping an eye on him, though, which means I do a random drive-by every day or so. His Toyota is still parked at the side of the trailer. There's a child's car seat in the back."

"Interesting. I appreciate everything you're doing, Richard." I thank him and hang up.

Dante, Selma. Aging white-haired men. A white van and a red Toyota, both with children's car seats. I have the data points but no connections.

I rise and heft Claire over my shoulder. "Come on, baby girl. You and Mommy are going to bed."

She giggles and kicks her feet with delight.

CHAPTER 66

FEMALE TRIAL LAWYERS TALK A lot about work-life balance. A few even mean it. But nothing kills the platitudes like a looming trial date. With the trial set to start Monday, I found myself consigning Claire to Edith's care and putting in long weekend hours at the office with Jeff, Alicia, and Shanni. And then, at 4:10 p.m. on Sunday, when we'd put our final notes to bed and our adrenaline pumps were priming in anticipation of the morning, Cy called to say that something had come up—he couldn't say what—and the trial wouldn't be starting until Tuesday.

"What do you mean?" I yelled into the phone. "You can't do this to us."

"I'm no happier about this than you are, Jilly," Cy replied tersely, and hung up.

I spent a fitful night, tossing and tearing at the bedsheets. On Monday morning I knew what I must do.

I call Edith and ask if she can get Claire from daycare tonight. I have to go up-valley and don't know when I'll be back.

I don my jeans and boots, bundle up Claire, and deliver her to Liz's daycare. Then I get back in my car and start driving. When you don't know where you're going, let the spirit take you where it will.

The morning light is breaking through the clouds as I emerge from the Massey Tunnel. My car takes me south and east through the dawning grey, toward the Peace Arch Border Crossing into the USA. I've left the urban sprawl behind; on either side, fields lie wet and fallow, awaiting spring planting. Beyond the fields to the east and north, a wooded bluff pushes up from the farmland framed by the distant silhouette of urban towers and coastal mountains. To the south, the languid Serpentine River ambles southeast through woods and fields. Dante's mother's friend lives out here somewhere. I find Richard's report on my iPhone, take a side road. After a couple of false starts, I find myself in a trailer park. I check Richard's report to verify the number.

Lot 216 is a modest structure on a modest concrete slab. Light gleams through a high window. I confirm the make of the car parked beside the home: yes, a red Toyota. I continue down the street and turn. I find a tree opposite and back from the trailer and park beneath it.

A side door of the home opens, and an older man with white hair emerges. He gets in the Toyota, backs up, and heads down the street in the direction I came from. I start my car and follow at a discreet distance. He is headed toward the border crossing, I think. But before he gets there, he takes a right and continues down a secondary road.

The sign says Riverside Golf Club. The Toyota turns in. Is my man here for a game of golf on a Tuesday? Soon enough, I find myself passing townhouses, the glimpse of fairways just beyond. I wait at a distance as the man pulls into a driveway and enters townhouse 240. I wait some more.

The man emerges at last. My heart skips a beat when I see he is carrying a child. But this child is a boy in a dark blue jacket and toque. From the door of the townhouse, a woman waves. The man opens the back door of the Toyota and buckles the child into the car seat.

My heart sinks. This is not my man and not my child. I am witnessing an ordinary domestic transaction—a man taking his grandson out for the morning to give the boy's mother a break. The Toyota heads out. This time, I do not follow.

Aimlessly, I drift north and west. I curse my stupidity. I should be in the office prepping for tomorrow's evidence; instead, I'm blindly wandering the back roads of south Surrey. Life has taught me not to follow blind hunches, so why don't I ever learn?

Still, Selma's grandfather's farm is somewhere out here. A day into the trial, and I still can't put the pieces together on Selma. On the surface, she is exactly what she professes to be—a good nanny who was devoted to Tess and her employer, Trist. But dig a little, and things seem stranger—her time in the cult and the unexplained transformation to caregiver, the chance meeting with Kate and Tess in the park that led to her employment, how she worked Kate out of Tess's life, how she just happened to not be available to go on the island vacation, her sudden appearance on television to subtly diss Kate, Tess's photo in her front hall. Perhaps a look at her grandfather's farm will help. And then another thought hits me—the man with the white hair. I had thought Rex, or Dante's mother's friend. But what about Selma's grandfather?

Heart racing, I hit my phone again, find the address Richard gave me, punch it into Google Maps, and head north.

It's all farms and bush out here in the greenbelt, crisscrossed by narrow roads you don't see until you're on them. It's going on midmorning, and my stomach is growling when I stop for a coffee at a service station and listen to the radio blather on about the weather. I sip my latte and study the map. The land is rough here, hill and gullies in the shadow of the ridge behind.

To judge from my map, Selma's grandfather's farm is in these hills. I start my car and take a narrow road north. Just when I think I'm running out of roadway, Google instructs me to take a left. I follow a trail to another trail, and then another. Then, abruptly, Google dies. Wherever I'm headed, I'm off the satellite map. Just like Richard told me.

Through dense greenery, I spy a sign that announces Wickham Road. The pretension of it, I muse, as I accelerate gently over the ruts toward the bluff. On either side, hedges loom, wild and unkempt. *Turn around, go back,* my brain says, *no one can live here.*

Then I find it. The hedges abruptly give way to a clearing. A metal gate rises before me, barring further entrance. A wooden sign hangs precariously from the gate post; 73, it announces in flaking letters. Beyond the gate, amidst a litter of rusting machinery and rotting refuse, sits an ancient farmhouse. One of those post-Victorian package homes you could buy in the 1920s, complete with gable, turret, and sagging front porch. Paint peels from the wooden siding, and the delicate cornice work on the porch is broken. One of the two windows that flank the sagging front door appears to be cracked. Once this was a place of pretensions; no longer.

I look closer. Despite its dilapidated state, the house is not abandoned. Richard was right; Selma's grandfather still lives here.

Curtains hang crookedly in the windows, and budding morning glories finger their tenuous way up a broken trellis. Someone has planted pansies in window boxes, and the porch is swept clean.

I kill the engine, step out of the car. I survey the gate: no way to get through, over, or under. I dive into a ditch to the side, roll my body under a broken fence, and head up toward the house.

A moving shape between the curtains in the right-front window stops me dead. A moment later, the front door creaks open and a man steps onto the porch. I gasp at what I see. He is wearing an old parka like the one in the CCTV photo, and his white hair sweeps down from his furrowed forehead and falls forward to his chin. Even from a distance, his blue eyes have the glaze of someone who does not see well. In his right hand he holds a shotgun. No, not a shotgun, a rifle. By the looks of it, the high-powered variety.

The man stares at me. I stand, frozen, twenty feet away. He lifts the gun to his shoulder and points it at me. His voice is rough, but his message is clear.

"Leave. Now."

The rifle wobbles, the man steadies it with difficulty. His eyesight and strength are not up to this. He might hit me, or he might not. Still, I don't like a gun aimed in my direction.

"Sure," I say, throwing up my hands and turning. I break into a run. I feel the gun boring into the back of my head, and I run faster. I hear a crack, and then I am dropping in the ditch and rolling under the fence.

My heart is beating fast, not only from fear but from what I have just seen.

CHAPTER 67

MY HANDS SHAKE ON THE steering wheel. I may be mistaken; I may be crazy. But my brain tells me what I thought I saw is real. Crawling under the bottom rail of the fence, deafened by the crack of the rifle overhead, I saw it: a tiny children's wagon, barn red, its broken handle a jagged finger against the waving grass. The red wagon in the photo I saw on Trist's shelf. Tess was here. Tess *is* here. I feel it.

I run to my car, reverse with a screech, and head down the trail. Only when I'm back on a proper road does my sanity return. Any number of farm homes have broken toys racked up against forgotten fences, I tell myself, stifling the instincts that have led me down false trails time and again in this case. But as I point my car back to Highway 1 and head east, the vision of the red wagon returns. Selma's place. Tess's wagon.

Selma is the key.

Agassiz is a pretty town, set where the plains of the Fraser Delta give way to hills and meadows surrounded by forest. Spruce trees line the streets. To the east and the north, the coastal mountains rise, dark and glowering.

I find an artisanal café off Main Street and treat myself to a salad and tea, munching while the local citizenry files by. Upscale urbanites fleeing the city sprawl. Local farmers and shopkeepers. The odd lumberjack pounding studded boots down the utility carpet to the order counter. *No studs or cleats on the hardwood*, a sign reads, but no one pays it attention.

I linger over my lavender tea. It's almost one, and the noon rush is over; people lunch early here. I chat up the waitress, a pretty brown-eyed girl in apron and jeans, and motion her to the chair across from me. *Jenny*, the badge on her right shoulder proclaims.

"Nice town," I say. "I've never been here before."

Jenny obliges me with a stream of trivia. How the town started a century and a half ago with the arrival of the CPR Railway. How it grew for a while and then stopped. How nothing has changed since. "Of course, that's just the European history," she says, brushing a dark bang off her forehead. "My people have been here forever. I'm Statin First Nation."

"My mother was Haida Gwaii."

Jenny offers a fist bump. "Sister," she says.

"I imagine a lot of different people come through here," I say.

"Yeah, a lot." Jenny fills me in on the hippies and weirdos that wash through Agassiz in overlapping waves.

"I heard about some religious cult that had a place somewhere near here."

"Oh yeah," Jenny says with a roll of her eyes. "Really weird. They lived communally, not that there's anything wrong with that, we've been doing it for millennia. But their Grand Poohbah—Zoron, he called himself—or something." Jenny leans closer. "They called themselves Christians, but it was a different brand than they taught at residential school. The rumours of what went on there . . ." She rolls her eyes to the ceiling again.

"I bet," I say to keep her talking.

"Most of them moved on," says Jenny. "Good riddance, I say."

"Fascinating. Where is this place anyway?"

"No address," says Jenny, rising. I catch a glimpse of her boss entering through the door behind the counter. "They didn't like addresses, those people, too public. But you can still find the place if you try. Take a right off Main, keep on going into the bush until you run out of road."

Behind us, Jenny's boss is clearing her throat.

"Gotta get back to work, Sis. Nice meeting you."

I follow Jenny's instructions and head down the road and out of town. I hit a dead end and stop before I make out faint tire tracks to the right. I follow the tracks; the woods on either side loom dark and deep. I come to a washout and tell myself I'm lost. Then I see the sign nailed to a spruce: *Church of the Sun and the Resurrection.* I study the peeling letters. No directions. No indication of how far it is. I push on.

Suddenly a gate looms before me. I slam on my brakes, inches away from steel. The padlocked barrier is well-built, as is the fence that runs to either side. Security matters here. Or used to.

I ponder what to do. My recent experience at the farmhouse has dampened my ardour for crawling under fences. And then I see a figure coming toward me. A woman clad in a long-sleeved beige shift. As she nears, I make out details. Her faded blonde hair is tied back at her neck, and a large cross hangs on her bosom. Looped loosely around the waist of her gown is a chain, from which keys dangle.

She opens a small side gate I hadn't noticed and peers in at me. I roll down my window.

"I'm Rachel. Can I help you?" the woman asks. Her voice is raspy, like it doesn't get used much.

I repress a shudder. There is something sinister about this woman, something sinister about this place. The thought of Claire floods my mind. The touch of her tiny hand, the smell of her hair when she wakes up in the morning. I am not going further.

"I'm lost," I tell the woman. "I need to turn around, but I can't back up. The track is too narrow."

She nods and opens the gate, steps back so I can turn my car around in the clearing. I watch her in my rearview mirror as I gun my way back, an ever-diminishing figure clutching her crucifix.

CHAPTER 68

KAN AND I ARE IN the back of a police cruiser, speeding up Highway 10. It's almost dusk, and the lights are coming alive in the countryside.

After leaving Rachel, I took the freeway back to Vancouver. My plan was to tell Kan about the house and wagon and persuade him to return with me to search for Tess immediately. But I hadn't counted on the thickening afternoon traffic, and it was three thirty before I pulled up at Kan's headquarters. It took him an agonizing half hour to get a search warrant—me swearing the supporting affidavit.

Kan's head is back, his eyes are closed. "You may have wondered why the trial was put over to Tuesday."

I don't answer. He carries on anyway.

"I spent the weekend going over Damon's footage and the

pieces that didn't fit, like the second shoe, and I realized what I should have realized long before—that we needed to deploy all our forces to search for the man with the white van and the child. A search of the partial plate gave us nothing. Sunday morning, I drew up a plan. I told Cy we needed another day to make sure our case was airtight. He was furious, but he had no choice but to agree. I applied for a search warrant for all farms in the area, but the judge said it was too broad and refused. We commenced an aerial search, looking for white vans. Come Sunday night we'd found nothing, despite intercepting twenty-three white vans."

If this is meant to be an apology, it isn't working. "What took you so long?" I say bitterly. "You sat on the first CCTV video for weeks and did nothing when I gave you the second. Then suddenly two days ago you wake up?"

He stares straight ahead.

"You have no reply," I say. "I thought as much."

Kan ignores my interjection and pretends he didn't hear me. "We continued the search through the night and all day today. If we find Tess today, Jilly, it will be because of your detective work. If she's on the farm . . ."

His words don't ease my anger. His refusal to follow up on the information I pleaded with him to take seriously has left Tess in limbo for weeks and jeopardized her rescue. So much needless suffering. Tess, separated from all she knew and loved. Kate, facing life behind bars. Trist, thin and wan. Not to mention the wasted effort of our trial preparation. I shake my head to clear my thoughts. If we don't find Tess tonight, will Kan continue his testimony against Kate? Will he convince Cy to carry on as if none of this has happened? What about the child's red wagon in the farmhouse yard? Just coincidence, Kan will say when I confront him on the stand.

I gaze into the landscape streaking past the window. The lights are more blurred than they should be. I brush my cheek, discover it's wet. I tell myself I'm a professional and don't let things like anger get to me. I swallow to compose myself. Two officers occupy the front seat of the cruiser, Constable Felesky and her sidekick, Eric Marten. Constable Felesky is the sort of officer who keeps her lips pursed and her hands behind her back at all times, unless she's at the wheel, as she is now. Still, I concede she's one hell of a driver. She has moved us through south Vancouver, Richmond, and the Massey Tunnel in less than thirty minutes, a not-so-minor miracle. Of course, it helps to have flashing lights on your dashboard.

"Nearing destination," says Felesky as we bump over the ruts. She slides to a stop at the farmhouse gate.

"I hope one of you has a gun," I say. "You may need to shoot the lock off the gate. Or defend us against the old man with the rifle."

Kan shakes his head again. But he gets out, pulls out a pistol, and shoots the lock off the gate. He swings it open, and Felesky barrels through. *Maybe Kan is finally getting it*, I think. This is serious.

I leave the vehicle, move to Kan's side, and scan the yard. "No white van," I say.

"Maybe it's in one of the sheds," says Kan. "No red wagon, either. You're sure it was there?"

"I swore it was there. Remember the affidavit?" Despite his apparent change of attitude, Kan is still ready to doubt me. "Looks like they've already gone."

"Share your thinking," Kan orders.

"What would I do in Selma's shoes if her grandfather phoned to tell her about a strange woman showing up unannounced at the farm? I would pack Tess up and bolt. Selma knows the jig is up. She has only one option: take Tess and flee. I showed up at the farm around eleven thirty. Grandpa would have called Selma shortly after that, and she would have come straight here to pack, clean up as much evidence as she could, and leave." I pause. "They can't have got far."

Constable Marten bangs on the door of the house. When no one answers, he gives it a shoulder shove that breaks the lock. The door falls open.

We push through to the kitchen. The remnants of someone's breakfast-for-dinner sit on the table. Cold toast, an egg-smeared plate. On the ancient stove sits a pot of coffee.

I take the steps to the basement three at a time. Its all cement, except for a painted door. Someone's built a room down here. I push the door open and gasp.

Walls painted pale pink, a ruffled pink coverlet. A small bookcase filled with little books, and basket of fuzzy bears and rag dolls. "Tess's room," I breathe.

"Let's go," says Kan. "If we're lucky we can stop them. Coffee's still warm."

Kan is in operational mode as we run for the car, shouting into a special phone he has pulled out of his pocket. "We need a helicopter. Police at the border crossing, police on number one going east and Highway 7, too. We're looking for a white van, last three digits of licence five-something-*M*. Do not shoot if you find it. Verify if child is in the van before taking any aggressive action. Female, about five years old. Mixed race. Two adults, one male in his late fifties, one female in her twenties. Caucasian."

Doors slam. We are in the car, gunning out the open gate, south and east. Cacophony in the car. Voices, high and low, male and female, coming in and out against the background wail of sirens.

And then the words I want to hear crackle in. "Van has been spotted, heading for the Peace Arch Border Crossing. Numbers match. Bringing it over now."

Felesky pulls in the coordinates on her display without missing a beat, and we change course.

"On our way," Kan says. "Approximately seven minutes."

We pull up behind a white van and two police cruisers. More police, to judge by flashing lights ahead and behind, are on their way. An officer comes over and leans in Kan's window. "There's a kid in the back, meets the description you gave. We took the adults out. They're standing against the van."

"Arms?"

The officer shakes his head. "We confiscated a rifle."

"Good."

Kan nods to Officer Marten, steps out. "You stay in the car, Ms. Truitt."

Of course. They don't want a rank amateur getting enmeshed in what could be a violent scene. Much less a lawyer. From the back seat of the car, I crane to see what is happening. I can't make out much; the police car ahead is blocking my view of the side of the van.

It seems to take forever, but then I see Kan's tall form. He is carrying something—a child, I think. My heart thuds in my chest, and I hear a thundering in my ears. Yes, he is carrying Tess.

Tess.

She is wailing, screaming, flailing in Kan's arms. Behind Kan, the police car moves, revealing the white van. Selma is breaking loose from the policewoman who is holding her and running after Kan. "Give me my baby," she half screams, half sobs. "Don't take my baby."

Tess's arms reach back to Selma. The anguish on Selma's face hits me in the gut. I flash back to the moment Mike lay dying in my arms, relive the wrenching feeling of the person I love being ripped away and being unable to prevent it. Sirens are blaring, blue lights flashing. I catch a glimpse of Tess's eyes, wide with terror. Kan tightens his grip, bends his head to Tess. Her screams subside into shuddering sobs, and her little hand curls around Kan's neck.

The officers are holding Selma, cuffing her. The cold wind tears at her flimsy sweater. "Don't take my baby," she sobs.

Kan hands Tess to Constable Marten and strides back to Selma. An officer hands him a coat, and he drapes it around her shoulders. She tries to shake it off, without success.

Kan's words cut through Tess's wails and the wind. "Selma Beams, you are under arrest for abduction and confinement of a child, one Tess Sinclair-Jones."

They push Selma into one of the police cars. Kan strides back to our car, opens the back door. He pulls out his phone again. I catch snatches of his words: "Kate, we have Tess . . . Children's Hospital on Oak Street . . . half an hour . . ." He ends the call and dials again; this time he speaks to Trist. I understand. Tess is terrified, and only her parents will bring her comfort.

Kan opens his door and gets out. "Constable," he barks at Felesky, "please take Ms. Truitt home."

The night is just coming on, but the retreating adrenalin of the chase has left me exhausted. Felesky's wheels spit gravel as she reverses the car, and once more we are headed back to the city.

Numbness overtakes me as the adrenaline dissipates.

"Need to stop?" Felesky asks over her shoulder.

"No," I say. "Just take me home."

A half hour later, we pull up in front of the house. "Thanks," I tell Felesky. "And by the way, you are one hell of a driver."

I mount the steps, pull off my boots, and cross the hall on cat feet. No need to worry, the stillness of the house tells me Edith hasn't brought Claire home yet.

I think of calling Kate. But by now she will be at the hospital, reuniting with Tess. I've reached the end of my long and improbable quest—Kate and Tess reunited—but I won't be there to see it. It will take Trist a while longer to get there, from his North Shore home. But that's alright. Everything in its turn.

I wander into the den and find the couch.

I pull Mike's throw over me and fall into a deep and dreamless sleep.

CHAPTER 69

"ORDER IN COURT," THE CLERK cries.

Justice Tesik climbs the steps to his dais, slides into his red leather chair, and casts a stoney gaze over the courtroom. The good citizens who have presented themselves for jury duty gaze at the judge expectantly from the benches below. The press at their side table bend over their laptops, fingers poised to record every word and act. Family and spectators look on. The day we have all been waiting for has at last arrived. Except it's not going to turn out the way we thought. A few of us know this; the rest wait for what the press has billed as the trial of the decade.

Kate, who remains in custody until the judge releases her, sits in the prisoner's box, wan and still. Her dark hair is pulled back from a centre part, and she wears no makeup save gloss on her lips. Her thin figure is swathed in a black sheath, a gold necklace her only adornment. I told her last night that if all goes to plan, she will soon be free. She shook her head, like she couldn't believe it. "Tess is alive," she breathed. "That is enough."

I make a point of not looking back, but I know where they are placed, the supporting cast in this drama. Trist and Lena, protagonists for the prosecution, sit immediately behind Cy. A handsome man with white hair is at their side—no doubt the agent, Rex, who Richard says didn't leave Trist's residence on November 29. Trist's face is lined and gaunt, and his dark suit hangs off his shoulders; he looks years older than his press photos, and I understand why he cancelled Vegas. If he is relieved to know his daughter is alive, he is too exhausted to show it.

Lena, by contrast, is in splendid form. She covers Trist's hand with hers and stares straight ahead, except when she's scanning his face in loving anxiety. She's wearing an expensive dark suit and holds her sleekly coiffed head elegantly high, every inch the lady. Lena in life possesses a glow that the photograph on Trist's mantel failed to catch. No wonder Richard was smitten. I note the glances the press and public send their way. The curious will go home tonight and tell their families that they have seen the famous Trist and his beautiful consort. But it's not just voyeurism—I detect sympathy in their glances. It is a terrible thing to lose a child, and Trist and his lady are bearing it with grace.

Behind me, Angela and Sammy Sinclair await what will come. Angela, makeup flawless, hair combed smooth in a pageboy, shields her eyes from public scrutiny with dark glasses. Sammy sits stiffly beside her, rooster chest puffed out beneath his well-cut suit, embers of anger at the ordeal the family has been put through burning in his coal-black eyes.

The court watchers have come out in force. Every seat is taken;

those who could not get in rumble outside in the Great Hall in hopes someone inside will leave. In the seat nearest the bench, an artist is already capturing Kate in coloured crayon.

Cy rises slowly, gathering his robes around him, gaunt but still a mountain of a man. His face is ashen, and dark shadows ring his eyes. He has yet to speak, but his forehead is beaded with sweat. Although the world doesn't know it yet, the case that he predicted would cap his career in a haze of glory has crumbled beneath his feet. Yet he must go on. He reaches for the crutch his junior cradles, pulls it toward him, and stabilizes himself. He bows to the judge and opens his mouth to begin.

Justice Tesik, anxious to proceed, preempts him. He nods at the clerk, "Read the charge and take the plea."

"My Lord, that will not be necessary," Cy says.

The judge leans forward and scowls at him through narrowed eyes. "What do you mean, Mr. Kenge?"

"The trial will not be proceeding," Cy replies tonelessly. "Yesterday, the child Tess Sinclair-Jones was found, alive and well, in the custody of her former nanny, Selma Beams. Ms. Beams has confessed to taking the child from the island. It was she, not the accused, Kate Sinclair-Jones, who abducted Tess Sinclair-Jones."

The jury issues a collective gasp; the room behind me breaks into madness but Cy doggedly continues. "The Crown hereby withdraws the charges against Kate Sinclair-Jones and asks that she be released from custody."

"This is preposterous," Justice Tesik rasps. "We are gathered here for a trial, at great expense to the taxpayer. Why was I not advised of this decision earlier?"

"Because the Crown itself did not know until an hour ago, when Ms. Beams's counsel confirmed that she will plead guilty to the charges against her." Cy sucks in his breath as if to gather strength. "Ms. Beams is present here and prepared to address the Court."

"How can I hear her if this isn't a trial?" the judge asks querulously, seeking refuge in the technicalities of criminal procedure. "And why does this Ms. Beams want to do this anyway?"

"Ms. Beams has been advised by independent counsel. She understands her right not to incriminate herself. Nevertheless, she has asked to be allowed to tell her story to the jury. Her own situation stands to be resolved in proceedings other than these. Her act today of setting justice right may stand her in good stead in those proceedings."

The judge nods. "As in, taken into account in sentencing," he says, his lip twisting cynically.

"Precisely, my Lord."

Justice Tesik shakes his head, as though he can't quite comprehend what is going on. I can't blame him. He came here today ready to handle the biggest case of his career. Now it is evaporating before his eyes. But as judges must, he accepts the inevitable.

"Very well. Bring Ms. Beams forward." He turns to Kate. "You may step down, Ms. Sinclair-Jones." Kate stares at him stonily and stays put. Maybe she doesn't understand, maybe she wants pride of place as Selma tells the world how she led the best legal minds in the city down the garden path. The judge shrugs and swivels again. "Members of the jury pool, it appears your service will not be required. You are free to leave."

No one rises; this show is too good to walk out on.

Justice Tesik shrugs again. He has never seen anything like this. He swivels back to Cy, and says with a sigh, "Mr. Kenge, bring on Ms. Beams."

CHAPTER 70

SELMA BEAMS MOVES UP THE aisle, a law officer on either side, head down. She finds the witness box, takes her seat, and looks out over the courtroom. She wears the same aging sweater and loose dark slacks I saw on the tarmac last night. Her short hair is neatly combed, but her face is wan and tired. Last night, she was frantic as she screamed after her child; today, her face is unreadable but composed. I feel admiration despite myself as I watch her bend to kiss the Bible the clerk proffers. Selma could have wrapped this up at the police station last night, but she has chosen to be here, to confess what she did to the world. Cy thanks her and launches in.

"Ms. Beams, did you take Tess Sinclair-Jones from the custody of her father on Bowen Island on September 25 of last year?"

"I did."

"Can you tell his Lordship why you did that?"

Selma pauses and looks at the judge. "It's simple. Tess is my child, not theirs. My responsibility is to my daughter. It was my duty to rescue my child from an unfit adoptive mother and an absent father. So, I decided to remove her. I took her to my grandpa's farm and kept her there, until the police took her away last night." Her voice drops. "Tess is well and has suffered no harm."

Justice Tesik leans forward; he's finally getting into this. "No physical harm. But you kept her from her parents for almost six agonizing months, perhaps doing irreparable harm to her emotional development."

Selma blinks back tears. "Yes. I kept her from Kate and Trist. But I do not believe this harmed her. It's true I couldn't go to the farm to see her except a night or two here or there—I was worried I was being followed. Gramps is good with Tess. Still, I am here to tell the jury I was mistaken. Though Tess is my daughter, I had no right to deflect blame for her abduction onto someone else.

"And I am here to apologize to Ms. Sinclair-Jones," Selma continues, turning her gaze from the judge to Kate. "All I could think about was getting Tess back to where she belongs and living with my baby in peace. But it got complicated. I didn't want the police coming after me, so I came up with the idea of pinning the abduction on Kate. I found a few of Ms. Sinclair-Jones's hairs on Tess's sweater left from their last supervised visit, so I saved one of them and planted it on the seat of the boat. But I never counted on Dante Bocci taking blurry photos, much less identifying Kate." She touches her clipped hair. "At the time, my hair was long and dark. Just like Kate's."

"You framed her for the abduction of her own child?"

Selma stumbles. "Y-yes. Except you need to understand, Tess isn't her child, Tess is mine."

"Can you take the jury back to the beginning—how you came to believe that Tess was your child?"

Selma bristles. "I *know* Tess is my child." She turns to address the jury. "I lost both my parents when I was seventeen. They were on their way back from a revival meeting when a truck hit their car head-on. My whole world changed. I had lost my mom and dad, and there was no one to look after me. I rattled around in the house eating canned beans and biscuits until they shut the heat off. I stopped going to school, and that was what did me in. The school sent out a truancy notice, and Child Welfare people picked me up and put me in a home. The kids there were bad. I was raised a Christian, taught to be truthful and responsible. These kids didn't understand that. They taunted me and I couldn't stand it there, so I ran away."

Selma bends her head, remembering this terrible time, lifts it and continues. "I had no where to go. One night on the street in a town called Agassiz, I started talking to a guy, a down-and-out kid like me. He told me about a Christian group in the bush north of Agassiz who would take me in. As I said, my parents were born-again Christians and had brought me up the same way. I thought it was a sign."

Selma fixes desolate eyes on the jury. "I hitchhiked out of Agassiz and walked north through the bush till I found the place. Some women took me into a big house painted white inside and out. There were crosses everywhere, reassuring me I was in a good place. I was taken to a room where a man named Zoron interviewed me. He wore a white robe, and on his chest was a cross in the circle of the sun. He sat very still, just looking at me, for a long time. Then he spoke to me. 'Daughter, you have suffered,' he said in a deep and quiet voice. I felt he could see into me, see all my sorrows, and it was like my fear dissipated. I knew I was in the presence of someone close to God. 'You may stay with us, daughter,' he said. 'The only condition is that you serve the Lord and obey the rules of the community.'

"The women took me to their dormitory and gave me a lovely warm bath and a fresh gown and a bed with stiff white sheets. They were tender and loving, just like my mother had been. I remember thinking, this is what Mom and Dad would have wanted for me.

"I spent almost three years at the Church of the Children of the Sun and Resurrection—that's what it was called. Eventually, I became a handmaid of Zoron. Out of that union, I became pregnant."

Cy looks meaningfully at the jury. Then he holds up a photo for them to see before standing in front of Selma. "Is this a picture of Zoron?" He shows her a photo of a handsome man with dark skin and Afro hair.

"Yes," breathes Selma, shaking herself as if to repress the memory. The clerk hands copies to the judge.

"What happened then, Selma?"

"When my baby was born—a little girl—they feted me. There was great rejoicing in the community. But then, after ten days, the women came and took my daughter away. 'It's what must happen,' they told me. 'A celestial child cannot be raised by her mother.'

"I went mad. I cried, I wept. I stole out of my bed at night and peered into the windows of buildings to try and find her. The women were alarmed and took me to Zoron. He told me I must accept the loss of my child because she belonged to God, and this was God's will. I screamed at him that she was mine, and I would never give her up. He said, 'Then you must leave, my daughter. There is no other way.'

"The women took me from the room and to the dormitory. They took my cross and gown and gave me baggy pants and a shirt and running shoes. I fought, but they were stronger. Finally, one put a needle in my arm. The next thing I recall, I was being set down in a town I didn't know, Chilliwack, they told me. I recognized the man who had driven me, one of the elders in the community. He pointed to a building. 'This is a hostel,' he told me, 'they'll give you a bed.' He handed me an envelope. 'Zoron wanted you to have this. May God be with you.' And he was gone.

"The next day, I blew part of the five hundred dollars in the envelope on a cab trip to my old house. It was still there—nobody had got around to claiming it. I found a key under the mat where we kept it and let myself in. I used the rest of the money to get the power and heat back up running, and I've lived there ever since— that is, when I wasn't nannying in someone else's home. Eventually, the town said the house was mine since there were no other claims, and a nice man got it stamped by a judge."

She takes a deep breath. "I didn't think I had any relatives. But one day Gramps showed up. My mother's father. I remembered Mom talking about him. They had a falling-out over religion. She said he was a simple man who didn't have a strong enough relationship with God, but a kind and lovely human being. So, I welcomed him into my life. After losing my daughter, he was all I had. We didn't live together—Gramps wouldn't leave the farm— but we've grown close. He helped me and stood up for me and made sure I had food. And I looked out for him. It was Gramps and me against the world.

"When summer came, I told Gramps I needed to do something, needed to get away. I got a job up the coast running boats at a resort through a guy Gramps knows. I liked that job. They gave me an iPhone and I got into the internet. But inside, I was aching. Aching for the baby I had left behind."

Selma pauses. "That's when I saw it."

"Saw what?" asks Cy.

"Saw the news that changed my life."

CHAPTER 71

*C*ULT LEADER DECAMPS FOR NICARAGUA.

"The story was months old, dated three months after I was thrown out of the compound. I scrolled down. I learned that Zoron and a core group of followers had left their compound in Agassiz in search of warmer climes. But it was the last paragraph of the story that sent a chill down my spine. *Four infants ranging in age from three months to two years, believed to have been fathered by Zoron, were left at the Agassiz Medical Centre for adoption.*

"I was stunned and angry. I put together the dates and realized that the three-month-old baby adopted out was mine. Without asking me, without even telling me. And it was too late for me to try to get her back. My beautiful girl was long gone, someone else's child."

I steal a glance at Kate. Her lips are parted, her eyes glazed and distant. She's thinking of the pseudo-lawyer who procured Tess for them, thinking of the money Trist paid. Her mouth sags, and she chokes back a sob. Now she knows what she never wanted to know—her child's biological parents—and what she has learned appalls her. Tess's father is a monster of manipulation called Zoron.

"I called the Agassiz hospital and talked to a lady in the office. She confirmed that a biracial three-month-old was among the children adopted out. I need to talk to the people who adopted her, I said. 'You can't, dearie,' the woman said kindly. She must have guessed I was the birth mother. 'This is just something you will have to accept. But I can assure you of this: the child has gone to an excellent home and fine parents. You have nothing to regret and nothing to feel guilty about.'

"But I didn't stop looking. I decided to take a nanny course at the local college with the money I made up north. The way I saw it, when I recovered my baby, I would need to know how to look after her. It was just a dream, and then, suddenly, it became real.

"One day, after I had finished my course, I was standing at the cash in the grocery store when I saw a magazine. On the cover was a photo of Trist Jones and his wife, Kate, holding a child with the face of angel and a halo of Afro hair. Their little girl, the headline proclaimed. *My little girl*, I thought. I bought the magazine and read the article; there was no mention of Kate being pregnant, just that she and Trist had come back from Europe and had a baby. I combed through the internet—no mention anywhere of their expecting a baby, like you usually see when a star's involved. I googled Tess's birthday and did the math. The timing fit. And suddenly, in my heart, I knew the truth. God was speaking to me. This was my lost baby.

"I knew the truth in my heart but I kept investigating. I looked for evidence that Trist and Kate had adopted Tess. The records were shut tight as a tomb, but I had another idea. I went into my iPhone and looked for photos of Kate in the months before the child was born. There weren't any. But then I found one. Two months before the birth of the child, a paparazzo caught her and Trist entering a musical event somewhere in London. Trist wore a sequined silver jacket, and Kate was in a form-fitting skinny dress. No baby bump. I knew then beyond any doubt that their baby was my baby, adopted three months after her birth when Zoron went to Nicaragua.

"That's when I put my plan into action, or part of it. At that time, I had no desire to take my baby away from Trist and Kate. It would be enough, I thought, if I could see her every day. I had my nanny training and had a couple of short jobs on my résumé. I found out where Trist and Kate lived, found the nearest park. Sure enough, Kate was there, sitting on a bench, rocking a pram. When she took the baby out, I gasped—it was my child. I found a way to get near, to comment on the child. Kate was nice, let me hold Tess. I remember Kate looking up and asking why I was crying. After all my careful planning, I almost gave myself away with a tear.

"We chatted a while. I told Kate I loved babies and had completed my nanny training. A couple of days later, I saw her in the park again. 'As it happens, our current nanny is leaving,' she said. She gave me a card with her email. 'Send me your résumé and a couple of recommendations.'

"That was how I came to work for Trist and Kate. I was ecstatic. I was with my baby. But after a while, problems surfaced. Trist and Kate loved Tess, but Trist was gone a lot, and when he wasn't home Kate was—how shall I put it—scattered. She went with the flow, whatever appealed to her in the moment, interrupting Tess's eating and sleeping schedules. It got worse and worse. I spoke to her about it, but she didn't seem to think it was a problem.

"When Trist and Kate split, they agreed on joint custody. I couldn't stand being away from Tess when she was with Kate. I worried about her all the time."

"Why were you worried?" Cy asks.

"Kate was already scattered. But the separation hit her hard. She started to get depressed. Forgetful, neglectful. I started to fear for Tess's safety. Finally, I told Trist Tess wasn't safe with Kate, that he had to apply for sole custody. Looking back, I can see I cared more than a nanny should. But I wasn't just a nanny. I'm Tess's mother, and I want only the best for my child.

"When Trist got sole custody, things were better," she continues. "I was able to keep to my routines and bring up my little girl properly without interference from Kate. Trist didn't get involved with the details, so I had her all to myself. Except when Kate had Tess on weekends. One Monday, I came to pick her up and found the house locked. When I finally got in, Tess was on the counter screaming with fright." Selma shoots Kate a long, contemptuous look. "I found Kate asleep upstairs, passed out on pills. I was shaken. I told Trist he had to end the weekend access. I swore an affidavit saying Kate couldn't be trusted with Tess alone, and the judge cut Kate down to a supervised visit twice a month."

"So, at last you had the perfect situation," Cy says. "You had Tess all to yourself, subject only to the casual oversight of her father. Why did you want to change that? Why did you decide to kidnap Tess when you didn't need to?"

Selma's face hardens. "It was Lena. Lena changed everything. She didn't like Tess; she had no idea how to parent." Selma gazes across the room to where Lena sits in shocked silence. "And then one day, I overheard Lena and Trist talking about getting married and moving to the States. I heard Lena say, 'I think a Black nanny would be better.' I'll never forget her laugh. 'One who's not quite so uptight.' A chill went straight to my heart. I decided there was only one solution—to take my little girl back before I lost her a second time.

"I saw my opportunity when Trist and Lena started talking about a week on Bowen Island after Trist's tour. Wouldn't it be perfect, I thought, if I stole Tess right out from under their negligent noses? At first it was just a crazy idea, but the more I thought about it, the more I convinced myself I could pull it off. Step one was telling Trist that I couldn't go to the island with them. I made up a story about having to take Gramps to the doctor, and that I was scared stiff of boats. They didn't argue. Lena was only too happy to have me out of the way, and Trist went along like he always did.

"The rest was easy. I told Gramps I had had a baby while I was in the religious community—he was pretty shocked, but he took it well—and that I would be bringing her back to the farm. He would have to help me look after her for a little while. I would visit when I could, until things calmed down and we could restart our life somewhere else.

"I worked out a plan. Like I said, I told Trist I was afraid of boats. It was a lie. I had worked with boats on the job Gramps got me up the coast. I prayed to God for forgiveness. I asked a neighbouring farmer who kept a little boat for fishing if I could borrow it for a week or two—going to the coast for some fishing, I said. Sure, no problem. I went to Ikea and spent a day fixing up Tess's room in Gramps's basement and buying her new clothes and toys. By this time, Gramps was all excited about meeting Tess, said he knew all about how to look after little ones.

"I took his van to haul the boat to Bowen Island the day after Trist and Lena and Tess settled in. I parked the van in a clearing at the top of a cliff above their chalet. I sat up there every day, watching. Sometimes they came out on the deck, other times Trist and Tess were on the back lawn, just beneath the place I was hidden in the bushes. But he never left her alone.

"They spent most afternoons on the beach, looking for shells and dabbling their toes in the water—it was too cold for swimming. Trist liked to lie on an old lounge chair they had down there. That was when I would go down to my secret cove and push the boat out. There was a big rock sheltering Trist's beach; I would sit behind it in the boat, poking my nose out every minute or two. He never even knew I was there."

I glance at Trist. He's pale. He looks like he's going to throw up.

"I was beginning to despair that my opportunity would never come, until that last afternoon, when Trist fell asleep. I edged around the rock, pushed my boat onto the sand, and scooped Tess up. She was happy to see me.

"Everything went to plan. I rounded the point and put the boat in at my secret cove, where I pulled Tess out. I took a moment to wipe my prints off the boat and plant the hair I had found on Tess's sweater, and then pushed the boat out into the receding tide with a long piece of shore debris. With luck, it would be far out into the channel before nightfall, and the police would find Kate's hair in it. I grabbed Tess in my arms and headed through the bush to the van. She laughed the whole way. I told her it was a game.

"At the van, I changed Tess into jeans and a sweater and pulled on the sneakers I had bought for her. 'Put your jacket on,' I whispered while I gathered up her swimming suit and little pink shoes. I could only find one. The other must have come off while I was carrying her, but I had no time to look for it. I told Tess to lie down under the covers in the back of the van and not move—a new game, I said. I drove down to the beach I had sussed out and parked in the trees. I could hear sirens—the search had already started—but the beach was deserted. I flipped open my pocketknife and tore a big rip in the swimming suit, then placed it with the shoe behind the log. If the police thought Tess had drowned, they would stop searching, and Tess and I would be home free.

"I drove my van to the ferry terminal. It was crawling with police and volunteers, but they waved me through. It wasn't until we were well out to sea that I told Tess she could take a stretch before she resumed her place on the floor under the blankets.

"We arrived at the mainland, and I drove straight to Gramps's farm. Tess was delighted with her new room, and Gramps loved her. He's simple, Gramps, like I said, but he knows about kids, how to wash them and feed them and show them story books. And I visited as often as I could.

"I watched the news, Kate being charged, Mr. Bocci identifying her as the woman in the boat. It was working better than I hoped. But then the police announced that the second shoe had been found at the top of the cliff behind the house, and I panicked. I decided I had to do whatever I could to make sure the jury convicted Kate. I didn't like the idea, but I realized that if she was acquitted, I would never be safe. So, when Global asked me for an interview, I agreed and said negative things about her. I didn't really lie." Selma looks at Kate. "I hated doing that, but I had to—had to do it to save my baby.

"And all was well until yesterday. I got a call from Gramps saying he'd had a strange visitor that day, a woman. From his description, I knew it was defence counsel for Ms. Sinclair-Jones, Ms. Truitt, there—she had come to see me earlier and I had ended up throwing her out of my house. My heart froze. She *knew*. Somehow she'd figured it out. She would tell the police and they would come and take Tess away from me again.

"I don't know how long I sat on the floor with the phone in my hand. And then it came to me. I prayed for guidance, and the Lord sent it. *Go to the farm. Get Tess and Gramps. Go across the border to the States. You will find a home there, a place to live in peace.*

"I phoned Gramps and said we were going to take Tess away, just for a little while until the trial was over. He didn't want to leave his farm, but he finally agreed. I got in my car and drove as fast as I could to the farm—the only thing I took besides some clothing was the portrait of Tess I cherish. It was mid-afternoon by the time I got there. I used my key to open the padlock on the gate and drove to the shed where Gramps kept the van. We would need the van for the three of us and Tess's stuff. I took the van out and left my beater in the barn. I drove back to the house, grabbed Tess, and got her dressed. I stuffed her clothes and some toys in a plastic bag. But Gramps—I could see he still didn't want to go. Then Tess decided she didn't want to go either and started wailing. I stuffed her in the van and told Gramps to get in the passenger seat. I jumped into the driver's seat and started driving. I was terrified the police would arrive any minute and all would be lost."

Selma blinks back tears. "We were almost at the border. And then I heard this noise above us, a horrible noise. I pulled the van over, rolled down the window, and looked up. 'A helicopter,' I screamed at Gramps. 'They've found us.'

"'Step on it, go,' Gramps yelled. He was enjoying this now, just like on TV. I hit the gas pedal and we bolted ahead. And then I heard the sirens. 'Don't stop,' Gramps yelled, but I killed the engine. 'See those lights in the rearview mirror, Gramps? See those lights ahead? Police. Everywhere.' 'What do you mean, Selma?' 'It's all over, Gramps.'"

CHAPTER 72

IT IS NEVER ALL OVER.

In the aftermath of Selma's testimony, we move to tie up the loose ends.

Justice Tesik turns to Kate, who is still in the prisoner's box, and tells her that she is free to go. "On behalf of the people of this province, I express my profound regret that you have had to endure not only the trauma of your missing daughter, but the infamy of being falsely accused of abducting and killing her."

As if this is what she has been waiting for, Kate rises, opens the door of the prisoner's box, and steps out. She's shaky on her feet. She comes toward our table, tears in her eyes. Just when I think she's going to sit beside us, she hesitates and moves on to join her parents.

The judge turns to Selma, still in the witness box. "You have had a bad start in life, Ms. Beams. Losing your parents, joining the Church of the Sun and Redemption, losing a child. But you did a terrible thing. You framed an innocent woman for the murder of her child. You did this without a care for how you were abusing her and misleading the justice system, cooperating with the Crown only when you were caught red-handed. Your belief that Tess is your biological daughter does not justify your actions; at law Tess is not your daughter. The abduction and confinement of a child is a serious offence. You have done a great wrong to the parents and the state. I am remanding you for further proceedings where a different judge will hear your plea and try your case. "

Selma nods, wipes her eyes, and is escorted from the witness box by law officers.

The judge thanks counsel and exits to the cry of "Order in court." The clerks set about packing the exhibits. The press box is empty. They've long since scrambled for the exit and the news cameras.

We are packing our bags. I look across the aisle, where Cy sits, head on the table. Jim Early, his junior, is gently shaking his massive shoulders. "Mr. Kenge, Mr. Kenge."

I go over, touch Cy's face. "It's over, Cy," I whisper. "Time to go."

His fists ball, he rears his head. "I didn't try to save the child. I deterred the search. And I would have put the wrong person in prison for life. I was so sure of my case." He swallows a long sob. "You were right, Jilly, you were right all along."

"It's alright, Cy. We found her."

Wordlessly, Cy heaves himself to his feet. His face is lined with defeat. "I thought I was your mentor, Jilly, but I failed. Failed the justice system. Failed you. And now it's over." His voice drops to a whisper; I strain to hear his words as he grasps his crutch and heaves himself to his feet. "It's over, all of it. Finished."

No, I want to say, you've still got it in you, Cy. But the words won't come out. I watch as Jim leads him away.

Kan, too, is still here. He sits alone across the room, his huge hands folded in his lap, his narrow eyes fixed on the middle distance. What is he thinking? Does he regret his part in this travesty of justice? Or has his facile mind already classified Kate's case an inevitable blip in the never-ending quest to finger culprits and put them in jail? *So many cases, you're bound to make a few wrong calls, and anyway, I did everything a good police officer should.* He finds my eyes, stares for a long moment, then rises, turns, and walks away. I swivel to nod to Kate, who is holding back tears as she gathers her bag and prepares to leave with her parents. Her joy at finding Tess is even now being replaced by a suite of new concerns. Will Trist fight her application for custody? And what if the judge agrees and lets Trist and Lena take her with them to Vegas? I make a note to call Olivia, my go-to family lawyer, and tell her to call Kate ASAP.

The room is empty now, save for the clerks and a few stragglers. Selma, flanked by her lawyer and guards, is still sitting on the front bench. Her head is down. Is she thinking about what lies ahead? It will be a short proceeding—arraignment, guilty plea, sentencing. A year or so in prison. Who knows? The Crown may decide no good will come of making Selma sit in jail and let her off with community service. *At heart, Selma is just a misguided girl who loves kids, a couple of years working with Child Protection will do the trick.*

I came into this trial determined to figure Selma out. I shake my head. I understand some of it, but not everything, and now I never will. On Selma's telling, she is a victim whose child was stolen from her, and who sought to right things by stealing the child back—a person more sinned against than sinning. Yet sin she did. She plotted to send another woman to prison for a crime she had committed. She planted Kate's hair in the boat to inculpate her, dissed Kate on TV to ensure her conviction, and sat by while the full array of state power focused against Kate, the woman she knew to be innocent. When her grandfather phoned to say I had been to the farm, she swung into action to put Tess beyond reach, Kate be damned.

Selma is standing now, leaning on her lawyer's arm. She looks over to the defence bench and eyes me. She takes a step forward, like she wants to talk.

For a long moment, we stare stonily at each other. Selma's lips part. She owes Kate and she owes me. She wants to say she's sorry, I think. Then the moment passes. Her lips settle in a hard, thin line. She wrenches her arm from her lawyer and steps toward me.

"You took my child away from me," she hisses. "You came after us, just when we were set to create a new life for ourselves. God will not forgive. May you burn in hell."

I step back in shock. I've grown inured to insults and slurs, but no one has ever *cursed* me. The law officers guide Selma firmly out of the courtroom.

I turn back to the counsel table, slam my briefcase shut, and look at Jeff. We could say a lot of things, but we don't. He slings an arm around my shoulder, and we head out.

CHAPTER 73

IT IS SUNDAY AFTERNOON. I sit in my den, contented. Upstairs, Claire is sleeping. The sun slants through the window, bearing promise of spring.

My doorbell is ringing. I try to ignore it—I am happy in this moment of solitary peace—but it rings again, insistent. I rise and go to answer.

I look up. Kan's broad face is looking down at me. "May I come in?"

I feel foreboding. This cannot be good. It's been twelve days since Selma confessed and Kate's charges were dropped. Just when I thought Kate's case was over, this man has come to tell me there is more. I sigh. "Of course, Detective," I say, and lead him to the den.

"How can I help you?" I ask.

"By listening. I have something to say. But first, may I ask how things are with Tess and her parents? After all that has happened, it has been on my mind. What will happen to Tess now?"

"Trist and Kate and their respective lawyers have met. They have agreed on custody. Trist will have custody for two months each summer and three weeks at Christmas. Kate will have Tess from September through June, the school year. Each parent will have access when the child is in the other's custody. Trist has agreed to not move to Vegas."

"The judge will accept that?"

"The lawyers think so. If we have learned anything from this saga, it is that snatching children from their parents is seldom a good idea. Kate loves Tess; Trist loves Tess. They will figure it out."

"I am pleased they have sorted this out." Kan bends his head, looks up. "How about those threatening calls? I assume they've stopped?"

I nodded. "Are you thinking Gramps was helping out Selma?"

"It crossed my mind." Kan pauses. "I have been searching my conscience these past days, Ms. Truitt. After Selma's confession, I was of a mind to resign. I felt I had failed to do my duty and was no longer fit for the force. But I have decided to stay on. I'll learn from this case and strive to do better."

I peer into his sad eyes. "That's all any of us can do. If it means anything to you, Detective Kan, I think you are right to continue in your work. You are a good detective, a good man."

His lips twist. "A humbled man. But I will go on. First, however, I must apologize. To you. That is why I am intruding on your afternoon, for which, by the way, I also apologize."

The sun catches his face, and I see the pain in his eyes. I had pegged him as a man of cold, arrogant efficiency, but I see now there is more to him. I wait.

"I apologize, Ms. Truitt, for ignoring your pleas that I continue the search for Tess. I was certain that Tess's mother had taken her, and whether by design or accident, Tess had been killed in the process. I told you we were still searching, but I reduced our efforts and continued building a case against Ms. Sinclair-Jones. If you had not persisted and got Damon involved, Tess would never have been found. An innocent woman would have spent her life in prison."

"Why were you so sure Kate did this, Detective?"

He bows his head, looks into my eyes. "In the absence of proof, it seemed the most logical explanation. Scorned, unstable mother afraid of losing her daughter, identified by a witness—"

"*Falsely* identified. Speaking of which, what are you doing about Dante Bocci?"

"Reopening his file," Kan says.

I am curious. "You say you believed Kate was guilty. When did that change?"

"I got to thinking about all the things that didn't fit, that you kept telling me didn't fit. The second shoe on the cliff, the CCTV sightings of the child. And for the first time, I entertained the possibility that I might be mistaken. I told myself the case was solid, but the fear that I could be wrong haunted me. Finally, I joined the officers on Kate's detail and followed her for a day—shopping mall after mall, service station after station. As dusk was falling, she pulled into the service station where the man and child were last seen. She got out of her car and stood there, looking around as though by some miracle she might see them, fists balled, tears streaming down her cheeks.

"That is when I saw my error. This was not the face of a mother who has killed her child. This was the face of a mother who believed her child was alive. I forgot my forensic logic and looked into Kate's heart." He looks me in the eye. "For my dereliction of duty, I am truly sorry."

I bow my head. In the end it was not me and my nagging that moved Kan to action, but Kate. Kate and her refusal to stop believing Tess was alive.

"Thank you, Detective," I say. "Thank you for the courage to question everything you believed about this case. And thank you for your insistence on finding the truth. My client will appreciate your apology." I halt, my voice dropping. "I too accept your apology."

"It's you who should be thanked, Ms. Truitt." Kan shifts in his seat. "There's more. Cases rarely end when you think they do, there's always an aftermath. So it is with Selma's case. When Selma claimed to be Tess's biological mother, we did rapid DNA tests to confirm. Tess is not Selma's daughter. Her belief was a fantasy."

My jaw drops.

Kan continues. "It's a sad story. We tracked down the woman at the compound. The one who let you turn around—Rachel. She remembers Selma. She says that Selma's baby died at three months and showed me a grave. A simple marker with the number 777. God's sacred numbers, she said. We've got a court order to exhume the remains."

I ponder Kan's revelation. Are we right to think genes matter? Or are they just a crude way of claiming property in a human being?

The baby monitor sounds with Claire's cry. "Excuse me, Detective. My daughter's awake."

He stands to go.

"No, Detective. Please wait." I run upstairs.

"This is Claire," I tell Kan five minutes later. Tidied up and fresh from sleep, Claire reaches out to him with a smile. Then shyly, she buries her face in my shoulder. Kan catches her giggle and smiles.

Kan gazes out the window at the greening grass. "What better time is there in our lives than when the two best virtues—innocent gaiety and a boundless yearning for affection—are our sole objects of pursuit?" he asks of no one in particular.

I must look puzzled because he smiles at me ruefully. "Tolstoy. He believed that childhood, that time of innocent joy and affection, is the best time of our lives. I also believe that to be true."

I remember the story of how a teenaged Kan returned from a ski trip to find his parents murdered. The moment his time of innocence and affection ended.

"I know about your parents," I say. "I'm so sorry."

Kan coughs and stands. "I must go. I'll leave you and Claire to your afternoon."

At the door, he bows to us. "Thank you for listening, Ms. Truitt. And for seeing that justice was done."

He turns and walks slowly to his car.

EPILOGUE

THE MAY SUN DAWNED BRIGHT this morning. A perfect spring day for my perfect spring daughter, who is one year old today.

Mike's clock in the hall strikes one, a ring that goes on forever. A special ring for Claire, I allow myself to fancy, like he's supervising things. I raise my glass to Mike, who would have cherished this day. He would be putting music on, wandering among the guests with Claire on his hip, pretending to dunk her in an imaginary basketball hoop before sweeping her to the ceiling and holding her high at the end of his long arms. A lump rises in my throat; I swallow it and raise my glass.

Cy has been given place of honour on the upper patio just off the kitchen, near the walker he now requires. He sits in an expansive chair, cradling a single malt in lieu of champagne.

"I am allowed to indulge myself now that I've finished my last case," he says.

"As if you haven't always indulged yourself." I smile.

"I *have* allowed myself a few indiscretions from time to time," Cy admits. "Never regretted any."

A long table on the lower terrace is spread with white linen and gleaming silver. At its centre stands a giant birthday cake. To the side, on a small table, red roses front bottles of birthday bubbly from Martha and Brock.

They are coming across the grass now, my friends. Tony from the bar across the street from the office offers each arrival a flute as they pass.

Jeff and Jessica are the first. Jeff gives a grand halloo and crosses to Cy and me.

Richard and Donna arrive, waving from across the garden where the blooming magnolia tree has caught Donna's eye.

Alicia and Shanni appear from nowhere, hand in hand as they descend the side steps and swoop toward the table. Who would have thought?

Debbie arrives, stately in lace and clutching Damon's arm. "Finally found the perfect man," she hoots. Damon only shakes his head and smiles.

Crossing the lawn toward me, I see Angela and Sammy. Angela, elegant in a dress of mauve crepe, Sammy awkward in the suit he has donned for the occasion. I move to them and offer hugs, then I stand back a loosen Sammy's tie.

Now that's better.

Edith appears behind me, proudly bearing the star of the day, Claire, who is decked out in a new engine-red, white-frilled tee. "She refuses to wear anything else," I say.

"She thinks she's a judge." Cy observes. "Already."

"We should get started," I say, conscious of Claire's short attention span. I lead the way to the lower table, Cy shuffling behind with his walker.

Edith cuts a piece of cake for Claire and places it on the tray of her highchair. Edith lights the candle.

"Quick," I say, clapping my hands. "Happy birthday!"

"Wait, wait!"

It's Kate, late as always, running toward us across the grass in her flowing floral dress, hand in hand with Tess of the halo hair. "Wait! Tess and I are here to lead the singing."

We hold off until Kate offers the first note, her tone clear and true. She's right; we could not have sung this song without her. When the song is finished, we all blow out the candle. Claire hoots with joy as the flame disappears and plunges her fist into the icing.

"You must all come to my concert," Kate is telling us as she settles Tess in the chair beside her. "I've been practising my song for Tess. Chan Centre, June fifth, two p.m., tickets at the desk for everyone."

"Lovely," I say, remembering Kate's music on the stand that time in her home and how her voice trembled in those days when we feared Tess was lost.

My left hand lies flat on the table; I feel another hand covering it.

I put my fork down and look up.

"Another chair," I call to Tony. "Another piece of cake."

Tony rushes to comply, pulling up a chair beside me with one hand and placing a coupe de champagne on the linen with the other.

Kan lowers his bulk onto the chair, sits back, and surveys the table. His eyes linger when they comes to Tess, then settle on

Claire. She grins at him through the chocolatey layers that wreathe her face.

Kan folds his hands and bestows a beneficent smile on the company, before finally turning it to me.

"All's well that ends well," he growls, and takes an enormous bite of cake.

ACKNOWLEDGMENTS

I am deeply grateful for all those who helped me shape this book and bring it into being. I am particularly grateful to my agent, Eric Myers, for encouraging me to go on when I might have given up, and for my editors, Sarah St. Pierre and Adrienne Kerr, for their insights and advice. Finally, I am grateful to my husband, Frank McArdle, for allowing me to absent myself from his life for long periods of writing and revision and for his constant support through thick and thin.

ABOUT THE AUTHOR

Beverley McLachlin is the #1 bestselling author of two novels, *Full Disclosure* and *Denial*, and a memoir, *Truth Be Told*, which won the prestigious Writers' Trust Shaughnessy Cohen Prize for Political Writing and the Ottawa Book Award for Nonfiction. From 2000 to 2017, McLachlin was Chief Justice of the Supreme Court of Canada. She is the first woman to hold that position and the longest-serving Chief Justice in Canadian history. In 2018, McLachlin became a Companion of the Order of Canada, the highest honour within the Order.

Read more
BEVERLEY McLACHLIN

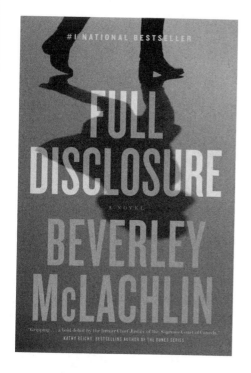

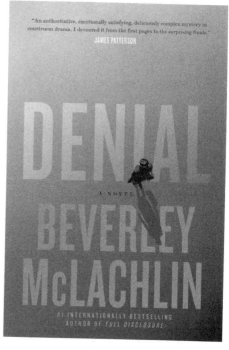

"A bold debut. Novelist Beverley McLachlin is a force to be reckoned with."

KATHY REICHS,
bestselling author of the
Temperance Brennan series

"*Denial* captures the life of a defence lawyer embroiled in a high-stakes murder trial, with twists and turns to the very last page."

ROBERT ROTENBERG,
bestselling author of *What We Buried*

The bestselling and award-winning memoir that chronicles Beverley McLachlin's remarkable life, on and off the bench.

WINNER OF THE WRITERS' TRUST OF CANADA SHAUGHNESSY COHEN PRIZE

WINNER OF THE OTTAWA BOOK AWARD FOR NON-FICTION

"Her legacy . . . is now part of the country's foundations."

The Globe and Mail